# NAMELESS

BOOK THREE: AGE OF CONQUEST

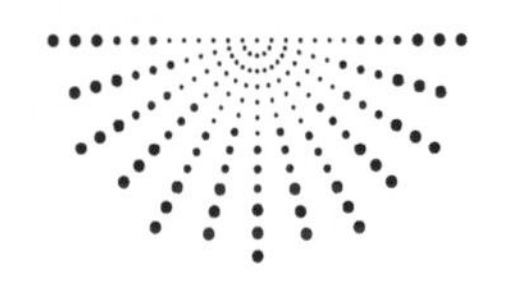

TAMARA LEIGH

WWW.TAMARALEIGH.COM

**THE WULFRITHS. IT ALL BEGAN WITH A WOMAN.**

A battle. A crown. The conqueror. The conquered. Medieval England—forever changed by the Battle of Hastings. And the rise of the formidable Wulfriths.

A NAMELESS NORMAN

Born of scandal, Sir Dougray of the family D'Argent defies his illegitimacy by championing the oppressed—until the prospect of winning the hand of a lady persuades him to join the Duke of Normandy in conquering Saxon-ruled England. When an injury sustained at the Battle of Hastings causes the woman he loves to reject him, an embittered Dougray turns his efforts to uprooting Saxons resistant to their new king. But among those he must bring to heel is Em, an escaped slave-turned-rebel whose suffering at the hands of a fellow Norman tempts him to reclaim the man he was before he betrayed his conscience. And captivates him though he vowed never again to fall prey to a woman. Might yet another D'Argent warrior take a Saxon bride? Or will the one who made a possession of Em destroy what remains of her?

A FUGITIVE SAXON

Forced into slavery to ensure her siblings' survival following the Norman invasion, Em escapes her abusive master and joins the Saxon resistance. Now trained in the ways of the warrior, she is determined to never again suffer the depravity of men. And will not, providing she can stay ahead of the one intent on recovering his property—and the usurping King William's warrior scout, Sir Dougray, who also seeks to capture her. But when he appoints himself Em's savior, thwarting an attempt to once more enslave her, she glimpses an honorable man beyond the conqueror and begins to feel that which is forbidden enemies—worse, forbidden one as ruined as she. Or so she believes until his kiss more thrills than frightens. And threatens to break a heart she would not have believed capable of being touched by a Norman.

*From the Saxon victory at York, portending the fateful Harrying of the North, to the walls of Wulfen Castle, Sir Dougray and Em's tale unfolds in the third book in the AGE OF CONQUEST series revealing the origins of the Wulfriths of the bestselling AGE OF FAITH series. Watch for HEARTLESS: Book Four releasing Spring 2020.*

**For new releases and special promotions, subscribe to Tamara Leigh's mailing list: www.tamaraleigh.com**

Cover Design: Ravven

Print ISBN-13: 978-1-942326-42-7
Ebook ISBN-13: 978-1-942326-41-0

*The son shall not bear the iniquity of the father, neither shall the father bear the iniquity of the son: the righteousness of the righteous shall be upon him, and the wickedness of the wicked shall be upon him. ~*
Ezekiel 18:20 KJV

# PROLOGUE

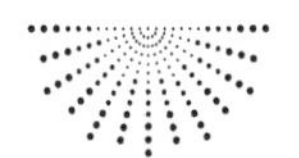

Normandy, France
Spring, 1067

You are baseborn. Despite my every effort to remedy that beyond our walls, it cannot be undone. No matter how many masses a man attends, no matter how many prayers he prays, in the absence of much effort to change his heart, he will act in accord with that to which he is disposed." Baron D'Argent sighed. "It is the same with women, Dougray."

"Non, Godfroi," his wife beseeched.

The man who possessed but a forelock of black hair to evidence he had ever been other than shockingly silvered, looked from her son before the dais to where she stood alongside the high seat into which he had been settled minutes earlier. "It must be told."

"Must it?" she whispered.

Taking her white-knuckled hand in his, he returned his regard to the one forced to his knees to prevent him from doing further injury to the men-at-arms. "It is not only Adela's sire who rejects you, Dougray. It is Adela."

His words did not surprise, but they were not to be believed. Dougray had not betrayed his conscience by aiding the Duke of Normandy in taking England's crown and lost half an arm for this to be the reason the one for whom he had done those things stayed away. It was Adela's sire who kept her from his side all these months while he fought infection that nearly put him in the ground. Her sire who, as learned this morn from servants' gossip, meant to wed her to one of legitimate, noble birth and sizable lands. *This* day.

Suppressing the impulse to resume struggling against those who kept him from the woman who had pledged her heart to him, what remained of reason warning it would only humiliate him further, he growled, "You lie."

"It is a hard truth, but more true because it is hard, my son."

"*My* son? Non, as you say, I am baseborn. As you say, it cannot be undone."

"Dougray!" His mother stepped forward.

It was good the baron drew her back, though it would be better had he sent her away when her son was returned to the castle.

Despite Dougray's anger, he did not want the one who had suffered from years of whisperings over the conception of her third child to hurt more. Albeit an act of indiscretion, it had been forgivable under the circumstances—though few men other than Godfroi D'Argent would have pardoned her. And even fewer would have given another man's child his name and raised him alongside legitimate sons.

Continuing to clasp his wife's hand, the baron leaned forward. "Even if you reject me as your sire, you *are* my son—another hard truth, though only hard in this moment of believing you are betrayed."

Feeling ache in knees pressed hard to the stone floor, though not as great as the ache of his absent lower arm, Dougray said, "I *am* betrayed."

"Not by your mother nor father."

"Am I not? You ordered me ridden to ground like a criminal. You speak lies of Adela. And unless you allow me to go to her, this day she will be wed to a man she does not love."

"But of whom her sire approves, as does she."

"Another lie."

"Non, Dougray. Do I let you go to her, all you will find there is humiliation at best when it is confirmed I speak true, grave injury at worst when her kin and betrothed retaliate for your offense. And think of what might be believed of her. If you halt the wedding, it will be only until it can be verified she is not your lover." The baron raised an eyebrow as if he himself questioned it.

That he thought it possible his *son* had dishonored the lady moved bubbling anger toward boiling. Here a reminder Lady Robine D'Argent had been tainted by a dishonorable man, as evidenced by Dougray's untimely birth that announced he was not of her husband.

The sins of the father...

Longing to break free of those who restrained him, he glanced at the hand on his right arm—bloodied, doubtless from being drawn across a broken nose. As for the soldier gripping what remained of Dougray's left arm—fractured ribs.

Though Dougray wished the injuries earlier dealt his captors confirmed he could throw them off, he had landed those blows only because they were not expected and the men were loath to injure one bearing the name D'Argent.

The body and reflexes that had made Dougray a warrior capable of besting most opponents had suffered much wasting these months abed. Of a weight he had not been since his youth, he was at their mercy—rather, that of the man who sat in judgment of him.

"Adela is where she ought to be, Dougray."

He returned his gaze to the baron who only appeared formidable. From the muscular breadth of his upper body, one would not know his legs were emaciated and immovable beneath the blanket. Though none witnessed the rigor to which he subjected his torso and arms, daily he exercised those muscles yet under his control.

"Robine," the baron said, "I know you prefer to tell him when he is fully recovered, but it must be done now, and I think it best heard from me."

"Non, I was there." She drew her hand from his. "It is for me to do."

*Where had she been?* Dougray wondered as she descended the dais. *And what was for her to do?*

"Release my son," she commanded the men-at-arms.

They hesitated, then receiving a nod from their lord, did as bid and stepped back.

Skirts gently billowing, Lady Robine sank to her knees before her son. The pain in her eyes and lining her face was greater than he had seen since his brother, Cyr, returned her maimed son to Normandy and told there was yet no word of her eldest son's fate. Though three of her four sons had survived the battle of Hastings, and she clutched at hope Guarin had as well, she mourned. And this day, she hurt more for whatever she meant to reveal.

For her, Dougray did not take advantage of his release. For her, he kept his knees to the floor.

Cupping his bearded face in her palms, she said, "Dearest Dougray, your father does not lie. Had you been awarded a sizable demesne in England the same as Cyr, it is possible Adela's sire would have allowed you to wed, but even then she would not have you."

He curled his fingers into fists, felt the ache of both hands despite the absence of one. "She does not care I was born on the wrong side of the sheets. She loves me."

"I do not question once that was true, but I believe it is no longer. Hence, her love was unworthy of our son."

The strain of remaining still causing him to tremble, Dougray said, "What lies would your husband have you tell?"

As tears flooded her eyes, the baron barked, "Dare not speak—"

"Non!" She twisted around. "Let me do this."

Godfroi's face was so dark it appeared he was in the throes of apoplexy, but he jerked his chin.

"The week after Christmas, while you were so senseless with infection we feared we would lose you, Adela came," she said.

Dougray startled. "Why did you not say?"

"Because you needed something to live for, and that day she snatched it away." She swallowed. "When she saw you lying in bed, so pale and thin she could not conceal her distress, she..."

"What, Mother?"

"She cried out and turned aside. I assured her there was hope you would recover and persuaded her to sit with you, myself set her hand upon yours. But when you roused and drew your left arm from beneath the cover as if to reach to her, she saw."

He narrowed his lids. "You did not prepare her?"

"Tidings of your loss was not cast far and wide, but since she had stayed away, we assumed she knew and, like her mother..."

"What?"

"Ever beauty the first consideration. Though Adela's mother could have wed any of a number of godly men, she chose the most handsome—and most ungodly."

"Adela is not the same."

"Is she not? As told your father, I was there. Upon her face was revulsion that could no longer disguise itself as shock as when first she looked upon you. I saw how quickly she loosed your hand and departed. And I heard tale of how horrid she thought your injury and that it was a pity you should be so unmanned—"

"Lies!" Dougray thrust to his feet, causing the men-at-arms to take back the step given. Pointing at the baron who surely wished legs beneath him, he said, "Lies he has you tell to keep me from her."

His mother rose. "Were they lies, they would be mine alone. They are not, and it is a blade to the heart to tell what I prayed I would not have to. Ill it makes me that loose lips gave you false hope ere unbreakable vows could be spoken."

He refused to believe it false hope. If he could get to Adela, she would go away with him, and they would make a life together beyond Normandy.

"She is undeserving, Dougray. In time, there will be one more true who does not first see your loss but her great gain in taking you to husband."

"Heed your mother," the baron said. "If a wife you desire, I shall make a match for you when you fully recover. A lady of constancy, kind heart, wit, beauty, and good dowry—perhaps even lands."

As Dougray stared at him past his mother, he put order to his face lest it reveal he calculated the chance of overwhelming the only ones present capable of intercepting him.

Make it past the men-at-arms and he had only to make it to one of the horses in the inner bailey. Make it to the drawbridge before it was raised and he had only to make it to Adela's home. Make it to her side before his pursuers arrived and they had only to make it to the wood. Then they would decide whether to head north, south, east, or west.

Non, not west. Never again would he cross the channel. Never again would he set foot on English soil choked with his countrymen's blood. And when Cyr returned from pilgrimage to atone for those he had slain in the great battle, neither would he return to England. Providing still they had no word Guarin lived, Cyr would assume his place as the D'Argent heir. As for the lands awarded him in England…

Hopefully, the duke now its king would grant them to one other than the youngest brother who administered them for Cyr.

Dougray did not wish Theriot denied lands of his own, but better Normandy lands acquired by way of marriage like that proposed for the baseborn one.

"Naught to say?" the baron asked, and Dougray sensed he suspected what was behind this mask.

*Lull him,* he counseled. *Tell him what he desires, and sooner Dougray not-of-the-same-silvered-hair as his brothers and sister will be gone from here.*

He drew breath, but before he could spend it on conciliatory words, the baron commanded, "Confine him. At peril of your positions, he is not to leave his chamber without my permission."

Dougray was moving before those last words were spoken—as were the men who sought to seize him as he swung away from his mother. Though he had not mastered what was required to efficiently move a body whose one side was out of balance with the other, he made it to the doors. But as he reached to one, it swung wide with the entrance of a young woman.

"Dougray!" Nicola exclaimed, then shrieked as a man-at-arms slammed into her brother and carried him to the floor.

With feet, knees, elbows, and fist, Dougray fought his one assailant who quickly became two.

"They will hurt him, Godfroi!" his mother cried.

"Get off him!" Nicola screamed, and he saw her drag on the tunic of the man-at-arms who struggled to restrain Dougray's upper body, felt the one grappling with his legs jerk as if kicked hard.

Sanity prevailed. Though angered it must in order to ensure his sister was not harmed, Dougray ceased struggling and was pinned as thoroughly as when he fell at Hastings. Strange he had not been able to feel his lower left arm then, though still it clung to the upper. Stranger, he could feel it now though long removed.

He did not resist when he was dragged upright, merely made fists—one visible, the other no longer—and looked to Nicola who was met halfway across the hall by their mother. Staring at the young woman who demanded to know the reason her brother was set upon and the older woman seeking to calm her, Dougray made the baron wait on the regard of one who ought to be grateful first, repentant second.

He *was* grateful for all afforded the son of the man who cuckolded Godfroi, but repentant? Not possible in this moment—if ever.

"Silence, Nicola!" the baron commanded, and when his daughter's impassioned words ended on a squeak, looked to Dougray. "I know you are not entirely healed. I know your loss makes it difficult to think well, but you offend—more than me, God."

"God?" Dougray stood taller. "Be assured, I but return the favor."

"Enough!"

"You say He knows the depths of my heart, so what harm in letting *you* know?"

The baron gripped the chair arms as if to keep from lunging out of the seat—as if *he,* longer and more grievously maimed than his wife's ill-conceived son, did not have cause to question God.

"I answered our liege's call to invade England," Dougray snarled, "salving my conscience over the longing for land with assurance the duke had the pope's blessing, and yet in battle..."

He tried to shoulder past those images, but they flashed before him the same as dreams entreating him to claw open his lids.

"Dougray?" his mother called as if from a great distance. And so she was—Lady Robine D'Argent in Normandy, her son's memories returning him to Hastings.

Amid the dark ere dawn, the ride to the meadow ahead of foot soldiers.

Amid the grey of first day, the formation of battle lines in mist mingling with the breath of men and beasts.

Amid the light of morn, the sparkle of silver so beautiful one could hardly conceive it was of blades and armor.

Amid the hours that followed, the flash and spray of crimson... clang and crash of metal...grunts and shouts of men fighting to live...cries and whimpers of men yearning to die.

Amid the waning of day, the desperation to secure victory ere nightfall.

Amid the exultation of keeping a sword from a fellow warrior, the bite of steel when an upward stroke caused his mail sleeve to fall back and expose his forearm.

Dougray staggered as pain radiated elbow to fingertips, glimpsed blood splash his tunic and the sun course his blade as his sword fell from a hand no longer under his control, saw the long-haired bearded Saxon swing his arm back to deliver the killing blow. But unlike other times inside and outside this memory, he saw something else. Another heathen came for him—of greater age, long hair, and beard.

Dougray tore the D'Argent dagger from its scabbard and drew back his right arm to cast it at the first Saxon whose battle-axe sought to sever what remained of his enemy's life. But before it left his fingers, the second Saxon's shield spiraled toward his Norman opponent and struck Dougray in the chest, dropping him onto a fallen warrior.

Losing his grip on the dagger, he reached to the sides for purchase and should not have been surprised one arm was useless. Then someone fell atop him.

As he shoved at the gasping, convulsing man, his wavering gaze took in two Saxons trading blows with each other, the same who had set themselves at him. He could make no sense of it, and more it shocked when the older one thrust a sword into the gut of his countryman.

The battle-axe plummeted to the ground ahead of its master, then the victor's golden eyes swept to Dougray. As that Saxon once more moved toward his enemy, Dougray's head lightened. Before all went dark, he saw his assailant veer to the right to cross swords with a Norman lunging at him. Then nothing.

Returned to Normandy, the great hall, his mother who sought to console his sister, the baron who kept him from Adela, Dougray wondered why only now he recalled a Saxon had slain the one who took his arm. And why a shield to the enemy's chest rather than a blade? Had a vendetta played out between those two? An attempt to end a blood feud by concealing murder amid battle?

"Given time and prayer," Godfroi tore Dougray from his pondering, "the memories that haunt and torment—of killing and near being killed—will become shadows in the corners of your mind. And providing you turn back to God, there they shall dwell."

Though Dougray knew he spoke from painful experience, he said, "Of what benefit to turn back? For William who had the pope's blessing of God, I lost the use of an arm to a heathen on whose side God should not have been. We lost an uncle and possibly a brother to more heathens on whose side God should not have been. Thousands of our people lost husbands, sons, and brothers to thousands of heathens on whose side God should not have been. And you say *I* offend?"

"I feel those losses more than you," the baron bit, "and more I shall feel them if Guarin *has* been taken from us, but I hold to my faith. If you are determined to reject what I taught you, at least honor the memory of Hugh by remembering what *he* taught you."

Godfroi's twin brother. More ungodly than godly, Hugh had trained up his son, nephews, and scores of other men in the ways of the warrior. Were it to be believed, he had suffered a dishonorable death on the same battlefield where Dougray fell.

"If your uncle were present," the baron continued, "he would say—*Let not your heart make a fool of you.*"

He would, after delivering a blow to impress those words on the offender.

"He would say—*Grind your failings and losses underfoot.*"

He would, after greatly shaming one who fell short of a mark set higher than most could reach.

"He would say—*Be a warrior, Dougray D'Argent.*"

He would, though never would he add his surname to his sister-in-law's baseborn son. Dougray had been treated nearly as well as those of legitimate birth, but ever Hugh had left him nameless.

"He would say—*Be a man.*"

He would, but that last pushed too far, Godfroi unmanning Dougray the same as it was said Adela thought him unmanned by his injury. Adela who was to wed within hours and would this night lie in another's arms.

Dougray tried to hold to reason, but the thread was too frayed.

With a roar, he threw off one man-at-arms. And was slammed to the floor by the other, straddled, his one and a half arms wrenched behind his back. Then the angry and beseeching voices of women were silenced by a fist to Dougray's temple.

Quick to recover from such blows, whether they dazed or rendered him unconscious, this was no exception. However, whatever hope remained for Adela and him was lost when he roused to find he was being bound to his bed.

Upon his release two days later, the woman he loved was another man's wife and possibly soon to be the mother of another man's child. *That* Dougray would not trespass upon. Never would he be the same as the one who made him on his mother. Never would any child of his be nameless.

And never again would he darken the home of the family D'Argent.

# CHAPTER ONE

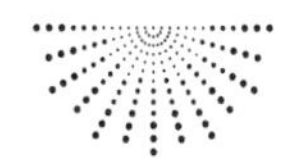

City of York, England
Early Autumn, 1069

They had taken York, and so completely and violently their Norman oppressors were diminished by the thousands. How many? Two? Three?

Regardless, far more Normans than Saxons and Danes were strewn outside and inside a city so devastated it was barely habitable.

"I am pleased," Em whispered. It was the same she told herself each day since the Norman garrison sallied out of the city they themselves set alight to confront the approaching army of Saxon rebels and Danish allies—and been overwhelmed.

"Verily, I mean it," she added as if challenged.

Not possible considering she stood distant from others of her guard who would soon relieve the first night's watch outside what remained of the city's walls.

Her isolation was self-imposed, so uncomfortable did the Danes among the Saxons make her feel. Unlike many of her people, few of those from across the sea looked upon her with fearful suspicion. They did so with something else, and sharp senses to which her rebel training had given a keener edge told it was dangerous in the way of desire. Though not yet ten and nine, Em knew all about the carnal side of men—rather, all she wished to know.

Memories rising like smoke above the city's walls, she straightened from the tree she leaned against and gave her head a shake to send her thoughts elsewhere.

Home. That was where she longed to go. But first she had to know where home was. Was it Gloucester in southern England from which she and her brother had departed three years past? There where they left behind a younger brother and sister whose survival depended on the coin gained from Eberhard and her selling themselves into slavery? Could she safely venture there? Or would she find herself returned to the man who searched for his *witchy-eyed* slave?

*My beloved lord,* she had been required to name him though she hated no one more—not even the conqueror whom Normans and traitorous Saxons now called *William the Great.*

Again, she averted her thoughts and this time settled them on Eberhard. He remained safe upon Wulfenshire with the Saxon lady who had bought him at auction and made a noble son of him. Though he no longer played that part, the ruse having been uncovered by the conqueror, Em had confirmed her brother was treated well—that as the lady promised, his warrior's training had resumed. Once he was awarded sword and spurs, a commoner who was to have been a tiller of soil would have the skills to defend himself and, if still Normans ruled England, be among those who sent the invaders to hell if not back across the sea.

"Please, Lord," a prayer slipped from her, so rare a spoken thing many believed her godless, albeit likely more for what they saw when they looked upon her than for what she would not say. Though the faith of many rebels formerly led by Eberhard's guardian was renewed by the Saxon priest who had attached himself to the Rebels of the Pale, Em avoided those gatherings.

*Contrary,* Father Julius named her and warned her faith was so loose that if she did not pull it back up, it would be trampled.

She *was* contrary, but not godless—merely, unwilling to share what had happened to her that day at auction, then that night and all the days and nights until her escape. Never would the priest know, though he said she would sooner heal were she to entrust her burden to one whose prayerful hands were more capable of delivering it to the Lord. Never would anyone know. They could only speculate—except other women slaves whose duties went beyond those of household and fields.

"Not godless," she whispered and wondered how many times she had gone to God these past years. Likely more than all the years before, whether standing, on her knees, or on her back.

Surprisingly, many were the answered prayers sent up by one of a heart so bruised often it felt black. Not surprisingly, they did not number as great as prayers whose answers must be verified and prayers that might never be answered well. Had the coin of her and Eberhard's sacrifice saved their younger siblings? Would Saxons rid themselves of Normans? Would England regain its glory? Would slavery and the need for the ungodly practice find its end upon this island kingdom? Would cruel justice be done Raymond—?

*That* name causing her stomach to clench, she pressed a hand to her belly.

"You are Em, hmm?"

The only good of the heavily-accented words that made her startle was they were of a Dane rather than Norman. Still, he might intend her harm.

Moving a hand to her dagger, she turned to the warrior who stood between her and others of the guard. Not much taller than she but thick of muscle, here was the one whose eyes had earlier served himself portions of her and smile had sought the encouragement of her own lips.

"Of what concern yours, Dane?" she scorned.

He touched his chest. "I am—"

"I care not how you are called. What do you want?"

He hooked thumbs beneath his belt and lowered his gaze over her moonlit figure. "You look lonely. I am lonely too."

She wished she could appreciate his show of teeth that turned him more handsome, but even her commander's smile that sometimes softened her made the greater part of her tense.

"Were I lonely, I would not have sought solitude, Dane." She jutted her chin toward those beyond him. "If it makes you feel a man, go back and boast of promises and caresses to come. Providing you bother me no more, I will not gainsay you."

Her commander would rebuke her for being offensive, but she was safe. Not only were the majority of the guard her fellow rebels, but when they went on duty she would be paired with Zedekiah whom few dared challenge. Too, likely half her Saxon words were lost on the Dane—just enough making it through to leave him in no doubt she did not wish company. And yet he remained unmoving.

Once more, she nodded toward those he blocked from sight. "You will not like it do I call to them."

"Who?" He turned to the side and looked to where the guard no longer gathered.

Though her retreat had not escaped this one's notice, those who ensured no man touched her surely thought her yet amongst them. Fearing she might pay an ungodly price for allowing her thoughts to drift far from the present, she started to draw her dagger.

The Dane raised a hand. "I am not like that. Another time, eh?"

"No other time."

"Bjorn could make you happy."

Bjorn could not. No man could. "Leave me."

He moved away, though not in the direction of the departed guard—rather, bushes to the left.

"What do you?" she called.

He laughed and put over his shoulder, "What I came to do, Woman. Make water."

Em nearly laughed herself. It was dangerous to ease her guard with a man, but she did not think this one the same as—

No sooner did she thrust aside her tormentor's name than a warrior with the long hair and beard of a Saxon rose from the bushes toward which the Dane advanced. But it was not his sudden appearance that caused her breath to stick.

Was moonlight responsible for a face so familiar her heart pounded? Or *was* he one of her own? Though his shoulders and chest were considerably broader than those of the man come to mind, too many lives were at risk to allow him to draw nearer. Or escape.

As the Dane touched his sword hesitantly, Em drew her own. "He is Norman!" she cried, then louder to alert others, "Norman!"

Bjorn unsheathed his blade and lunged. A moment before the two men met over swords, a shift of the blond one's mantle confirmed here was the man she had not seen in more than a year—a warrior missing half an arm, and on his belt a dagger set with a gem that sparkled blue the same as those worn by others of his family.

What surprised as much as his muscular physique was how quickly he dropped his opponent. When last she had seen him, he was the one put down by the greater strength of the miscreant who tolerated no interference with his slave. Though Em had told herself the words this warrior had spoken were merely meant to provoke a fellow Norman, they had freed her from her master's attentions—that night only.

Now, drawing his blade from the spasming Dane, he met her gaze.

She had been trained to respond quickly and viciously to the enemy, but she could not think what to do. Though she might not be indebted to this D'Argent, she owed others of his family.

His chin snapped to the side, and she also heard the advance of those her cry had summoned. As it would be many against one, the Norman's need to outrun them would render useless the stealth with which he had slipped past sentries set about this wooded, marshy area beyond the city. Soon, his enemies would take him to ground.

"I am pleased," she whispered as he pivoted. "Verily, I am." Then she followed, though for what purpose she dared not ponder even when she, the swiftest of the Rebels of the Pale, drew near.

WERE HE CAPTURED, it would not be because stealth failed him. It would be because he failed it. Though he was only to observe and gather information as commanded by the king, upon catching sight of the slave of remarkable eyes, he had lingered. Thus, he had seen the Dane approach her after others of the guard departed and, risking his mission, determined he would not let happen what it appeared the warrior intended—once being too many times to fail her.

More for that failure than what Godfroi demanded of him, a year past Dougray had begun reclaiming the warrior he cast off—not in Normandy, but in this country he had vowed never again to go.

After mutually agreed banishment from D'Argent lands following Adela's marriage, the nameless one had made his home in a hovel. During a year of near solitude, so hobbled was he by anger and self-pity that any who happened on him thought him twice aged, even decrepit with his tangled hair and matted beard. Then his brother came one last time.

Dougray had refused to accompany Cyr to claim the English

lands awarded the second-born as demanded by King William, but with that demand came tidings their eldest brother had been sighted.

The possibility Guarin lived and was held by Saxon rebels had given Dougray reason to return to the world of men and England. However, Cyr had required more of him than aid in recovering their brother, which Dougray resisted until humiliated in front of the woman who now gave chase.

At Castle Balduc upon his brother's lands, Dougray had first laid eyes on her when the keeper of that fortress, Raymond Campagnon, ill-treated a servant he named *Wench* and for which Cyr berated him. Smugly, the knave had revealed she was his slave. Hence, none could gainsay him.

Dougray, subjected to derision by those who disapproved of Godfroi raising him as a son, had often championed those scorned for the lack of nobility, money, or legitimacy. Upon witnessing the abuse of Campagnon's slave, he had been nudged toward compassion for the suffering of one Saxon at the hands of one Norman, which began opening his eyes to the suffering of numerous Saxons at the hands of numerous Normans.

Then came anger, not only toward his own people but himself, causing him to look close upon the Dougray who had turned his back on his conscience to win the woman he could not otherwise attain and remember who he had been before Adela and why—a far better man than the bitter one he had become.

Unfortunately, now the Saxon rebel who had moved the immovable within him could prove his downfall, something at which his cousin warned English women were particularly adept. However, were he undone, it would not be by way of her drawn sword. It would be by way of legs that, though not of great length, kept pace with his. She had only to repeatedly sound the alarm, and he would be surrounded by those called to her and sentries he had evaded earlier.

Why was she silent but for the fall of her feet behind and to his right? And of greater curiosity when she veered in front of him, what did she intend?

"Suivez-moi," she tossed Norman-French over her shoulder.

Though tempted to alter his course lest she lead him to his death, it made no sense she sought to do so. Considering she had shouted no further warning, he guessed she had recognized him belatedly. She might hate him for a Norman, but more she hated being indebted to his family for the compassion shown her brother and her. Familiar with where her fellow rebels were posted, she betrayed her own in clearing a path for the enemy.

Beginning to feel the slice to his thigh that would slow him were it not bound soon, he followed the woman whose dark hair was braided into a plait of such length it circled her head twice.

They skirted dense trees and wide marshes, plunged through sparse copses and forded narrow marshes. Only once before they cleared the heavily patrolled area did any call them to account. Though the sentry was unseen, Dougray's sure-footed guide led their pursuer astray and did not slow even when the man was no longer heard.

After putting another half league between the Norman and his enemies, the woman halted alongside sodden ground and spun around. The same as Dougray, she had kept her sword to hand, and now she angled it at him where he had ended his flight a dozen feet distant.

Both bereft of breath, neither spoke, the only movement about them rising and falling chests. And eyes.

Out of one he knew to be blue, the other brown, she surveyed him, doubtless noting he was as changed as she.

During earlier encounters, she had worn a shapeless gown and stood only as tall as necessary to serve guests, as if bowed head and hunched shoulders would allow her to escape Campagnon's notice.

Now Dougray saw her true height reached as high as the underside of his nose. And no longer was she shapeless, a belt defining her narrow waist. Changed indeed, but had she not immediately recognized him, it was because he was more changed.

After Campagnon humiliated him by besting him in front of his slave, Dougray had begun the journey to recover what was left of the warrior their uncle had made of the baseborn one and find ways to compensate for one-handedness.

The training had been arduous and infuriating, but just as the D'Argents had finally recovered their eldest sibling, they recovered Dougray and saw the D'Argent dagger returned to his belt. He could never again be as accomplished at defending family, home, and country, but once more he was of solid build and weight. Other than long hair, short beard, and the absence of a lower arm, he appeared the same chevalier who had crossed the channel with Duke William.

However, the greatest change was not visible to the eye. Nearly as much as the recovery of Guarin, his return to England had been motivated by revenge against the heathens, but the Dougray of old had struggled back to the surface and remained in England not for vengeance but atonement.

"Did you slay the Dane?" the woman asked in Anglo-Saxon rather than the Norman-French used to command him to follow her.

He shifted the shoulder of his left arm. The weight of the mantle draping it confirming it concealed his loss, he said, "Great the temptation, but since one ought not fault a man for seeking to relieve himself, the Dane is injured only enough to ensure it will be some weeks ere he can do serious harm to a Norman." What he did not say was had the man sought to ravish her, it was not mere temptation with which Dougray would have been afflicted.

Her chest sank as if with relief. "Still, you make use of a Saxon's disguise," she said.

Then she had heard of the deception worked on the one who now led the Rebels of the Pale—Vitalis, a Saxon warrior who had only begun to repay the indignity Dougray had dealt him more than a year ago. If this woman had not led the way past the sentries, worse than indignity might have been done this Norman.

"It has served me well, and more so this eve when you recognized me. Tell, why did you give aid?"

"Be assured, I did not do it for one who hates my people."

He could not fault her for believing that of him since it had been so in the beginning and he had not attempted to hide it. Now what he hated were those whose acts of rebellion caused England's wounds to gape larger. Thus, once more he served a man for whom he had no liking.

Having uprooted and caused the scattering and stamping out of a handful of rebellions these past months, word of his efforts in the name of King William had surely reached the Rebels of the Pale. And made *him* greatly hated—though not as much as he would be should this mission yield the rebels and their Danish allies who had slaughtered thousands of Normans in taking York. So great was that offense that were William not delivered the perpetrators, Saxons who had no hand in that city's fall would pay, whether with their own lives or further oppression.

Containing anger over what this woman and others of the resistance caused to spin faster, Dougray said, "If you did not do it for me, for whom?"

"For Sir Guarin who kept my brother out of the usurper's hands at Darfield."

Recalling the angry youth who infiltrated the Norman camp to slay Campagnon for abusing his sister, Dougray said, "You did not know I aided my brother in that endeavor? Indeed, methinks still I have the bite marks."

Ignoring that, she said, "And I did it for Sir Cyr who showed me kindness when I was a..."

*Slave* was the word, but she backhanded the air as if what she had endured were a bothersome fly.

Ache and the sticky moisture soaking his chausses a reminder his injury needed tending, Dougray shifted his weight. "You are sure you did not do it for me—even a little?"

"If you refer to the night at Balduc you happened on…" She swallowed loudly. "…*him* and me in the kitchen, I am quite sure. It was only a distraction."

It offended she named his encounter with Campagnon that, but it *had* ended in his humiliation.

"As you but delayed what was to be done me," she continued, "it was of no use and no comparison to what I have done for you this eve." She put her head to the side. "Had the Dane sought to force his attentions on me rather than relieve his bladder where you were concealed, would you have shown yourself?"

"I would have."

She shrugged. "Even did I believe you and had you stopped him, a small thing it would be."

His innocent—rather, nearly innocent—sister rising to mind, Dougray said sharply, "You consider ravishment a small thing?"

"As you must know, the use of my body by grasping men is no longer of consequence. For other women, aye, but me… It would be like bemoaning a lost crust of bread when an entire loaf has been stolen from another."

Was she ruined? Dougray wondered. Were he allowed to draw near, would he see only the dark of Campagnon in her wondrous eyes? Though she had freed herself of that knave, perhaps she was so calloused she bestowed sexual favors on whoever appealed.

"Thus, my debt to your family is settled," she said, "and so thoroughly I do not think it exaggeration now *you* are in my debt."

Thigh throbbing, he pressed a hand to it, drawing her gaze there.

"You are injured," she said with what sounded concern, and quickly added, "Obviously, it was more than the loss of an arm that made it easier than usual for me to outrun the enemy."

Again, she offended, though not as greatly as she would have had he not glimpsed soft emotion behind hard—as if a remnant of who she had been before Campagnon survived.

Curling the fingers of the hand beneath his mantle into a fist, acknowledging the wonder that still he could feel what was no longer present, he struggled against the impulse to aid her as she aided him. If he yielded, his mission could be compromised. If he did not, she could fall into the hands of one more dangerous than the young Dane.

So be it.

"I give warning, Em," he spoke her name and resented the longing to savor it on tongue and lips. So slight were those two intimate letters, it was like taking a small bite of something soft and sweet, but not so soft and sweet one did not wish another taste.

"I wait," she said.

"Sooner than expected, what happened here will deliver the king and a great host to York."

Her eyes widened.

"They march now, and Raymond Campagnon and his mercenaries number among them. If you are not gone ere they arrive, the paper that knave carries may see returned to him one whose eyes shall betray her should she be captured. Thus, you must leave the rebels and take yourself as far from York as possible."

Despite palpable unease, she raised her chin. "Your warning hardly covers the interest on your debt, Sir Dougray, but there is honor in the effort."

Would she leave the rebels? Likely not. Would she pass his warning to her commander though it would mean constructing a lie to cover having aided the enemy? Likely. Still, for as much as Dougray disliked Vitalis, he hoped she *would* share the warning, causing the Saxon to take his Rebels of the Pale distant.

Though once those men and women had been of Wulfenshire whose lands were now mostly held by Dougray's brother, Guarin, a division among their ranks had forced them to flee north. Now they remained in no place long and never departed without plaguing Normans—earning the ire of King William who had believed that pocket of rebellion cracked wide open when he relieved them of their leader by wedding the lady to Guarin. Unprepared for the rise of Lady Hawisa's former housecarle, there were few rebel leaders William wanted more than Vitalis. Had not the Saxon warrior aided in freeing Guarin from rebel captivity, Dougray would not hesitate to see him undone.

"As I must return to my own and report you escaped," Em said, "I shall leave you to tend your wound and recover your mount."

She stepped to the side and paused. "One thing might aid in paying down your debt."

"Speak."

"When next you are at Wulfen Castle, would you tell my brother I fare well and expect to journey to our siblings soon?"

"I will. Where will you go?"

"He will know," she said and ran.

As Dougray watched the night breathe her in, he hesitated over prayer to which he remained more a stranger than an acquaintance, then beseeched the Lord to keep her out of Campagnon's clutches. Regardless of how ruined she was, the mercenary would further damage her. And then Dougray might have to kill him.

"Dear Lord." Trembling, perspiration dripping from nose and chin onto fists pressed atop thighs, Em rocked herself where she had dropped to her knees on sopping ground a half league distant from Dougray D'Argent. "Dear Lord, nay."

She pressed a hand to her mouth. She would not heave. That she no longer did—excepting when she slew her first Norman outside York to keep his blade from her belly. So much blood. And death so greedy it had dimmed the man's eyes before he hit the ground.

*That* unsettling was understandable, this was not. Unlike when first she escaped *him,* she was strong and every day grew stronger.

*Not as strong as you shall be when you can speak his name,* she reminded herself of counsel given by one who had trained her into a rebel—Lady Hawisa who kept Eberhard safe and, alongside her new husband, Guarin D'Argent, made a warrior of her brother.

Em drew her hand from her mouth, let rise an image of the one whose name she must speak. It should not be difficult, having lurked around her every corner during the encounter with Dougray D'Argent who *had* spoken it, but it was like imbibing too much sour wine. Regardless of how thirsty one remained, it was impossible to take another sip. But if she could speak the name now, surely she would be stronger.

She tried. And failed. It was absurd, especially since he was near—indeed, on her shoulder though much pain she had inflicted on herself to remove the vile thing that not only identified her as his possession but boasted the blessing of God.

Sitting back on her heels, she slid a hand beneath her tunic and touched the ridge capping her shoulder, next moved her fingers into the round depression from which she had flayed that skin after her escape.

So loudly she had sobbed it had been necessary to gag herself lest anyone near try to save her from herself—worse, see what she wanted none to see. She had cut it away in its entirety, for a time lost consciousness, then bound up the bloody wound that evidenced on the day *he* acquired a slave, he had paid extra to permanently mark her.

*Not* permanently, she had told herself after removing the ink, but still there was the scar. Still *he* was on her shoulder.

"Speak it," she commanded. "'Tis not *he* nor *him.* It is that over which he would exult to know you fear it on your lips." She swallowed, whispered, "Raymond...Campagnon." She nodded. "Never my beloved lord. Ever my enemy. Raymond Campagnon."

Her belly unclenched, and its spare contents began to settle as if it were but a basin of water set atop a level surface.

Letting her hand fall from her shoulder, she rasped, "A good beginning, is it not, Lady Hawisa? Even if I cannot make you as proud of me as you are of Eberhard, a worthy start." Another nod, then consideration that the one she had led through the marshes was no longer indebted to her.

Not only had Dougray D'Argent given warning she would share with Vitalis, unknowingly he had challenged her to speak the name of he who would do worse to her than ever he had should he lay hands on her again—at the end of which, likely he would make good his threat to pass her around his men.

Em pushed his name past her lips again and unthinkingly followed it with, "Dougray D'Argent," a name not difficult to speak though more and more he was a scourge to the rebellion. What was difficult was recalling what she had led him to believe of her—that ravishment was a little thing by implying she was known to others beyond the one who searched for her.

No little thing. And no others. She had said it to unsettle him and feigned indifference to relations with men because his pity shamed her. Still, it had been dangerous since he might have thought it an invitation to seek sexual favors and, when she refused, stolen them.

That last made her scoff. Though a Norman and her enemy, he was a D'Argent. And even were he not of that family, she would not believe such of him. At least, that he would turn thief, which was the only means by which any man would ever again lay hands on her.

# CHAPTER TWO

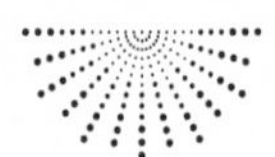

Had hell a currency, the king's coffers brimmed with that coin—payment from that place to which William agreed to send those who continued to oppose his rule, whether they did so by deed, deceptive ignorance, or merely crossed his path when they should have waited for him to pass out of sight.

As Dougray had reported upon overtaking the army as it neared York, that city was mostly gutted by fire, though not by Saxons and their Danish allies. The Norman defenders, fearing the timbers of the buildings outside the castle would be used to bridge the defensive ditch, had set them afire—only to lose control of the blaze.

When the rebel army arrived, nearly all inside the walls was alight. Hardly surprising it took little effort to put as many as three thousand Normans to the sword. As also told William, the majority of the Danes had returned to their ships after plundering what remained of the city and crossed to the opposite side of the Humber estuary, leaving the Saxon rebels in control of the city. But now those led by Edgar the Aetheling had departed, whether concluding their charred prize was indefensible or Em had shared tidings of the Norman army's impending arrival and effected the withdrawal.

It was good Dougray had forewarned the king about the state of his stronghold. Had he not, William might have been unable to contain his anger.

Turning in the saddle, Dougray's liege called, "Chevalier Maël D'Argent!" As the commander of his guard urged his destrier forward, two others were summoned. "Guy Torquay, Raymond Campagnon!"

The last called forth should have been Theriot, the youngest D'Argent brother whose honed senses would serve better than Campagnon's thirsty blade. And less distracting it would be, so great was Dougray's longing to avenge the humiliation dealt him by this man in front of Em.

As his cousin, Maël, reined in on William's left, the other two halted to the right of Dougray.

"The sooner to meet the enemy in battle," the king said, "I would know where the Danish army have gone and if any Saxon rebels remain with them."

Since the ships of those come across the sea were no longer visible on the Humber, it was possible they had returned to their homeland, but unlikely.

"Without making your presence known, discover their whereabouts." William jutted his chin at his scout. "Sir Dougray shall lead you."

Though two murmured agreement, the third said low, "At least in this the false D'Argent is of some use to our king."

*Hold!* Dougray commanded anger roused by Campagnon's taunt as if such things he had not thought first—that he was not a true D'Argent nor as useful as once he had been. Both were unassailable, but the second he had brought upon himself.

Had he not violated the lesson taught by his uncle to celebrate victory after it was complete—and even then with one eye roving —he would not have taken an axe to the arm during the great battle. True, he had recovered the warrior rejected following the removal of his lower arm, but he could never be as before, so expert at wielding two blades he was entrusted with the lives of fellow warriors, often putting down opponents they could not.

Though he accepted this, he yearned to slam a fist into Campagnon's teeth. It was no easy thing to have been lauded first a mighty warrior, second skilled at scouting and tracking, and now the reverse. However, there was an advantage in catching unawares any who underestimated his proficiency at arms.

"As surprise is an ally worth courting," the king said, "put to the sword any Danes or Saxons you happen upon."

Danes, Dougray silently conceded, since those lurking near were warriors who sought Norman lives. But he would not slay Saxons unless clearly they sought to kill his countrymen.

William returned his regard to the smoldering city, muttered, "Many the plans to be laid the sooner to see debts due me settled."

Talk of debts called Em to mind. Though two nights past Dougray had not been allowed near enough to become further acquainted with her marvelous eyes, often he recalled them as he did now with Campagnon at his side, the paper that would prove the miscreant's ownership of her likely that which bulged his purse.

*Be gone, Em,* he silently entreated. *Far gone, even if never I see you again.*

~

Isle of Axholme
Lincolnshire, England

Sir Guy Torquay was a quiet one. The question yet to be answered—was it by nature or circumstance?

Dougray guessed the latter. Not only did it seem an unnatural state for the man who had been a companion to the celebrated

Bloodlust Warrior of Hastings, but the chevalier had suffered a great loss months past following what had nearly been the Battle of Darfield.

The rebels led by Edwin Harwolfson had gathered opposite the king's army. Despite nearly equal numbers, another Norman victory had seemed imminent, William's forces mostly comprised of warriors, Harwolfson's of commoners trained at arms. But might had yielded to reason and negotiations ensued, saving thousands on both sides.

Among the concessions Harwolfson had gained was pardon for the rebels who had taken up arms against their king, a sizable barony, and custody of his misbegotten son birthed by the sister of the Bloodlust Warrior of Hastings. That lady had claimed she was willing to relinquish her half-Saxon infant, but the day she was to place him in his father's arms, she could not be parted from him. And so her betrothal to Sir Guy was broken and she wed Harwolfson.

Though surely for the best, that this chevalier had left his friend's service and entered the king's guard suggested his loss of the lady was great—the kind of loss with which Dougray was familiar.

As he thrust aside memories of Adela who had likely given her husband a child by now, Sir Guy's gaze shifted to him. Because he felt watched? Or because once more he thought to watch the king's scout as often done since first Dougray made his acquaintance shortly after the averted battle of Darfield?

Though Dougray resented being a curiosity, as he himself had indulged in the same, he returned his attention to the mission.

*Lord, stay our side,* he appealed to the one above looking down on these below who had drawn dangerously near the Danish army—possible only because the enemy's patrol was as pitifully lax here on the isle as it had been in the surrounding marshland. Though the area was difficult to negotiate, if the Danes wished to engage William in battle, which their retreat from York made it appear they were loath to do, their losses would be considerable.

"Saxons," Maël said as Dougray also caught sight of those whose garb was different enough to mark them as outsiders among Danes also given to long hair and beards.

Two score strong, though there could be more elsewhere on the isle, they moved toward the center of the immense camp as the three Dougray had led here looked down on them from a ridge so thick with foliage a worthy commander would have ordered it razed.

Dougray's cousin grunted. "And there is the one who thinks himself a man and capable of ruling England."

"Edgar the Aetheling," Sir Guy murmured.

Campagnon snorted. "Toothless pup!"

Though Dougray had no kind regard for the nephew of the departed King Edward who had pledged himself to William and been greatly rewarded and treated as a son, he longed to drive a fist into Campagnon's face.

Still, it was true Edgar was toothless. Not yet twenty, he was so inexperienced he could not have taken even a burning York without the guidance of two of the most powerful resistance leaders and the aid of Danish allies who the youth foolishly believed would place him on the throne.

"Do you see Gospatric and Maerleswein?" Dougray asked, never having set eyes on those more in command of the rebellion than the Aetheling they counseled.

"Unless they are among those beneath hoods," Maël said, "they are not here. Unlike Edgar, who likely acts against their advice, I believe they have taken their men north."

Sir Guy nodded. "I concur. In coming here, Edgar tests the width and length of a ruler's mantle, but though King Sweyn's brother may enjoy allowing him to believe it a good fit, it swallows him."

Guessing the one who emerged from an immense tent ahead

of a dozen Danes was that brother, Dougray took measure of the warrior who strode toward the Saxons. Boldly confident, he might play at deference toward Edgar, but that was all.

"The earl," Maël named him as Edgar and the Saxon rebels halted.

At a distance of fifteen feet, the Danes ceased their own advance.

There was too much ground between the camp and the ridge for their exchange to be heard, but it seemed friendly, though falsely so at its conclusion when the earl strode forward and embraced Edgar. Had the latter the substance of kings, he would not permit a show of affection reserved for close kin, offspring, and inferiors in need reminding they were as children even were they scores aged.

When the earl drew back, the Aetheling grinned and puffed his chest as if unaware of how insignificant he was to one he believed served him.

More discussion, then Edgar turned to the hooded man on his right. That one's height and breadth familiar, Dougray hoped there was more than one rebel of that exceptional size.

Whatever was spoken between the two caused the Aetheling to slice a hand through the air as if he lost patience. Then the one who displeased him turned and summoned forth a half dozen rebels who followed Edgar toward the earl's tent.

As they neared, the big Saxon dropped his hood, revealing red hair and beard.

"Vitalis," Dougray and Maël murmured the name of the warrior who, had Em warned him to take the Rebels of the Pale distant, had ignored her. However, his presence became of less consequence when he halted before the tent and motioned to the one on his far side.

A relatively slight figure stepped forward and also dropped her hood. Blessedly, the woman with a dark braid disappearing beneath the neck of that garment had her back to the ridge where lurked one she had great cause to fear. But then she turned to face Vitalis.

*Lord,* Dougray silently appealed, *let Campagnon's eyesight be poor.*

"Wench!" the mercenary barked loud enough that were the area properly patrolled, there would be blood. If not for his fellow Normans' reflexes, those below might have caught sight of him when he thrust up off his belly.

Dougray, Maël, and Guy dragged him down, muffled his shout of protest, pinned his flailing arms and legs, and dealt a blow to the head that rendered him senseless lest a patrol was near—or so Dougray reasoned away what satisfied despite pained knuckles.

Maël released Campagnon's arms and looked to Dougray. "It is she?"

"Who?" Sir Guy asked as he loosed the knave's legs.

Dougray flexed the knuckles of his visible fist. "It is," he answered his cousin who had never been as near Em as he. "And so desperate is Campagnon to reclaim his slave, he risked our lives."

"Slave," Sir Guy growled, evidence he found the trade distasteful and surely more so that a fellow Norman engaged in it.

Dougray looked to the purse on the mercenary's belt. "I do not know about you, Maël and Sir Guy, but this miscreant owes me for endangering my life. As he cannot be trusted to pay, methinks it best to collect whilst the pig is fat and drowsy."

Neither understood, but before Campagnon regained consciousness, they did. And approved.

# CHAPTER THREE

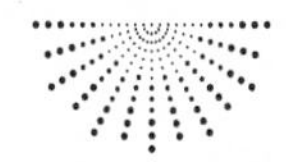

Em had believed it was for protection of the Aetheling the Rebels of the Pale were enlisted to escort Edgar to the marsh-enclosed isle to meet with his allies. Now she feared it something more.

In the weeks since they were called to join with other forces to take York as Edgar had failed to do earlier in the year, often the young man had turned his attention upon her.

Those with whom he surrounded himself disapproved, but like the Danes, he regarded her without narrow-eyed suspicion. And once, two days' march from the city he meant to take from the Normans, he had said he would like to see her in a gown. Drawing so near her she had struggled to hold her feet firm, he told when she came to his tent that eve, she could choose one of four bliauts fashioned for a lady.

Only because she wished to believe he would make a far better king than the conqueror had she remained civil, resisting the impulse to slap a face that did not yet require a razor.

She had not scorned him for trunks stuffed with riches that slowed the entourage, one of which contained garments intended to polish the rough edges of common women otherwise unworthy of notice.

She had not berated him for believing a handsome face, noble blood, a position of influence, and soft cloth against dry skin could transform her into a harlot. Even Raymond Campagnon, despite his every effort, had not succeeded in making her that.

Instead, she had forced a smile, said she could better protect England's future king clothed in tunic, chausses, and boots, and feigned hearing her commander call to her.

It had not stopped Edgar from looking at her since, though he had not approached again. But now this.

Why had he insisted a woman, far from the most proficient or lauded of Vitalis's rebels, be among his guard? Why was she here where the Aetheling and the earl were to discuss what was feared to be a crack in their alliance?

Standing behind Edgar and alongside Vitalis and five other rebels that included the stout Zedekiah, Em moved her gaze around a canvas interior unlike any tent she had seen. It was vast, covering perhaps four times the area of her aunt's cottage, its exact size difficult to gauge due to tapestries suspended ceiling to floor.

Reaching her senses beyond the movable walls, she determined others were here, but were they to be feared? She looked sidelong at her commander.

Gaze fixed on the earl who stood before a chair with a wide-footed base that resembled the letter X whose sound Eberhard had taught her, Vitalis's stance and hand on hilt told he was battle ready.

Hopefully, the King of Denmark's brother had a good reason for being averse to confronting the usurper's army. It was one thing for the Danes to withdraw to their ships following the city's fall, leaving behind only two score to aid in putting down further resistance, another thing to sail farther down the Humber at William's approach. Without the Danes' aid, the Aetheling's advisors had determined the city was indefensible and abandoned it before Vitalis could advise doing so. Considering York was mostly a shell, it was no great loss, but the foothold gained in defeating its defenders was slipping.

"Before we discuss our plans," the earl said in Anglo-Saxon, "may I?" He swept a hand before him.

Edgar dipped his chin.

"Vitalis?" Em breathed when the Dane strode toward her.

"Hold," he said low.

Hoping she was not trembling as much on the outside as the inside, she met the earl's gaze.

He halted and considered her so long that, were it other than her eyes and face he scrutinized, she might have ducked behind Vitalis. *This* was nearly how it had felt before the auction when buyers came to the tents to inspect merchandise made of humans.

"You are very pretty," he pronounced. "Are you a seer? Is that how you knew it was a Norman who drew sword on my son?"

Two things nearly staggered her—the first, he thought it possible she possessed the ungodly power to venture into the future, which could as soon see her slain by her own people as were she Norman. The second thing was the Dane whom Dougray D'Argent injured was the son of an earl.

The King of Denmark's brother smiled. "I am right, hmm?"

"I am no seer. I am Christian." Something to which she had not owned in a long time.

"As am I, but you need not fear me. I think it a good thing you see beyond sight."

"I am not a seer," she said forcefully and, sensing Vitalis's unease, added, "my lord."

The earl put his head to the side. "Then how did you know it was a Norman?"

Only with Vitalis had she shared the truth of the night she aided in Sir Dougray's escape. He had not been angered, though of all those of the family D'Argent he had encountered, the misbegotten brother was the one he truly disliked. As for the sister... Mere mention of that one made him grunt as if to laugh.

"As reported to my commander," she said, "he looked a Saxon, his hair long and face bearded. However, as I did not recognize him and he rose as if from hiding and had a sword to hand, I determined to sound the alarm and apologize later were I mistaken. As now known, I did not err."

"I understand you gave chase."

"Myself and others of my guard, but it was dark and the Norman familiar with the land."

"Perhaps he was no Norman but a traitorous Saxon, of which I am told there are many."

She moistened her lips. "I see no difference between a Norman and a Saxon who betrays his own." At least she had not until *she* betrayed her own, she silently corrected, and wondered how many she had ill-judged for acting in the interest of Normans though they found themselves in positions similar to hers.

"Come." The earl turned away.

When she did not move, the Aetheling looked around. "You heard the earl—follow, Woman."

Had not Vitalis taken her elbow and led her forward, she would have disobeyed.

A glance back at Edgar revealing his displeasure over her commander leaving his side, Em whispered, "I thank you, Vitalis." More thankful than she could say, and that his hand on her did not frighten as once it had. It was a hand made for violence, though only whilst training rebels and in the presence of the enemy.

Not for the first time of recent, she considered it might even be gentle upon a woman he loved. And wished she had not allowed her mind to wander such corridors. He could not care deeply for one as ruined as she. And she was too ruined to return the kind of devotion with which her parents had been blessed.

When Vitalis drew her to a halt in a back corner of the tent, she chided herself for neglecting to attend to her surroundings and wondered how many tapestries they had negotiated.

"She is here, Bjorn." The earl lowered to his haunches before a pallet near the head of a body covered with a linen sheet. "As told, Edgar values our support."

Em looked up at Vitalis, from his grim mouth knew he concluded the same as she that for more than their good reputation the Rebels of the Pale escorted the Aetheling. A young man's whim had been answered by a doting father.

"I told she is pretty," said the one unseen.

"And such eyes she has though they be bruised," his sire said.

Not bruised, Em nearly protested. Though others mistook the dark shadows beneath for bruises, it was fatigue, so lightly had she slept whilst Campagnon's possession—and still slept for fear of once more wearing his collar.

The earl looked over his shoulder. "Come nearer."

At Vitalis's nod, she obeyed. When she halted alongside the earl, he stood and removed his shadow from his son.

Propped on pillows and looking fairly well for one dealt a blade that had dropped him, the young man smiled. "You saved me."

Not true. All she had done was give him time to draw his sword so he could go down fighting rather than shamefully defenseless. If anyone had saved him, it was Dougray D'Argent in showing mercy to one who merely wished to relieve himself.

She cleared her throat. "I but sounded a warning."

"And then, like a true warrior, pursued the enemy."

She clasped her hands before her. "It is unfortunate I could not overtake him."

"You would have killed him, eh?"

"I would have tried," she lied.

"I am glad he got away."

She raised her eyebrows.

He chuckled. "Do you not see? He might have succeeded with you where he failed with me, and you would not be here."

She drew a deep breath. "I am pleased you recover well. Now I must—"

"As you know, I am Bjorn. Though not of my sire's wife, I am fondly regarded."

Baseborn, the same as Dougray D'Argent.

She tried to smile. "As you know, I am Em."

"Just Em? Or Emma?"

"Em." Not exactly a lie since she had not been called the latter since selling herself into slavery.

"A very short name." He shrugged a shoulder. "But I like it."

"My lord," Vitalis said, "should we not rejoin Edgar to discuss that for which we came?"

The earl inclined his head. "We shall commence our discussion whilst the woman tends my son."

Em swung around, but before she could protest, Vitalis said, "She is a soldier not a nursemaid, of better use in service to the Aetheling than spooning broth in your son's mouth."

The earl raised his hands to the sides. "I do not mean to offend. I wish only to give Bjorn and Em privacy in which to become acquainted."

"For what purpose?" Again Vitalis spoke ahead of her.

"It is time my son take a wife and make sons. He likes this daring one, and providing she is—"

"Nay!" This time Em spoke for herself.

"Nay?" It was said with such disbelief and offense, one might think the earl had offered the crown of England and been refused.

"Earl," Vitalis said, tone conciliatory.

The Dane slapped the air. "Let speak the one who insults my son and me." He stepped nearer Em. "Nay, Woman?"

He was not as aggressive as Campagnon, but she had to tell herself the miscreant was not here—that as Dougray D'Argent told, the mercenary was with the usurper.

"For what do you say nay, Em?" Bjorn asked.

She startled when he caught her hand and would have pulled free had his sire not stood between Vitalis and her. Too, he sounded confused rather than angered.

*Vitalis will protect me,* she assured herself, only to ponder what price he would pay should her refusal of Bjorn affect the alliance.

Telling herself she could be someone she was not, she turned back to the young Dane and set her other hand over their two. It made her stomach churn, but less violently than expected.

"You honor me, Bjorn," she pushed out words that also proved easier than expected, not only because of his encouraging smile but that it was true. He seemed a good man, and she had been certain never would a good man want one who—

She frowned, recalled the earl's words over which she had spoken when he said it was time his son take a wife—*providing she is,* he had begun to state a requirement, doubtless that she be virtuous.

Standing taller, she said, "Regrettably, until England is England again, rebellion is the only path for me, no matter how tempting your offer of...happiness. Thus, no husband will I take nor children will I make until the Normans are gone."

"That is why we are here, Em. To help your people."

"And we are grateful. When we are free, let us speak again of you making a life for yourself in my country."

Though that last was meant to discourage him by asserting she would not go home with him, he said, "Be assured, a good life I will have here. With a vast demesne, fine home, and slaves to work the land, I will be a lord and you a lady."

Em hardly heard his last words, struck as she was by his reference to slaves which she would not expect from one whose country had abolished the practice the same as the Normans. But then, Campagnon was Norman.

Though she had been raised to accept slavery as necessary since those unable to feed and clothe themselves might otherwise perish, inwardly she recoiled. No matter the need for labor that could not be found beyond slavery, she herself would starve or freeze to death before benefitting from chattel made of humans.

"You do not like this?" Bjorn asked, and she was glad for his distress. But she would not be foolish.

"What I do not like is that it could be years ere such is possible, but if you can be patient, I can." She drew her hand free, turned to the earl. "Forgive me for any offense. None was intended."

"Still it was dealt," he grumbled. "Though I do not wish a commoner for my son's wife, I would accept you if it is what he desires."

"I am grateful for your willingness to overlook my lowly status," Em said, "but there is another obstacle. The son of an earl, even one born of a lover, ought to wed a virtuous woman. Alas, that I am not."

It was strange to be both pleased and pained by the distaste widening his eyes.

"Still you could be my woman," Bjorn said. "Could she not until a suitable wife is found, Father?"

Bile, so acid she feared it would eat through her throat, kept her from spilling angry words.

"'Tis time we return to Edgar," Vitalis said. "Come, Em."

She hastened to his side, and they began negotiating the tapestries.

"I am proud of you," he said low. "You are stronger and sharper of mind than you believe."

Since part of her training was to accept the criticism and praise of those more learned than she, she pressed her lips, nodded, and stepped out from behind the tapestry ahead of him.

The earl did not immediately follow. Indeed, he kept Edgar waiting an hour—a portent of the Danish alliance, it was feared.

~

It was a relief to part ways with the brooding Edgar. Though the earl had appeased him in the moment, the Aetheling and his men riding center of Vitalis's guard had discussed the meeting and the youth questioned their ally's assurances that seemed of such thin substance they were likely but a salving of pride and concern.

Since Normans scoured the lands near York to flush out the enemy, once they were a league from Axholme, Edgar and his men went one direction and the Rebels of the Pale another, the latter to reunite with its second contingent.

Now where Vitalis stood distant from the campfire, gazing at the stars on this cool night absent cloud cover, he said, "A time of reckoning."

Em thought he conversed with himself, but then he added, "I am sorry to say it, Em, but more and more it appears that way—and not in our favor as Dougray D'Argent warned."

She halted alongside him. "Neither do you trust the earl."

"Even less his brother, the king. When the Normans came across the sea, the one who would be king led them and battled alongside his men. Never was there doubt he intended to make England his. But King Sweyn... His absence from the Danish force eased our concern about his motive for giving aid, but I believe we were lulled."

"What troubles you?"

"What should trouble all the resistance. I wager the Danes are not here to return England to the English. They wish to replace King William with King Sweyn."

As believable as it was, she did not want to accept it, even if it made her appear a simpleton. "But if Danes seek so great a prize, why did the earl withdraw from York? Why does he not battle the Normans to overthrow William?"

"Had it been possible to take the city intact, likely they would have established a base there from which to roll out their own war machine. Thwarted, methinks now he and his men settle in to determine the direction the wind blows by taking measure of

Saxon resistance and the strength of William's grip on our country so they may prepare for the coming of their king."

"I do not believe it."

"You do not *want* to believe it. Though you did not see the earl's disapproval when his enamored son spoke of a good life here in England, you heard Bjorn the same as I." He sighed. "The Danes lay plans to carve up the bone they think to take from the jaws of Normans."

"What of Edgar?" she struggled for argument.

"A pawn who allows them to place Saxon rebels on the front lines ahead of their own men, making it easier to finish off the Normans left standing. Do they allow Edgar to rule, it will be to calm the Saxons just long enough to ensure a good fit for our new yokes." He considered the stars again. "Providing Edgar behaves, his reign could last years, but there will be an end to it. And Sweyn will sit the thrones of two countries."

Fearing Danish rule would be little better than Norman, Em whispered, "What are we to do?"

"Wait, keep watch, ourselves determine the way of the wind." He met her gaze. "And pray we can stomach the direction it blows."

"Surely not that of Normans," she beseeched.

"As ever, God will reveal all in His time." He jutted his chin toward the camp. "Father Julius worries over you. Perhaps you ought to—"

"I ought not." She did not snap at him, though she might were this not the first time he pushed her to seek godly guidance. "The priest may not approve, but I am well with speaking directly to the Lord, and I believe He hears me even when there is no evidence my words have the strength to reach Him."

"Then you have not abandoned your faith." It was said with mild surprise.

Her shrug was defensive. "Often I misplace it, but each time I think it irretrievably lost, just enough prayers are answered to keep it 'round me."

Something of a smile moved his mouth.

And something of a thrill moved her heart.

"I do not think I could have said it better. I have felt the same, Em."

"Truly?"

"Aye, though my sufferings do not compare to yours."

She knew not to step nearer, but she did, causing his eyes to narrow and mouth to flatten.

"You know you are like a sister to me, do you not, Em?" he spoke words meant to discourage without offending.

But she needed no discouraging, that one moment of being drawn to him as far as she would allow herself to go with a man—and that was fearfully far considering only a year past the fleeting touch of the opposite sex made her long to peel that skin from her bones.

"As you are like a brother to me," she said. And here a means of turning the conversation. "Though not as precious as my brother, Eberhard, and my younger brother and sister." She clasped her hands at her waist. "You recall I told I wish to go south to verify the little ones are well?"

"I do."

"Now that I am trained to defend myself and others, I am as safe as can be. Thus, it is time."

"You are safer than a year past, but still in grave danger, especially with Campagnon searching for you."

"A risk I must take. If my siblings are in need, I may be their only hope."

Vitalis set a hand on her shoulder. "Remain with us until we know if this uprising births others."

He referred to Edgar's messengers who carried tidings across England of the victory at York in the hope of encouraging great numbers of Saxons to rise up against the oppressors.

"We should know within a sennight," Vitalis said. "If what we achieved here was not in vain, it is possible the Rebels of the Pale will go south to aid efforts there and you will have our protection for a good part of your journey."

"A sennight," she whispered.

"What is one more, Em?"

She agreed, and he dropped his hand from her. "Gain your rest. On the morrow, we break camp."

To stay ahead of the Normans who would put to the sword any believed to have participated in York's fall.

Em wished him a good eve and returned to the bed made of a blanket spread upon armfuls of gathered grass. Unfortunately, no matter how comfortable it was, it would not gift her the deep sleep denied her for years.

~

City of York
Yorkshire, England

"Axholme." William stared at the map that showed the isle surrounded by marshland. "How well fortified, Sir Maël?"

Campagnon snorted. "Hardly at all, my liege. Were it, we could not have—"

"I did not put the question to you, Sir Raymond!"

The mercenary who had been close-mouthed until now pressed his lips so hard they drained of color. Much he wanted to say, but he had good reason not to speak unless given cause.

Thus far, Dougray, Maël, and Sir Guy gave him no cause. It was an exchange of sorts. They would not reveal that by behaving a child denied his toy, four of the king's men might have been slaughtered, and he would not make complaint against those he believed had stolen his slave's paper. But this uneasy truce did not mean he would not seek to discover the preservation or destruction of written proof he owned Em. For that, Dougray must watch his back, sides, and front. If Campagnon did not himself come for this D'Argent of the family he detested, one of his fellow mercenaries would.

"Fairly well fortified," Maël answered, "and each day that passes, more so."

"Poor Edgar," William scorned. "He knows not how remiss his advisors in not warning it bodes ill the Danes refuse to meet me in battle." He frowned. "You say Gospatric and Maerleswein were not among his escort?"

"They were not. I think it true they and their men fled north."

"Mice! They scurry from their holes when the cat is away, scurry back when the one with teeth and claws reappears. Hence, the moment I take my army elsewhere, the cowards will strike again." He crossed to a leather-covered chair recovered from the city's ruins and dropped into it. "Who escorted Edgar to Axholme?"

At Maël's hesitation, once more Campagnon overstepped. "Rebels of the Pale, my liege. I am certain they were among Edgar's men."

Annoyance flashed across William's face. "How certain?"

"Though I have only seen Vitalis at a distance, the one at Edgar's side was as described by my fellow chevalier, Merle—exceedingly tall and of red hair and beard. It was him."

William looked to the other three. "You agree?"

All concurred, and Dougray noted Campagnon did not mention Em. Not surprising since the king did not approve of slavery. Unfortunately, as long as revenues from the trade funded the army required to repress insurrection, William would not outlaw it in England.

"Did you follow them when they departed the isle?" the king asked.

"We did not," Sir Guy said. "There was too little cover and we determined it best we deliver you tidings without delay."

Mostly true, Dougray reflected. What he did not say was the greatest risk in following the Aetheling and his escort was Campagnon who had to be further restrained upon regaining consciousness.

Dougray looked to the mercenary whose gaze he felt and smiled the smile of one who warned, *I will not tell if you do not.*

"I understand the others not following," the king said, "but you should have, Sir Dougray."

The reprimand expected, Dougray said, "I beg your forgiveness."

"Given once earned, which you shall do by discovering where Edgar and those of the pale have gone." His hands curled over the chair arms, and in a voice dark with threat, he said, "I have spilled my last drop of patience. May God bear witness, I will be done with these rebels ere year's end."

William not one to idly call on the Lord to witness the word he gave, Dougray felt a constriction about his soul. As feared, the king's appeasement of his new subjects that had failed a dozen times too often had found its end at York though, were William honest with himself, time and again he had given the English abundant cause to reject him.

But was Dougray responsible for the suffering to come—at least in part? Had he not warned Em, would the rebels have been at York when the Norman army arrived? Thus, a battle fought and wrath unleashed on those who acted against the king and that the end of it?

*In veering from my mission so I might protect one, did I endanger thousands?* he wondered.

"With your permission, my liege," Campagnon said, "I shall join your scout in tracking the Rebels of the Pale."

"Denied," the king said, to the relief of Dougray who was certain injury or death would result if Campagnon and he kept company again. "On the morrow, you will join your fellow mercenaries in putting my enemies to the sword." William pushed up out of the chair. "We are done. Sir Maël, resume your command of my guard."

The warriors turned away.

"Sir Dougray," the king called as the others departed ahead of him.

"My liege?"

"No rest for you. Provision yourself and find Edgar and the Rebels of the Pale."

That he must, as soon as possible delivering them to William so fewer innocents suffer the punishment of others.

Dougray inclined his head, and as he exited, gripped the purse on his belt and heard the protest of parchment. Hoping Em had left the rebels, he lengthened his stride.

# CHAPTER FOUR

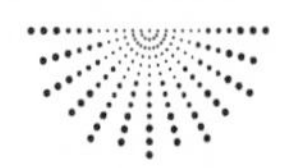

Nottinghamshire
England

Four days of tracking, on the second day evidence of Rebels of the Pale—that of a great number of horses for which they were known. Since that day, Vitalis and his followers stayed only far enough ahead of Dougray the ashes of their abandoned fires remained warm. But now he had them as he did not wish but must. Just over the border in Nottinghamshire, it appeared they numbered fifty, among them a half dozen women.

For an hour, he watched for Em, and though several times he caught sight of Vitalis, no glimpse was afforded of Campagnon's slave.

Had she left their ranks as hoped? If so, where had she gone? To her younger siblings which the paper he carried indicated were in the South? Her brother upon Wulfenshire?

Regardless, it was good she was not here. Once he mapped these rebels' movements that, hopefully, led to the Aetheling, he must do his duty—even if those he uprooted were his sister-in-law's people. Were William delivered enough of those responsible for the Normans slain at York, he might not loose wrath on men, women, and children merely encountered on the path to his enemies.

Dougray set his back against the tree, took the skin from his belt, and finished the last of his wine. He had dried meat and fish aplenty so he not render himself vulnerable while cooking fresh game, but henceforth his drink must be drawn from streams and rivers that offered the cleanest water possible.

Once more, visually he marked the sentries posted around the camp, then departed. Ere dark fell two hours hence, he would make a place for himself upstream to pass the night. That was the plan—until a quarter hour later he sensed he was no longer alone.

Having followed the river toward where he had secured his horse, he paused behind a tree and delved the opposite bank ahead.

Shortly, a shift of light became movement, and a mounted warrior emerged from a copse. No Saxon this, but neither an ally. Here was Campagnon's fellow mercenary who had great cause to dislike this D'Argent.

Not only had Dougray captured Sir Merle during his attempt to set fire to a crop upon Wulfenshire, but force had been required to gain the miscreant's written confession he acted on Campagnon's orders. Unfortunately, he had recanted when brought before the king, allowing his friend to escape punishment while he and others captured with him took the blame. A further travesty of justice was all they had suffered was months of imprisonment, after which they returned to Campagnon to do his bidding—in this instance, retrieval of his slave.

As Dougray retraced steps that once more distanced him from his destrier, he raked through memories for evidence he had led Merle here. He had covered his advance as much as possible lest the tracker become the tracked and attended to those whose paths nearly crossed his. Either Merle excelled at stealth, or his skills were limited to tracking that had placed him in the vicinity of his prey.

No great worry, Dougray assured himself, especially since Em was not here. He had only to ensure Merle continued onward. However, if the mercenary discovered the encampment, which was possible considering his success thus far, it would become a matter of ensuring he did not reveal himself to the rebels—and Dougray being first to reach William who would be displeased Campagnon's man had sabotaged the tracking.

Leisurely, Merle guided his mount over ground that at times offered enough cover to conceal horse and rider, at other times starkly exposed them. The farther upstream he journeyed, the more Dougray's tension eased. But to salvage his original plan, he would have to follow for hours to be certain Merle did not retrace his steps. And still the knave might return when he found no further sign of his quarry.

Dougray bent low to traverse a span between trees on this side of the widening river formed by the convergence of several smaller ones and straightened behind an aged oak. He had gained ground ahead of Merle who yawned and stretched in the saddle—unaware the two here he believed one had become three.

"God's rood!" Dougray rasped.

Upstream, a woman dressed as a man, unbound hair rippling down her back, eased off a large rock on this side of the river. He was not close enough to look near on her where she bobbed in the water, mouth open as if gasping over the cold, but it was Em who distanced herself from others to bathe in privacy—albeit fully clothed.

Though Dougray beseeched the Lord to turn Merle aside, he saw the moment Em came to notice.

The mercenary halted his horse and leaned forward, grinned, and dismounted. Blessedly, he did not unfasten the bow from his saddle. But there was no need since he was unaware he had a rival.

Now she submerged, the undulating water evidencing she swam toward the opposite bank which Merle approached.

Though Dougray's first thought was to sound a warning, there was no time when she reached that bank, so swiftly she came up for air, turned, and went under again. Hopefully, when she returned to this side, she would come out—and the river was as deep as it appeared, giving her time to flee Merle before he found a good crossing.

The predator was moving now, much the same as Dougray in spurts, hunkered flight, and pauses.

It was a challenge to advance ahead of him without being seen. Were he sighted, the mercenary would abandon stealth and all would be decided by which side of the river Em was on when the men drew level. Though Dougray believed upon finding herself trapped between them she would choose him over Campagnon's man, were she nearer the latter, Merle could have her astride before Dougray made it to the opposite bank. Timing was all.

From cover of a tree directly across from Em, Dougray saw the mercenary was a hundred feet distant—fortunate for his prey since she neared the bank on his side and he would be unable to reach her before she started back. Surely aware of that, Merle dropped out of sight before she surfaced, and as soon as she went under, resumed his advance. When next she returned to his side, he would try to take her.

Dougray stepped out from behind the tree. Knowing the mercenary would catch sight of him, he fixed his gaze on the woman swimming toward the center of the river and feigned ignorance of his fellow Norman as he ran to the rock by which Em had entered the water.

Sidelong, he saw Merle drop, it benefitting him none to reveal himself unless his quarry was near. Thus, if Dougray succeeded, Merle would believe he had surprise on his side when he attempted to take Em from his fellow Norman.

It being imperative she not return to the opposite bank,

Dougray bent low as he neared the river lest she glimpse him through the water. He reached the rock just ahead of her, dropped to his haunches alongside her scabbarded sword, adjusted his balance, and gripped her wrist as she came up for air and started to turn.

Blue and brown eyes splaying, upper lashes tracing the under curve of her eyebrows, lower lashes tracing the dark shadows beneath, she screamed.

Unable to silence her call for help that would bring rebels running were any near, he pulled her toward him and began straightening to add the strength of his legs to the effort.

She screamed again, drew up her knees, and thrust bare feet against the rock's edge.

Despite a relatively slight figure, the force of her leverage threatened to dump him in the river. Risking injuring her to keep her from Merle, he wrenched her toward him—just as she slashed at his chest with a dagger brought to hand.

Surprise more than the sting of scored flesh eased his hold, and she yanked free.

As she propelled backward, fury shot through him. She had acted as she should in the face of an enemy. *He* had acted as a warrior should not. And blame for his shortcoming did not entirely rest on the loss of an arm.

"Stop!" he shouted.

She continued to distance herself, keeping him in sight and having no care for watching her back.

As she would soon be within the mercenary's reach, Dougray called, "Sir Merle is that side!"

He feared her too shaken to make sense of his words, but she paused and, treading water, looked around.

Since she lacked Dougray's vantage, and even he glimpsed the miscreant only because he knew where to look, he said, "He is in the grass beyond the reeds. My word I give."

"The word of a N-Norman." Her teeth clicked. "Of no use to me or any Saxon."

"It is the same word Lady Hawisa and Lady Aelfled accept from their D'Argent husbands."

Her throat convulsed with a swallow. "I am not one of them. I was common, then a s-slave, next a criminal for fleeing m-my master, now a rebel. As well you know, honesty is n-not my due."

It seemed he would have to test the ability of one who had once been a strong swimmer against one who, in this moment, felt half a man as he had not since beginning the journey to salvage the warrior. It was not possible he would ever again be whole, but half was unacceptable. Though he could not reach Em before she gained the bank, Merle would not take her without a fight—nor with.

Dougray reached up, the sudden movement causing her to startle, then did as done only when he practiced at arms and bedded down at night. He unfastened the clasp at his neck and let his mantle fall to reveal the absence of a hand protruding from his left sleeve.

"What do you?" she demanded.

"What I must to keep you from Campagnon. If you will not come out, I shall come in."

Her eyes widened, then she flipped around, ducked underwater, and swam opposite.

Dougray stepped forward, but before he could go in after her, a voice struck like steel. "Do you move, I will shoot you in the air, D'Argent, drop you like a bird bound for the spit."

# CHAPTER FIVE

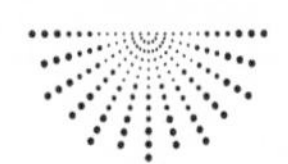

Vitalis had arrived, doubtless armed with a bow. Bad for this Norman who had long ago made an enemy of Lady Hawisa's man, good for Em.

Dougray looked from where she neared the opposite bank to Merle's tunic visible amid the grass and reeds, then turned his head toward the red-haired warrior who stood with bow extended, string to cheek, arrow centered on his enemy's back.

"It is good you have a full quiver, Vitalis. You will need at least one for Campagnon's man. He lies in the grass opposite, twenty feet to the right."

The warrior shifted his gaze where directed just as Em announced her surfacing with a gasp.

As she pulled herself onto the bank and struggled to get her feet beneath her, Dougray shouted, "Back in the water!"

Unaware Vitalis had answered her call, she started forward. Blessedly, she still had her dagger to hand.

"Em!" Vitalis called just as Merle thrust upright.

She spun around. And faltered at the sight of the mercenary.

An arrow sped past Dougray. It missed Merle as the man wove

toward Em. Lest the next found its mark, he would have to make a shield of her.

"Put him to ground, Soldier!" Vitalis bellowed.

She drew back an arm and, with grace Dougray had never before seen, flew the dagger.

It struck Merle in the shoulder a moment ahead of an arrow entering his side. His fall altered by the side impact, he jerked and dropped.

"Do you even twitch, D'Argent," Vitalis warned, "the next shall be yours, severing your spine and leaving you a cripple does it not also pierce your heart."

The same as Godfroi, Dougray silently acknowledged the helplessness of the warrior who had risen above his crippling to raise alongside legitimate sons a boy not of his loins—even more unbelievable than that Vitalis did not mock Dougray for already being lamed, one whose strokes through the water would have been so impaired it was unlikely he would have reached Em ahead of Merle.

Returning her to focus, he saw she stared at the fallen Norman, the fist made of the hand that had flown the dagger pressed to her chest.

"Come this side!" Vitalis shouted.

Em heard her commander, but her head buzzed, causing the sounds all around to crackle like distant thunder. Wondering if this was another dark dream, she watched Campagnon's man dig his heels into the grass as one shaking hand sought to remove the dagger from his chest while the other dragged on the shaft protruding from his side.

"Soldier!" Vitalis shouted.

She heard his anger but could not take her eyes from one of several tormentors she had suffered whilst enslaved by Campagnon. They had not been permitted to do to her the same as their leader, but they had taunted and leered—and out of sight of Campagnon, touched, squeezed, and pinched.

"Come!" Vitalis ordered.

She shook her head, then more deeply feeling the chill of wet garments dripping onto hands and feet, stepped forward.

"Em!"

Though fear edged her commander's voice, she continued forward.

Her shadow across the mercenary opened his eyes, and he gave a grunt of laughter that caused crimson to slide from one corner of his mouth down his jaw.

Bleeding into his lungs from Vitalis's arrow, he croaked, "When Raymond is done with you, vengeance will be mine." He coughed hard, then ceased trying to free the blade and shaft from his body.

Shaking, Em lowered to her haunches. "Never again will that knave lay hands on me."

He showed bloody teeth. "He will more than lay hands on you. Over and again, he will make you suffer. And how I would like to be there." As he had been the one time she alerted Campagnon those he believed faithful to him did more than taunt and leer.

She leaned in. "It is time to answer for your lies and theft, the ravished and the murdered." She drew another breath. "Go, nithing. Go, poltroon. Go, sinner."

"Whore!"

She did not flinch when his fingers grazed her jaw, and moments later his eyes rolled up and bloodied palms unfurled.

Slowly, she stood and turned to Vitalis who was twenty strides distant from the bank, an arrow trained on the Norman who had warned her Campagnon's man was here.

Gazing upon Dougray D'Argent, she wondered at the bloody slash across his upper tunic, then recalled she had done it to one who had not lied but…

*But what?* she sought to clear her muddied thoughts.

*But he is here with Merle. They trapped you between them. Was it a contest made of you? Or did this Norman truly seek to aid you?*

"He is dead?" Vitalis called.

"Aye. Gone. Never to return."

"Come back!"

She wanted to, but the prospect of returning to the water made her shake harder.

"Now!"

As she skirted the corpse, she hesitated over her dagger but could not bring herself to free it. Whoever disposed of Merle's body would retrieve it and anything else of use to the rebels.

Though earlier Em had welcomed the challenge of a strong current, it required great effort to return to the other side. Body quaking, teeth chattering, she reached the rock where she had unbelted her sword.

As she engaged protesting muscles and limbs to drag herself from the water, she saw Dougray D'Argent now stood a half dozen strides from Vitalis, and on the ground was his sword belt surely removed under threat of the arrow trained on him.

"Gain your sword and don the chevalier's mantle!" her commander ordered.

*I ought not be so cold,* she told herself as she donned her own sword belt and adjusted her tunic to ensure her scarred shoulder remained covered. *Is this shock, or was I too long out of the water without movement to warm me?*

The latter, she determined and snatched up the Norman's mantle. Ever she bathed clothed regardless of the season, mostly for fear of baring herself, even when it appeared she was alone. Of added benefit, it cleaned her fouled garments. Providing she remained in motion—swimming and afterward running to camp—she warded off the worst of the cold and had only to sit before a fire to warm and dry herself.

Frustrated by the clasp of D'Argent's mantle, she gripped the garment closed at the neck and did her best to walk a straight line to Vitalis.

"You are well?" he asked as she halted alongside him.

"How could I not be?" She met Sir Dougray's gaze and, in a language she hated but had well enough learned whilst a slave, said, "After all, another Norman is dead."

"Retrieve his belt," Vitalis said. "And Sir Dougray, pray you do not have an itch that needs scratching."

As taught her, Em kept her eyes on her enemy, using side vision to guide her to where he had tossed his belt from which hung sword, the dagger set with a blue gem, and a sizable purse of worn leather. Closing stiff fingers around the belt, she was surprised by the weight.

D'Argent's weapons were twice as heavy as her own—and certainly his purse, though she heard no coin song. Doubtless, he used fleece to muffle the silver within.

His eyes, whose color she questioned for the first time, lowered to the belt as she retraced her steps. "I will want those returned."

Vitalis snorted. "A pity Saxons are not inclined to give Normans what they want."

"Greater the pity for the losses of Saxons who refuse to submit to their king," D'Argent retorted.

Em's commander shrugged. "It cannot be helped. Resistance to thieves and murderers is in our blood." Keeping his arrow nocked, he released the string's tension and drew his sword from its scabbard. Though he did so swiftly, Em sensed Dougray D'Argent could have challenged the rebel leader were he of a mind to chance it in the absence of having a weapon to hand. But he had not even tensed. It was as if he settled into the role of captive—and yet not with resignation but the confidence of one who believes he has naught to fear.

Sword pointed at D'Argent's chest, Vitalis hooked the bow over his shoulder and slid the arrow into its quiver. "Tell why I should not end you the same as your fellow Norman, D'Argent."

"I would think it obvious—I sought to protect your *soldier* from Sir Merle."

"Did you?" Em challenged and saw his eyes were of a gold so liquid it had to be contained by rims wrought of bronze. "More, it appears I was stalked as if it were a contest to see who could capture me."

His eyebrows rose. "Just as I am here by order of King William and Sir Merle by order of Raymond Campagnon, our missions are different. Mine was to discover the location of the Aetheling and Rebels of the Pale. Sir Merle's was to return a runaway slave to her master. But whereas Campagnon's man knew the task given me, I became aware of the task given him only when I caught sight of him after I departed your camp. To ensure he did not reveal himself and sabotage my efforts, I followed him upstream and discovered you had not left the rebels as it appeared."

Em frowned. If he spoke true, her decision to remain beneath Vitalis's protection awhile longer could have seen her returned to slavery, but the fault would be hers. Vitalis had warned her not to venture far from camp, but since she was a sennight without a bath, needful of privacy, and believed William's men would not venture beyond Lincolnshire's borders, she had thought it safe. If Vitalis had not come in search of her, her screams would have gone unheard.

"When I drew you from the river," D'Argent continued, "it was to keep you from the other side where Sir Merle planned to take you."

"I am to believe you laid ruin to your mission to aid a lowly rebel?" she scorned.

His lids narrowed. "Not only did the knave's attempt to return you to Campagnon cause my mission to run aground, but as should be apparent from our every encounter, I find men who prey on women offensive—worthy of themselves being made prey. Too, there is the debt you believe I owe you. If ever I did, it is settled."

She noted he did not mention how it was acquired and would

have been relieved had she not told Vitalis she had made a path for D'Argent past the sentries at York.

"So well, indeed," he added, "I do not think it exaggeration now *you* are in my debt."

If not for the glint in his eyes, it might have escaped her it was the same she had said to him at York. But though it seemed mockery and she longed to argue, she knew just as he had caught hold of her when she replenished her breath, Merle would have. Even had Campagnon's man provided an opportunity to summon Vitalis with a scream, the expanse of river could have provided enough time for him to knock her senseless and carry her away.

Hopefully not to her detriment, she believed what Dougray D'Argent told. There was good in this man, even if not enough to outweigh the bad of one who hunted rebels.

"I think he speaks true, Vitalis."

He raised an eyebrow.

"In my purse you will find a parchment," D'Argent said and shifted his shoulders, causing the half-empty sleeve to sway. "Further proof I intended you no harm."

Em loosened the drawstring and withdrew a cream-colored cylinder.

"Now returned to you," he said.

She frowned. "Never have I possessed anything of this sort."

"Be assured, it is yours."

Did he play with her? The nearest she had come to parchment were hides so thin the black scratched upon them seemed almost to float on the air, whether held by an official speaking the words or nailed to a tree.

Fearful D'Argent entertained himself by making her feel a simpleton, she said, "What is it?"

"Open it."

She untied the string affixed to it by a broken wax seal and unrolled it. Many were the words boldly written like the scattered pieces of a drawing, and beneath them, more wax pressed down on a crook of crossed ribbon.

She knew she should pass the parchment to Vitalis who was proficient with the written word, but she was further unsettled by shame different from what Campagnon had heaped on her.

"I do not see how this numbers among my possessions," Em said.

His brow lined, a moment later smoothed. "I assumed you could read the same as your brother. Forgive me."

Her confidence wavered amid rising discomfort she should not feel since few of the common—even the nobility—were learned in letters, but she felt exposed.

Vitalis stepped nearer. "I will read it."

"Nay." She turned her shoulder to him and tried to sound the letters in her mind to form words. And failed. She looked to D'Argent. "I *was* learning to read, but there has been no opportunity to continue my study these past months."

Had she to name what shone from his eyes, she would call it pity, but as anger rose through her, he said, "Can you recognize your written name?"

The first thing her brother had taught her. "I can."

"It is above the seal at the bottom."

She recognized the first and second letters as belonging to her, but this was of four letters and closely followed by three other words. Though she knew many of the sounds of those letters, they were too numerous. "Em is not here."

"But Emma Irwindotter of Gloucester is. That is your name in full, is it not?"

Now she could see the first was *Emma,* a name brought across the channel by Emma of Normandy who had wed two kings of England. "It appears my name in full, but why is it written here?"

"That is your bill of sale."

She startled.

"Under the king's orders, myself and three others tracked the

Rebels of the Pale and the Aetheling—with whom it appears you have since parted—to your meeting with the Danes upon Axholme."

Certain Vitalis was more alarmed than she, Em glanced at him and saw his face had darkened.

"It was there I took that from Campagnon," D'Argent said.

Em gasped. "He was on the isle?"

"Aye, and so determined to retrieve you, he nearly revealed us. Thus, it was necessary to silence him."

Em looked to the parchment. "My paper."

"Proof of his ownership," he more terribly defined it.

"If I destroy it, am I free?"

"I fear not. As long as there are witnesses to the sale, he could assert his claim, and even were there none to attest to his ownership, at such a time as this and since you possess eyes eager to betray you, you are not safe."

"Then of what use is this?"

"Its absence allows fellow Saxons—and Normans—opposed to the trade to aid you without openly defying the law of the land. Hence, if Campagnon must produce proof of ownership, the delay in securing witnesses could provide time in which to escape him again."

It seemed of little consequence since, had Sir Merle seized her this day, there would have been none to whom she could appeal. Still, a thrill went through her knowing the knave she had been forced to title *my beloved lord* was deprived of what she would put to flame.

"I believe this Norman speaks true," she said and slid the parchment beneath her belt.

"Regardless, we have a problem, Sir Dougray," Vitalis said. "I do not doubt you detest Campagnon the same as Sir Merle, the latter most obvious at Stern Castle when you..." His mouth curved. "...*coaxed* a confession from the knave, but still you are William's man. To ensure the safety of Edgar and my rebels, I ought to kill you. Fortunate for you, Lady Hawisa and her husband stand between you and death. Not only would I not have my lady's marriage suffer should your brother learn her housecarle severed your life, but Sir Guarin has earned my good regard as much as possible for a Norman."

*And mine,* Em silently acknowledged what had been unthinkable until six weeks past when the Rebels of the Pale paused in northern Wulfenshire. Past middle night, she had ventured near the castle to verify her brother fared well. The long wait proved worthwhile when those training at Wulfen assembled outside the walls for a pre-dawn run.

At the great waterfall, she had intercepted Eberhard out of sight of the others. He had flung his arms around her and both had wept. In their short time together, he revealed the same which Sir Dougray later told when Em helped him at York—Sir Guarin had saved Ebbe when he sought to slay Campagnon at Darfield and he had been aided by the third D'Argent sibling.

The parting of brother and sister had been painful, Ebbe so insistent on joining the rebels despite her assurance Lady Hawisa had done the right thing in continuing his training, it had been necessary to be cruel in refusing him. But he was where he needed to be and, God willing, would continue to excel so no matter what came of the conquerors, he would be able to defend himself and his country.

"I could make a captive of you," Vitalis mused, "but I am loath to once more be the jailer of a D'Argent."

Sir Dougray raised his eyebrows. "I am to believe a Saxon in possession of a Norman found it distasteful keeping my brother chained in a cave? That there was no satisfaction in permitting him sunlight only when it served the rebel cause to fix him to posts and force him to defend himself so common men and women might learn the ways of enemy warriors?"

Vitalis shrugged as if it were a small thing of which he was accused, but Em knew better. She was not well versed in Guarin

D'Argent's captivity but was acquainted enough with her commander to know had he felt any satisfaction in punishing a man for the sins of his fellow countrymen, he had not long indulged in what had surely been more bitter than sweet.

"I would think you sufficiently informed to know what role I played in holding Sir Guarin," Vitalis said. "If you are not, it will have to wait until next you reunite with your brother. Now, as I can neither slay nor take you prisoner, it is best you pass the night here."

"Then I am, indeed, a captive."

"A temporary state. Not only will my men and women gain a restful night unaware there is a Norman in our midst, but on the morrow we shall have adequate time to withdraw ere you bring Le Bâtard's army down upon us. Of course, all is conditional on you giving the word of a D'Argent that rather than continue to track us you will return to your king with whatever tale best serves the demise of Sir Merle."

So great a risk it seemed to Em, she was certain Vitalis would not take it with any other.

"If I do not give my word?" the chevalier asked.

"Give it, and I will ensure you are able to escape your bindings within hours following our departure so you may retrieve your mount and return to York. Refuse, and you will escape your fettering only if a fellow Norman, rather than a vengeful Saxon, happens on you within the next few days."

A smile bent Sir Dougray's mouth. "It seems I must give the word of a D'Argent."

"Beneath the eyes of God," Vitalis qualified, "lest you think your oath easily broken by one who is not truly of the D'Argent line."

Em noted Sir Dougray's stiffening. Obviously, much tale there since he had a younger brother and sister who were of the same male line as his two older brothers.

"Lend me my sword," he said.

At Vitalis's nod, Em stepped near. Gripping the base of the belted sword's hilt lest he snatch it from its scabbard, she extended it.

He remained motionless, his eyes delving hers, then he considered the shadows beneath which some believed were bruises.

Returning his gaze to hers, he turned his hand around the wire-wrapped hilt. Lower finger pressing against her upper, he said, "In the sight of God, I give the word of Sir Dougray, known by the name D'Argent, that once my bonds are loosened I shall refrain from tracking the Rebels of the Pale until after I have reported to King William."

Reprieve only, but perhaps enough he would lose their scent.

"Search him for other weapons," Vitalis ordered.

She placed the weapon-heavy belt in the grass beside Vitalis. Though she continued to feel the cold, she removed D'Argent's mantle lest it hinder her search and dropped it alongside the belt.

Then she set herself at his back. It was not the first time she had run hands over a man, both Lady Hawisa and Vitalis requiring it when Normans whose lives were to be spared were relieved of weapons. However, this was different—as it should not be, but surely due to his left arm over which he tensed when she set a hand on that shoulder.

She did not wish to feel for his loss, but she did and quickly moved her search lower before coming around to his front. Keeping her chin down, she drew her hands over his chest. More lightly, she probed the ribs she had slashed to gain her release, as evidenced by the bloodied tear in his tunic. The cut was not deep, but it would require tending.

She took two daggers from him—one from a second belt beneath his tunic, the other his left boot.

"Thorough," he said as she straightened.

She looked up and wished she had sooner when she saw his

eyes did not await hers. They were fixed on her shoulder, and the reason required no inventory of her body.

As she swung away, she snatched the neck of her tunic up over the scar that had come uncovered. Had it happened when she removed D'Argent's mantle? If so, likely Vitalis had seen it as well.

Gaze averted, she accepted the coil of rope her commander unhooked from his belt and, blessedly, met no resistance in fettering D'Argent. Still, several times she hesitated while fixing him to the tree against which he sat, what he did not speak in words asked in the silence between them—how had she been so terribly disfigured?

"What of my sword and dagger?" he asked when she finished.

Vitalis returned his own blade to his scabbard and lifted the chevalier's belt. "I am tempted to add such fine weapons to our cause." He touched one, then the other. "For a time, a sister of this D'Argent dagger was in my keeping. I understand since Sir Guarin's marriage to my lady, its sapphire has been replaced with a ruby to represent the house of Wulfrith whose Saxon name your brother has taken."

"As required of him by King William," Sir Dougray said with resentment.

Vitalis was not given to smiles, but his lips curved. "Since it is no longer safe for any to travel these lands, I shall not yield to temptation." He dropped the belt atop the mantle and looked to Em. "Return to camp. If any ask after me, tell them we crossed paths, and I am in pursuit of game."

"You will remain here with him?"

"Nay, I must conceal the mercenary's body, secure his mount for our use, and search the area to ensure neither he nor Sir Dougray have traveling companions."

Then Dougray D'Argent would be left alone and defenseless. It bothered as it should not that even if he did not become the prey of men, among the beasts lurking here was the boar who could as effectively end a man's life with tusk and tooth as could steel. But there was naught for it.

"Within the hour," Vitalis continued, "you are to discreetly depart camp and return here with drink and viands."

Em kept refusal from her lips by assuring herself she had nothing to fear from a defenseless Norman, nor need she answer any questions he might put to her. More importantly, Vitalis provided an opportunity to prove herself worthy of his trust.

"Within the hour," she agreed and ran.

# CHAPTER SIX

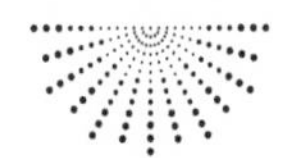

He despised his loss, but whether the absence of his lower arm distracted, reviled, or caused the warrior to be underestimated, opportunities abounded to turn those vulnerabilities against an opponent.

Em should not have averted her gaze nor hands from his half-empty sleeve, and Vitalis should not have allowed it. Had they been diligent, he would have been relieved of the scabbard strapped to the inside of his upper arm that held a dagger whose hilt was flush with what was no longer a joint.

Of further advantage was the manner in which he was bound lacking the powerful vise made of roped wrists. Em was to be commended for securing him to the tree, but the expansion of his chest during that binding allowed enough space upon emptying his lungs to work his right hand beneath the ropes to his left arm—and remove the dagger.

Vitalis having taken longer than expected to conceal Merle's body, retrieve the chevalier's horse, and begin his search of the area for other Normans, speed was of the essence were Dougray to escape before Em's return.

He would not make lie of the word he had given, only free

himself to ensure his release. Though Guarin might be on fairly firm footing with Vitalis, not Dougray who had cause to doubt his Saxon rival would do as professed.

He set the blade against the lowermost rope beneath his left arm, but as he began slicing through tightly twisted hemp, above the river's song he caught what might be sound or merely sensation. Were it of *something,* the sooner he must work the blade. Were it of *someone,* better he conceal it.

Glimpsing no movement, wishing his senses as perfectly honed as his youngest brother's, he strained to identify whether the one who approached was two-legged or four-legged. There, the sound of one who moved on two legs.

He dragged his right arm beneath the straining rope to return it to that side, then rotated the dagger up beneath his sleeve, pressed the flat of the blade against the inside of his forearm, and curled his fingers over the hilt's pommel.

The woman who appeared was the same he had saved from once more being enslaved.

Easing his head back against the trunk, Dougray watched her advance. Hair fashioned into two braids, wet garments exchanged for dry, she carried a cloth bag across her body whose strap rode the scarred shoulder she had guiltily concealed. Recalling the ravaged skin whose acquisition appeared fairly recent, once more he tensed over the possibility Campagnon was responsible.

"I brought food and drink and gathered wood to set a warming fire," she said, halting before him. "Also salve and bandages."

That last unsettled, the familiarity required to tend his injury risking discovery of the dagger. "If it is true I am to find my release on the morrow, food and drink will suffice, and my mantle is all the warmth I require. Later, I shall tend my injury."

She lifted the bag over her head and placed it on the ground with a clatter that evidenced the makings of a fire. "As it can be no other way, I count you my enemy, Dougray D'Argent, and yet I know you aided in keeping my brother safe at Darfield, believe you sought to save me from Sir Merle, and am grateful for my… bill of sale."

"Did you destroy it?"

Her eyes above dark shadows wavered. "I shall tend you as best I can," she ignored his question, "and when you return to your king, neither debt nor vengeance need ever again draw you unto me nor me unto you."

He shifted his regard between the blue eye and the brown and was so struck by indecision over which to look upon, realized just as the loss of his lower arm made others vulnerable to him, the same was true of her eyes. They would distract the curious, revile the superstitious, and cause fools to underestimate her.

"Do you not agree?" she prompted.

"Neither debt nor vengeance is in play here, Em. What *is* in play is ending the unrest devouring your country."

Though day waned, he saw anger streak her eyes. "Aye, *my* country. Not yours nor Le Bâtard's. Why can you not…?" Briefly, she closed her eyes. "'Tis useless to argue with a Norman."

Neither did Dougray wish to argue. Though imperative the rebellion end were England to be salvaged, which might prove impossible if the Danes further tore at its fabric, clearly it was not the time to persuade her what had been done at Hastings could not be undone.

Turning her face away, she began removing items from the bag.

Though he was tempted to be harsh with her so she would depart sooner, he let her do as she would, the reward of it watching her, the punishment feeling something move in him—and not for the first time.

Impossible was Cyr and his Saxon wife, Aelfled.

Impossible was Guarin and his warrior wife, Hawisa.

Beyond impossible was Dougray and a slave-turned-rebel no matter how much he was attracted to her. And this one who had been Campagnon's plaything ought not move him at all.

After building a fire to ease the chill of coming night, she set out cloth-wrapped bread and cheese and a skin that, whether it bulged with wine or ale, would be welcome. What was not welcome was the pot of salve.

"First your injury?" she asked. "Or food and drink?"

Assuring himself she had no cause to venture near his right arm, he said, "My injury."

Em stared. Something about this man disturbed that should not with him so well bound that even were this Campagnon, she would have no cause to fear drawing close enough to feel his breath on her face.

*No cause other than memories of when last that foul breath was upon you,* the thought slipped in.

She shoved it out, told herself she was no longer without recourse, and feeling the weight of the dagger on her belt, brought the wineskin, salve, and bandages near.

Though she knew it was best to free D'Argent's tunic from beneath the ropes to access that portion of his ribs she had cut, her stomach cramped at the prospect of exposing so great an expanse. Thus, she tugged several lines of taut rope farther up his chest and two down, gripped the edges of the slashed material, and enlarged the opening.

"That is one way to tend me," he muttered.

Grateful his breath shifting her hair did not make her shudder, she cleaned the cut with wine, patted it dry, applied salve, and covered it with linen that eagerly adhered to the medicinal.

Though difficult to yield her gaze to his after laying hands on him, blue and brown met gold. "Drink, Sir Dougray?"

He inclined his head, and she put the spout to his lips. He drank deep, then she exchanged the skin for bread and cheese.

She had not considered how intimate a thing it was to feed a man, and more so each time a morsel placed in his mouth brought her fingers into contact with his lips. But though the heat coursing her skin made it feel as if she were too long in the sun, she did not falter.

"I thank you," he said when his meal was done, then asked, "Do you not sleep well, Em?"

Further confirmation he had noted the shadows beneath her eyes. Unable to temper defensiveness, she snapped, "What Saxon in this England sleeps well?"

He nodded slowly. "Still, your sleep may improve do you destroy the bill of sale."

Feeling the burn of that parchment as if flames leapt around it, she murmured, "Three years. In all that time, I do not think I have truly slept."

His brow lowered. "Put it to flame. It is of no use to you—and of great use to Campagnon. You have it with you?"

"I do."

"Burn it now."

It seemed appropriate to do so in the presence of the one who delivered it to her, but she hesitated. Why?

*Because I have something Campagnon wants,* she thought. *Because in* my *hands is proof I own myself again.*

"Now, Em!" commanded another Norman who thought to bend her to his will. But before she could rebuke him, he sighed and said more gently, "The ashes made of it will be a balm to your soul."

Emotion threatening to shame her, she lowered her chin, removed the parchment, and unrolled it to look one last time on that which was to depart this earth in a manner more violent than what had taken Sir Merle.

It was impossible to read, the words too numerous and some letters barely familiar, but surely there was one she could make sense of.

"Burn it," D'Argent repeated, and she knew he wearied of her just as she wearied of herself. Still, she searched for the word that began with the same letter no longer inked on her skin.

"If it will sooner see it put to flame, I will read it to you, Em."

She hesitated but glimpsed no mockery in his eyes. "His name is all I seek."

"Bring it near."

She lowered between the tree's buckling roots and held the parchment before him.

"The second line from the top, third word," he said.

She leaned in. There it was, of more letters than expected.

"And at the bottom above the names of the auctioneer and his witness, it is signed by his own hand—Chevalier Raymond Campagnon."

She stared, then shot to her feet, hastened to the fire, and dropped the foul thing atop it.

Was it an ill portent the flames tentatively touched tongues to it as if seeking to determine if it was to their taste?

*I am being superstitious,* she chided, and yet she was nearly starved of air by the time the blackening edges caught fire.

Satisfaction dampened by the stench, she moved to the opposite side of D'Argent.

"It is done," he said.

In his eyes she saw a reflection of the flames as they devoured proof of her slavery. "I am grateful, Sir Dougray, but I do not understand why one who hates Saxons did this as if...for me."

Light flickered in his gaze, but it had naught to do with the fire. "It *was* for you, just as for you I gave warning at York of how near the king's army—which I regret."

"Why?"

"Had your rebels and Danes been present when William arrived, it is possible one great battle would have put finish to the resistance and what has yet to be done would be done."

She almost smiled. "You have naught to regret, Sir Dougray. Though my commander intended to urge Edgar to withdraw lest your warning prove true, since the city was indefensible, already the decision was made to abandon it."

He allowed a glimpse of relief, then said, "And all the more indefensible when the Danes withdrew—disappointing allies, do you not agree?"

She did, though she would not speak it.

"For what were you at Axholme with Vitalis?" he asked. "Why were you admitted to the earl's tent?"

She nearly ignored the question, but there seemed no harm in answering. "The young Dane you injured at York was there. Bjorn is his name, and he is the earl's much-loved misbegotten son."

As understanding rose on D'Argent's face, she continued, "It seems he is much taken with me. Thus, the Aetheling honored the earl's request I be present at the meeting. Though marriage was proposed, once I revealed I did not meet the requirement of chastity, the offer became one of… *Bedmate* is the kinder word for a woman valued by a man only for what she brings between the sheets." She forced a smile. "I declined."

"I am sorry."

"As I did not wish to wed him, there is naught to be sorry for. And why should one who hates Saxons care?"

"It is true I hated your people, and occasionally I am moved again that direction though reason rues I condemn the many for the axe of one who sought to keep my blade from *his* neck, but—"

"You slew him?" She looked to his left arm.

"Nay, he fell to another."

"Someone came to your aid?"

He hesitated, said, "Opportunity only." A peculiar answer, but before she could delve it, he continued, "Though it has been difficult to accept my loss, it is not Saxons I hate. What I hate is no end to the rebellion."

"But the rebellion is Saxon. What difference?"

"What difference? Is it not more acceptable to God to hate an act rather than a people? Especially when the act is committed by the few?"

Such reasoning made her consider her hatred of Normans was

due to an act committed by one, but not so. She hated his people for the invasion that stole her sire's life and all the suffering and atrocities committed by the Normans before and after she and her brother sold themselves into slavery. But though it angered that he sought to blame England's ills on the rebellion, she had seen enough suffering of innocents caught between rebels and conquerors to know there was some truth to what he said. For this, Lady Hawisa and numerous others had abandoned the fight.

*That does not mean they were right to accept Norman rule,* submitted the desperate Saxon.

*That does not mean the fight cannot yet be won,* submitted the hopeful rebel.

Still, she dropped to her haunches and said with pleading, "As persecuted as our people are, what choice have we but to resist?"

Regret shone from his face. "Two choices—pursue futility or yield."

"Futility." She nearly choked on the word. "I do not believe you."

"You do not wish to believe me."

Recalling Vitalis had also challenged her disbelief following the meeting between Edgar and the Danish earl, she ground her teeth.

"Unlike when first I returned to your shores, I accept your rebellion is justified, Em," he surprised. "However, there is a time to fight and a time to cast aside arms. As the opportunity to take back your country is long lost, continued resistance will only lead to more deaths. Though some will be Normans, most will be Saxons."

"You cannot know that."

"What I know is the king's patience and anger. After what befell the Normans at York, the first is nearly depleted and the second eager to sweep up its dust. Though the resistance think they have seen his darkest side, they have not. If the rebellion does not end soon, Saxons will discover how pitch black that side of him, and what your people suffer now will hardly compare to what comes. Thus, a longer, more crooked road it will be to England's healing."

He sounded so certain, desperation gripped her. "We cannot yield, Dougray!"

His lids narrowed.

Realizing his name had passed her lips without title, she shook her head and whispered, "We cannot."

"But *you* must. If not for yourself, for your siblings distance yourself from what is to befall those who aid the Aetheling and his allies. Go south."

She glanced at the fire. Though the parchment retained its rolled shape, it was a thin shell of black. Once it collapsed into ash, that proof of Campagnon's ownership would be more thoroughly obliterated than what she had removed from her shoulder.

She moistened her lips. "Vitalis believes as long as Campagnon pursues me, I am safer with the rebels, that it is more dangerous for me to travel across occupied England alone than fight alongside my own, even if we are surrounded by Campagnon and his mercenaries."

"What of your siblings?" he pressed.

"When I stand a good chance of confirming they are well, I will go south. Until then, I must be satisfied they are safe with my aunt."

Dougray stared at Emma of Gloucester. Though he had resented her return had delayed his release and was frustrated she refused to heed his warning, with dusk moving toward dark, he wanted her to stay. And did not understand why.

She was no Adela. Though she had shown grace in flying a dagger, she did not glide when she walked nor did her hands dance when she talked. Though lovely despite the absence of smiles, sensual laughter, and fluttering lashes over sparkling eyes, she was no fragrant flower. Though pleasing of figure, neither bosom nor hips swayed in a manner that made promises a man wished kept.

She was simple Em, not refined Adela. She was a girl thrust into womanhood ahead of her time, not a girl groomed into a lady many a man wished on his arm.

"I must go," she said.

When she started to rise, Dougray said the first thing he could think might cause her to linger. "I understand it was by choice, rather than debt or abduction, you and your brother entered into slavery."

Her unworldly eyes sprang so wide he glimpsed flecks of brown amid blue and blue amid brown. Then as if accused of wrongdoing, she said, "There is no dishonor in that. The coin ensured our younger brother and sister remained sheltered with food in their bellies, of great necessity after you and yours came to our shores. The dishonor belongs to the Norman who made the honest labor I owed him ungodly. Though he sought to make a harlot of me, I am not and never will be." A loud swallow. "Only by force will a man take from me what I do not wish to give."

She told more than expected, as if anger, hatred, and hurt spilled over her sides. Though the timing was poor, he wanted to know who the Normans had made her. Since this might be his only opportunity, he said, "The day my brother, Cyr, and I rode to relieve Campagnon of his command of Castle Balduc, we found all in disarray. He was enraged that the one who injured him could not be found."

Her gaze wavered, and once more it felt as if she looked through him. "He discovered I passed information to the rebels. Though it was not the first time he beat me, never before had he done so with such violence I feared death."

*Death due him,* Dougray seethed, guessing it was then she acquired the unsightly scar.

"I snatched the dagger from his belt, but I hesitated and he knocked it from my hand. I dropped to avoid his fist and crawled under the bed after the dagger." She swallowed loudly. "He dragged me out, and I stuck him when he flipped me onto my back." She shuddered. "He screamed and called for help. I thought…feared…hoped he would die. But I knew if that were his end, it would be mine as well, though only after his men…" She closed her mouth, confining a sound of distress to her throat.

Dougray waited, and finally she said, "I do not know how I slipped past them, but I made it to Wulfen Castle where I learned Lady Hawisa had bought my brother at auction to play the son she lost at Hastings, that in all the time I feared him sold across the sea, he was near." She lowered her chin. "So very near."

Would she continue a tale already known to him, just as was known what followed that night when the woman now his sister-in-law was betrayed by her rebels and forced to flee with her people?

"Though she knew I was Campagnon's slave, she kept it from my brother," Em whispered. "I did not think I could forgive her, but…"

"It was for the best," Dougray said.

She blinked, caught her breath, and thrust to her feet.

She *had* been looking through him, but he had not erred in speaking her back to him. Already she had begun the journey. Merely, he had sooner seen her returned.

She swept up the bag, dropped the salve in it, and skirted the fire. Halting alongside his possessions, she said, "You wish cover of your mantle?"

*And risk slicing it the same as the rope?* he considered. "I thank you, but the fire will suffice."

She nodded, then left him to the solitude required to free himself.

THAT A WARRIOR, especially a D'Argent, had means beyond

training to compensate for the loss of an arm did not surprise, nor that it sooner freed him from his bonds—albeit only because the leader of the Rebels of the Pale had not corrected Em when she neglected to search that side of him.

Not for lack of faith in her nor fear for her well-being had Vitalis set himself a watch over the chevalier. He had done it to salve curiosity—and as a test of sorts.

This day, Sir Dougray had shown he possessed some of the honor of his brothers. This eve, he provided further evidence. Still a Norman, still an opponent, but less the foe he had been during their first encounter when the third D'Argent brother's infiltration of the rebels had seen all those seeking sanctuary at Lillefarne Abbey captured. Vitalis had nearly slain him—or perhaps the chevalier had nearly slain *him*. Regardless, had not his brother and cousin intervened, one might have died that night.

Strange now there existed the possibility of making something of an ally of him...

Vitalis had been privy to most of the exchange between Em and this D'Argent, missing only her words when her voice dropped to a whisper.

Much he had known of her, but more he had learned—and been surprised she shared any of her tale with D'Argent, let alone those pieces heretofore withheld from one who had earned enough trust she no longer feared being alone with him and at times confided in him.

Little had Vitalis known of Sir Dougray, but more he had learned of one he was inclined to believe had not spoken false to Em. The bound Norman had no cause to seduce her into releasing him and, following retrieval of his mount, had ridden in the direction of York in accord with the word given. No longer was it hatred that moved the third D'Argent brother against Saxons. He regretted what was done the people of this country, and just as he was overly concerned for Em's well-being, he was attracted to her.

Not that anything could come of it. Even were they on the same side and of the same class, barring divine intervention, no man would know the sweet of her unless...

*Heal her, Lord,* Vitalis silently appealed, then returned his thoughts to Dougray D'Argent.

If what he predicted came of the fall of York—and Vitalis feared it would—good use might be made of the Norman who was exceedingly adept at quelling English resistance.

Vitalis finished coiling what remained of the rope he had watched D'Argent slice through following Em's departure, hooked it on his belt, and extinguished the fire he had not instructed her to build since he had been fairly certain the Norman would not pass the night here.

Now to make a lesson of D'Argent's early departure that could one day save Em and others.

~

VITALIS HAD NOT BERATED HER, though he should have.

Even if Dougray did not fulfill his duty to bring William's army down upon the Rebels of the Pale, she had failed them all. And so great her shame over a lesson it should not have been necessary to learn—again—she had felt only discomfort knowing her exchange with him had boasted an audience.

How weak and unworthy she must appear. How pitiful it was not appearance only. Were there any consolation, it was that she had not exposed her fellow rebels to one such as Campagnon. Whereas Dougray could offer up a defense for what he did in service to Le Bâtard, the one from whom he had stolen her bill of sale could not. What Campagnon did, he did for himself, taking coin and satisfaction as payment for the suffering of her people.

Finding a hand beneath the neck of her tunic, fingers digging into the scar Dougray had not asked after, Em wrenched it away. Fingers gripped in her palm, she turned on the blanket spread atop grass, fixed her gaze on the clouded night sky beyond thinning branches, and listened.

Though Vitalis said Dougray appeared to have kept his word to cease tracking them until after he reported to his king, the sentries patrolling the wood had been doubled. One would not know it from how still and quiet the night, so well trained were those moving amongst the trees.

"Worthy," she whispered. Then vowing she would prove their equal else leave their ranks so she not cause them harm, she closed her eyes.

She did not expect to find rest that night and was jolted to wakefulness each time she became aware of scarred flesh beneath her fingers, but at last she drifted.

When next she opened her eyes, she did so upon a ceiling—that of Castle Balduc's solar. And once more, her hand was on her shoulder, though not a scarred one.

*I dream,* she told herself. Still, she listened, counted the seconds between draws of breath and exhales, and gauged their depth.

He slept. Deeply. At last.

She ceased raking nails over her inked skin, the pain of which distracted her from other hurts while awaiting the opportunity to slip away, thanked the Lord there was something for which to be thankful, and eased onto her side. She paused, assured herself there was no change in his breathing, then moved her feet and legs off the bed. Once her toes touched the floor, she turned her hips and, gripping the mattress, slid her belly and chest down the side.

It was too soon to sigh, twice that sound having roused him as if the rush of air were louder than the creak of the bed.

Knees and palms to the floor, head down, tangled hair blocking the light of torches beyond the solar, in near darkness she crawled to the most distant corner. *Her* corner, where she would huddle for a time, sleep for a time, and awaken first so he would think her gone only so she might serve him in another capacity.

She turned her back into the corner, drew up her legs, and pressed her forehead to her knees. In the warm space between breasts and thighs, she breathed long and slow and tried not to think on all the places she ached and why she ached. To do so risked weeping, which risked awakening him, which risked…

A sob expanded her chest, but she held it in. When another nearly betrayed her, she dug her nails into her shoulder. There would be blood, though naught compared to the day when she rid herself of his mark. Until then, the letter inked into her and emboldened by a cross was of use, the pain distracting her from a different kind of pain until she could escape it altogether.

"Lord, if You are there," she whispered, "if You hear me, if You do not fault me for what is lost that I did not give away, help me. Help Eberhard. Help the little ones. Help my people. Show us there is yet day on the other side of this night. Please Lord."

Now to sleep lightly. Very lightly.

# CHAPTER SEVEN

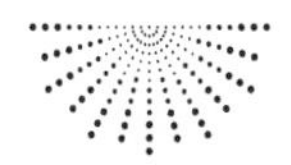

Stafford, England
Mid-Autumn, 1069

It was not enough for the Northern resistance to lay ruin to York, moving William nearer the place where not even a shadow of mercy cast itself. In answer to the Aetheling's call to rise up against the usurper, now others of the king's enemies had begun besieging the West Midlands. And the ones sent to suppress it had failed, much of the blame for that failure due the Rebels of the Pale who added their numbers to those distant rebels.

Thus, the king had declared he would himself put down the insurrection. Leaving his half-brother in charge of forces near York who were to continue searching out rebels while keeping watch on Danes yet of no mind to do battle, William had marched the bulk of his men and mercenaries west—among the latter, those led by Campagnon though much favor he lost when the slightly altered tale of Sir Merle's end was told. Not surprisingly, the knave denied sending his man to retrieve his slave and suggested the king's scout, enamored of the *whore,* had slain the chevalier.

Dougray had controlled himself. William had not. He had backhanded Campagnon, thrust his face near the one he dropped to his knees, and spat, *Enamored or not, I myself would put through Sir Merle for thieving the opportunity to bring those rebels to ground.* Then he had ordered the mercenary from his sight.

As expected, neither had Dougray escaped his wrath. But in the weeks since, once more he found favor by effecting the disbanding of two more rebel factions north of York and delivering the Aetheling and his guard into the king's hands. Unfortunately, Edgar escaped when those sent to seize him proved incompetent. Had not the sire of the leader of those troops been amongst William's esteemed companions, that one would have suffered more than the disgrace of being returned to Normandy without reward.

Now at Stafford, Dougray was ordered to further prove himself by fighting alongside fellow Normans against Mercians, Welshmen, and rebels who had not expected so great a show of force—nor that William would command his army.

During the first quarter hour, as the sun shifted from mid-afternoon to late, memories of the battle that took his preferred sword arm slashed at Dougray, causing him to falter. But upon realizing now it was he who benefitted from the protection of those he fought alongside, he was moved to terrible anger of which he made use. Thereafter, each swing and thrust of his blade was so devastating, his struggle was not only against those of the resistance but bloodlust.

Less than an hour into the battle, it was obvious the king's victory was imminent, hundreds of rebels put to ground and hundreds having fled and continuing to flee.

Blessedly, Dougray had yet to catch sight of any who wore grey on their sleeves to identify them as Rebels of the Pale. That did not mean they were not here, so spread out was the battle and great the dust rising from parched and trampled earth, but there was hope Vitalis and his rebels were elsewhere. A traitorous hope Dougray should not entertain. Though capture of the Aetheling would likely bring rebellious Saxons under control, an end to the Rebels of the Pale was among the wounds from which the resistance might not recover.

And now a wound from which Dougray might not recover did he not turn it aside. Before the Saxon's sword could take his remaining arm, he spun, ducked, and arced his blade up. As he straightened to the left of his opponent, he landed his sword to a back absent armor.

The man screamed and dropped to his hands and knees.

The Dougray of Hastings would have ensured his death, but not this Dougray even were there no other Saxons coming for him. It was enough his opponent was no longer a threat to the king's men. Unlike the accumulating dead, this one had a chance to depart the battlefield, recover, and live out his days in a country that would adjust to the new order, just as it had hundreds of years earlier when the conquerors were Saxon.

Dougray warded off the blows of his next opponent, after much effort rendered him harmless, then set himself at a Saxon charging Sir Guy who fought alongside Theriot. A warning shout brought the chevalier around, and together Dougray and he ended the threat.

More lunged at them, desperation in the eyes of men determined to fight to the death—the reward of it taking as many Normans with them as possible. A futile endeavor, the three chevaliers who set their backs to one another fending off those whose ranks continued to thin by way of death or withdrawal, both of which caused the dust to thicken and billow. In the midst of it, a scream sounded, this one of note because it was not of a man.

God forbid it was Emma Irwindotter.

CAMPAGNON.

She had seen him. He had seen her. And the shock proved her downfall. She had not swung when she should have, and the sword she could have fended off sent her stumbling backward.

"Em!"

Hand to her head, knees knocking, feet churning up dust, she commanded her jittering eyes to follow the voice to the one who called.

Fighting his way toward her, the warrior of red hair and beard was far nearer than the devil who sought to reclaim her.

"Forgive me," she gasped, though Vitalis would not hear her above shouts, curses, metal on metal, metal on bone…

She had not kept her word. And now, her commander drawn away from where his efforts were better spent, he ran to save her as she could not save herself.

Blood trickling into one eye, she swiped at it with the hand she realized no longer gripped a sword. "Lord, let me not be his undoing," she rasped. Then hoping he would turn aside and leave her for dead, she let her legs fall out from under her.

Were she of glass, her meeting with the ground would have shattered her. Certes, her head felt shattered. A good thing, she told herself and closed her eyes against the dust. No more Campagnon. No more fear. No more tormenting memories. Gone from this world the same as those slain this day and all the days before.

*But what of the little ones?*

Reminded of the siblings left behind, she drew a sharp breath and struggled to crawl back onto the edge over which she had lowered herself, but all she could do was sink her nails in and hold on.

Hands upon her. Fear the hands were *his.* Breath sweeping her face. Fear the breath was *his.*

"I have you, Em."

Not Campagnon.

Vitalis lifting her onto his shoulder and setting the blurred ground in motion. Her sobbing as the jostling threatened to further split open her skull. Then darkness, on the other side of which could lie hell for one such as she.

~

"It is so," Maël said. "The Rebels of the Pale were here."

Dougray looked up from the cup he gripped and swept his gaze around the camp Theriot and he had made distant from others, many of whom would continue to revel in the Norman victory until William sent them to their beds. Not long now.

Seeing his youngest brother yet conversed with Sir Guy near the tent, he prompted, "And?"

His cousin lowered beside him on the log before which a fire had been built hours earlier. "Ten were slain."

"Any women?"

"Though nearly a score of that sex yielded up their lives this day, thus far it appears none were of the pale."

Momentarily, Dougray closed his eyes, then he raised his cup and across its rim said, "I thank you."

"There is more."

He took a draw of ale. "Tell."

"Campagnon claims he saw his slave on the battlefield, she took a blade to the head, and Vitalis carried her away."

Beneath his mantle, once more Dougray felt the fist that was not there. Had her injury been fatal? Were Vitalis's efforts wasted on one who might soon see earth heaped upon her?

"Non," he said, then again, "Non."

"It is obvious you care for her, Dougray, but she belongs to another man. Even if she survives and gains her freedom, one has only to know Campagnon to accept she is lost to good men."

Though tempted to strike his cousin who did not seek to harm nor offend, Dougray said, "Oui, I have a care for her. Oui, I ought not."

A smile tilted Maël's mouth, likely born of relief he would not have to fend off an assault. "I am pleased you come back to yourself, but methinks she is one lost sheep you ought not go after."

Dougray set aside his cup. "I but wish to keep her from Campagnon."

Maël's eyebrows rose. "That is all?"

"All that is possible—does she live."

The silence that fell between them was rent by Theriot's shout of, "To arms!" Then the ring of his sword exiting its scabbard ahead of Sir Guy's.

Whatever alerted him, his senses were too honed not to heed, especially since the camp's location might tempt defeated Saxons to seek vengeance here.

All four were battle ready when half a dozen warriors moved out of the shadows. Though heavily armed, their weapons were sheathed, and at their fore strode one whose hair and beard were nearly the color of the dried blood he wore.

Vitalis halted, and as those behind did the same, looked over the Normans. Settling on Dougray, he said in Norman-French, "No more blood and vengeance need be taken this day. Unless you will it."

Maël adjusted his stance and pointed his sword at the one who eluded William. "You entreat us not to raise the hue and cry?"

"Entreat? Non. Strongly suggest? Oui." Vitalis nodded over his shoulder. "We are many."

Whether or not it was true others awaited summoning, much blood could be spilled on both sides before fellow Normans rose above revelry to move against these rebels.

"As I wished to meet with you alone, Sir Dougray," Vitalis said, "several hours I have awaited the opportunity. But I can delay no longer."

"Of what do you speak?"

"Of Em."

Dougray gripped his sword tighter. "She lives?"

"Injured and senseless, but she breathes."

Ache in Dougray's jaw alerting him to the grind of his teeth, he questioned if the scream of a woman heard on the battlefield had been hers. And if that was the beginning of her end because of this Saxon.

"As we can do naught more for her," Vitalis said, "and she will slow our retreat, we have come." He turned, and as Dougray was struck by realization of what he intended, gestured someone forward.

Two answered the summons—a Saxon warrior cradling a limp body whose head was wrapped with cloth, and a woman garbed in a gown rather than chausses and tunic.

"It could be a trap," Maël rumbled.

Dougray looked to where his youngest brother stood alongside Sir Guy. "How many are they, Theriot?"

"Of greater number than those we see here. A score, mayhap more."

Hence, as it was unlikely four Normans would prevail were this a trap, there was little to lose in indulging Vitalis.

Easing his stance, Dougray elbowed aside his mantle and returned his sword to its scabbard.

"What do you?" Maël snarled.

"It appears the lost sheep has come to me."

His cousin's nostrils flared. "That does not mean this sheep can be returned to the flock."

"Perhaps not, but neither can she be returned to Campagnon." Dougray strode past the fire to where the one who held Em stood to the left of Vitalis and the others.

He recognized the stout rebel as being among the guard at

York from whom Em had separated before the Dane approached her. Recalling what the others had named him, he said, "Zedekiah."

A blink of surprise became a one-sided grin. "The nameless one," he said, proving he was as versed in the D'Argents as the D'Argents were versed in the Rebels of the Pale.

Determined to contain anger that wished to add this man's offense to the flames sprung from Em's injury, Dougray jutted his chin. "May I look nearer?"

Zedekiah turned to the side as if holding an infant whose sleep he did not wish to disturb whilst another looked upon it.

By moonlight, Dougray considered the half of Em's face not pressed against the man's chest. Her eyes were closed and lips parted, and though the blood of her injury had run down her face as evidenced by stains on the neck of her tunic, it had been cleaned away. As told, it appeared what could be done for her had been. And it might not be enough.

Glimpsing movement, he looked around.

Vitalis broke stride within feet of Dougray. "I would have you deliver her to Lady Hawisa and her brother at Wulfenshire," he said.

Would she survive the journey? If so, would she fully recover? Anger toward Vitalis that had never been so great—and great it *had* been—made Dougray long to test the odds of drawing sword on him in the midst of the rebels. Instead, he said, "I am to make right what you made wrong in allowing her to take to the battlefield?"

He heard the grinding of teeth, then Vitalis nodded at the young woman to the right of Zedekiah. "She will accompany you."

Dougray recognized her. At the rebels' camp upon which he had spied before Merle set himself at Em, he had seen her, of note because she was the only one who wore a gown. Though her chin was raised as if in challenge, her only visible weapon was a dagger. Had Em required a chaperone, this one would not save her.

"For what purpose?" Dougray asked.

Vitalis turned to the side. "You will wish to hear this, Sir Maël."

"I listen!"

"As much as possible, the Rebels of the Pale will disband. Some will stay my side, but most will return to their homes, the greatest number of which are upon Wulfenshire. For Lady Hawisa and her D'Argent husband, I ask they be allowed to do so without fear of retribution."

"Possible only without the king's knowledge," Maël said.

Vitalis inclined his head. "Ignorance that shall benefit him and England. Providing the rebels who wish to return home are allowed to live in peace, they will accept Norman rule."

"Yet still you and your faithful will oppose William," Sir Guy said, a reminder it was not only the D'Argents who must be persuaded to hold close what was asked of them.

"A dozen men at most and, as ever, we shall move against Normans only when provoked by those bereft of honor." Vitalis drew a breath that further broadened his shoulders. "As Hastings and all in between foretold, and now Stafford, I think the conquering nearly done."

Only if the king agreed, Dougray reflected. At Darfield, William had refrained from vengeance that, even with victory assured, could have seen hundreds if not thousands of his own men slain. At Stafford, had there been an opportunity to come to terms with his enemies, he would not have. And Dougray suspected if the Aetheling and his supporters surrendered on the morrow, William would not pull back what he reeled out. This was not nearly as done as Vitalis believed.

*Accursed William,* Dougray silently rebuked. *Accursed rebels. How many more will die before the suffering ends?*

"As I can say nor do more, Sir Dougray," Vitalis said, "I leave it to you to persuade your fellow Normans here to allow

Wulfenshire to be made as whole as possible." He turned to the young woman. "Margaret has not been with us long enough to receive adequate training. Though she understands our language, she speaks no word. Either she is mute or has taken a vow of silence. Regardless, since she is versed in healing herbs and does not fear the stitching of flesh, she will care for Em until a physician is found." Vitalis returned his regard to Dougray. "You will do this?"

He would, the only questions being the tale told the king to account for the departure of his favored scout and how to gain Sir Guy's cooperation. Though Theriot and Maël would not speak of this, that chevalier did not share the allegiance of kinship. Fortunately, there was enough to recommend him that often he kept company with one or more D'Argent. Albeit given to few words, and at times Dougray felt as if a crude map beneath the chevalier's gaze, the man behaved respectably, fought well, and exhibited no fervor in suppressing the rebellion of those amongst whom long he had lived. Had Dougray to guess, he would say Torquay but did his duty to his king.

Mistakenly taking silence as refusal, Vitalis prompted, "You made yourself her savior, Sir Dougray. If you are truly worthy of the D'Argent name, you will finish what you began."

"I will do it." Ignoring the bore of Maël's gaze, Dougray looked to Em. "Was it the flat of the blade dealt her or the edge?"

Vitalis shook his head. "Though I saw the injury done her when she caught sight of Campagnon and he caught sight of her, I was too distant. But though it cracked her skull, the line is so fine I believe it dealt by the flat. Were it the edge, it had to have been a glancing blow."

"Then she has a good chance of recovering."

"That is the hope. Still, our priest prepared the way for her should hope fail."

Then they were done here. Just barely, Dougray suppressed the impulse to take Em from Zedekiah. Not since before learning

Adela was lost to him had he questioned how to hold a woman well with only one fully functioning arm. And this went beyond holding.

Anger toward Vitalis shifting to anger over the realization that, in the absence of Margaret, it would be impossible to deliver Em to Wulfenshire without risk of further injury, Dougray said, "Carry her to the fire."

Zedekiah stepped past, and Margaret followed.

"Ere we part ways," Vitalis said low, "I would have you know it is for more than the aid previously given Em and the need to quickly depart Stafford I entrust her to you."

Dougray raised an eyebrow.

"Before keeping your word to discontinue tracking us, you revealed you are not cold to Saxon suffering and have a great care for her."

Dougray stiffened. Had Em told of their exchange and destruction of proof of Campagnon's ownership? Or…?

Vitalis inclined his head. "A warrior finds ways to compensate for his losses, and you are no exception. Had I trusted you then as I trust you now, I would not have kept watch to ensure Em came to no harm. Though you are a Norman, more you are a D'Argent. If not by breeding, then deed."

That surprised more than learning Em and he were watched, and not for the first time since rejecting Godfroi as his sire, Dougray regretted words spoken that could not be unspoken—as much for the cruelty dealt the only father he had known as the pain dealt his mother.

"I thank you, Vitalis. Be assured, I will do all I can to reunite Em with her brother and younger siblings."

"Of utmost importance," the rebel leader said, "keep her out of Campagnon's hands, even if you must kill your fellow Norman."

"He has only to give cause the same as Sir Merle."

Vitalis inclined his head and called, "We are done, Zedekiah!"

The man rose from where he knelt beside Em, said something to the hovering Margaret, and started back.

"Watch for me, Vitalis!" Maël called as the leader of the Rebels of the Pale withdrew.

"Watch for me, Sir Maël!" Vitalis answered.

Shortly, where he and his rebels had been, the breeze alone walked the night wood.

# CHAPTER EIGHT

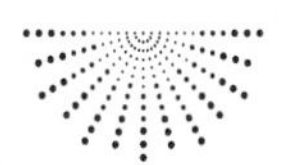

"Soon we cross into Derbyshire," Sir Guy said. "You recall I told my sire and uncle have lands there?"

Dougray did. When the king paused his great army in that shire's southernmost corner to pass the night en route to Stafford, the chevalier had suggested that, like William and other nobles who lodged at nearby castles, they seek accommodations with his kin. Dougray had declined, it being a better use of time to gain more sleep on the ground than ride leagues distant for pallets they must sooner depart to overtake the army come morn. His companion had been disappointed but also prevailed upon dirt and grass to gain his rest.

Dougray looked across his shoulder at the woman with whom Sir Guy shared his saddle. Head propped on his shoulder, she had yet to awaken. Was she paler than earlier, or was the light of morn responsible for skin that looked cold to the touch?

"She worsens?" he asked.

"Certes, she is no better. Hence, I suggest we turn north and make for my uncle's home. It will add leagues to the journey to Wulfenshire, but this day a physician will tend her."

Dougray considered the man who had accompanied him east.

Pride had tempted him to reject the chevalier's offer. However, the need to protect Em and Margaret across unsettled lands made him accept. And disgruntled Maël had agreed it was best under the circumstances. Once the tale to be told William was complete —that Dougray had found signs of Rebels of the Pale and set off after them accompanied by Sir Guy—the journey toward Wulfenshire had begun beneath a moonlit sky.

"Why your uncle rather than sire?" Dougray asked.

The chevalier adjusted Em's seat between his thighs, causing her lids to flutter. "My sire is a good man and much admired, but less likely to risk a rebel in his home than my uncle who sympathizes with their cause."

"Your uncle keeps a physician?"

"He does, now more out of habit than need, the physician mostly occupied with tending villagers' complaints."

"Habit?"

"My uncle's wife passed years ago, but throughout much of their marriage was abed with illness."

"I am sorry."

"To Stavestone, then?"

"Oui. We shall reach it ere nightfall?"

"At this pace"—he glanced at Em, then Margaret who rode alongside—"it will be full dark."

"Lead and I shall follow."

Stavestone-on-Trent
Derbyshire, England

THE MOON WELL-RISEN by the time Dougray and his entourage reached the great wooden fortress, the men on the walls were wary of those requesting entrance, though one was known to them. Thus, Sir Guy was required to pass Em to Dougray before being admitted.

Surprisingly, holding her astride was not as precarious nor awkward as expected, the half of Dougray's arm a good support. At a sedate pace, he would be able to forego reins and guide his mount with voice commands and the press of his thighs, but only that. Were speed required or must a weapon be brought to hand, she would have to be conscious and capable of keeping her seat.

Margaret, who had drawn her horse alongside his, leaned near and raised her eyebrows.

"She is well," Dougray said. "Whatever you put on her tongue when we paused has deepened her breathing, and if torchlight is to be believed, she has color in her cheeks."

She straightened in the saddle and yawned. There was voice on her exhale—a single note, but surely evidence she was capable of speech. Her gaze returned to Dougray, and whatever was reflected on his face made her press her lips.

A vow of silence, Dougray guessed, and wondered if she was a displaced novice or nun. If so, likely Normans were to blame for the attack on another of God's houses.

The chains of the portcullis that had lowered following Sir Guy's entrance a quarter hour past sounded again, and this time rose fully to permit the visitors to enter astride.

Sir Guy stepped beneath it, traversed the drawbridge, and mounted his destrier. "The physician has been awakened and prepares to receive Em." He looked to her. "I should take her?"

"Non, I have her." Dougray nudged his destrier forward.

They crossed the outer bailey to the gate of the inner bailey, and there Dougray relinquished Em, dismounted, and adjusted his mantle to ensure it covered his left arm.

Men-at-arms leading the way, they ascended the steps to the donjon set atop a motte raised higher than most. Behind Sir Guy and Em, Dougray and Margaret entered a high-ceilinged hall where a lone figure stood on the dais, legs braced apart, hands behind his back.

The Baron of Stavestone, a good-sized man likely roused from his bed to receive his nephew, wore a fur-trimmed robe, his calves and feet bare. Of note, the one said to have long resided in England looked equal parts Norman and Saxon. His graying blond hair was long, though not of a length that could be gathered at the nape, his beard close-clipped.

He offered no greeting, merely observed those advancing—most intently Dougray and the woman his nephew carried.

Strides from the dais, Sir Guy halted. "Uncle, here my fellow chevalier, Sir Dougray of the family D'Argent." He nodded at him, looked to his other side. "This the injured woman's caregiver, Margaret."

"You are welcome here," the baron said in Norman-French, his accent not of the strength it would have been years past. Then he dismissed his men-at-arms.

When the great doors closed, Dougray said, "I thank you for receiving us, Baron..." He trailed off at the realization despite Sir Guy's talk of his kin, the man had not been identified beyond his title and the lands held. Guessing his name the same as his nephew's, kinship by way of a brother rather than sister, Dougray said, "Baron Torquay."

What seemed a smile of regret moved the man's mouth, and Sir Guy tensed beside Dougray.

"Non, my brother-in-law is Torquay," their host said. "I am Roche. Michel Roche."

What moved beneath Dougray's skin moved no more. Here a name never spoken in the home in which he was raised, but made known to him nonetheless. And surely there was only this one whose hair might once have been as blond as Dougray's. Had the golden brown of his eyes ever been as golden as those that now beheld him?

"You know the name," the baron said. "Hence, we are partway

there. However, what remains must wait." He looked to his nephew. "The physician awaits her and her woman in the first chamber abovestairs. The second chamber will sleep Sir Dougray and you."

His words sounded very distant to one who could only stare though he commanded a fist of flesh and one of air to open and his body to follow Sir Guy.

Baron Roche watched Margaret and his nephew's progress, but at the creak of the first step, returned his gaze to Dougray. "On the morrow," he said gruffly and traversed the dais to its backside and pushed through curtains into a darkened solar.

Dougray watched the panels swing into place. Just as he no longer believed the tentative friendship extended by Sir Guy was genuine, he did not believe the man intended harm. Still, the chevalier had much to answer for, and from Michel Roche's reception, there was another to whom he would answer.

Dougray pulled air into his lungs, pushed it out, and strode to the stairs.

"'Tis good you did not continue on to Wulfenshire," the physician said in the language of the Saxons. "If she is to recover, she must be tended and move as little as possible."

Dougray straightened from the door frame he had leaned against a half hour watching the wiry man aided by Margaret. "Then you believe she will recover?"

The physician halted before him. "More, the question is—to what extent?"

Ache in his teeth, Dougray put past them, "What say you?"

"Blows to the head can alter a life worse than loss of eyesight or a limb."

Beneath the mantle concealing his empty left sleeve, Dougray shifted his shoulder. "When will we know?"

"When the Lord tells her and she is ready to tell us, beginning with opening her eyes. It could be this night, it could be days. If it is much beyond that, it could be not at all." The man smiled sympathetically. "With God's aid, I will do all I can for her. Now gain your rest so this woman may gain hers." He nodded at Margaret who surely wished to stretch out on the pallet beside the bed. "And pray," he added.

"I shall." Dougray stepped into the corridor and crossed to the room he was to share with Sir Guy who had withdrawn from Em's chamber after settling her on the bed.

By the light of a single candle, he saw the one who owed him an explanation sat in a chair beside a glowing brazier. His eyes were closed, but as Dougray seated the door, he lifted his lids.

"I was aware of what I did this day, as I have been since I determined to know what could be known of you, Sir Dougray. Though you have questions, they are not mine to answer. They are for my uncle who may be less inclined to forgive me than you." He pushed up out of his slump and stood. "What I have done is done. Now it is for you and Michel to decide what to do with it."

He dragged off his tunic and tossed it on the chair. Garbed in undertunic and chausses, he lowered to the pallet, yielding the bed to Dougray as though he had more right to it. He did not.

Then, as if relieved of a great burden, he sighed. "Good eve, Cousin."

# CHAPTER NINE

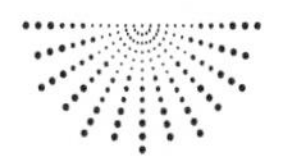

Dougray watched. And was watched.

Though invited to sit at high table to break his fast with the baron and the most esteemed of the household, he had taken a seat at the lowermost table.

Breaking off another piece of bread, he moved his regard from Baron Roche, past the man's nephew, and settled it on the physician who had merely shaken his head when Dougray asked after Em earlier.

Still she slept, each hour she did not open her eyes drawing her nearer to never doing so.

*It is not even two days,* he reminded himself. *There is time to heal. Time to awaken.*

Meaning there was also time to discuss what the baron had called *what remains.* Or not.

For the first two and a half score of Dougray's life it had not needed discussing, it being enough to acknowledge the end result for which mother and son paid a price—as had Godfroi who was named a fool for sending neither away. Why speak of it now, especially since last eve Michel Roche had seemed no more pleased than Dougray with this…?

What did one call it? It was no reunion. Introduction?

Oui, and it was more than sufficient considering the mess Roche left behind for a more honorable man to clean up.

*Still I am trapped,* Dougray thought as he followed the bread with ale. But providing the baron also accepted it was best to remain strangers, the days would pass.

At meal's end, Dougray started for the stairs.

"Sir Dougray."

He turned, guessed the man who had sat near the baron at table was the steward. "Aye?" he answered in the language spoken to him.

"My lord requests you attend him in the solar."

Dougray looked to Roche who conversed with one of his men on the dais before curtains that concealed the solar. "Give him my regrets. Tell him...what remains ought to remain." He pivoted and ascended the stairs.

When he entered Em's chamber, Margaret turned from the unshuttered window. Acknowledging her with a nod, he strode to the bed.

Earlier, a bandage had been wound several times around Em's head. Now there was a single strip that held a thick pad in place where a small portion of her hair had been cut away.

Dougray glanced at Margaret. Seeing she had returned her attention to the bailey below, he lowered to the mattress edge.

There was color in Em's face, and when he set fingers near her mouth, her exhale was long and full. He knew he should not, but he touched the bow of her upper lip, then the lower.

No exhale of her next drawn breath.

"Em?"

No response, as if...

He pressed a hand to her chest. There, the beat of her heart.

As he released his own breath, he felt hers on his brow and looked up. Her lashes lifted, and he saw light in the narrow space through which he could not be certain she looked upon him. Then her lashes lowered, and she spilled more breath in speaking what sounded his name.

Immediately, Margaret was beside him.

"She opened her eyes, and I believe she spoke my name," Dougray said as he rose. "A good portent she recognized me, is it not?"

The woman set a hand on Em's brow, inclined her head.

"Keep watch," Dougray said. "I shall inform the physician."

A half hour later, the man emerged from the chamber. "She will not be roused further, but 'tis good she did so for a short time. I have examined her injury, and the swelling lessens and stitches hold. There is naught to do but wait." He adjusted the bag on his shoulder. "Now I am for a village to tend the bellies of those taken with an ill humor of autumn."

As Dougray stared after him, he wondered how to fill what could be days of avoiding the man who grudgingly wished to discuss *what remained.*

He touched his sword hilt, nodded. It wanted swinging—vicious swinging—even if only against a pel.

PERSPIRATION DAMPENING HIS TUNIC, Dougray tilted his blade left and right and ran his gaze down the edges as once he had lightly run a thumb to gauge the need for sharpening.

Eyes confirming what the severed post told, he continued to ignore the interest shown him by others on the training field and considered the smithy across the bailey.

Since departing the donjon, he had heard a hammer striking its iron song while the refining fires wafted heat across the distance. Certain the smith would have one or more apprentices capable of putting a fine edge on a blade, Dougray sheathed his sword and strode toward the fence over which he had tossed his mantle.

Though he remained uncomfortable revealing his empty sleeve—ever a draw for the curious—it was necessary during arms practice.

As he neared the fence, he glimpsed the approach of one from the direction of the inner bailey. Sir Guy, resolve in his stride.

"Almighty," Dougray muttered. Though the chevalier professed it was for the baron and Dougray to determine what to do with what the meddler had done, doubtless he meant to trespass further.

"Sir Guy," he said and pulled his mantle from the fence.

The chevalier halted. "I find much to admire in you, Sir Dougray, but we are not yet friends. Though it was with motive I drew near you, it was done to determine if you are worthy of friendship. Had you proven otherwise, I would have suggested we pause elsewhere to sooner see Em receive a physician's care."

Dougray shifted his jaw. "Much you meddle."

"I do—in the hope you will take the opportunity gifted you to speak with my uncle."

"Did he send you to me?"

"Non, he said it is best this way. I do not agree. Some things are better left unspoken, others not. Since it seems I am the only reasonable one, I have determined this is something best spoken. Thus, by rights of kinship both sides, I take it upon myself." At Dougray's silence, he added, "There is too much loss and regret in this world, especially for things lost that could be found."

Dougray stared. Would he regret eschewing this opportunity to look near on the man who had cuckolded the only father he had known? To give ear to his excuses? He shook his head. "Never has Roche been in my life as never he should have been. Thus, he is naught to me."

The chevalier sighed. "Pray, indulge me, and in doing so know what I ask of you is not self-serving—that the door I open could hand me more loss than already I know."

Doubtless, what the man had already lost was the woman wed to another. Though Dougray sympathized, he would have refused again if not for curiosity over Sir Guy's pending loss. "My sword requires sharpening." He nodded at the smithy. "I have naught else with which to occupy myself until it is done."

"I thank you, Sir Dougray."

Shortly, they stood at the well. While a whetstone was applied to Dougray's blade, he satisfied his thirst and poured what remained of the bucket's contents over his head. He gave a grunt of satisfaction, swept the wet hair back off his brow, and looked to Sir Guy who leaned against the stone ledge. "Enlighten me."

"You are wrong to believe Michel Roche is naught to you. Beyond your existence, he is much, and great the gratitude owed him."

"Gratitude?" Dougray glowered. "One must be a good force in another's life for that to be their due."

"It is his due. Simply, you do not know it, though I wonder if you would were he of longer hair and beard. If he looked more a Saxon as once he did."

Feeling something move out of the dark of his mind, casting a shadow long enough to flirt with the threshold of light, Dougray narrowed his lids. "What say you?"

"This is not the first time my uncle and you have met."

Suppressing the impulse to walk away, Dougray said, "He would not have been present at my birth."

"Hence, it is the great battle of which I speak."

"Where you fought alongside the one lauded the Bloodlust Warrior of Hastings," Dougray said, "and I fought alongside my brothers."

Sir Guy raised his eyebrows. "And your sire."

Dougray nearly pointed out that was impossible since not only was Godfroi in Normandy but no longer capable of warfare, but it was petty.

"I saw you on the battlefield," Sir Guy continued, "and there is a reason one unknown to me came to notice ahead of thousands of my fellow Normans—because another first came to notice, one on the side of the Saxons whom I was looking for and prayed I would not see. And *you* came to his notice."

As the shadow ceased flirting with the light, Dougray tensed. "Your uncle sided with the Saxons?"

"He did, but he did not stay their side. He turned on them—rather, one of them."

The memory that had eluded Dougray until the day he lost Adela to another man returned, and he began to make sense of it. It was no vendetta that caused the older Saxon to slay his countryman who sought to finish what he had begun in ruining a Norman's arm. It was...

Dougray did not realize he sought the support of the well until the knuckles pressed hard into the stone rim shot ache up his hand.

"A father protecting his son," Sir Guy said, "the only opportunity ever given him snatched hold of, albeit at the cost of an ally. Though once a fearsome warrior, now of an age and temperament that should have seen him felled by a younger, stronger warrior."

As Dougray struggled to contain his emotions, the chevalier smiled, though not with joy. "Ever I am awed by the strength and determination of men and women rising to feats unimaginable when one for whom they have a great care is in danger."

Briefly, Dougray closed his eyes. "Though these things I did not wish to know and still do not, I am grateful."

"I wish something in return," Sir Guy said. "That you speak with my uncle."

Dougray would not commit to that without thinking well on it —and knowing more of the man who had sinned outside of wedlock. "You are close with him, so much he revealed my existence to you."

The chevalier grunted. "No one is that close with him. I knew naught of the Norman whose life my uncle saved until I sought out Michel weeks following the battle to confront him over what I had seen and hoped no others had. A dangerous thing it is for a Norman to side with Saxons, but then to return to the side of his own..."

He shook his head. "It appeared a ruse of William's to catch the English unaware, the same as I understand you have done in disguising yourself as a Saxon, but I knew of the great affection my uncle had for those among whom he came to live as a young man and that he had fought with King Harold to defeat the Norwegian invaders before William invaded. A Norman by birth, he is a Saxon by choice—and appearance, though not as great as he bore at Hastings. It was not easy to persuade him to explain what he had done, but he revealed I had another cousin and the reason the one who had taken an axe to the arm bore the name D'Argent though he has no silver about him." He considered Dougray. "Those of the silvered hair with whom you fought is what drew my uncle to your side, not only to look upon his grown son but ensure no blade cut him down. That he did—and suffers for it."

"Suffers?"

"He does not speak of it, but I know him. He fostered me from the age of seven to twelve, after which my sire determined his youngest son's training should be completed with one whose loyalty to William was unquestioned—Baron Pendery of Trionne."

The father of his friend, the Bloodlust Warrior, Dougray mused.

"My uncle regrets he could not more than save your life and to save it he had to slay one who is more his countryman than any Norman. On one hand he believes himself a failure, on the other a murderer."

Dougray tried not to feel for one whose actions had cast a greater shadow over his mother than her misbegotten son. Whereas in the eyes of many, the latter was deemed foul for his conception, the former more so for his making. Returning his regard to Sir Guy, he said, "Why do you care so much for one who sided with your enemy?"

"Not my enemy. I have also lived long among the Saxons and feel for them, but first I am Norman the same as my sire, my loyalty bound to William ahead of an English king, be it Edward or Harold. Still, I care for my uncle. Though my father is a good man, fond of his wife and children, Michel Roche is a better man. Childless but for the son denied him, he has been as a father to me. Thus, with the aid of the one to whom he *is* a father, I would see him made as whole as possible."

"He is not nor has ever been my father."

Anger glinted in the chevalier's eyes. "I know you were born of sin, for which you have suffered, but it was not ravishment. It was a mistake the same as I have made and likely you, one the Lord not only revealed to all by swelling your mother's belly but by way of indescribable forgiveness in seeing you bear the name D'Argent."

None of this Dougray needed to be told, and yet hearing it from this man who was as much a cousin as Maël helped to contain his resentment.

"You will go to him?" Sir Guy asked.

"I will think on it."

A muscle jerking in the chevalier's jaw, he said, "I believe prayer will move you in the godly direction, *Cousin.*"

As he strode opposite, Dougray realized he had not learned what Guy stood to lose in championing his uncle. But he shrugged it off, settled against the well, and watched the chevalier enter the training yard.

His sword also needed swinging, as evidenced by the match

made with a man-at-arms who, were he Norman, looked more a Saxon the same as his lord.

Dougray frowned. Had William's conquering caused Roche to shorten his hair and beard? It *was* a dangerous thing in Norman-ruled England to look more the conquered than the conquerors, and if the king even suspected the Baron of Stavestone fought against him…

Dougray told himself it was not his concern and he had no cause to be alarmed. But he was.

# CHAPTER TEN

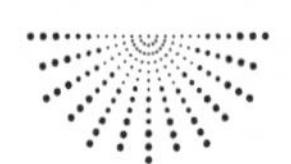

Hunger. Though greater the longing to return to wondrous sleep than take food or drink, her belly gnawed.

She shook her head, whimpered as a throb flared behind her eyes, and told herself morn would be soon enough to satisfy this ache. But a murmur sounded to her right, followed by the breath of sleep. It was near, meaning she had drifted off as she never dared before distancing herself from *him*. And that breath was lighter than it should be in the depths of night.

Heart thudding, mouth going drier, she questioned if it was still night and opened her eyes. It was difficult to make sense of a ceiling that seemed nearer than it was but, blessedly, it remained deeply dark.

*That does not mean dawn does not draw nigh,* her inner voice warned. *You do not want to be here when he awakens.*

She rolled onto her side. And nearly gasped when the throb in her head sharpened. Was she ailing? Not that it would matter to him…

*Slowly,* she counseled and put her legs over the side and set her feet on the floor, turned her hips and slid down the mattress, lowered her hands to the floor and crawled toward the farthest corner, bumped her aching head against the wall and muffled a cry, turned her back into the wall and drew up her legs, wrapped her arms around her knees and pressed her forehead against them, closed her eyes and thanked the Lord she had reached her sanctuary without awakening *him.*

Now if only He would heal the pain in her head that was so vast she felt none of the other hurts inflicted this eve, so intense she risked weeping which might awaken *him* and once more see her…

Em tightened her throat muscles for fear of releasing the pressure in her chest. The effort making her shudder, she slid a hand into the neck of her garment. And jerked when her fingers found a slight depression where she had thought to dig her nails to distract herself.

She fingered it all around. Perhaps she had not fallen asleep beside *him.* Perhaps she had come to her corner hours past and but dreamed of the day she rid herself of *his* mark. That was it, and so welcome was the dream, she began to relax. But the ache in her head doubled as if a dull-edged blade had been sharpened.

Another cry laying siege to the backs of her lips, she caught hold of the hair spilling over her shoulder, twisted it around her hand, and dragged on it. When that pain did naught to distract her from the one in her head, she clamped her other hand over her mouth to muffle her sobs and entreated the Lord that if He would not deliver her from Campagnon and this terrible ache, He deliver her from a life in which she was of no use to her siblings. Nor her people…

WHAT ROUSED Dougray from a semblance of sleep sounded again. Non, this sound was different. Not a knock from the other side of the wall against which his bed was positioned but a soft staccato sound.

Had Em roused? Did Margaret tend her? Might she require aid since the physician had not returned by the time all bedded down for the night?

He tossed back the cover and dropped his feet to the floor. As he dragged on chausses amid moonlight come through the window, he sensed Guy's awakening.

"Em," he said by way of explanation and drew his dagger from beneath his pillow, slid it in the waistband of his chausses, and strode to the door.

In the corridor lit by a single torch, he looked to the door beside his own. Glimpsing no light beneath it, he opened it.

With the torch casting a soft glow over all, he sent his gaze around the room, and his heart lurched when he saw the bed was empty. The only occupant here was Margaret on her pallet.

He opened his mouth to awaken her and demand she reveal where Em had gone, but a noise like that heard whilst abed sounded from the right. Seeing a figure huddled in the shadowed corner, he stepped inside just as Margaret sat up on her pallet.

Motioning the woman to remain where she was, he strode toward Em whose knees were drawn up, one hand muffling sobs, the other wound around her hair at her shoulder.

Counseling measured steps, he slowed.

Her head came up, and when he heard a sharp breath drawn behind her palm, he turned to the side to allow the corridor to light his face.

She stared, eased her hand from her mouth, then blinked as if to mend his blurred edges.

"Em?"

"'Tis *you,*" she croaked, then with less certainty, "It is, is it not?"

He closed the remainder of the distance and lowered to his haunches. Seeing her face was damp and flushed, he suppressed the impulse to reach to her and said, "I am here."

Her hand in her hair tugged at the dark swath. "Dougray D'Argent?"

"The same."

"Then where is *he?*"

"Who?"

She sent her gaze past him, swept it all around, then said with wonder, "'Tis not the solar. Not Balduc."

Previously, Dougray had considered he might have to kill Campagnon, but in this moment it could be as much out of desire as necessity. Though at York Em had led him to believe the use of her body by men was no longer of consequence, causing him to question if she was so calloused she had turned wanton, no longer did he think it possible. If any man had been intimate with her since Campagnon, it was by force.

Of a sudden, she gasped and caught up a handful of the chemise covering her knees. "Where are my chausses?"

"Being laundered with your tunic."

"For what?"

"They were fouled at the battle of Stafford where you took a blow to the head. Do you not remember?"

She blinked. "*He* was there. I knew to keep my eyes on my opponent, but I saw *him* coming for me."

"He is not here, Em."

"Wh-where is here?"

"Stavestone upon Derbyshire."

Her eyes widened further, and he wished more light so he might look upon the blue and the brown. "What of Vitalis?" she whispered.

"He himself delivered you from the battlefield."

Her brow furrowed.

"When the resistance was defeated," Dougray continued, "Vitalis withdrew the Rebels of the Pale. After seeing your injury tended, he sought me out and gave you into my care."

"He did?" Disbelief, though not great.

"And Margaret as well. She aids the physician in tending you." He set a hand on her arm, and when she did not pull away, said, "You were not abandoned. Vitalis did what was needed to protect you and the others." Should he tell her the Rebels of the Pale were disbanding? he wondered, then decided it could wait.

Still holding to her hair, she lifted her other hand, felt it over her head, and fingered the bandage. "I would have slowed them."

He nodded. "You must return to bed, Em."

She lurched back. Sounds of discomfort muffled behind her lips, she pushed upright against the wall.

As he also stood, her free hand shot up, beseeching him to keep his distance.

*Non,* Dougray silently amended, *I will not kill Campagnon as much out of desire as necessity. More out of desire.*

Staring at the pain rendering her face almost unrecognizable—teeth clenched, eyes narrowed, brow lined—so great was the longing to put an arm around her and assure her she had nothing to fear, he nearly ignored her beseeching. But she wrestled with a demon as once he had done, and lacking an invitation, such battles were best fought one-on-one.

Dougray looked to Margaret who had moved to the foot of the bed. "I do not think the physician has returned," he said. "Blessedly, it appears Em is not in great need of his services."

Or perhaps she was, he corrected when a hand wrenched at his tunic and he saw desperation vie with fear as she gave more of her weight to him to keep her legs from folding. Abandoning caution that could see her heaped at his feet, he stepped near and slid his arm around her.

She dropped her head back and ran the blue and brown of her gaze over him as if to confirm it was he who held her.

"I will not hurt you, Em. I want only to return you to bed."

A shake of the head made her whimper and free her hand from her hair to add its efforts to the one gripping his tunic. "I am hungry."

Though twice he had caught the rumble of her belly, he wondered if what she truly wished was to avoid the bed. If so, because she had believed it was the one at Balduc?

"I will help you to a pallet," he said, "and Margaret will remain with you while I go for food and drink."

"Nay, I would eat in the kitchen."

"It is late, Em, the household at their ease."

She shook her head again, whimpered again. "Pray, carry me."

Already he was tense over how near her body, now more so over what was asked of him as if she forgot he was not whole. It was one thing to hold her astride, and that had been safe only insofar as the pace was sedate, but to raise her into one and a half arms and negotiate dim stairs and a hall whose floor was strewn with dozens who passed the night there?

"I do not like this room, Dougray."

He warred with pride, then resenting his victory, said, "I shall awaken my companion who aided in delivering you from Stafford. Sir Guy will carry—"

"Nay, I will hold to you." She released his tunic, put her arms around his neck, and pressed her head beneath his chin.

He considered the bandage affixed to one side, then raised his half arm to support her upper back, slid the other arm beneath her thighs, and swept her up against his chest.

Her head rolled on his shoulder, and he saw she squeezed her eyes closed. "I hurt, but I will not let go," she rasped.

He stiffened in remembrance of the last time a woman said she would not let go. Hoping to make a future with Adela by fighting alongside the duke, he had met with the lady before departing and warned it could be months before he returned and he might not return at all. Arms around his neck, she had leaned up and said, *Whether you are long in returning to me or never return, my love, I will not let go.*

She had done worse than let go, casting aside what remained

of the man who had believed his heart was in her keeping the same as hers was his.

"I will not, Dougray," *this* woman entreated.

For a moment, he thought her promise went beyond aiding in carrying her belowstairs. But she was not Adela, not even one to be pursued in place of the noblewoman he had wished for his wife. She was a woman ruined for a life together—perhaps more ruined than the warrior whose pieces he had put back together as much as possible.

Drawing her closer, he crossed the chamber and put over his shoulder, "Bring blankets to the kitchen."

Hearing disbelief in the catch of Margaret's breath, he turned sideways to fit Em through the doorway. Almost effortlessly, he traversed the corridor, and upon reaching the stairs said, "Tuck your feet."

Though their descent was slow, it was without misstep. The hall, patrolled by two men-at-arms who paused over the sight of them, was more of a challenge. All but one torch had lost its flame, and the pallets of sleeping men and women were scattered, making the path among them a winding one.

Shortly, Dougray shouldered open the kitchen door and stepped into a cavernous room lit by the glowing embers of three ovens whose fires had ceased being fed following the evening meal.

"We are here," he said, and when Em met his gaze was struck by a memory not of Adela but of this woman when last they were in a kitchen.

Sleep eluding him in Balduc's hall, he had heard and seen movement opposite. Guessing it Campagnon who rose from his pallet and crept among the occupants, Dougray had watched lest the man intended his brother harm. However, his destination was not the solar but Em whom he had dragged from her pallet.

Dougray had told himself it was not his concern, that she was a slave to do with as her master pleased, but he had followed and entered the kitchen just as Campagnon pressed her back against a table though she beseeched him to cease.

Lest directly defending her encouraged the knave to do her greater ill, Dougray had chuckled.

Campagnon released her, and she sprang away as he swung around. "What do you here?" snarled the one whose barony had been forfeited to Cyr.

"I would make use of a kitchen as it is intended, not slake another kind of thirst on a filthy Saxon." Peripherally, he saw the slave startle where she pressed herself into a corner, evidence she was better acquainted with Norman-French than hoped. Reminding himself he hated the heathens of England, he chuckled again. "Here proof of what is said of Raymond Campagnon—only by way of coin does a woman suffer his attentions."

He thought himself prepared for the attack, but as chairs tumbled, pots clattered, and tables scraped and teetered, the truth that rendered him barely capable of moving beyond defending himself became clearer. And that eve, before his brother and cousin intervened, great his humiliation witnessed by the woman he had been unable to deliver from that dark corner, one from which she later delivered herself in fleeing Balduc.

"I remember," she whispered Dougray back to Stavestone, and he saw she watched him through pain-narrowed lids.

"I did hate Saxons then," he said, "but they were only words to move him off you—futile, as you told at York, what he intended done another day."

She drew a hand from around his neck, but when she reached as if to touch his face, the door opened and she snatched her arm back.

Dougray jutted his chin at the central oven whose embers were brightest. "Make a bed for her there, Margaret."

The woman gave a grunt of disapproval but stepped past and arranged the blankets one atop the other. Lastly, she folded them over. Though it created a more comfortable pad, he guessed she did it to ensure space enough for one alone.

"Now food and drink," he said as he carried Em to the blankets.

Margaret hastened to the cupboard that, were the Lord of Stavestone respected by his household—else feared—would be free of lock and key.

Em startled when Dougray lowered to a knee and realized she had begun to drift. That she did not want, just as she did not wish to feel as if…

What? She was safe with him? Aye. Though she should be afeared to be so near him, she was not. Because of how great her relief at discovering he was not Campagnon? It must be, and yet it was more. Never had she gone willingly into the arms of a man not her kin. And with Dougray, she had done so not only to gain aid but comfort.

Now with the warmth of his arms to be traded for that of embers, reluctantly she unhooked her hands from around his neck and pressed a palm on either side of the blanket to remain sitting.

"You are well?" he asked.

She nodded and was pained by the movement, a reminder she was not well at all.

Shortly, Margaret appeared, lowered a cup of wine, and turned back a piece of cloth to reveal bread and cheese.

"It hurts to move my head," Em said when the woman raised her eyebrows. "But less than when first I awakened."

Another arch of the eyebrows.

What did she ask? Em wondered and searched through the fog of all that had happened since her awakening. What had been hazy beginning to clear, she recalled more of what the woman had witnessed and Dougray had looked even closer upon. Doubtless, both questioned the soundness of her mind.

But it was sound, was it not? Throughout her training with the rebels, she had sought to reclaim the Em who once had moved amongst men as easily as women. Gradually, she had become accustomed to the relatively close company of the opposite sex. And this eve, rather than sink to the floor, she had sought Dougray's arms.

She moistened her lips. "Truly, I am well," she said, then in response to her grumbling belly reached for the bread.

"You may return to the chamber, Margaret," Dougray said.

Her widening eyes beseeched Em to protest.

Attempting a reassuring smile, Em said, "The same as Vitalis, I believe I am safe with Sir Dougray."

The woman, liked well for how unaffected she was by Em's eyes when first they met, departed the kitchen.

Looking up at Dougray who stood over her shoulder, Em narrowed her lids against the pain and acknowledged he was handsome as she had not at York when she saw he no longer wasted away. Despite his halfway-empty sleeve, the formidable warrior appealed as no man should were she truly ill of mind.

"Drink, eat," he prompted as if uncomfortable beneath her *witchy eyes.*

Rather than resent him for it, she wanted to assure him she was no more devil-bent than he. Instead, she hid behind the cup she raised to her lips, and managed a single sip before slopping wine down her front. She gasped, and Dougray took the cup and set it aside.

With scrabbling fingers, she gathered up the bodice of the chemise that had replaced her tunic.

"Em." He extended the cloth that no longer held bread and cheese.

She snatched it from him and blotted at the stain. When she could do no more, she ventured a look at him where he rested on his haunches, the glow of the embers at his back making his hair appear as golden as his eyes.

He had been looking to the side of her, but before she could determine whether something had captured his regard or he merely sought to save her humiliation by averting his eyes, they met hers.

"Will you let me help you, Em?" At her nod, he put the cup to her lips.

She sipped, time and again betraying her resolve not to peer at him over the rim.

"Now something to sop up the wine, else you may not keep it down." He broke off a piece of bread and placed it between her lips, followed by cheese and more bread. It was peculiar to be fed by a man, causing strange flutterings between chest and belly. Was it as peculiar for a man to be fed by a woman?

Remembrance made her catch her breath, and now it was Dougray who said, "I remember, though I believe I was more at your mercy bound to a tree than you are at mine."

"Not so. You had a dagger." She glanced at his empty sleeve. "Even now?"

"Even now, though this one is tucked beneath the waistband of my chausses."

She opened her mouth, closed it, then blurted, "Why do you aid me?"

He considered her, then said, "I but seek to right some of the wrongs done you."

*Is that all?* she was tempted to ask and was glad he offered another piece of bread followed by wine.

"I would like to lie down, Dougray."

"Should I carry you abovestairs?"

Though that chamber was far from the solar at Balduc, she did not wish to return to it at night lest she react in a way that further added to the belief she was ill of mind. "Nay, I will rest here." As she began to lower to her side, the shoulder of her chemise dug into her upper arm, and she realized where Dougray's eyes had ventured earlier.

She wanted to wrench the material over the scar, but she was weary and already it was seen. And now again it captured his regard.

"One day you will have to tell me how you came by that," he said.

Doubtful. Even if she wanted to share the tale, *one day* was so distant he would be long gone.

She looked up at him. "Will you stay with me, Dougray?"

"I shall. Now sleep."

*Lightly,* she told herself. *Ever lightly.*

# CHAPTER ELEVEN

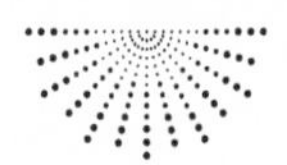

Dougray slept in minutes, none of which could number greater than a quarter hour. Though he believed Em was safe here, he had seated himself against the wall near the door. Even if he dozed, no one could enter without rousing him.

It was becoming evident night shifted toward day when the door opened.

Tightening his grip on the dagger at his side, Dougray tensed in preparation to use it should the one who entered pose a threat to the woman sleeping before the oven.

It was not one of the household seeking to calm a rumbling belly, nor the cook intent on beginning preparations for the day's meals. It was the Baron of Stavestone who turned his head first in Em's direction, then her protector's.

"Sir Dougray," he said low, and stepping farther into the kitchen, let the spring-hinged door swing closed.

Dougray stood and slid the dagger in the waistband of his chausses. "Baron."

By the light of what remained of the cooking fires, Michel Roche considered the one who had refused his summons on the day past, then said, "I did not expect you would still be here."

"Still?"

"Hours past, I was informed you had carried the Saxon woman belowstairs." He shrugged. "Though I knew it the opportunity my nephew desires for us to speak, I delayed in the hope it would be lost."

"As neither of us share Sir Guy's desire, Baron, what is not found cannot be lost. Hence, best you return to your bed."

Roche's eyes narrowed. "And you to your watch over this Saxon?" He glanced at her. "My nephew tells she is a rebel, but what is she to you?"

"Obligation."

"Rarely a good reason to adjust one's loyalties," the baron said, "but often honorable."

Though the question that rose to mind should not be spoken, Dougray said, "Was it obligation that caused you to align yourself with the Saxons at Hastings?"

Of a good height and breadth nearly equal to Dougray's, the baron stared at the one his sin had brought into the world. "If we are to make an opportunity of this, we ought to sit." He gestured at a table in the far corner.

Dougray hesitated, then assuring himself Em would continue sleeping providing their exchange did not become heated, he crossed the kitchen.

Shortly, Roche lowered to a stool on the opposite side of the table and placed between them a candle he had lit. Clasping his hands, he leaned in, and golden eyes stared into golden.

"Is Hastings truly where you wish to begin, Dougray?" he eschewed formal address. "I can, but it is better to begin in Normandy more than twenty years ere that battle."

Would it be better? Dougray wondered, then deciding it made no difference, said, "Begin where it best serves, Baron."

The flickering light revealing the planes, hollows, and lines of a face Dougray wished were not an older version of his own, the man said, "Your mother was coming out of mourning when a journey undertaken with her young sons was interrupted by brigands. Hearing the cries of women and children, my hunting party gave answer and put their attackers to the sword."

"This I know, Baron."

"Good. What you do not know is I loved your mother the moment—"

"You set eyes on her," Dougray scorned.

His nostrils dilated. "Non, but nearly. It was the moment she tore herself from her children and ladies to herself bind up injuries dealt my men. She was courageous and kind and, like the sun, so beautiful it hurt to look long upon something so far out of one's reach. And then I learned she was a widow." As if returned to that time, his eyes glazed. "Certain I had found a woman worth eschewing all others, I pursued her. Though great her love for her departed husband, in some measure she began to return my feelings. When I told her I wished to take her to wife, she who never lacked for truth said if she accepted, above all it would be to keep the word given her husband that in the event of his death, she would provide his young sons with a worthy father. It was enough for me, confident as I was her love would grow. But as our wedding neared, I sensed uncertainty and feared she would decline to speak vows."

He lifted a hand to the candle's flame and ran his fingers through it. "There was fire between us, and though I heeded my conscience and pulled back from kisses that sought to become more, that last time I did not. I led Robine into temptation believing were we one in body, naught would prevent us from becoming one in wedlock, especially if..."

"You got her with child," Dougray growled.

Momentarily, he closed his eyes. "I did not know it, so close she held what came of our one night though it should have seen us wed sooner. I contented myself that since she seemed less uncertain, she was mine. And I believe she would have become my wife had not the ghost of Godfroi D'Argent become flesh and blood weeks ere we were to speak vows."

His eyes were moist, and though Dougray did not wish to feel his heartache, he did, having himself lost a woman to another with a better claim on her—that of legitimacy and wealth.

The baron gave a bitter laugh. "I lost what I never truly possessed to a man come back from the dead. I told myself it was a blessing he returned before unlawful vows were spoken, but then I learned a healthy boy was born months too soon to be a D'Argent. I sent word I would take the infant and raise him as one who fights were he of that disposition, one who prays were he not." Again, he skipped fingers through the flame. "In the fewest words, Godfroi answered that the infant was a D'Argent and would be raised alongside his brothers."

His jaw shifted. "It sounded generous, but I feared for my son, certain Robine's husband would not long tolerate evidence of being cuckolded. Though I desired to put the sea between me and what I could not have, those first years I kept watch over you, sometimes with my own eyes at a distance, other times with the eyes of others sympathetic to my loss or desirous of coin."

Silently, Dougray rebuked himself for also feeling sympathy for the man who had seduced Robine.

"Then your mother came to me."

Dougray startled. From Robine and Godfroi, he knew the bones of this tale, but no splinter of this. "What say you?" he demanded, and regretted the strength of his voice might awaken Em.

"It was with her husband's knowledge and consent," the baron clarified.

"Why would he allow it?"

"Discreet though I was, he knew I kept watch and wished an end to it. Your mother assured me he had forgiven her, and I had no cause to fear for you and your future. She said you were happy and loved and her husband was fond of you." His brow furrowed. "You were well-treated, were you not?"

"By my family, but you must know my mother suffered for your seduction since it could not be hidden I was not Godfroi's."

"I know, just as I know you must have suffered when you were old enough to understand the whisperings."

Though tempted to shrug it off, Dougray said, "The D'Argent name is a shield not easily shattered, not even marked. However, enough blades made it past to prick, on occasion gouge, even incapacitate." Adela evidence of that last.

"Though I dare not ask for forgiveness," the baron said, "I pray you know I am sorry for your suffering, your mother's, and Godfroi's."

That last surprised, and more so for how seemingly sincere his regret for the man who had denied him Robine and his son. Ignoring his apology, Dougray said, "My mother asked you to leave Normandy?"

"That she would not do. She asked me to entrust you to the care of her husband and her and encouraged me to live as if never we had met so I could find happiness with another. I let myself believe it was possible and crossed to England as my sister and her husband had done by invitation of King Edward who gifted them with land. After years of fighting for Edward, he rewarded me with marriage to the Lady of Stavestone."

Dougray did not wish to care what followed Roche's departure from Normandy, but he did.

"She was a good Saxon lady with little prospect of bearing children. As she was considerably older, frail, and often abed, she was more a sister than a wife. Before she passed, she beseeched me to defend her people, even against my own should Duke William attempt to make good his claim on England." He sat back. "For her and love of these people, I fought with the Saxons in the great battle and would have done so to the death had I not yielded to the desire to search the enemy for sight of one of light hair among young men of dark silvered hair."

He shook his head wonderingly. "You, son of my blood, were formidable. Though left and right, before and behind, you cut down those I defended, I was proud. Folly, I knew and told myself to fight elsewhere, but I drew nearer, dropping Normans as I came and knowing you might slay me and never know who fell at your feet." He shoved a hand back through his hair. "If that day I hesitated over the killing of one of those I vowed to protect, I do not recall. What I remember is the desperate need to keep you from your opponent's rage. Failing that, to prevent him from taking more than your arm. You saw me, did you not?"

"I did—a grizzled bear of a warrior coming to the aid of his fellow countryman. I was certain if the one who landed his axe did not finish me, you would. When you turned on him, I thought it a vendetta under cover of battle. You looked even more a Saxon than I did two years later upon my return to England with Cyr to..." Surprised he had joined the conversation, Dougray trailed off, then said, "Now you appear more tame than I."

Roche ran a hand over his short beard. "I am ashamed to say necessity, rather than preference, dictates my appearance. With William thieving the lands of those who stood against him at Hastings, I dare not show the face I presented on the battlefield. To keep the people of Stavestone safe so they not suffer these lands being awarded to a dishonorable Norman, it is better I look one of my countrymen who has grown lazy with his grooming than a Norman-turned-Saxon—a traitor whose lands would be forfeited though he nearly emptied his coffers to pay the ransom to redeem them."

Though curious over what might yet be told, Dougray did not like how quickly his resentment toward this man eased with the tale of how, in battle, he had sought to be the father he was not. "If we are done, Baron—"

"Only if you are, Dougray. Do you allow it, there is more."

Was it cowardice to refuse? Dougray looked over his shoulder. Noting Em's breathing was less evident, he wondered if she had awakened. Though the possibility tempted him to end the conversation, he said, "Continue."

"Upon departing France, I resigned myself to Godfroi D'Argent being the father to my son I could not be. Thus, in all the years since, only rarely have I had word of you from well-intentioned kin and friends. But that changed after Hastings when I sought tidings of your recovery, and one of those who watched and listened for me revealed what you lost besides an arm."

Dougray tensed.

"I know you believe it none of my concern, but I praise the Lord you are rid of so unworthy a woman."

Dougray stood. "I do not regret having listened, but I have heard all I wish to hear. Now we need never again seek the company of the other."

"Oui, that ought to satisfy Guy," the baron said gruffly and came around the table. "I regret it was necessary to slay a man who sought to keep England out of William's hands, but never will I regret my son remains among the living. If ever you did, I pray no longer."

Dougray knew what was due Michel Roche, but it was not easy. "Long I rued surviving Hastings, but that is in the past. I *am* grateful."

The baron raised his hand as if to set it on Dougray's shoulder, but he closed his fingers into his palm and lowered his arm. "It is difficult to see your mother in you, but I do. When a man loves as I have loved, he knows where to look." He smiled tautly, then strode from the kitchen.

"It is done," Dougray rasped as the door swung closed, then he crossed to the window and opened the shutters to let in the dawn.

~

OBLIGATION. That was all she was to him.

*And I wish it no other way,* Em told herself. And yet…

As she had listened to a tale that made her ache as if it were her own, including Dougray's loss of a woman he must have cared for, she had felt something for him. She thought it new, but an air of familiarity forced her to acknowledge it was not. Simply, it was more felt than before, and possibly of greater depth than what she tried not to feel for Vitalis.

*Fool,* she rebuked. *You can feel this for no man, especially one who is Norman and noble to your Saxon and common—and you are not even common in the eyes of Campagnon and others. You are a slave, a possession.*

"You are awake."

She ceased breathing and rebuked herself for not attending to sounds and sensations that would have alerted her to Dougray's approach. He had halted at her back where she lay on her side facing the oven, but though she was tempted to feign sleep, he sounded too certain to be fooled.

Easing onto her back, she suffered only a throb from one side of her head to the other.

Dougray was of good height, but in this moment standing so far above her, he seemed a giant.

"I have been awake for a time now," she admitted.

He bent down, by the light of dawn lingered over her eyes, then touched a finger beneath the right. As she struggled against trembling, he traced her cheek from alongside her nose to the outer corner of her eye.

"These now appear more shadow than bruise." He withdrew his hand and draped it atop his thigh. "I would not wish you to fall ill, but some good has come of your injury."

Despite what was now more discomfort than pain, she did feel better rested than she had in a long time.

"And now I believe you know far more of me than I know of you, Em."

She swallowed. "I heard most of what your father and you—"

"Not my father," he said more wearily than harshly.

Though it was not for her to defend the man forced to yield his son to another, especially since she could not know how true that one's words, she said, "He seems a good man."

"Methinks you are swayed knowing he fought with the Saxons."

"So I am, and so he did until his Norman son needed him. Upon Nottinghamshire, you said it was opportunity that caused the one who took your arm to fall to a fellow countryman. Now you know different. Deny the baron though you do, that day he sacrificed his beliefs and loyalties to claim you as a son."

"I will not argue that, and I am grateful, but there it ends. When you are recovered enough to resume our journey to Wulfenshire, he and I will return to our separate paths."

"Even if he wishes to know you better?"

His nostrils flared. "He wants that no more than I—will be as glad to see my back as I shall be to see his."

"It did not sound that to me."

"Then we hear different things. Now I am done discussing what concerns neither of us. As it will not be long ere the cook appears, I shall return you abovestairs."

Hoping to postpone until more light could be had through a window, she asked, "Have you served your king well since you escaped your bindings in Nottinghamshire?"

He stilled. "I have."

"How?"

"After disbanding two rebel factions north of York, I delivered to William the location of the Aetheling."

She caught her breath.

"Fear not. As those sent to capture Edgar were poorly chosen, he and his guard slipped away."

Em sighed. "I do not like Edgar, but I am glad."

"Why do you not like him?"

"He is impetuous, spoiled, and nearly as given to flattering as he is to being flattered. This I saw even before he sought me out to be a bedmate, just as the Danish earl wished me to be his son's. I declined his offer as well."

In the silence that followed, she sensed Dougray's displeasure, then he said, "You do not think the Aetheling would make a better king than William?"

"I did not say that," she exclaimed, "nor would I after what William has wrought. Edgar would have to be the devil to loose worse evil on Saxons."

She expected his anger to rise to hers, but what she glimpsed on his face was fleeting. "It is past time I carry you abovestairs," he said and reached to her.

Wariness cleared her anger, and he saw it, the good of him—whether from the sire he spurned or the one who accepted his wife's ill-gotten child—making him pause.

"There is naught to fear in that chamber, Em. Margaret is there and will stay your side when the physician comes to examine you."

She wished he did not read her well, especially as it moved her toward wishing something possible that was not.

"Put your arms around me," he said.

She wanted to refuse lest she add to memories of him, but she could not traverse the distance unaided. Linking her hands behind his neck, she settled into the support of his half arm across her shoulders and nearly sighed when his arm in full scooped her against his chest.

He did not strain in getting his legs beneath him, nor was her position precarious as he conveyed her from the kitchen through the hall and up the stairs. So secure was she, she almost felt a girl in her father's arms, and ache for the sire lost to her made her long for Dougray to embrace the sire he had found. And reminded her of those she should not have forgotten.

"The little ones!" she gasped when he reached the landing.

"They are not in the direction of Wulfenshire. They are in Gloucester where soon I would be had I not turned back."

He halted before the first door on the corridor. "You were heading to Gloucester?"

"I was. Vitalis delivered me as near as possible and said it was not for me to fight at Stafford but to ensure my brother and sister's well-being. After I departed, I happened on Normans clearing the way for their contingent by taking to ground any who could forewarn the resistance. I stayed out of sight and learned it was Le Bâtard who led an army twice as great as anticipated—and they were hours away. Thus, I returned to Stafford to give warning."

"And fought as you were not meant to."

"Aye, Vitalis ordered me to resume my journey, but it was too late. With William's men all around, it seemed more dangerous to flee than fight."

"I owe Vitalis an apology."

"For?"

"I thought him responsible for your injury."

"He is not. That is Campagnon's doing."

Dougray inclined his head, then directed her to open the door.

Ignoring his request, she said, "I cannot go to Wulfenshire. Though the greatest resistance was in the midlands, it extends south, possibly where my—"

"We shall speak more of it later. Open the door, Em."

Setting her teeth, she did as told.

Inside the chamber which she had no cause to fear, it was dark and silent, the shutters fastened over the window and Margaret on her pallet. But still that corner beckoned.

"We are at Stavestone," Dougray said as he lowered her to the bed.

Half pleased, half alarmed once more he read her well, she said, "I am glad." Still, she was wary—until the soft mattress gave beneath her and she caught the scent of lavender cast over it. In that moment, her body seemed to double its weight and her lids lowered in defiance of the command to sleep light.

"Rest, Em."

The coverlet drifted down over her, settling so softly its warmth was more felt than its weight.

"Heal, Em."

The throb behind her eyes receded, and something like peace swept over her.

"Trust me, Em."

*I do, Dougray,* she thought. *I dare not, but I do.*

# CHAPTER TWELVE

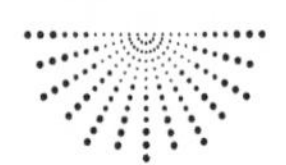

William was on the move again, as told by a score of Norman nobles granted entrance to Stavestone three days following the victory at Stafford.

Certain to be recognized, Dougray and Guy had absented themselves while the baron provided his uninvited guests with food and drink, next pallets in the hall when his excuse for not offering chambers abovestairs—confinement of knights showing signs of pox—had not caused the Normans to seek lodging elsewhere.

Now they were gone, having departed before dawn to rejoin William's army that would return to York to finish what was left unfinished with the Aetheling and the Danes.

Later this day, Guy would overtake the king and deliver tidings the surviving Rebels of the Pale had mostly disbanded, leaving Vitalis with too few men to present a great threat. To explain Dougray's absence, he would say William's scout had once more turned his efforts to tracking the Aetheling—as Dougray would after he delivered Em to Wulfenshire.

Though still he resented Guy for forcing an introduction to the man who had cuckolded Godfroi, much good had come of the detour to Stavestone. It had given Em access to a physician and time to heal—perhaps even saved her life.

Though he had not seen her since the morn he carried her from the kitchen to her chamber, the physician told she was much improved and on the day past suggested she walk the inner bailey. If not for the Normans' arrival, she would have, but this day Dougray would escort her.

That was the thought—until what had not been revealed to Michel Roche was revealed when Em, accompanied by Margaret, appeared in the hall for the nooning meal.

It unsettled Dougray to see her belowstairs, and more so attired in a gown that had likely belonged to the baron's departed wife. Though of good material and simple cut, it was too large. Still, it showed many of the curves previously hidden beneath tunic and chausses—and more obvious those curves with her veiled hair fashioned into thick braids that coursed her breasts.

The baron was also visibly unsettled, though not until he descended the dais and halted before the woman he had only glimpsed the night Sir Guy carried her into the hall.

Had Dougray been seated at the high table, Roche's reaction would not have been as evident, but like others who occupied the tables before the dais, he had a frontal view of the Lord of Stavestone—the jerk of his body, widening of his eyes, slackening of his smile.

As Em's back was turned to Dougray, all he could see of her response was her stiffening.

For as little as Dougray knew of the man, he should not be surprised he was given to superstition. And it was surely that, for what else could account for so great a change in his demeanor?

Dougray was gripped by anger of a depth not felt for the baron since first they met—and gripped harder when he recalled Em's defense of the man.

"I am Baron Roche, dear Lady," he titled her what she appeared to be. "It is kind of you to accept my invitation to join me at meal, but as you do not look as well as hoped, allow me to return you to your chamber so you can gain further rest." He took her arm, and when he turned her back, Dougray saw her stricken expression shift toward anger, and Margaret's as well.

It mattered not the baron had invited her to the hall, nor he titled her a lady. What mattered was his revulsion.

Hence, the sooner Dougray took Em from here, the better. Unfortunately, it could not be this day since they dare not risk encountering the stragglers of William's army. On the morrow, they would depart and never return.

It was difficult remaining seated as Em neared, and painful when she looked to him with what seemed accusation in the blue and brown of her eyes. Then she was past, Margaret trailing.

*Be discreet,* Dougray counseled. He hated it was necessary, but already there was too much curiosity and superstition amongst those who had seen what their lord saw. Thus, he waited until conversations resumed.

Doubtless, some noted when he withdrew abovestairs, but it caused no perceptible change in the resumption of eating, drinking, and fellowship.

Though he expected to meet the baron on the stairs, certain Roche's revulsion would not long tolerate keeping company with Em, he was neither there nor outside her chamber.

Dougray opened the door, and his gaze fell first on the man's back where he faced Em and Margaret before the window.

"What is this?" Dougray demanded.

The baron turned. "I seek to explain my behavior to impress on a runaway slave the importance of departing Stavestone as soon as possible."

Dougray ground his teeth. He knew Guy had revealed the injured woman was a rebel and assumed he had also told she was a slave. "Guy did not tell you?" he said.

"He did not. Unfortunately, neither of you could know how dangerous it is you withheld that information."

Dougray considered him, next Em whose own anger had abated. Now she looked uncertain, even fearful. "Explain to *me,* Baron Roche," he said, "how a learned, tolerant man—if you are, indeed, that—fears rare beauty is of the devil's doing rather than the Lord's. And so greatly fears it he subjects a guest to humiliation."

"He does not fear me," Em said. "It is Raymond Campagnon he fears, the same as I."

Dougray hesitated, demanded, "Speak, Baron!"

"As you know, last eve Normans demanded food and lodging following their withdrawal from Stafford. Nearly a sennight past, others demanded the same en route to Stafford."

The night Guy proposed they seek accommodations with his uncle.

"They were mercenaries—vile, godless men, among them a chevalier so full up in his cups one could hear his belly slosh between boasts of the reward offered for the return of his *witchy-eyed* slave who had joined the Rebels of the Pale—a young Saxon woman with one blue eye, one brown." Roche jutted his chin at Em. "In all of Christendom, I do not believe there is another."

Now Dougray understood.

"The physician having kept me apprised of her recovery, I had a gown delivered her so she might join the household at meal. Harmless, I thought, especially if I ranked her a lady." The baron shook his head. "Not harmless with such eyes. They are beautiful, but they mark her as prey."

"You believe one of your own might seek Campagnon's reward," Dougray said.

"I do not want to think that of any loyal to me, whether they are Saxon or Norman, but though I am fairly certain the first consideration would not be a purse of coin, superstition..." He sighed. "It breeds fear, and fear loosens tongues. Hence, it is unforgivable to ignore the possibility word this woman is at Stavestone will travel to the knave who seeks it, whether it does so on the feet of one who beheld her this day or of one told of her."

"I must leave," Em said.

"I am sorry," Roche said, "but if you are to remain free, the sooner you resume your journey the better."

"This day we make for Wulfenshire," Dougray said. Though they risked encountering those of William's army bringing up the rear, if they went wide around Derbyshire's southern border and bypassed Nottinghamshire, they might avoid the slow-moving wagons and carts bearing the least of the injured expected to fight another day for the king. A dozen or more leagues would be added to the journey, but it would increase the distance between Em and any who gave chase. Hopefully, none would, and soon he could pass her into the keeping of Guarin's wife and resume his efforts to end English resistance.

"I will see your horses prepared and packs provisioned," the baron said.

"I thank you."

Michel Roche stepped near the women and reached to Margaret.

She hesitated, glanced from Em to Dougray, and yielded her hand.

He drew it to his lips. "Godspeed," he said then reached to Em.

She also hesitated, also yielded.

His kiss was brief, but he held to her fingers. "Truly, I think your eyes beautiful, fair Saxon, that only the ignorant are blind to the hand of God having wielded the brush and paint."

Em stared at the man she had nearly hated when first she looked close on him in the hall. Upon his face she had seen what she thought the same as that of others who feared she was shaped by hands other than God's. More now than then, she felt as if she gazed at a younger Dougray. There were differences in their faces, but the similarities made her wonder how great the ache of

Dougray's mother and her husband when they looked upon the misbegotten son.

"I thank you, Baron Roche," she said.

"Godspeed, Lady." He stepped before Dougray. "Remain abovestairs until I send word. You alone shall depart in view of all and ride to the wood. Then the most trusted of my men will bring the women down the backstairs which are hidden—"

"I know their location. Had last night's guests insisted on chambers abovestairs, Sir Guy and I would have taken Em and Margaret down them."

The baron grunted. "I am glad my nephew—your cousin—has cause to trust you as you have cause to trust him."

Em was surprised he acknowledged their kinship in her presence. Either Michel Roche had been told she attended to his conversation with his son in the kitchen or he had sensed it.

When Dougray did not respond, he said, "The women will be brought to you in the wood."

His son inclined his head and remained unmoving long after he departed, then he crossed to the door.

"Dougray," Em called, "Wulfenshire will further distance me from my brother and sister. As I am recovered, it is to Gloucester I would journey."

He looked around. "Though much improved, you are not recovered. Thus, what has waited this long can wait a while longer. Too, I believe my brother, Guarin, will aid in confirming your siblings are well."

"I do not ask you to accompany me to Gloucester. As I know that would take you farther from your duties to your king, I can—"

"You cannot. I follow my conscience in this more closely than I follow the charge given me by Vitalis."

She stepped toward him. "A charge given whilst I was senseless and he feared for my life. As he was well with me journeying to my brother and sister before Stafford, I—"

"Non, I will deliver Margaret and you to Wulfenshire, and there you shall remain until you are fully recovered and it can be determined what is to be done with you."

"Done with me? I am a Rebel of the Pale."

"No longer, Em. The Rebels of the Pale disband." Ignoring her gasp, he continued, "Unless Vitalis lies, and I think not, most will return to their homes upon Wulfenshire and accept Norman rule."

The contents of her stomach burning a path up her throat, she swallowed. "Most?"

"Vitalis said no more than a dozen will remain with him and will continue to act against Normans when provoked."

She shook her head. "Why would he do this?"

"At least ten of your numbers died at Stafford, but it is barely of note considering how many others of the resistance spent their last day there. Vitalis believes the rebellion is nearly done."

"You lie!"

He looked to Margaret. "You were present when he said it. Do I lie?"

Sorrowful eyes meeting Em's, she shook her head.

"I know you do not believe it for the best, Em, but it is. Now make ready to depart." He stepped into the corridor and closed the door.

Em dropped her chin. Of course it was done, had been since York—nay, Darfield—but knowing it and accepting it were different things.

Margaret touched her arm.

Em looked up. "'Tis to Gloucester I go, and that may require your aid. But fear not, Sir Dougray will do well by you."

DOUGRAY HAD NOT EXPECTED to see the baron again—this day or any other—but he was in the stables fitting the bridle of the destrier who acknowledged his master with a toss of its head.

Roche looked around, patted the horse's neck. "A fine mount."

"Norman bred," Dougray said, "gifted by my father during my recovery following the great battle." Acknowledgement of Godfroi as his sire was unintentional, though often he had denied the man since his mother's husband set in motion the revelation of Adela's rejection. If not for the weighty silence, he might not have realized how thoughtlessly he returned to the form of address he had used since his first words were spoken.

He stepped around the baron and a lad adjusting the saddle straps, fastened his pack to the saddle, and looked to Roche.

A muscle convulsing in the baron's jaw, he looped the reins over the pommel and instructed the lad to saddle the second horse that would carry Em and Margaret. Then he retrieved two of four packs of provisions and returned to the destrier on the side opposite Dougray and began fixing them to the saddle.

Dougray moved to the destrier's head, plucked the remains of an apple from the pouch on his belt, and fed it to the beast.

"Dougray."

He peered over the horse into golden eyes. "Baron?"

"I would not have you depart Stavestone without knowing my greatest hope is we shall meet again."

Once more, Dougray felt for this man, but he did not resent it as much as before. "Providing I remain in England, it is possible."

"Why would you not?"

Dougray gave a curt laugh. "You ask that with Stafford a portent of what shall come of the resistance's continued rejection of William? By aiding in uncovering pockets of resistance and scattering them—most often in William's direction—I do what I can to sooner see this land heal. But even if the end of the resistance is nigh, it will be years before England is truly at peace and Saxons and Normans live and work alongside one another without suspicion or fear."

"Were there more Normans like you with a care for the people born to this land, the sooner it would come to be," the baron said.

"Ah, but those of the resistance would not agree I have a care for Saxons."

"The *dwindling* resistance. It is true most Saxons do not like Norman rule, but so greatly they weary of the unrest and punishment falling more heavily on those who do not resist, they want an end to the rebellion—even if by force or lost battles."

Dougray shrugged. "Regardless, when I am no longer of use to the king, likely I shall return to France."

"What in France have you to return to?"

Adela was between the baron's words—rather, her absence. "There I shall make a new life. If I gain lands, I may wed and father children." He nearly added *legitimate* children, but it seemed a cruelty of which Michel Roche was unworthy.

"You could have that here, Dougray."

Why did his thoughts move to Em, a woman beyond his reach?

The baron came around the destrier. "Em," he said.

Dougray jerked. "What of her?"

"You want her."

Perhaps cruelty *was* due this man. "Not only do you err, Baron, but you overstep."

Roche raised his eyebrows. "Whereas much you lie—and not well, which of itself may be a virtue. Certes, I am more accomplished at making truth out of naught, especially as done in telling myself I was worthy of your mother, she would come to love me, and a better father I would be to my son than Godfroi." He sighed. "Lies better told than the one you tell of Em whom I looked near upon this day. I have been as protective of a woman as you are of her and felt what I believe you feel, and so I know what lies behind the face you present."

Dougray glanced at the young man bridling the women's horse. Though he appeared too distant to catch words spoken here, Dougray stepped nearer. "Even were it true I have such a care for Em, any claim I make on her is more impossible than your claim on my mother. Not only does she belong to another man, but I fear she is ruined for any other."

The baron considered that, said, "Guy told you took her bill of sale from Campagnon."

"I did—and watched her put it to flame. But as you yourself observed, her eyes make prey of her. Despite the absence of written proof of ownership, likely Campagnon can produce witnesses to attest to his purchase of Emma of Gloucester. Hence, the best I can do is keep her out of his hands."

"Or purchase her freedom."

Recalling when his brother, Cyr, had offered to buy her from Campagnon, Dougray shook his head. "He will not sell her, even to one other than me."

"Then take her to France and wed her."

He stiffened. His first thought was, lacking great incentive, she would not want a one-armed husband just as Adela had not. But it was self-pitying, and so it was his next thought he spoke, which was just as true. "You would not suggest such had you seen her return to consciousness the night I brought her to the kitchen. Where men are concerned, I do not believe her mind is fully right."

"That may be so, but you cannot know for certain until she herself determines if you are but one of many men or a man alone whose face is the only one she sees when he touches her."

Once more, Dougray considered his words as if they were of a father counseling a beloved son. "You do not know Em. More, you do not know me."

"I know you more than you think, Dougray, not only from what is told me by those I trust, but from what I see."

Deciding no response was best, Dougray gripped the saddle's pommel, slid a foot in the stirrup, and swung astride. "I shall await Em and Margaret in the wood," he said and put heels to his mount.

Though he did not look back, he felt watched out of sight.

*And here the end of it,* he told himself. *No reason to meet again.*

Bending low over his destrier, he spurred across thirsting grass upon which autumnal leaves had found their resting place—until hooves kicked up oranges, yellows, and reds, forcing them to remake their beds for the coming winter.

# CHAPTER THIRTEEN

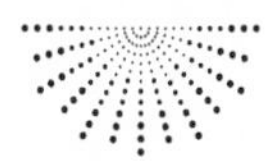

Her self-appointed champion was displeased by how little ground they covered before nightfall forced them to make camp. Had it not been necessary to adjust their course to avoid Normans bringing up the rear of William's army, they would have crossed into Leicestershire and be nearer their destination—rather, Dougray's.

Lest Em cause his eye to fall more heavily on her, she had not further protested distancing herself from her siblings. Blessedly, she herself lost little ground in reaching Gloucester, but the morrow would be different if she did not slip away this night.

As it could prove impossible to do so without alerting Dougray, at best she would have a few minutes' lead if he left Margaret unprotected to overtake one more capable of defending herself than a woman with so little training her dagger was of better use at meal than against an enemy. Em was counting on him not endangering Margaret—and her fellow rebel making it difficult for him to protect her.

Unfortunately, as Em was parted from her sword at Stafford, all she would take with her was the dagger given by the Saxon warrior who escorted Margaret and her to the stables, a pack of provisions into which she had stuffed her laundered tunic and chausses and, God willing, a horse to speed her journey.

That last depended on how well she moved furtively compared to Dougray's ability to sense that movement. Though greater the challenge since he knew her destination was Gloucester, she had to believe it was possible to escape.

As a girl, she had been graceless, rarely thinking ahead of a body eager for movement. Campagnon had changed that, there being few worse regrets than too soon recapturing his attention. Thus, she had learned to attend to her surroundings, go utterly still when the devil took a turn toward awareness, and move her breath and body with the least amount of disturbance.

Dougray was no devil, but given the chance, he would thwart her escape more effectively than Campagnon whose love of drink had greatly aided her.

Margaret touched Em's arm where they sat on blankets before a fire that barely warmed for how little it was fed lest it draw attention.

"Aye, Margaret?"

The woman glanced at Dougray who had gone to tend the horses near the stream following a meal of dried meat, biscuits, and little conversation, then knit her eyebrows.

Fairly certain of what she asked, Em said, "I shall try. With so many uprisings in the West and South, I must ensure my sister and brother are safe."

Margaret pointed at where the bandage had been removed from Em's head before they ventured to the hall to sit at meal with the Baron of Stavestone.

Em nodded. "'Tis sore, but otherwise I am recovered."

The woman's frown deepened.

"Vitalis and Lady Hawisa taught me well," Em assured her. "You need not fear for me—nor yourself." She looked to Dougray who bent to loosen saddle straps only enough to make the horses more comfortable without compromising the ability to be quickly astride were a hasty retreat necessary—a consideration that would benefit Em soon. *If* she could untether a horse and get astride before she came to his notice.

It would be hours before she dare risk it, she acknowledged as he straightened, the only light about his shadowed figure that of the moon slipping past towering pines to caress the blond of his hair and broad of his shoulders.

She knew not to linger over him, but rare was the opportunity to look at him unseen. She had thought his brother, Cyr, more handsome with his fine face and shock of silver amid dark hair, but that was mostly surface. The one who bore a good resemblance to Baron Roche was more than surface.

Recalling the conversation between the two men in the kitchen, Em wondered what had caused Dougray to lose what Roche believed a woman unworthy of his son. The injury that returned a vengeful Dougray to England? If the woman was so blind she could not see the whole of him in spite of that, she was unworthy, indeed.

Reason catching up with thought, Em rebuked herself for believing she could see the whole of a man who was her enemy.

*Enemy in name only,* said the voice within.

It was impossible to overlook Dougray's role in uprooting the resistance, but also impossible to ignore he did not do it to gain what belonged to others but to sooner end the destruction wrought on a rebellious people.

"He is worthy," she whispered and was alarmed by brimming tears.

Concern on Margaret's brow, the woman leaned nearer.

"Be assured, Sir Dougray will deliver you safely to Wulfenshire," Em said, "and I will rejoin you there as soon as possible." *Though only because of Eberhard,* she did not say.

Margaret set fingertips to Em's chest and tapped lightly as if on the door of the heart beating beneath, nodded at Dougray, and raised her eyebrows.

Em longed to feign ignorance, instead said what she feared more a lie than the truth, "I do not feel that for him."

Disbelief narrowed the woman's lids.

"Mayhap I am broken," Em said defensively. "So broken no good man will ever want me. But since never will I want a man, I am well with that."

"Nay, I do not b-believe—" The woman sucked a breath, pressed her lips.

"You speak!" Em exclaimed, then shot her gaze to Dougray.

She could not know if he made sense of her words, but they brought his head around. For some moments he considered the women, then returned to his task.

Em scooted nearer the one who had tensed as if caught doing something wrong. "Margaret?" she spoke the name she had discovered months past, the first letter learned by presenting examples as she worked through the alphabet and the young woman nodding when asked if her name began the same as *Maud.* Then other names were suggested that began with that letter and the nod was more vigorous when *Margaret* was submitted.

"'Twas a vow of silence you took," Em ventured, "and you fear having broken it?"

The woman averted her gaze, covered an exaggerated yawn with her hand.

The matter would wait. "We should gain our rest," Em said.

In the midst of preparing to bed down, the woman patted Em's arm to alert her to Dougray's approach.

"Aye," she breathed and noted the swing of his arms one would not know was mostly singular unless they looked lower to where only one hand was visible beneath the sleeve's hem.

He halted before the fire. "I believe we are safe, but be assured I shall sleep light."

*Hopefully, not as light as I,* Em thought, then lay down behind Margaret who had turned onto her side facing the fire as earlier instructed and drew the blanket over them.

Thus began a vigil like those at Castle Balduc. And yet not.

~

IF DOUGRAY SLEPT AT ALL, it was so light Em caught no sound of his breathing where he lay opposite, not even when the dying fire ceased crackling.

What was evident was when he rose to patrol the area—every hour, she guessed after thrice he had done so. Though she had hoped to escape when he was a half hour into his rest, guessing that his deepest sleep, during his last patrol she had peered over Margaret to follow his progress and discovered a better chance of reaching the horses ahead of him.

Dougray circled wide, starting just beyond the horses and often going from sight. Less than halfway through his patrol, he was behind Em. Thus, she must move opposite well before she was in sight and hope he was unable to detect it was only one figure beneath the blanket. However far she made it, crawling and hunkering, when he was most distant from the horses she would run for them.

Though her dark mantle ought to be of some benefit in the night, she would come to his notice. But providing she made no errors, soon he would have to decide between the rebel Em and the defenseless Margaret.

~

*ACCURSED WOMAN!*

Gown and mantle lifted clear of her feet with one hand, her pack in the other, she sprang toward the horses.

"Em!" Dougray shouted as he lunged through the trees. "Do not!"

She did, fluidly slowing, untethering, and gaining the saddle of the mount she had shared with Margaret—a horse of less strength and speed than his own, but unanswerable to Dougray who could have called back his destrier had Em been unwise in her choice of ally.

He was less than a hundred feet distant when she spurred away. Astride he could overtake her, but she was an accomplished rider, and it could be an hour or more before he forced her back to camp, during which the one left behind could become prey to four-legged beasts if not two-legged.

"Margaret!" He turned to the woman who had sat up. "Make haste!"

She shook her head and drew the blanket close around her.

Though she might not speak, she was not so fearful to allow ill to befall another. She aided in her fellow rebel's escape.

Silently cursing, he ran.

The woman proved she had a voice when he yanked her to her feet and she screeched. Proved she had words when he flung her over a shoulder and she cried, "Nay!" Proved she had fight when she attempted to turn the loss of his arm to her advantage—and nearly succeeded in causing him to lose his hold on her.

Dougray dropped her to her feet alongside his destrier and pushed her up against it. "Get astride. Now!"

Eyes wide, she hesitated, then turned and fit a foot in the stirrup.

Once she was in the saddle, he untethered the destrier, but as he started to mount in front of her, she slipped off the other side.

Had she not landed wrong, as evidenced by a yelp, he would have been forced to chase her through the trees. "I should leave you," he snarled as he pulled her up from the heap she had made of herself.

Whimpering, she put her weight on one foot. Hopefully, she had only twisted her ankle, but even were it broken, it would have to wait.

He put his arm around her waist, hastened her around the destrier, and turned her toward the stirrup.

Again, she hesitated.

Finding patience in the dregs of his deepest well, he said, "Though you seek to aid her, more you harm her. She is not entirely recovered, and a woman alone—even one with warrior skills—can be taken with little effort does she cross paths with men of ill repute, whether they are Norman or Saxon. Now you have given her enough of a lead, and more you will give her in sharing my saddle. Get on."

She gripped the pommel, fit her uninjured foot in the stirrup, and swung a leg over.

Moments later, she clung to Dougray's back as he guided his destrier through the trees as quickly as possible without losing the trail Em's mount left behind.

# CHAPTER FOURTEEN

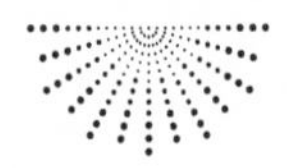

City of Gloucester
Gloucestershire, England

They were no longer little ones. At play amid the waning of day before wattle and daub huts so closely set they appeared to share walls, brother and sister kicked a leather ball with four other children, two of whom were cousins.

In the alley between cottages opposite, Em pressed a hand over her mouth to muffle gasps of relief her siblings were well and appeared happy—proof her sacrifice and Eberhard's had been worthwhile.

She had thought she might die if no good came of the coin traded for Tristan and Flora's older sister and brother, but this was more than good.

Swallowing hard, she slid her hand from her mouth into the neck of the tunic she had exchanged for the gown and fingered the depression. What had been inked into her skin, flayed from it, and all that came before, in between, and afterward—every last shame, degradation, and ache—was worth it.

"I am home," she whispered, but saying it did not make it so.

No longer was this home and likely never again. Even had the passing of years greatly changed her face and figure, she would be known for her eyes, and the merchant on the other side of town who had arranged the sale of brother and sister would catch word a most unusual slave had come home as slaves rarely did. And further removed was she from this town by what she had glimpsed as she slipped street to street, shop to shop, house to house.

The Gloucester left behind had been mostly Saxon, the Norman invaders a great, albeit fearsome, minority. They remained a minority, but their numbers had swelled, and not all were warriors. She had seen over two score common folk whose hair, style of dress, and speech revealed they had traded the country across the narrow sea for England.

Hearing a cry of excitement, Em returned to the present in time to see Flora intercept the ball passed to a boy and move it toward her brother. She halted, kicked, and Tristan took control of it. Moments later, he sent it spinning toward a girl who failed to keep it from passing between wooden buckets. More cries of delight amid groans, then the next round began.

The little ones no longer little were safe and happy. *They* were home.

Remembering her defense of the slave trade to Cyr D'Argent when he came to Dougray's aid after Campagnon bettered him at Balduc, she whispered, "Here proof 'tis not all bad—survival of those who might not otherwise." Still, it was very wrong any human be reduced to the state of animals merely to survive, even if labor was the only thing required of them. And yet, to save Tristan and Flora it had been the right—and only—thing to do.

Now that her fears were eased, the cautious side of her urged her to leave and this night begin the journey to Wulfenshire that had been delayed by two days' ride south and would be delayed two more to get back to where she escaped Dougray. However, the heart side of her longed to pass the night in her aunt's home.

Tristan and Flora would be shocked to see her, but they had not been so young they would have forgotten her. And if they missed her half as much as she missed them, it would do them good to know Eberhard and she were well.

*Leave,* prompted the voice Vitalis said it was best to heed. But not always…

Em adjusted her hood and looked from the children to others outside their homes. Assuring herself she would not draw attention providing she kept her head down, she stepped from the shadows.

Once she distanced herself, she would cross the street, slip between two homes on that side, and work her way back to the rear of her aunt's hut. Likely, the woman would be inside at her loom or preparing supper. They would speak, and unless her aunt had good reason to reject Em's wish to reunite with her siblings, three of the four would be together again. One night only.

Had not Em erred in ignoring the voice within, she erred in letting her thoughts blind her to what was more important in this moment—assessing and adjusting to her surroundings.

There was no creak of door to herald the young man who stepped from his hut, but she should have seen him soon enough to keep surprise from raising her chin. Recognizing small eyes, a broad mouth, and a deeply dimpled chin, she veered as if she had intended to cross the street here and prayed her hood had thrown enough shadow to hide the color of her eyes.

Hearing his boots move opposite as they scraped over packed dirt, she ventured a look behind.

Stride unbroken, he traversed the long street that led to the mill and castle, the latter raised by Le Bâtard to control the town and surrounding area by threat of force. Then of a sudden, he broke stride.

Lest he look around, she leapt between two huts and heard him resume his course.

*Leave,* the warning sounded again.

Should she? Nay, it was fear speaking—tempting her to do what she would later regret.

*Leave!* it sounded again, this time more beseeching than demanding.

She wavered, then struck a bargain. She would heed it if, when she peered around the hut, the man appeared to linger or had gone from sight since he might hide the same as she.

She counted to twenty, eased forward, and searched past the children. Purpose in the stride carrying him away, he was a good distance gone.

"Only fear," she murmured and traversed the alley to the back of the huts where summer gardens that had months past yielded their bounty were now pitiful patches of wilted and trampled leaves and stems. Ahead, her aunt's garden was easily identified by the carved bench where Em had perched when she needed to be alone to mourn her parents and pray for a way to ensure the survival of what remained of her family.

The answer to those prayers was supplied by her aunt—enslavement, even it if meant the loss of Em's virtue that was already endangered with invaders taking what they wanted from a beaten people.

"Worthwhile," Em reaffirmed. "No regrets."

Lest her aunt kept company with a neighbor, cautiously she unlatched the rear door and eased it open to the sound of humming. Between the gaps of woven reeds in the screen this side of the single room, she caught movement on the right where her aunt's loom was positioned before a window open on the street. Sitting on a stool before it with her back to Em, working the shuttle side to side, was the woman whose attempt to sacrifice herself to save them had failed. Instead, that burden had passed to her eldest niece and nephew.

*She tried,* Em reminded herself so she not succumb to resentment and anger as done often when her days and nights were spent beneath the hands of Raymond Campagnon.

She drew a deep breath, lowered her hood, and stepped from behind the screen.

Her aunt continued to hum as she wove cloth whose sale would keep the children and her fed and clothed—and well, it seemed, from the appearance of all within. Despite the Normans' stranglehold on England, life in Gloucester had greatly improved since the early days of the invasion. If only it had sooner.

Telling herself there was no good in wishing for what could not be, Em stepped to the center of the room and cleared her throat. "Aunt?"

A gasp, a dropped shuttle, then the woman leapt up and swung around. Eyes wide in a face that was still pretty, she choked, "Emma."

Pleased to be recognized, Em smiled. "Aye."

Her aunt's hands splayed. Then closed into fists. "Ah, nay."

Em lost her smile. "Nay?"

"You cannot be here." Her throat bobbed. "Did any see you?"

"Why?" Em snapped.

Her aunt strode forward, halted, and searched her niece's face. Eyes moistening, she raised her hands and clasped Em's face between her palms. "I see before me a lovely young woman. As expected, you fulfilled your promise." Her brow furrowed. "What of Eberhard?"

"We were sold separately."

Briefly, she closed her eyes. "I feared that."

Then she had known it was unlikely the word given would be kept. Struggling against anger, Em said, "Eberhard is well, purchased by a Saxon lady who treats him as a son."

"Praise the Lord," her aunt said, then caught her breath. "A Norman came looking for you."

Em stiffened.

"The one who owns you—the one you ran from."

"When was he here?"

"Over a year gone. He threatened to harm me and the children did I not reveal you. Blessedly, my husband returned home."

Em gasped. "You are wed again?"

Her aunt's face flushed. "Aye, to the Norman second in command of the castle's guard."

Then she had gained what desperation had made her seek to save her family before it fell to Em and Eberhard to save them—marriage to one of the conquerors. Despite her aunt's determination, each Norman she had attempted to gain as a protector and provider had wanted nothing more than to ease his carnal appetite with one of lovely face and figure.

"Truly, a good man," her aunt said. "He loves my children and your brother and sister as if his own. And he is formidable." She nodded. "He tossed out Campagnon, but I fear there is naught he can do to aid you as long as King William permits slavery."

*King* William. Of course she accepted him as her sovereign—the same as her husband.

Her aunt dropped her arms to her sides. "And aid you will need if any recognized you. Ere Campagnon departed Gloucester, he spread word of a reward for the return of his *witchy-eyed* slave. So I ask again, did any see you?"

"Mayhap Hearst."

"Hearst," she hissed. "A mischief-maker as a boy, a misery-maker as a man. You must leave immediately."

"But Tristan and Flora—"

"They have a good life, Emma. And as you must have seen"—she nodded toward the window through which the sounds of play drifted—"they are happy. But that will be spoiled if their sister is taken before their eyes."

Hurting for how right her aunt was, Em said. "You will tell them Eberhard and I are well?"

She hesitated. "They cannot know whilst you are near, and even when you are gone from Gloucester it could bode ill should they unthinkingly speak of you."

*Well thought,* Em silently acceded. What might be told here could reach Campagnon who, if he believed her dead from the blow dealt at Stafford, would no longer.

Her aunt set a hand on her shoulder. "I will tell them when I am fair certain they can hold it close. Certes, it will be of comfort. Even after all this time, Eberhard and you are in their prayers." She kissed Em's brow. "Godspeed and God's grace so we meet again in years better than these."

"I thank you for caring for the little ones," Em said and turned away.

She expected to feel hollowed out when she closed the door, but she was more hopeful than sorrowful. All was well here. Tristan and Flora had their cousins, an aunt, and now an uncle.

That last gave her pause. The children appeared happy, her aunt as well, the woman's face and grooming evidencing she had reclaimed some of what was lost to worry and weariness. Surely here proof her husband was a rare Norman the same as those of the D'Argent family.

*Leave,* the warning came again. *Night gathers its stars. Best you are gone ere they sprinkle themselves across the heavens.*

She gauged the sun's position, then telling herself it would do no harm to await the return of her aunt's husband, retraced her steps to where she had watched Tristan and Flora at play.

An hour later, as the sun's setting saw the children begin to return to their homes, a tall soldier took shape as he moved in the direction of her aunt's hut. Was it him?

Gripping the hood of her mantle closed at the neck, Em looked to Flora and her girl cousin who lingered on the stoop outside their home. Did they await his return?

She had her answer when they ran to him.

Em saw his broad smile as they tumbled into his embrace, heard his deep laugh as he scooped one under each arm and resumed his stride.

While they chattered excitedly where they hung from his arms, he grunted, harrumphed, and spoke words that made them giggle and exclaim.

He was not at all handsome—indeed, of a brutish form with a round face many times scarred, a bulbous nose, and missing teeth visible when he exclaimed over something Flora said—but clearly he adored and was adored in return.

*Now leave, Em.*

"Soon," she whispered.

Moments later, the hut's door opened and her aunt bustled out.

Her husband's smile fell and he lowered the girls, then it was his wife in his arms. "What is wrong, my pearl?" he said in Norman-accented English.

She shook her head.

He slid a hand down her braided hair. "You will tell me when the children are abed?"

Her words were muffled, but his nod revealed they were in agreement. Then he kissed her brow and took her hand. Trailed by the girls, he guided her into their little home.

"I praise you, Lord." Em dashed away tears, then retreated to the rear of the huts and began making her way toward the crumbling portion of the town's wall that had yet to be repaired though all the children knew it lay between dense, thorny undergrowth on either side. Albeit easier to go through the gate to reach the River Severn, that way was farther and less exciting.

In a copse well beyond that portion of the wall, Em's mount awaited her. They would not travel far, so weary was she from pushing hard to stay ahead of Dougray should he follow with Margaret. She would sleep long this night and rise with the sun to resume the journey to Wulfenshire.

The soft grey of the sky had transitioned to slate grey when she came in sight of the town walls' greatest vulnerability. Now she must be twice as cautious to ensure those who patrolled them did not see her before she saw them. Rather, she should have been more cautious sooner, she acknowledged when the hairs on her arms rose. She was far from alone.

*How many?* she wondered as she turned a hand around her dagger and forced herself to continue forward so whoever followed remained confident they were as unfelt as unheard and unseen.

There—a sound from the left, and was that a draw of breath to the right?

Two here, perhaps more. And she would be a greater fool to doubt she was their prey. Were Hearst the predator as hoped, she had a good chance of escaping him since he would be unaware of her rebel training, Campagnon having offered a reward before learning she had joined those of the pale. But were it her tormentor…

*It is not,* she assured herself, then drew her dagger from its scabbard. As she slipped tree to tree, she resolved though she would not slay Hearst nor those who aided him, they would hurt as they meant to hurt her.

"Lord, be with me," she whispered and, when the first attacker came at her from behind, swept open her mantle and spun around.

They numbered three. And were unprepared for a far from helpless woman.

~

Stavestone-on-Trent
Derbyshire, England

Raymond sniffed the air, wished he could smell her fear to confirm she was, indeed, here—that the rumor which beat a greedy path to him in search of reward was not rumor. Were it, someone would pay for causing him to leave the march toward York, especially if William learned he had done so.

"She lives," he told himself for the dozenth time.

When he had seen her fall at Stafford, he had thought her survival unlikely, but Vitalis had carried her from the battlefield. Surely a warrior would not waste precious time nor render himself vulnerable for a dead or nearly dead woman. Of course, were they lovers...

His upper lip curled. Though he knew it exposed a tooth so decayed it needed pulling, in this moment he did not care if his fellow mercenaries saw. Vanity had no place here, not with his wench hiding behind these walls. And if Vitalis was with her...

He ground his teeth, groaned when the decayed one sent pain shooting up his cheekbone, stilled when he saw movement atop the torch-lit wall above the gate.

A good-sized man with a short beard and long hair relative to the Norman style peered down. He could be mistaken for a Saxon with good grooming, but as Raymond had learned en route to Stafford when he lodged here for the night, this Norman had come to England many years past. And he had not liked Raymond nor the other mercenaries he let into his hall. Did he like better the Saxon rebels who entered here? The runaway slave?

"Sir Raymond," the baron called, "what do you outside my walls at middle night?"

"As told your man, I will not impose on your hospitality at so late an hour. I but seek entrance to confirm or refute the presence of a runaway slave who may be posing as a lady. You recall I offered a reward for her return?"

Light flickered across a lined brow. "I recall. You were quite drunk and made a song of the reward you would pay for...what did you call her? Your *witchy-eyed* wench."

Unable to remember having done so, Raymond shrugged. "The offer stands."

Baron Roche set his arms atop the wall and leaned into them as if attending to a good conversation. "There is no witchy-eyed slave here, albeit there was a Norman lady and her entourage who availed themselves of my hospitality en route to her husband's lands in the North. True, she had unusual eyes, one brown, the other somewhat lighter, but she was no slave in disguise."

"You may think you speak true, Baron, but I have journeyed far out of my way and would verify it for myself."

"Most unfortunate, she departed two days past. Hence, even were she the one for whom you search, she is long gone."

Did he lie? Certain of it, Raymond said, "Be it so, it will take me and my men less than a half hour to ensure she has not fooled you."

The baron sighed. "I suppose there is no harm in granting you entrance. Return at dawn, and not only will I allow you to search inside my walls but break fast with me and mine."

Raymond trembled with the effort to suppress anger. "Dawn will not do!"

"Of course it will." The man smiled and straightened.

"Baron!"

"Sir Raymond?"

"If you think to steal her away in the night—"

"In the absence of your slave, no such thing can be thought, Chevalier," the baron spoke over him, then swept a hand forward. "Avail yourselves of the protection of my walls and make camp before them. Ere first light, we shall dine together. Good eve."

Pain once more shooting up his cheekbone, Raymond parted his teeth, shifted his jaw, and promised himself if Emma Irwindotter of Gloucester was not to be found here, someone would pay mightily for the disrespect shown by the Baron of Stavestone.

# CHAPTER FIFTEEN

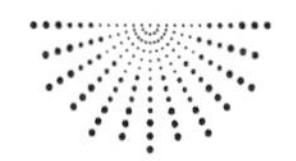

City of Gloucester
Gloucestershire, England

Light burning bright against the fronts of her lids. Tempting her to learn its source. Tensing her in anticipation of striking out.

*Power in patience,* Vitalis's words returned to her. *Power in lying in wait—in being still.*

"She will live," a man said with a defensive whine.

Hearst, she identified the voice, not from memories of the boy he had been but the man he had become. *Someone is looking for you, girl!* he had called as he and two others set themselves at her this night. Were it still this night...

The light and heat on her face shifted, then retreated as two sets of feet caused the wood floor to creak.

Feeling herself go adrift, she dug her nails into her palms to remain alert and make sense of where she was—and her state of captivity, she added upon realizing her wrists were bound in front of her. What of her ankles? A slight movement confirming they were roped, she shuddered at how helpless she was and how much more she could be depending on where she was.

As it was not yet safe to open her eyes with her face turned toward those moving opposite, she dredged up the clash that had nearly gone her way.

Surprise and low expectation had been on her side when her opponents struck. She had fought well, dropping one by driving the heel of a hand into his nose. After much dagger swiping and dancing between Hearst and the other man, a kick between the latter's legs and a slash to the back of his blade-wielding hand had sent him to his knees, next his face. Had not the first downed man recovered and charged, Hearst would have ended the same.

While she fended off the broken-nosed one whose slashing blade sought to do greater damage to her face than she had done his, Hearst found the gap needed to bring a hilt down on the same side of her head injured at Stafford. The ground had rushed at her, and that was all she remembered before awakening here.

Senses reeling again, she commanded, *Listen, learn, scheme, else you are Campagnon's again.*

She might be regardless, but for certain if she did not try.

*Lord,* she silently entreated, *if that was You—not fear—urging me to leave, forgive me for not heeding You. Forgive me for not knowing Your voice from my own. Help me.*

"I want my reward," Hearst said.

"Delivered as soon as the reward is given me," the second man spoke with the crackle of one of good age. Now Em knew where she was—in the shop of the merchant who arranged the sale of desperate men, women, and children, the same who had assured her aunt that brother and sister would be sold together. "Of course, first my fee will be deducted."

"What is your fee, old man?"

"Two-thirds."

"How much is that?"

A chuckle. "For every coin placed in your palm, two placed in mine."

"Almighty, you would thieve me blind!"

"Nay, I would be given my due."

"Your due?" Hearst's voice turned shrill. "I saw her, followed her, captured her, and promised coin to those who aided me—men who will want more for what she did to them."

"Then take her and yourself deliver her to the Norman mercenary."

"I shall." The wood planks creaked again as Hearst returned to her.

*Dear Lord, not now,* she sent heavenward. *I need time to recover and plan.*

"'Tis good you are so courageous, my friend," the merchant said. "You will need that and more if you are to return to Gloucester not only with your life intact but a purse full of coin."

Hearst halted.

Sensing he had turned, narrowly Em opened her eyes.

Her captor stood with his back to her in the doorway of a small room lined with empty shelves and set around with barrels. Beyond him, a portion of the merchant's bulk was visible. "What say you, old man?"

"Like me, you are a Saxon in Norman-occupied England. Like me, you have little skill at defending yourself against a warrior. Unlike me, you lack the means to buy the sword arms of those fluent in negotiating with men more given to putting a knife in a man's back than coin in his hand."

Hearing Hearst swallow, Em rethought her plea to the Lord. Better she was taken now by Hearst than later by brutes to whom the merchant would entrust her—men like those on her journey with Eberhard who used the bodies of women lacking virtue as they traveled toward the coast.

"But mayhap Campagnon's reputation is more rumor than truth," the merchant slid the blade of fear deeper.

*Be foolishly courageous, Hearst,* Em silently pleaded.

"Very well, two-thirds," he moved her to tears. "But I require payment now."

"I am agreeable—for a fee."

"What?"

"'Tis proportionate to risk, Hearst. Whereas I have all to lose do I pay you this day, you have only to gain."

"What is your fee?" the younger man hissed.

"Three quarters. For every coin you gain, three for me."

Hearst cursed him, snarled, "Done!" and crossed the threshold and slammed the door.

Em startled when she heard the bar drop. "Lord, help me," she breathed. Not only was she bound hand and foot, but locked in the dark with memories of the one to whom she would be returned and the longing to seek a corner in which to press her back so she had only to concern herself with what was in front of her.

Silly, she knew, there being no advantage to being cornered. And yet, there was comfort in protecting three sides of her, even if only for the moment.

"All for naught," she whispered. "Tristan and Flora do not need me. I could be with—" She gasped over memories of the man from whom she had run. "If you are coming for me, Dougray, even if only to keep your word to Vitalis, come soon. Find me. Deliver me."

*If,* such a powerful little word, more often hopeless than hopeful. Tears beginning to pool alongside her nose, she rasped, "What have I done?"

*Kept your word,* she told herself. *Eased your fear. Gained proof your sacrifice was worth it. And proof the Lord listened and answered well the greatest of your prayers.*

True, but still fear cut like a knife so dull the hand holding it had to saw back and forth to work its way to the bone.

"Worth it," she said, then dragged to mind better memories—

her brother and sister at play and her aunt who had further secured her family's survival by wedding a good Norman.

These memories she must dwell on...sink into...drown in...

SHE HAD BEEN HERE. No surprise. She was still here. That did surprise considering the state of two of the three men who boasted they had captured the *witchy-eyed* Emma Irwindotter.

Having arrived at Gloucester shortly before the gates closed for the night, it had taken little effort to confirm Em had fled here, drunken men and fools ever boasting of things they ought not. And when they were both drunken and fools...

Dougray inhaled the strong vapor of mead whose cup he peered over. Fortunately for the leader of the three, a man who had suffered fewer injuries than the others in underestimating Em, Dougray dare not beat him bloody. Did he, it could cause the merchant said to have purchased Hearst's interest in Campagnon's reward to more closely guard his investment.

A half hour past, Dougray had left his table at the tavern to search out the merchant's shop. The possibility of freeing Em was rendered impossible by an argument in the street between the merchant and a Norman soldier that drew a crowd of Saxons.

It was soon apparent the Norman sought to use his influence to free Em, though it made no sense until the merchant thrust his face near the warrior's and bellowed it mattered not the runaway slave was the niece of the man's wife, that as long as the laws of slavery remained intact, they prevailed.

The Norman had punched the merchant in the mouth—and drawn his sword on the Saxons who lunged at him.

Sanity had prevailed by way of the merchant. Past bloodied teeth, he implored his fellow countrymen not to break the peace.

Compared to other towns in England, it seemed life was good in occupied Gloucester. The merchant might wish to see the streets run red with Norman blood, but not at the cost of more Saxon lives nor, surely of greater concern, his business.

The Norman had sheathed his sword and stalked opposite, unaware of the damage done Em's cause, the merchant quickly enlisting four armed Saxons to keep watch over his shop through the night to ensure her return to her owner.

Hence, this night Dougray could do naught for Em, but if the merchant did as Hearst heralded, on the morrow she would be set on the road with slavers who were to intercept Campagnon on his journey toward York.

Being a warrior alone, it would not be easy for Dougray to take Em from them, but far more difficult—perhaps impossible—had he company.

Margaret having greatly slowed his pursuit of Em, he had taken the first sound opportunity to rid himself of her. It had come in the form of nuns returning to their abbey in Derbyshire following a pilgrimage to Saint Oswald's Priory. Their escort of Saxon soldiers had been suspicious of Dougray, but the eldest nun had listened to his request they convey the mute Margaret to Stavestone along with a missive directing Baron Roche to see her delivered to Wulfen Castle.

The woman had drawn Margaret aside, and whatever was asked of her was answered with a nod or shake of the head. Thus, the nun agreed to take a less direct route home in order to deliver the young woman to Stavestone. By the morrow, Margaret would be under the baron's protection.

Dougray drank down the last of his mead, then left Hearst and his friends to spend—or see stolen—whatever remained of their ill-gotten coin.

There would be no room at the inn for him this eve. Instead, he would make his bed in the alley between buildings opposite the merchant's shop to ensure Em and her escort did not slip away unseen.

A half hour later, his back against an overturned trough, the merchant's shop visible beyond the alley, he adjusted the blanket around his shoulders and glanced at the star-pricked sky. Blessedly, no clouds that portended rain.

"I thank you, Lord, for delivering me to Em ahead of Campagnon," he rasped, "and easing this anger that benefits her none. Be my left arm on the morrow. Aid me in freeing her from those who sin against You in sinning against her. Amen."

He returned his regard to the merchant's shop where two of those guarding it were visible, imagined her bound inside, and felt her hopelessness and fear.

"Hold, Em," he whispered. "I come for you."

# CHAPTER SIXTEEN

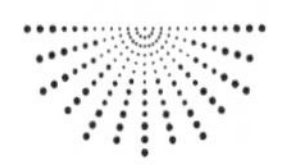

Stavestone-on-Trent
Derbyshire, England

Campagnon was a dog, not of the faithful sort worthy of bed, board, and affection—of the rabid sort that must be put down.

This morn, having provided Dougray and his charges further time in which to distance themselves, Michel had granted entrance to the mercenaries. They had searched every known room and corner—and there were some that would never be known to an enemy lacking wit and license to destroy—then made a mess of his hall in expressing frustration while satisfying their hunger and thirst.

And here was how Campagnon repaid the Lord of Stavestone's tolerance and hospitality.

Michel tried to talk down emotion dangling him out over its edge. He told himself it would be far worse had the Saxon warriors escorting a pilgrimage of nuns across his lands not set the attackers to flight, and it was true. Word of what was done here would have come too late to save men, women, and children to whom Michel owed protection. Blessedly, because Em had run from Dougray, the pilgrims had been persuaded to alter their course to return the mute Margaret to Stavestone.

"A blessing, indeed," Michel assured himself.

So what were mere injuries compared to deaths? What was harassment of women and their young daughters compared to ravishment? What was the loss of a half dozen homes compared to dozens?

*Still much,* he seethed. And he was to blame for underestimating Campagnon. He had tasked men with discreetly following the mercenaries from Stavestone lands, but whether the soldiers for hire were aware of those keeping pace or merely guessed they were not alone, it was they who had done this to the outermost village, turning back once no longer watched.

Michel spat on the charred, smoldering ground between two cottages set afire, opened his clenched hands one finger at a time, then turned to his men standing on either side of two warriors whose lord had tasked them with accompanying nuns from a nearby abbey on pilgrimage.

"That Norman dog must be put down," Michel said in Anglo-Saxon.

The Saxons did not speak, but their eyes did.

"Aye, I am also Norman." Michel nodded. "But that does not make us the same." He jutted his chin at the villagers who had gathered upon his arrival. "These are my people. If they are wronged, I am wronged, be it a Norman who trespasses or a Saxon." Abruptly, he turned on his heel and strode toward the villagers to assure them he would make good their losses.

"God help you if ever I lay eyes on you again, Raymond Campagnon," he muttered when he saw his physician tended a lad who would never be as handsome as before a blade sliced the top of a cheekbone and took a piece of his ear. "And God help me if I cannot leave you merely hurting."

~

Gloucestershire
England

*Every degradation worth it. Every ache worth it. Every dark corner worth it. And all yet to come.*

Em nodded, certain the bob of her lowered head would be attributed to the horse's gait. Not that she feigned sleep. Were she to do so, she would be unable to believably stay astride though her wrists were bound to the saddle's pommel. Thus, one of the slavers would seat her before him and touch her in places only his eyes went thus far.

How she prayed these men were worthy of the merchant's trust, all three instructed not to *play* with the merchandise and warned Raymond Campagnon would know if they sampled what belonged to him and would suffer for it. But not as greatly as Em was to suffer.

"Still I will fight him," she whispered. "Still I will seek to escape him." And if it was the death of her, better that than endless days in his presence and endless nights crawling away from him and into corners. "Aye, good reason I will give him to kill me—if I do not kill him first."

She focused on bound wrists shadowed by the curtain of hair she had unraveled from what remained of her braids. It was too dim to look near on flesh chafed by fibrous rope, but she felt the red of the abrasions. And hated Campagnon more.

*Heavenly Father, would You forgive me for slaying him were it not out of vengeance but to save others?* she sent heavenward. *Others like Flora?*

No answer, but she sensed disapproval.

*You must see his evil, that no matter he speaks Your name and bows his head in prayer, he knows You not. Exalts You not.*

Further disapproval.

*He inks Your holy cross into flesh alongside his mark of ownership of another made in Your image. Can there be redemption for one such as he? If You will not strike down the sinner, is it not for me to do—or any number of those he causes to suffer?*

*Can you do it?* asked her inner voice.

She wanted to remind it she had stuck Campagnon once and proclaim she could do worse without blink or falter, but…

In defense she had slain and injured several men. Could she do so offensively? And might it be counted defense if, after next Campagnon abused her, she stole upon him, stuck him, and watched the life fade from his eyes?

Perhaps. Perhaps not. Regardless, she would not be long with him, whether their association ended by way of his death or hers.

Em lifted her head slightly. Between gaps in her hair, she considered the burly slaver riding ahead. From the back, he resembled Zedekiah who was surely with Vitalis, but not from the front. He was younger, and there was no kindness about his eyes to make one think him attractive despite an unappealing face. He was ugly both sides of him.

As if he felt her gaze, he looked around.

Certain he could not see her eyes, she did not react in any way to reveal her awareness of him, not even when he smiled in a way that reminded her of Campagnon—though more the threat of that smile than the shape. Would the slaver heed the merchant? Or risk the reward and Campagnon's wrath to take what he wanted?

If the latter, surely he would strive not to mark her, and there was some power in that. It might do no good to fight him, but she would mark *him.*

He chuckled. "Methinks we ought to water the horses soon," he called to those at her back and turned forward.

Praying that was all her escort would do, Em gave her neck the entire weight of her head and resumed what was nearly a chant in reminding herself what had been and what was to come was worth what was gained by those no longer little.

~

DOUBT. Once more it sought to make him feel half a man—to extinguish the confidence required to bring Em out of this alive and unharmed.

He must not succumb. Must believe even one-armed he was more skilled at dropping foes than those leisurely riding over the dirt road with Em between them.

Three men. He alone had faced as many before, most recently at Stafford, but saving Em was different from the clash of two heavily armed forces on a battlefield. This would be no contest of warriors swinging and thrusting blades and, in between putting down an attacker and engaging another, defending the lives of fellow warriors. As well Dougray knew, the cost of great error in battle was his own maiming or death. The cost of great error here was failing Em, whether he lost her to Campagnon or a life-stealing blade.

He eased his destrier sideways. When it stamped a hoof, he murmured, "Patience, my friend. We shall free her."

The beast snorted, and Dougray returned his attention to the four traveling the road below the tree-lined slope that offered good cover in places where evergreens dominated, poor cover where the trees of winter's glory were sparse among their cousins who had shed much of their autumnal finery.

As Em and her escort were nearly level, he would have continued advancing ahead of them had not the slaver at the fore announced it was time to water the horses. Soon they would turn into the wood in search of the stream at which Dougray had satisfied his own mount's thirst a quarter hour past. Hopefully, it would prove the opportunity he had sought since dawn six hours past—one too long in coming and which, he prayed, was not overly dependent on Em.

From the moment she was led from the merchant's shop, feet under her command only enough to keep her upright, she had been mostly unresponsive. Hands bound to the saddle, back bowed, head hanging, there was little movement about her that could not be attributed to her mount.

Had something vile been done her? Had it further broken her? Or was she merely wracked by capture and the prospect of once more being in Campagnon's power? One or the other, was the damage irreparable? And would these men attempt to break her pieces into smaller ones?

Dougray closed his hands into fists. Though still he felt the absent one, more he felt the dagger strapped to what remained of that arm. If they sought to abuse Em, they would fail. He would use that distraction to his advantage, and in turning it against them sooner retrieve Em.

They were directly below now, the leader moving past, next Em's horse that required no hand to guide it, then the two slavers who conversed when they ought to attend to their surroundings on so narrow a road bordered both sides by wood. Here proof too much confidence could be as dangerous as too little, but it also served as a warning to Dougray. Men experienced at arms as these had to be since they were entrusted with delivering Em across unsettled lands, had little cause to fear the unseen. They would be fierce.

"Do not be too broken, Em," he rasped as she continued forward, her curtain of dark hair indistinguishable from her mount's mane. "If you are dead weight, this may not end well."

He touched the sword and dagger on his belt, next the dagger beneath his sleeve. And when he saw the riders turn off the road and enter the trees, he beseeched the Lord to use him to save Em.

~

"SIT UP, WOMAN!"

In the hope she would be deemed too senseless to present a threat of escape, Em ignored the command.

Unfortunately, after what she had done to Hearst's friends, there was little chance she would pass as harmless. Thus, her hands would remain bound while she relieved her aching bladder, and no privacy would she be afforded. Worse, she might need aid in lowering her chausses.

She nearly shuddered over imaginings of what might happen were she unable to drive a knee up between the legs of her assailant… were she unable to further incapacitate him by slamming her bound hands down on his neck as he bent over his pain…were there not time enough to run before the others descended upon her…

"Sit up!" This time the command was delivered with the back of a hand that knocked her head to the side.

Closing her mouth against a cry, once more she let her head settle between her shoulders.

The man cursed, with one hand gripped the hair at the back of her head and yanked her upright, with the other fumbled at the rope woven between her bound wrists and fastened to the pommel.

Terribly aware of his thigh against hers where he had brought his horse alongside, she fixed her gaze on the blue sky. It was more beautiful than a day like this warranted. It ought to be grey, as nearly without hope for sunshine as she was without hope for…

What?

"Dougray," she whispered. Dougray who had not come. Dougray who would not deliver her. And she did not begrudge him.

"She speaks to herself," said the man whose efforts to release her from the saddle caused the rope around her wrists to dig deeper.

Hearing wariness often roused by her eyes, she decided to feed it more. Were he superstitious, it was less likely he would violate her. "I bleed," she added only enough voice to ensure her words were heard and, continuing to stare into the blue, said, "It stings. It burns."

"Devil speak," the man hissed and shoved her opposite. "Take her behind a bush," he snarled as Em began a descent for which she had no time to steel herself. Fortunately, rough hands snatched hold of her shoulders and dropped her so hard to her feet her knees buckled. Again, her descent was arrested, the grip on her cruel.

"'Tis what she wants ye to think," this man said.

She tipped up her face and, past disarrayed hair, saw it was the one who had brought up the rear of their party—a muscular man of middle years.

"Is that not right, girl?"

Not superstitious, but would he move against the merchant? Would the others allow it?

"Let us be done with it," he growled.

Done with what? she wanted and did not want to ask. Though her bladder threatened to loose itself, she forced him to bear much of her weight as he led her toward a thicket thirty feet distant from the stream where the horses took water while the other two slavers remained astride.

Noting the bushes ahead were dense and of a height one would not know what transpired behind them if those there bent their heads, Em silently entreated, *Lord, aid me in rendering him harmless without alerting the others. Give me time to steal away ere they discover I am gone.*

She glanced over her shoulder and saw the one who had released her from the saddle dismount and hunker before the stream while the leader walked his horse opposite, head slowly turning side to side.

Did he sense something was amiss? Or merely ensure neither man nor beast had the opportunity to steal upon them?

A thrust flung her around the backside of the bushes. Dropped to a knee, she pushed upright and swung around to face the slaver.

"Do it!" He nodded at the ground.

Then he would not aid with her chausses? There was relief in that if it meant he would honor the merchant's order, but disappointment over the absence of carnal urgings that could draw him near enough to temporarily cripple him.

"You heard me!"

She pinched up the tunic between her joined hands, trapped the bulk beneath her forearms, and began plucking at the ties ever she secured with one knot atop the other.

As sometimes happened when her mind gave her body advance warning soon it would empty a bladder that should have been emptied sooner, she strained against messing herself as she sought to free the ties.

"Simpleton!" The man pushed aside her hands and bent his head.

Em slammed a knee up between his legs. He did not cry out, and as he wheezed and bent over, she curled her hands into fists and slammed them down on the back of his neck as taught her by Vitalis.

He toppled, and she jumped back to avoid him taking her down with him.

How many minutes before the others determined their absence was too lengthy or the man at her feet recovered sufficiently to alert them?

Seconds only. No sooner did she bend low to distance herself from the stream than she heard the pound of hooves on the left and the one whose bulk resembled Zedekiah's shouted the downed man's name.

"Heavenly Father!" Em cried and straightened to give her legs their full reach.

With so little lead, she did not doubt she would be recaptured, nor her punishment would be more severe the longer she evaded the slavers, but she would not go willingly into that corner. She would fight until rendered unconscious.

Two horses now—one coming at her from the left, the other her right. Or was it three? Surely not. The slaver she had unmanned could not recover so quickly, and even had he, sooner he would have her if he pursued her on foot rather than first retrieve his horse.

Em did not need to look around to know the one—perhaps two—on her left was nearer than the one opposite. Eyes mapping a winding path, she jumped a log and veered between towering oaks.

Sidelong, she glimpsed the horse on her right, but it was not this side of the stream. For what had its rider crossed over? Of what benefit to take the long way around to apprehend her?

She had no time to ponder it further, the two on her left drawing near. She veered again, this time toward massive rocks at the center of which stood a narrow opening a horse could not pass through. The riders would have to go far one side or the other to resume their pursuit. It would give her very little lead, but it was more than she had now.

"To me, Em!"

She nearly stumbled as she drew her arms close to negotiate the passage between the rocks. Was it Dougray on the other side of the stream? Or had her mind cracked?

Hearing the curses of the two on this side, she propelled herself past the jagged edges that grabbed at her hair, tunic, and chausses. Then she was through and moving toward the lone rider.

"Be Dougray," she rasped and looked to the man spurring toward her. As his destrier jumped the stream, his golden hair whipped back off his shoulders.

It *was* Dougray. But what chance had he against the slavers who would soon appear on this side of the rocks? He had no sword to hand, and could not were he to do as suggested by the lean of his body and arm thrown out to pluck her from the ground. Was there enough time to get her astride and a sword to hand before the others reached them?

She glanced over her shoulder and saw the leader of the slavers come around the far side of the rocks. Only he, meaning the other would likely appear this side.

"Dear Lord!" she cried, certain that with her hands bound, Dougray would have to seat her before him rather than behind. Though he should have time to draw his sword, her presence would hinder his ability to land and fend off blows. And that could mean his death.

She faltered, slowed.

"To me!" he bellowed again as the second slaver came around this side of the rocks.

She breathed deep, ran harder, ran faster. And beseeched the Lord's mercy for this D'Argent who was a D'Argent regardless of who fathered him.

# CHAPTER SEVENTEEN

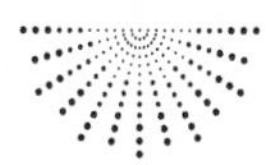

Not entirely broken and, God willing, no more than before her capture. Despite all Em had suffered before him and since, her unexpected bid for freedom made what barely seemed possible very possible. And as Dougray gripped the saddle with his thighs to lean down and snatch her up, he loved her all the more.

He startled at the thought surely planted by Michel Roche. He could not love her more when he had not loved her before and did not love her now. Whatever this feeling, it was too different from what he had felt for Adela.

Moments from entrusting the strength of his thighs to gather Em to him and keep them aloft, he told himself he would think on such things later. Were they worth thinking on…

He saw the blue and brown of her wide eyes as she thrust her bound wrists high to allow him to catch her beneath the arms, then his arm slammed around her, and he heard her gasp as if pained.

She was not heavy, but his lack of a second hand to keep his balance made his thighs burn as he dragged her up his destrier and leaned opposite to pull her onto his saddle.

Teeth ground, he twisted to the side and turned her forward. She started to slip, but before he could order her to throw a leg over, she did so and thrust her back against his chest.

"Hold to the pommel!" he commanded and looked to their pursuers.

The last to come around the rocks was nearer than the other, but though Dougray's hand longed for the sword to put down the one who had struck Em, even had he the use of two, fighting astride whilst sharing a saddle was dangerous. Thus, he retrieved the reins, urged his destrier around, and when it once more cleared the stream, moved it back the direction Em had come.

He heard a curse and saw the nearest slaver's attempt to follow had gone awry, the man's mount rearing in protest. Such a thin line between applying the right and wrong amount of spur and snap of reins...

Ahead was the slaver Em had overwhelmed behind the thicket. Limping, he moved toward his horse and hers grazing alongside the stream.

As those behind rounded the rocks, once more Dougray guided his destrier across the stream, this time through a shallow portion.

The man ahead drew his sword, swung around, and crossed his blade over his body to deliver a backward uppercut.

At the last moment, Dougray turned his destrier opposite and sharply inward, causing his horse's haunches to strike the slaver, the miscreant's blade to fly, and what sounded like the crack of bone when he landed.

Confirming the two mounted slavers gained ground, Dougray removed the D'Argent dagger from its sheath and halted his destrier alongside the toppled man's horse that would serve better than Em's aged palfrey. Of added benefit, a second sword was affixed to the saddle the same as Dougray's.

"Raise your hands, Em!"

She complied and strained her wrists opposite to allow him to slice the dagger up between them.

When the rope fell away, she leaned to the side, gripped the saddle of the other horse, and put a leg over.

Dougray thrust the D'Argent dagger at her. "I will find you. Now go!"

As her eyes widened ahead of protest, he slapped the horse's flank and turned toward the two thundering toward them.

"Go!" he shouted, and that was all he could do were he to have a chance of keeping these men from recapturing her.

Unsurprisingly, the leader set himself at Dougray while his fellow slaver rode after Em who bent low over her horse.

First her pursuer, Dougray determined and spurred after him. Blessedly, his destrier's strength and speed were superior to the other mount, and soon he was between predator and prey.

Teeth bared, the one who had struck Em yanked the reins to go wide around her savior.

Dougray followed, and the slaver veered toward the leader.

Two strokes, Dougray determined as he drew his sword. It was all he would have time to deliver before the leader joined forces with this one—and they would have to be good strokes. Unlike these Saxons who had only boiled leather vests to protect their innards, Dougray had the advantage of chain mail between undertunic and over tunic. However, they had the greater advantage of a single opponent lacking a left hand to guide his mount while the right kept keen steel from his neck.

Further tightening his thighs, he charged toward his target.

The man slowed, and steel met steel in passing, the force causing both men to snap opposite.

Though Dougray's bid to remain astride was more hard-won than his opponent's, he brought his destrier around and was upon the other man before he could get his mount fully turned to protect his back.

The second stroke to the shoulder cut through leather armor, but even if it sliced flesh, the man's loss of the saddle was his undoing.

Dougray caught no sound of broken bone that might incapacitate him as it had the first slaver near the stream whose struggle to rise had dropped him to sitting. Providing this one did not quickly regain his horse, the contest was now between one Norman and one Saxon.

And so it began, Dougray's muscular opponent with a face that looked as if flattened by a shovel proving though his ability to fight astride was crude, it was effective.

Amid grunts and flying saliva, their blades sought flesh. Amid bellows and curses, each brought his mount around before the other could strike from behind. On and on it went as it would not had Dougray a second hand to wield a second blade. And now that the unhorsed man was on his feet, greater the need to end this contest.

"Almighty!" Dougray shouted and set his destrier at the leader. Another impotent clash of swords, but when next they met, he found his opening. As his blade slid down his opponent's, he thrust and its point traced a path from jaw to neck. How deep he did not know, only that it was not mortal—yet.

The slaver wheeled around. Crimson running down his neck, he charged again. Had this savage not been at Hastings, he would have been of good use to the Saxons.

Dougray was ready for him—or would have been did he not catch movement where there should be none. Hoping it was another opponent rather than Em, he glanced in the direction she had fled.

"Heavenly Father!" he barked.

Having drawn the sword fastened to the saddle, she spurred not toward Dougray but the slaver who ran toward his mount, his own sword in hand.

Were she a fellow warrior, Dougray would be grateful he must only concern himself with the opponent before him, but now the woman whom he could not possibly love but cared for more than he should, could bleed out here.

Dougray returned his attention to the man swinging at him and deflected the keen edge seeking his neck, but this time when the slaver's blade came off his, it was the one to draw blood, its tip catching the edge of Dougray's chain mail tunic, slipping inside, and slicing the shoulder of his half arm.

He felt a sting and the warmth of let blood, neither of which he had time for were he to put down this man and get to the other before Em engaged him. He did not doubt she was capable, but her opponent had to be twice her weight, much of it muscle, and had the further advantage of greater height. If the slaver forgot her value, he might kill her.

"Lord, preserve her!" he rasped as he came around again and glimpsed her headlong flight toward the one who fit a foot in the palfrey's stirrup, then once more he prepared to challenge the leader.

Their blows tested the strength of muscle and jolted bones, but neither prevailed, and when next their swords clashed, he heard what sounded an echo and knew Em met at swords with the other man.

Desperation gripping him, he commanded himself as many times his uncle had done, *Think here, think now. Be only as aware of what is beyond as is necessary to ensure it does not steal upon you. And when what you do has not the desired effect, do the unexpected.*

Determining the unexpected was worth the risk of what he might lose since he possessed a spare, he drew back his sword in readiness to meet the next swing and was encouraged by the shoulder the slaver drew toward his ear as if to stem the blood earlier drawn from his neck. Hoping whatever lightheadedness he suffered slowed his reactions, Dougray swept his sword forward well before they met. And released.

As he jerked his destrier aside and reached to the second sword on his saddle, he saw the first did not fly true, but it need not. Rather than its point land center of the man's chest, the flat struck him across the face. The slaver's arms splayed, sword dropped, and his horse rode out from under him.

Certain were he to recover it would not be for some minutes, Dougray rode toward where Em and the last slaver danced their mounts around amid the crossing of steel.

The sight of her gave his pounding heart pause. She was more ferocious than imagined, and it was her blade whose edges were as crimson as they were silver.

Hearing her grunts and growls, he wondered if she was in the grip of bloodlust. If so, might she see him as an enemy before she saw him as an ally?

Dangerous this, but whether or not she wished his aid, he was hers.

EM HAD NOT BELIEVED fighting astride among her strengths, but neither was it a weakness, as evidenced by how swiftly she moved between offense and defense, the slaver's sword at the end of her hand feeling more a part of her than the fingers turned around the hilt.

To sooner aid Dougray, she must put this man down, then—

"Fall back, Em!"

Dougray was near, meaning the one whose thrust narrowly missed piercing her side was the only one left to fell. And she who had thought she wanted to ensure never again he served the merchant, longed to do as Dougray ordered—let him be the one who deprived the slaver of limb if not life. But she had come this far, and his blood was on her blade.

"Fall back!"

Chancing exposing the back of her neck, she bent forward and thrust her blade beneath her opponent's sword arm. She felt the tip penetrate leather armor at the same moment steel clashed overhead.

Dougray was here, keeping the blade from her. Then her mount turned to the side, forcing her to release the hilt.

Yanking the reins to bring the horse around, she saw the slaver fall forward over the palfrey's neck and his sword drop from one hand while the other gripped the blade piercing his armor. Not only did he bleed beneath the arm but the belly.

Em met Dougray's gaze beyond the bloodied blade he held. Anger there, quite possibly toward her, but she did not care. What mattered was he had made her escape possible, and he lived.

Fear of losing him to the slavers had driven her to leave the safety of the trees where she had watched him fight for her with the savagery of Vitalis. She had known he would not welcome her aid, but had he died trying to save her, life hereafter would be emptier than ever thought possible. But now that fear was behind her, fatigue was before her.

Gripping the saddle to steady herself, she realized she perspired so greatly her clothes were damp. Though she parted her lips to thank Dougray for coming for her, she blurted, "I could not leave you!"

Great draws of breath added to his height and breadth one moment, took from it the next, then his anger receded and he returned his sword to the scabbard on his saddle. "You should have, Em."

"Of what benefit?"

He frowned, and she tensed at the possibility he feared what was behind her words—perhaps the same as she feared.

He shifted his regard to the slaver they had defeated, then the others. The leader whom Dougray had overwhelmed before coming to her aid had also gone still, while the one who escorted her behind the thicket no longer sat upright. Though he was on his back, she guessed he but sought to escape further notice, heart pounding in anticipation of a death blow.

"What of him?" she asked, the abused slave wanting him dead so he could never again engage in the trade of humans, the Em of old flinching over ending the life of a defenseless man.

"I am tempted to put him through," Dougray said. "What say you?"

"I..." She pressed her lips. Never did Rebels of the Pale slay the defenseless, Lady Hawisa having decreed life should be taken only in defending one's own life or the lives of others, and Vitalis had embraced the same upon assuming leadership. "As he has been rendered harmless, leave him."

Dougray hesitated, said, "To ensure he does not soon alert others to what went here, we shall take the horses and release them distant." He drew from the slaver the sword Em had used, then thrust a booted foot against the dead man and sent him over the horse's side. "We must resume the journey with which Vitalis tasked me."

It was then she realized someone was missing. "Margaret?"

"She is well."

"Where—?"

"Later, Em." He urged his horse near and slid her sword in its scabbard, then looked close on her as she looked close on him. Of all his injuries, none appeared as serious as whatever caused blood to seep through the left shoulder of his chain mail.

"You are hurt badly?" she asked.

He rolled that shoulder. "Not a mortal wound. Are you well enough to ride?"

"I am." She wished she sounded more convincing. She had suffered no grave injury, but she was weary from a sleepless night, sleepless day, and controlling emotions that had made her long to scream and writhe. "What of you? Your shoulder needs binding."

"It can wait," he murmured as if his mind were elsewhere, and she followed his gaze to her white-knuckled, trembling hand on the pommel. "You are not well." He extended his hand. "Ride with me."

So great was her longing to sink against him and sleep away what remained of the day, she nearly refused. Instead, she pressed her weight into the stirrup and raised herself to swing a leg over. An instant later, she dropped back into her saddle.

"Em?"

She shook her head. "I am well enough to ride by myself."

"What is wrong?"

Was her face as bright as it felt hot? "Naught."

"Em—"

"I am well!" From beneath her lashes, once more she glimpsed his anger. Then the flare of his nostrils.

*Dear Lord, he knows!* "I vow it was not fear!" she exclaimed and felt her stomach toss as when she had begun training with men and had to draw so near there was contact between her body and theirs. It was bad enough her bladder had betrayed her this day, but all the worse she did not know when. While on foot pursued by the slavers? When Dougray swept her onto his destrier? When he moved her from his horse to this one? While she watched at a distance as he fought the men from whom he had taken her? During her battle with the one who now lay dead?

"The ride was so long, and I…"

"It matters not." Still he reached, inviting her to share his saddle though she would soil him.

"But—"

"It is the least of things that happen when one fights for their life, Em. Now come to me."

Heart aching, she said, "Let us ride further upstream. When we are a good distance, I will bathe."

He growled low, slid his arm around her waist, and pulled her to him.

"My shame will be greater, Dougray!"

"You have no reason to be ashamed." He set her atop his thighs. "Now hold to me."

So horrified was she, she did not know how it was possible all the stiff went out of her, but it was as if he were the flame to her candle. Melting against him, she wrapped her arms around his waist, and as her lids lowered, saw him take her mount's reins, feed them out, and loop them over the pommel.

Then she yielded to darkness, but of a different sort from any she had known. Was this what it was like to be in the night with one you did not fear? One who made the absence of light a place of comfort?

"I am with you, Em," she heard as if from afar.

# CHAPTER EIGHTEEN

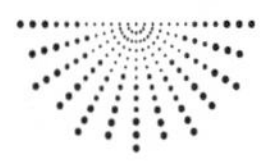

She bathed unclothed—something not done in years, and she had not feared doing so though a man was exceedingly near.

Bending her knees, Em sank her shoulders beneath water so cold she was nearly numb. She knew she should not linger, but the chip of soap Dougray had given her had slipped through her fingers shortly after she began scrubbing her skin. Too, the water lulled, especially the top layer yet warmed by the lowering sun.

"Come out, Em!"

She peered over her shoulder at the man who had assured her he would keep watch after he himself briefly ventured here. Between strands of wet hair, she saw he stood on the edge of the camp where they would pass the night, his back to her the same as each time she looked around.

"Answer me, Em, else I shall come in after you."

"I..." Her teeth chattered. "I am coming out."

As she moved from the pond's center up the incline, she rubbed her torso and limbs, as much to warm her skin as to clean it.

Cooling air against wet flesh made her gasp, but she forced

herself up the bank and dropped to her knees beside the blanket and tunic Dougray had given her.

Quaking, she caught up the blanket, dragged it around her shoulders, and sighed into its warmth.

"You are out?"

"I am." Gripping a handful of the blanket, she patted her skin to remove moisture that would make it difficult to don the tunic.

"Do you require aid?"

"Nay, I…" A shudder went through her, causing her to lose the handful of blanket and drop to her palms. Blessedly, the blanket remained draped over her, keeping the worst of the cold from her.

"I come to you, Em."

She was not afeared when he strode toward her, not even when he bent and rubbed the blanket over her. His touch was wondrously impersonal, and yet…

*I want more,* she silently admitted. The thought alarmed as much as it offered hope. *We can never be, but mayhap I am even less broken than believed. Mayhap what my training with men began to set aright is all the more mended by Dougray.*

"Did you hear me, Em?"

She had not. "Say it again."

"I shall raise the tunic. You have only to stand, slip beneath, and release the blanket."

She nodded, and he lifted the tunic between them, creating a barrier between his eyes and her.

Em pushed upright, as she held the blanket with one hand, lifted the other to raise the tunic's hem.

The garment was cut to accommodate broad shoulders and chain mail that might be worn between it and an undertunic. Thus, she had no difficulty fitting herself inside before releasing the blanket to pool around her feet.

As she slid her hands into the sleeves and pushed her head through the neck's opening, Dougray let the garment drop to her shoulders.

"I thank you," she said.

He swept up the blanket and wrapped it around her. "Now where are your garments?"

She caught her breath, flew her gaze to the heap near the water's edge, and started forward. "I forgot to wash them. It will not take long."

He pulled her back. "I will do it."

Once more flushing, she said, "'Tis for me to do." As she should have washed his that he had exchanged for clean ones, the former now drying before the fire.

"Sit," he said.

She wanted to argue, but she was tired and cold. Lowering to the bank, she whispered, "Forgive me."

"Enough," he rebuked and strode to the pool. From atop her clothes, he lifted the jeweled dagger he had given her earlier, returned it to his belt, and began washing her tunic and chausses.

"I think I must love him," she breathed and hated how much the possibility hurt and how much more she would ache when he slipped from her life.

*Lord, why did You not break my heart ere now so all such feeling would slowly leak out its cracks?* she sent heavenward. *Now when it breaks, I shall feel every drop of its spill.*

"It is done, Em."

She raised her chin and slowly focused on Dougray where he stood before her. Had she slept? She must have.

In the light of dusk, she noted a dark spot on the upper left of his fresh tunic. Though they had paused during their ride so he could affix a bandage over the injury, he continued to bleed.

Would it require stitches, or would a fresh bandage suffice? Regardless, she would aid him if he would allow her as he had not earlier. That being the side from which he had lost his lower arm, he might be self-conscious.

He drew her to her feet. As he guided her over uneven ground, she wondered what it would be like to walk at his side every day the rest of her life.

After settling her on a log near the fire, he stepped to its end and spread her wet garments alongside his. "My wound is not deep," he said as he turned back, "but unlike when you tended the injury you dealt me, methinks this one will heal sooner if it is stitched. Are you experienced at sewing flesh?"

Pleased he asked it of her, she said, "It was taught me in the rebel camp. Be assured, the stitches will be small and close without sacrificing speed. Of course, a good quantity of drink will lessen the pain."

"And render me vulnerable, which we cannot afford in this wood."

Remembering the last time she had been in a wood with him, she said, "I am sorry I ran from you, but I had to ensure Flora and Tristan were well."

"And so they are."

She frowned. "How know you?"

He lowered beside her and told of arriving in Gloucester the night after enlisting a pilgrimage of nuns to return Margaret to Stavestone, listening in on the drunken and boastful Hearst and learning where Em was held, and locating the merchant's shop and witnessing the failed attempt by her aunt's husband to free her.

That last nearly made her cry.

"Surely such a man is a good husband, father, and uncle," Dougray submitted.

She nodded and told him what had transpired at her aunt's home. "I must find a way to send word of my escape," she said. "My aunt will fear—"

"I sent word."

She blinked. "How? When?"

"By way of a lad this morn when the slavers rode you out the gates. I instructed him to tell the aunt of Eberhard Irwinson that what was done on the day past would be undone ere this day's end."

"Dougray," she breathed, "ever I shall be indebted to you."

He raised an eyebrow. "There is a way to pay down your debt —indeed, clear it completely."

She turned to fully face him, and though the blanket slipped from a shoulder, she let it be. "Tell me."

The lightness about his face fell. "Never again run from me. If you must run, run to me."

Should so simple a request hurt as much as this? After all, it would be short-lived.

"I will not run from you again."

"And if you must run?"

"I will run to you."

He nodded, then retrieved a saddlebag and passed it to her. "There all you need to tend me."

Em shrugged the blanket off and began pulling out items.

"It will be easier if I remove my tunic. Are you well with that, Em?"

She wondered why he asked. Because of what Campagnon had done that made her fear intimacy with a man? Or perhaps Dougray feared she would be repulsed by what remained of that arm.

"I am well with it," she said, though when she had tended the injury she herself dealt him she had torn open his tunic and not only because he was bound to the tree.

As she threaded the needle, she heard his tunic rustle and saw it drop atop the log, next the bandage. When he lowered beside her, yet garbed in chausses and boots, so disturbed was she by a glimpse of abdominal muscles, she forgot to breathe.

*I have no cause to fear him,* she reminded herself, then wet a cloth with alcohol, set aside the flask, and turned to Dougray. And stared.

Every muscle of his abdomen, chest, shoulders, and neck was

defined, as well as both arms though one lacked the reach of the other.

Were all battle-tested men as beautiful? She could not know, having never looked near on one, not even the rebels who cast off tunics in the heat of training—albeit never had they done so when she was their opponent.

Though once she had seen Vitalis's bared torso, it had been at a good distance, and she had averted her eyes. Had he looked like this? Had the one whom she could never bear to gaze upon no matter how close they were, looked like Dougray?

Thrusting Campagnon from her thoughts, more intently she surveyed the man before her. Beautiful, indeed, so much the perfection of him hardly paled alongside old scars, bloodied flesh soon to form new scars, and that which he had lost at Hastings. Certes, that last shocked, but not because it repulsed. Because its absence roused anger against the warrior who had taken it—her countryman who but sought to keep the invaders from claiming England.

Finding Dougray's gaze upon her, she said, "Forgive me for staring. Since York, I have become acquainted with your strength, but I would not have guessed it so beautiful."

"Beautiful?" he said with disbelief.

She had thought the word fitting, but when he spoke it, she knew it did not flatter. However, there seemed no better word to describe what he had bared. "I do not mock you, Dougray. I speak as I see."

"Then your eyes lie, Emma Irwindotter."

Ever aware of the ills and sins attributed to those eyes, she said, "They do not lie. Albeit mismatched, they see well, and what they see is you are beautiful." Once more, she regretted the words, though only for how petulant they came off her tongue. Were she standing, the stamp of a foot would fit one who had soiled herself.

She looked down. "I know I must seem a girl to you, childish and tiresome."

"You do not." He slid his fingers along her jaw and tilted up her face.

There his mouth, a curve to his lips. There his nose, a flare to his nostrils. There his eyes, pupils wide as they delved hers. "You are all woman, lovelier and truer than most I have known."

Once more breath was denied her. Such words she had imagined being gifted to her when she began awakening to womanhood. But then came Campagnon, shredding all hope she would be wanted for anything other than what he had stolen.

"Truly?" she whispered.

His calloused thumb moved up her cheek. "Truly."

"More than—" She closed her mouth against speaking of the woman he had lost whom Baron Roche had named unworthy.

But Dougray knew and released her. "Ere I am made more loose of tongue by the loss of blood, you had best stitch me closed."

Meaning he spoke words he should not have? Or words he did not mean?

*Leave it be,* she told herself. *Whatever the truth, only for a short time must you keep your word to run to him rather than from him.*

She lowered to her knees alongside him. Struggling to separate her mind from her hands as she cleansed his wound and seamed its edges, she kept her chin down so he would not see how flushed she was. Two dozen stitches were required, and throughout each poke, push, pull, and tug, he but tensed and grunted.

"There will be a scar, but not unsightly," she said when she finished bandaging the wound, then sat back on her heels and wiped crimson-stained fingers on a cloth as he donned his tunic.

"I thank you, Em."

She peered up at him. "For mending that for which I am responsible? 'Tis the least I can do."

His eyes moved down her face and over her neck. As once more she warmed, he shifted his regard to her shoulder. "Then you could do more?"

For a moment, she thought he spoke of carnal things, but he was not such a man. Then of what did he speak?

As if in answer, night air caressed that which his eyes had settled on—the shoulder bared by her skewed tunic. She reached to cover it, but he caught her hand.

"Nay, Dougray!"

He leaned forward, and she saw the fire at her back dance across the gold of his eyes. "Let me see, Em."

This was the *more* he asked of her, but what if it was not enough to look upon what she had done with what had been done her, something she found more abhorrent than ever she would find the loss of his arm?

"Pray, show me."

"Already you have seen it," she said, but when he eased the material from her fingers, she did not resist.

He slid the tunic down her arm, then came off the log and bent so near his hair brushed her cheek.

She closed her eyes and tighter when his fingers traced the rounded edge and ventured into the depression.

"How did it happen?"

She looked sidelong at him. Seeing his concern, she longed to give him what he asked of her, but memories stirred and made her throat so tight there seemed only enough space to draw air needed to survive.

"Campagnon?" he growled.

"Nay!" But that was not entirely true. "And aye."

Dougray ground his teeth. How could it be that knave and yet not? Sliding his hand from her shoulder to her chin, he turned her face to his and noted the shadows beneath her eyes were nearly as dark as the night he persuaded her to burn her bill of sale. "I must know."

"Why?"

He nearly said it would give him more cause to end the miscreant's life, but he sensed it would make a greater mess of the emotions teeming beneath his fingers.

"I wish to know you better," he said, and it was no lie, just not as great a truth as the other.

Still, she hesitated.

"You need not fight your demons alone, Em. I am here, and I know what it is to battle the dark side of one's self with only the Lord to hear one's groaning as He makes us wait on proof He has not abandoned us."

She blinked, causing the moisture rimming her eyes to spill.

"Did or did not Campagnon do this to you?"

Her nod was slight. "And more. Much more."

Worse than this, it sounded. But then, injuries seen were often less painful than those unseen which could tear at the soul and one's faith—the kind that at Stavestone caused her to seek a corner far from the bed she feared the same as the one at Balduc.

"The day he bought me at auction," she said, "he had me inked. When I fought it, he ordered Merle and Waleran to strap me down and..."

Giving her time to gather herself, Dougray mulled the name of the second man he knew only by sight and reputation and had thought a recent edition to Campagnon's mercenaries.

"Waleran, you say?" he prompted.

She nodded. "Though he is slow of wit, he is swift of foot and exceedingly cruel."

"The same as Merle."

"Worse."

"He was not at Castle Balduc whilst Campagnon held it for Cyr," Dougray said. "I would have noticed him."

"He was there before your brother and you arrived. When Campagnon became Baron of Balduc, Waleran served him two months ere being sent away."

"For what?"

"He overheard another mercenary boast he would make a better lord than Campagnon and for it almost thrashed the man to death. Campagnon was well with it until others in his service threatened to leave. Though Waleran was forced to depart, months later Campagnon took him back with the promise he would behave. But after a time, he roused again and once more was sent away. The third time was shortly ere your brother and you arrived to take Balduc from Campagnon."

"Were he such a problem, why was he allowed to return time and again?"

"I overheard Campagnon tell Merle that when he was a boy he fell through pond ice and would have drowned had not Waleran gone in after him. For it, Waleran himself drowned. Though he was revived, his head was never right again, and ever since he has been protective of Campagnon as if that knave were more a savior than he." She drew a deep breath. "He is very dangerous. If he can get his hands on me—"

"He will not."

She searched Dougray's face as if for further assurance.

"Neither will Campagnon," he said. "Now if you can, tell me the rest of how Campagnon marked you."

She moistened her lips. "The inking hurt so much I cried, vomited, and lost consciousness, but he would not stop. He wanted me marked so ever it was known I belonged to him. And ever I wanted it gone from me."

At the realization of what it meant that she was no longer inked, pressure built in Dougray's chest, so great it felt as if a rib might crack.

She raised a hand and explored the depression the same as he had done. Then with one finger, she drew a half circle. "The letter C was here. And here"—she slid her finger from the top of that letter to the bottom, then drew a horizontal line—"the cross." There was wonder in her voice, not of the joyous sort but of disgust tempered by disbelief. "It made no sense that in one breath he proclaimed me his property and in the next boasted of the Lord's approval. And even less sense after what..."

She lowered her hand, looked to Dougray. "Do I not know God, or is it Campagnon who knows Him not?"

"You know Him, Em. He hated the cross pressed into your skin more than you."

*And yet, why do You not strike down such a man?* Dougray silently demanded. *Campagnon did this to her in Your name the same as William invaded England in Your name. Could You not at least relieve the suffering of this one Saxon?*

He knew it was wrong to take the Lord to task—needed no priest to tell him that—but in this moment he felt more for Em's loss than his own. Of course, were this the day he awakened to find a stump where there should be muscled forearm and a long-fingered hand for wielding all manner of weaponry, he would surely believe his loss greater.

After a struggle to tell the rest, she said, "What you see I did after I escaped him. It would not be scratched off, so I cut it off. But still he owned me, and though I burned the bill of sale, still he owns me. No matter how I protect my back, ever I will be running. Be it days or years from now, he will corner me, and then he will have me again, and I..." Her voice broke.

"We must get you out of England, Em."

Her eyes flew wide. "My family is here."

"They are well and safe. You are not. Providing naught alters our course and we ride dawn to dusk, in two days' time I shall deliver you to Wulfen Castle. With my brother's aid, we will get you across the sea."

"To Normandy?" she gasped.

"I know not where in France, but there will be a place for you where Campagnon cannot find you. You will be safe, I vow."

She searched his face. "At Stavestone, you told you aided me to right wrongs."

"I did."

"For that only or...was it something more?"

Did she ask because she felt for him a measure of what he did not want to feel for her? That it did not matter he was not whole? That unlike Adela, she truly was not repulsed by the loss of his lower arm? That her pronouncement he was beautiful was as genuine as it sounded? If so, perhaps Campagnon had not ruined her for other men.

*Non, you were there for her awakening at Stavestone,* he reminded himself. *You saw the terrified woman that knave made of her. Outside of intimacy, she may not be untouchable, but within the bounds of intimacy...*

Though Michel Roche had suggested Dougray wed Em, it would be folly to bind himself to a woman who would, at best, tolerate intimacy.

"Was it something more?" she asked again.

Though he ought to end talk that could go nowhere good, he said, "What do you want it to be?"

"I wish a man to feel something for me besides desire—to be more than a bedmate."

As the Danish earl's son had sought to make her.

Dougray hurt for Em whose virtue should have been gifted a man whom she loved and who loved her in return. Instead, Campagnon had made her a plaything, his use and abuse of her body rendering her undesirable beyond satisfying—

*Not so,* he silently corrected. *For what she was to that knave, I did not think I could want her beyond desire, but I do.*

"Dougray?"

"I am attracted to you, Em, and I assure you it is not all desire."

Her mouth curved. "That gives me hope," she said and slid her arms around his neck and set her head on his shoulder.

Far too aware of her woman's body, he said gruffly, "We should eat and bed down."

She nodded but did not move away.

Dougray considered, considered some more, then put his arm around her waist, set his back to the log, and drew her against his side.

She tilted her face up.

He looked down, and when her lips parted, shifted his gaze to hers. Wariness there, meaning this was no invitation. Or had it been, it was no longer.

But her eyes softened and she said, "I have been kissed only once."

That surprised—first, that it sounded the invitation it did not look; second, that only once had Campagnon tried her lips. But then, considering what the knave had made of her, it fit. Was not a kiss the beginning of greater intimacy beyond the touch of hands, not only the man but the woman giving the other hope for more? And with it, hope for a future together?

"He was a boy, two years older than me," she said, correcting his assumption she spoke of the mercenary. However, it was no assumption. He had seen the kiss Campagnon forced on her that first day at Balduc to impress on his uninvited guests she belonged to him.

His face surely reflecting confusion, she gasped and said, "That was no kiss. That was his mouth on mine—only that. And it hurt and tasted of blood."

Because Campagnon had ground her lips against her teeth. Longing to feel the man's throat between his fingers, he said tautly, "Tell me of your first and only kiss."

Wariness returned to the eyes searching his face, but just when he thought she would speak no more, she said, "It happened before my mother passed after falling ill. When she and my father heard of the boy's boasting, they were disappointed in me and warned no good man would want me should a kiss lead to the loss of innocence—unaware the virtue not lost to that one kiss would one day cause Campagnon to make a possession of me." She bit her lip. "Though I reasoned my fate would have been worse had my life been that of a joy woman, never with him did it seem possible."

"Leave him in the past, Em, and trust me to ensure he stays there."

"But you would have me abandon my country."

"Because it is your best chance of ridding yourself of him."

Momentarily, she closed her eyes, then she set a hand on his jaw and looked to his mouth.

Though Dougray told himself to put distance between them, he listened to his body and said, "Do you wish me to kiss you, Em?"

She tensed, then leaned in. "I do. A man's kiss, not a boy's."

*Fool,* he named himself, and yet he slid a hand around the back of her neck and bent his head. When she returned her eyes to his, allowing him to watch for distress, gently he set his mouth on hers.

Catching a glimmer of uncertainty, he made no attempt to make more of what was not enough of a kiss to have hope for anything beyond. And dared not with his body stirring as if great that hope.

Em drew back. "This is pleasant, even despite the rough of your beard, but is it a man's kiss?"

"I do not wish to frighten you, Em. As told, this attraction is not all desire, but still I am much moved by temptation."

She frowned. "You fear losing control?"

"Nay, I fear the torment of *keeping* control."

Em stared at the man she no longer merely thought she loved, he who was breaking her heart through no fault of his own. How wanton she must seem to so boldly speak of a man's kiss and seek his, especially considering what she had allowed him to believe that night in the marshes of York when she claimed a man's use of her body was no longer of consequence. Were he not honorable, he could hardly be blamed were he to try to take what another had taken—and leave her with a child to forever remember him by as, blessedly, Campagnon had not.

Aching over the unbidden question of what color eyes a babe made of her and Dougray would have, she pulled free and stood.

Glimpsing relief on his face, she was struck by the possibility something other than honor caused him to resist. Were he truly attracted to her beyond desire, perhaps he could not reconcile being intimate with one whose body was first and many times over known to a man he detested.

Aye, more likely that. As thought, no good man would ever want her. She had told Margaret she would be well with that, and she believed it was true—were it any man other than this one.

As she turned away, she said, "You are a good man, Dougray D'Argent." *Too good for one as soiled as I,* she silently added, then retrieved her blanket and made her bed opposite.

She was glad he did not press food on her, and more glad she was so tired she did not suffer sleeplessness. And a restful sleep it was with him watching over her through the night.

# CHAPTER NINETEEN

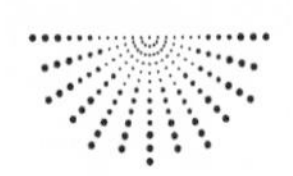

Wulfen Castle
Wulfenshire, England

Two days they had ridden hard dawn to dusk, but that hardly excused her for falling to her knees halfway across the hall when she saw her brother part from Lady Hawisa and run forward.

Quickly, Dougray returned her to her feet and set his arm around her waist though it was inappropriate for a nobleman to show such regard for one not even a commoner.

"Are you ill?" he said low.

"Nay, just overjoyed to see him. And look how he has grown these months!"

"Squire Eberhard, forget not your training!"

As her brother slowed, Em swept her gaze to the one whose silvered dark hair was all the confirmation needed he who stood alongside Lady Hawisa was her husband—Guarin D'Argent, whom the king had forced to renounce his surname.

Now titled Baron Wulfrith, it was his enemy hands that had intercepted Eberhard when her brother infiltrated the Norman camp at Darfield to slay Campagnon. With Dougray's aid, he had kept the youth out of other enemy hands. Too, he had ensured the Saxon warrior who betrayed Lady Hawisa never would again, albeit in doing so, he kept that man's blade from knocking Le Bâtard out of the saddle and into the grave. That last was regrettable. What was not was that both Eberhard and Lady Hawisa were here and safe.

As Em's grinning brother neared, and she saw he had surpassed her height, Dougray released her.

Though Wulfrith training applied to her as well since much of what she had learned defending herself and others had been gifted by Lady Hawisa, Em ran into Eberhard's arms.

"You are well," he exclaimed. "I have prayed, so much my knees ache."

She nodded her head alongside his and breathed in the scent of one who labored hard and long to transform the soft of him into muscle. Now he was far more man than boy.

"As I have prayed for you, Ebbe." She cupped his face in her palms and examined every line of it. "The Lord heard me. You are well, as are our brother and sister."

His eyes widened.

"Aye, with Sir Dougray's aid, I bring tidings from Gloucester our aunt has wed a Norman soldier who has made her a good husband and father to our cousins and brother and sister."

"God be praised!" He released her, stepped back, and looked nearer on her. Eyes narrowing on the side of her head where the physician had cut away a portion of hair, he said, "You are well, are you not?"

"All heals."

"How—?"

"We shall speak of it later." She looked to the Lady and Lord of Wulfen Castle, next the housecarle who stood to the right. When Lady Hawisa had yielded to William, leaving the Rebels of the Pale to Vitalis, Ordric had returned to Wulfenshire with her and her new husband. As a warrior, he was not as ferocious nor accomplished as Vitalis, but he was formidable and surely of benefit in training young men to defend their country.

Em frowned. She had been so intent on Eberhard, only now she noted the absence of his fellow warriors in training who at this hour should be bedding down. Too, there were few servants about. Lady Hawisa and her husband must have ordered them elsewhere upon learning who came to their walls, their alliance with William a precarious business. And more precarious it would seem when Dougray revealed the lie sent William by way of Sir Guy that the king's scout pursued the Aetheling.

"Sir Dougray," Eberhard said, "I thank you for aiding my sister."

Em followed his gaze around.

Dougray, having pushed his mantle back off his shoulders to reveal the emptiness of his lower left sleeve, inclined his head. "It was my privilege, Squire. Now as the ride was long and hard, I think it best your sister find her rest."

Lady Hawisa stepped forward. "I shall tend her."

Em looked to the woman to whom she owed much apology and gratitude then to her brother. Sensing his objection to being so soon parted from her, she leaned in and kissed his cheek. "I am very tired. We will speak on the morrow."

"As soon as you are rested enough to receive me," he said.

*Receive*—so formal, as if she were a lady. Was that part of his training?

When he relinquished her to Hawisa, the lady turned her toward the stairs. "A chamber is being prepared for you, Em."

Surely begun when the man-at-arms on the wall carried word to his lord Dougray had arrived and not alone. Em would have been content with a pallet in the hall, but she thrilled at the prospect of a private chamber and bed as afforded her at Stavestone. Once assured she was not at Balduc, she had slept fairly well there, so comfortable and quiet it had been—and safe.

Of course, she had also slept well these past nights in the wood. Though far from comfortable and many were the night sounds, still she had felt safe with Dougray though never again had they been as close as the night she all but begged a kiss.

*Pitiful,* she silently chastised as done a hundred times since being denied a man's kiss.

Struck by a thought, she turned back and saw her brother had stepped before Dougray. But the latter's eyes were on her. "You are not leaving, are you?"

"Not this eve."

Little relief in that since it did not mean Dougray would be here when she awakened in the morn, but feeling the weight of others' curiosity, she did not ask for assurance this would not be their final parting.

"I will not allow him to leave without bidding you farewell," Lady Hawisa said low as she urged her toward the stairs.

The chamber into which she led Em was small, but it was clean, the bed inviting, and the brazier from which a lad coaxed warmth would soon see her shed of her mantle.

"You are very kind to one who does not deserve it," Em said. "I—"

The lady held up a hand and crossed to the lad. "I will stir the coals. Go to the kitchen and collect the platter being prepared for our guest."

"Aye, milady."

When he departed, she said, "Truly, you are welcome here, though we must ensure we do not give the one who searches for you cause to venture here." Stirring the coals with the iron, she nodded at the bed. "While we await your drink and viands, make yourself comfortable and tell me of the Rebels of the Pale who I understand were present at York's fall."

Em unfastened her mantle. "We were there, and great the victory, but..."

Lady Hawisa smiled sorrowfully. "In the end, futile, the Danes unwilling to meet William in open battle."

Em set her mantle atop a chest. "Vitalis believes they aid us only to secure England for King Sweyn."

"I fear it as well." The lady crossed to the bed, turned down the coverlet, and gestured at it.

"I wear the dirt and dust of many days' travel," Em protested.

"Sustenance and rest this night," Hawisa said firmly, "a bath on the morrow."

Em hesitated, then as she bent to remove her boots, the lady went to her knees and began unlacing one.

"My lady, 'tis not for you—"

"It is." She pulled off the first boot. "Tell me of Stafford."

Em felt the sting of tears. "We were there as well. And defeated."

Moisture in her own eyes, Hawisa said, "Many the dead, we were told."

"Aye, among them Rebels of the Pale."

"Vitalis?"

"He lives, himself carried me from the battlefield when I took a blow to the head. Had he not, Campagnon might have had me again."

"Then that miscreant was there as well."

Em nodded. "I saw him across the distance, and he saw me."

The lady drew off the second boot, stood, and as Em settled back against the pillows, pulled the coverlet over her.

Shortly, the lad returned and placed the platter on the bedside table. Upon his departure, Hawisa settled in a chair and began kneading the shoulder that had taken an arrow when the man now her husband sought to escape his Saxon captors. "If you are willing," she said, "I would hear how you came to be Sir Dougray's charge."

Much to that tale and all that came afterward, much that did not reflect well on Em. However, excepting Dougray's reluctant kiss, it must be told, and that the Rebels of the Pale were mostly disbanding and many would return home. She did not doubt the lady would be glad to resettle her people, but still great the ache of further proof the Saxons' cause was lost.

After drinking the cup of milk and nibbling at viands, Em gave the lady what she asked. Though throughout the telling, she talked wide around her interactions with Dougray, when questions were put to her that brought to mind the sight, scent, and touch of the man she should not love, she flushed, words stuck in her throat, and it was a struggle to hold the woman's gaze.

Worse, her attempts to hide her feelings were futile as told by the sorrow and pity glimpsed in Hawisa's eyes.

## CHAPTER TWENTY

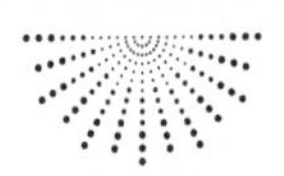

Assurances were given Theriot and Maël fared well, then Dougray began the tale of Em to be told nearly in full. *Nearly,* there being no reason to reveal the name of Sir Guy's uncle—one all D'Argents knew—nor forbidden feelings that denied Em the kiss she had sought.

In the midst of the tale, Guarin's wife entered the solar. Though Dougray did not want to like the woman after all his brother had suffered during his captivity, once more he was drawn to her strength and dedication to her people. As he continued to recount events between the Saxons' victory at York and the Normans' victory at Stafford, he noted she appeared unsurprised and guessed Em had revealed much of what transpired.

There was something else about her worthy of note, he mused when he finished the tale that had wound its way to Wulfen's walls. Despite a solemn expression where she sat beside Guarin before the hearth, her left hand clasped between his two, there was a lovely flush to her face. And from time to time, her other hand sought her lower abdomen.

In her belly the first of the line of Norman-Saxon Wulfriths?

Dougray would wager it. Since it was unlikely King William would lose his crown, making their peoples one through marriage and children was among the greatest means of healing England. By next spring, Cyr and Aelfled's child, the first of the line of Norman-Saxon D'Argents, would have a cousin.

Dougray looked to his brother and was not surprised by his smile.

"It is so," Guarin said, "my lady wife is with child."

Dougray saw she had stiffened, and in her eyes the challenge of one who anticipates disapproval. As he had given her and Aelfled cause to expect such, so bitter had he been when he made their acquaintance, he could not be offended.

He set his goblet aside, stood, and stepped before husband and wife. "I did not believe good could come of your union. I was wrong." He saw disbelief, then suspicion replace the challenge in her eyes. "I hope in time you will forgive me, my lady." He looked to his brother. "I am happy for you both, as I am for Cyr and Aelfled."

Guarin released his wife's hand, rose, and once more embraced Dougray. "We are gladdened, as would be Cyr and Aelfled were they yet here."

Dougray drew back. Though he knew the second eldest had become Godfroi's heir when the king wed Guarin to Lady Hawisa, he had not expected they would depart for Normandy so soon. "When did they leave England?"

"They have not. I speak of their visit to Wulfen. Three days past, they returned to Stern to await news of you, Theriot, and Maël. Though now we have it, and soon they shall, methinks with winter approaching, they will not chance crossing the channel with an infant."

For the best. When William and his army had set out to conquer England in September three years past, the crossing had been difficult. More treacherous it could prove this time of year.

"As I must make for Yorkshire on the morrow to resume my

duties ere the king learns of my lie," Dougray said, "I shall entrust you to send word to our brother and his wife that all D'Argents are accounted for."

Lady Hawisa moved to her husband's side. "Though you aided Vitalis—and Em—still you shall hunt those of the resistance?"

Months past, Dougray had explained to Guarin his reason for serving as William's scout. His brother had not been pleased but conceded something must be done to end the resistance's bid to take back their country which saw more and more innocents pay the greatest price. Though he must have explained it to his wife, if ever she accepted what her brother-in-law did achieved greater good than harm, no longer.

"When I returned to England, it was with a vengeful heart," he said, "but after witnessing the suffering of your people, now I do what I can for the many lacking the protection of lords and ladies like my brother and you. It does see rebels scattered and punished, but far better those who act against the king than innocents who seek to resume their lives only to find themselves caught between the blades of past and present."

Her gaze wavered.

"I am sorry it burdens, my lady, but you have met William, you have seen who and what he is. What you have not seen is what he can become when all patience is poured out. Not all rumors of his wrath are founded, but enough they breed lies worthy of being truth. If it is not too late, mayhap further disbandment and punishment of rebels will turn William from the direction he heads that could harm a hundred-fold more innocents."

Uncertain if he should be encouraged by the fear in her eyes, Dougray was grateful when Guarin put an arm around her.

She turned into him. "Tell me he is wrong, Husband."

"I wish it, Hawisa, but as you saw, William upon Darfield was nearly beyond mercy and contained his wrath only because Edwin Harwolfson yielded. The fall of York having prompted more uprisings, William's answer was the slaughter at Stafford, and now he returns to Yorkshire to finish what the Aetheling and Danes began. And likely more."

"You think it too late, that he cannot be turned back?"

He sighed. "If there is any possibility, I agree with Dougray the greatest chance is giving him the rebels he seeks."

She nodded jerkily.

"I will leave you to your rest," Dougray said and turned toward the curtain between solar and hall.

"Dougray," the Lady of Wulfen called.

"My lady?"

"What of Em?"

"As told Guarin, I believe she must go where slavery is unlawful. Since she is proficient in our language, France seems the best place."

"Were she willing to leave England, but she is not, and if we force her, methinks she will return."

As feared. "Providing you can keep her inside Wulfen's walls, away from any who would carry tale of her to Campagnon, she need not cross the narrow sea until Cyr determines it is safe to take his family to Normandy. That should be enough time to persuade her, and greater the likelihood if Eberhard supports the decision."

"And if still she will not go?"

He glanced at his brother and saw Guarin also wished an answer, but Dougray had none—and a long ride on the morrow. "Let us speak more on this when I return from Yorkshire. Good eve."

"Are you as fond of her as it seems?" The lady's question was so sharp it sounded an accusation.

Had Em revealed his attraction for her and the kiss that was hardly a kiss? Or did Hawisa make much of the unseen and unheard? "I but try to right the wrong done her by my countryman, my lady."

She stepped out of her husband's embrace and strode forward.

Halting, she scrutinized him, and more bared he felt when she lingered over his lower left sleeve. Since the night Em showed no revulsion for his loss, he had determined he would no longer seek to conceal it beneath a mantle and, when time permitted, see those tunic sleeves altered to the elbow.

Lady Hawisa returned her gaze to his. "Em must have a reason to turn her back on England, and I am thinking you could be it. When your duty to your king is done, whether or not your efforts to stop the suffering of innocents are in vain, take her to France, but do not leave her. Marry her."

He tensed at hearing what Michel Roche first suggested. And appreciated the meddling no more now than then.

She nodded. "*That* is how best to make right what Campagnon did to her."

"Marry her," he said between his teeth. "Is that the solution to all troublesome Saxon women? If so, England has quite the problem."

Her eyes flashed, but he did not care if he offended one who presumed to know the situation—who had not seen Em that night. "What problem is that, Sir Dougray?"

"That there is not an endless supply of D'Argents."

Guarin strode to his wife, set a hand on her arm, and slammed his gaze to his brother's. "Enough!"

As Dougray stared at one who had suffered all manner of ill, including torture, in seeking to protect kin who refused to be dissuaded from aiding William in claiming England, his indignation began to drain. And further when he saw the wolf in his brother's eyes that had ever been there, though not as fierce since he had given his heart to *this* most troublesome Saxon and she had given hers to him. Proof not all things impossible were impossible.

"Forgive me." He looked to Hawisa. "That was exceedingly ill-mannered. What I should have said is you cannot know of what you speak." He breathed deep. "I do have a care for Em, but even if she wished to wed one who is Norman, landless, and less than whole, what that miscreant did to her..."

He saw again that night at Stavestone, next the scar on her shoulder. He remembered their kiss, the longing to make more of it, and his fear of the torment required to keep control of desire for one who might wish greater intimacy but was likely ruined for it. Marriage was far more than lovemaking, but to spend a lifetime with Em knowing the bed they made was not theirs alone —that ever Campagnon was there?

"Dougray?" His sister-in-law set a hand on his arm.

Seeing no trace of the anger he had sown, he said, "Though Em is far stronger than when first we met, I fear she is yet broken in places from what Campagnon did—and may ever be."

She smiled softly. "Are we not all broken in places? It is true not all the wrongs done us can be made entirely right, but perhaps they ought not lest we become blind to the suffering of others who have yet to go where we have been."

"You are right, but that does not mean a husband is the answer to her. When she was injured at Stafford and returned to consciousness at Stavestone, she believed she was at Balduc. Her sobbing awakened me, and I found her in a corner of her chamber. She was untouchable. Even when she recognized me and was assured Campagnon was not near, I could not persuade her to return to bed. Thus, I carried her to the kitchen where she slept—"

"You said she was untouchable," Hawisa interrupted. "If in so vulnerable a state she went into your arms, she is not untouchable. She required patience, and that you surely gave her —the same as Vitalis and I when she joined the rebels."

It was true, he acknowledged, but Em had been mostly helpless then and gaining her trust to carry her from one room to another was far different from gaining her trust so she might be a wife.

"Training her into a warrior those first months was almost futile," Hawisa continued. "She made good progress with other women but could not stand to be near enough men to trade blows—was so fearful she forgot how to wield weapons, visibly shook, and vomited. Hence, of little use in engaging the enemy. But she was determined and eventually able to train with Vitalis and other men. You have seen her fight, have you not?"

"I have."

"And well, aye?"

He inclined his head.

"Time and patience, Dougray. If Em wants something, I believe she will overcome what stands between her and her longing."

Was it possible? He recalled Michel Roche's words in response to his own that he did not believe Em's mind was fully right where men were concerned—*You cannot know for certain until she herself determines if you are but one of many men or a man alone whose face is the only one she sees when he touches her.*

Despite momentary tension and uncertainty, it had seemed Dougray's face was the only one she saw when he kissed her, but that touch of lips was just the beginning of intimacy.

"Methinks you assume Em wants me, my lady."

She raised her eyebrows. "Some assumption, mostly observation. As it is obvious she has a care for you, I believe she would wed you."

A care for him… Was that incentive enough to overlook he was a Norman, landless, and one-armed?

"You tell you are not whole," Hawisa said, "but again, we are all broken in places. As I can attest the same as my husband, two broken people can make a whole, possibly stronger than the two wholes ere they were broken."

Dougray looked between the two who loved as neither Em nor he loved. Or did he? Non, he had a care for her, but this was not what he had felt for Adela, and that had been love.

Or had it? It was not the first time he asked it of himself, but previously he had indulged only in response to Adela's betrayal—

not wanting to love one who ought to be unlovable for what she had done.

*Just as you ought not love Em who ought to be unlovable after what Campagnon did to her?* submitted a voice within. *Certainly it is safer never to love than later learn it was wasted on one who could not return love.*

So unnerved was Dougray by his ponderings, he was grateful when Guarin stepped forward, but not when he said, "I believe what my wife proposes has merit. We and our charges are unfortunate to have lost our priest last month, but if you linger a day, we will send to Stern for Father Fulbert who can wed you ere you depart for Yorkshire."

"Nay!" Once more, sharp words from his wife. It surprised considering she had suggested marriage.

"Hawisa?" Guarin said.

She looked between him and Dougray. "Great the risk does your brother openly bind himself to a slave. Should Campagnon prove Em belongs to him despite the absence of a bill of sale, it is possible your brother will answer to him as well."

"What say you?" Dougray demanded.

"That it is folly to bind yourself to her with holy vows. And stronger that bond will be when the marriage is consummated. Even in William's England, there are men who will uphold a slave owner's right to compensation for so great a trespass, and the cost could prove your own freedom—that ever you shall be beneath Campagnon's heel."

"Not if he is dead," Dougray growled.

"You speak of the murder of one's master, Dougray, a greater obstacle with more terrible consequences."

In that moment he felt the weight of slavery as if already he had wed Em despite Hawisa's warning.

"I wish her free of that devil," she said, "but there is no advantage to wedding her in England. If you will be the reason she moves forward, it must be done where his only recourse is to try to take her from you, be it in France or another country that forbids slavery."

Dougray tensed further at the realization he moved in the direction Hawisa sought to move him. And yet it did not alarm as much as it should.

"Dougray?"

She sought an answer, but he needed time to think, and his resumption of the hunt for rebels would provide it. "Just keep her safe until I return."

As he started to turn aside, she said, "I promised her I would not allow you to depart without bidding her farewell."

He nearly told her such promises were not for her to make, but he would not further offend one who had defied his expectation she would prove unworthy of Guarin. He nodded at her and his brother, then strode into the hall in search of a pallet among the warriors in training whom Eberhard had returned to the hall.

There were thirty boys and youths, their numbers equally divided between Normans and Saxons, a stipulation to which William had yielded to gain the advantage of Wulfrith training for those coming up after the warriors who had aided him in conquering England.

What would it take for the king to end slavery here? Dougray pondered a while later as he stared across the dim hall that was quiet but for softly snoring occupants and the tread of two patrolling youths.

Would the end of rebellion whose suppression required an army twice as large as would otherwise be required cause William to yield? Would that be enough? And were it, how long before slavery was outlawed?

He sighed. Not soon enough. As long as Campagnon and his mercenaries benefitted William, Em could not remain in England. But would she willingly leave if she did not do so alone? Would she wed a landless Norman not whole of body? Would time and patience mend what was broken? Would what could not be love become love?

That last summoned a memory of his uncle striking him upside the head for forgetting he was a warrior ahead of what he was then—son, nephew, brother, cousin, friend—and what he might become—husband, father, uncle, grandfather.

He grunted, turned onto his side, and wished the night away the sooner to distance himself from all that threatened the warrior who should not concern himself with love.

But his last thought ere sleep was of Em. And his first upon awakening.

# CHAPTER TWENTY-ONE

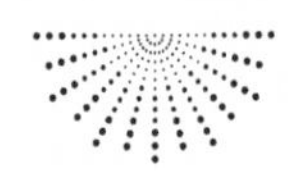

So this was the Wulfrith-D'Argent training Le Bâtard had sought and gained. Blessedly, what was to be made of the determined boys and fierce youths would not be fully realized for years to come. By then, would Saxons and Normans fight the same side without hitch to conscience? Would the enemy be other than Norman or Saxon?

"Thus begins their every day," Hawisa said where she stood alongside Em atop the gatehouse overlooking the land before Wulfen's walls that was lit by torches. "Prayer in the chapel, the breaking of fast en route to the training field, exercise to warm and stretch muscles, then a run to the waterfall and back."

In this instance, led by Eberhard who had gone from sight, whereas a score of his fellow warriors in training were yet visible as they churned bodies weighted by sacks of rocks fastened around their waists. And bringing up the rear and quickly gaining on them was Baron Wulfrith and Hawisa's housecarle, Ordric. But not Dougray, who had accompanied his brother to the training field only to observe. Likely, by the time the youths and boys returned, his journey to Yorkshire would be underway.

Hurting in anticipation of his absence, Em leaned into the

embrasure and saw he yet stood on the drawbridge staring after his brother. Feeling Hawisa's gaze, she eased back. "What of when they return, my lady?"

"Wrestling, weaponry, riding, hunting, the study of battles wondrously won and horribly lost, and in between and at each day's end, serving others, fellowship, and more prayer."

Em peered sidelong at her and saw Hawisa did the same. "More intense than my own training."

"And more complete, which is necessary for those not yet of an age to be fully accountable for their actions." The lady returned her regard to the handful of boys who were nearly out of sight. "Wulfrith training strengthened by D'Argent training."

"You have a hand in it?"

"I do. Much my wolf respects my knowledge and opinions, far more than my first husband."

"Your wolf," Em murmured.

Hawisa smiled. "Mine and our cub's."

"Your...?"

The lady turned toward Em. "I carry the first of the House of D'Argent-Wulfrith."

Em felt as if dealt a blow to the heart. This was to be expected—and welcomed—but what of Eberhard who had become as a son to the lady following the loss of her own?

"Em," she said, "I love Eberhard and will not cease loving him. Indeed, he has been offered the name of Wulfrith and need only accept it for all to know how precious he is to me and my husband."

Another blow to the heart, this one making her long to embrace so fine a woman whom once she had scorned for keeping the truth of Em's captivity from Eberhard so he would not foolishly attempt to aid his sister.

Em dropped to her knees and grasped the hem of Hawisa's gown. "I thank you, my lady. You know not how your kindness and generosity ease my mind. I—"

Hawisa gripped her elbow and drew her upright. "'Tis his due. A good and faithful son he has been and will continue to be."

Em frowned. "Why has he yet to accept your name?"

She sighed. "He loves me as a mother. I know he does, but he cannot entirely forgive me for withholding my knowledge you were with Campagnon at Castle Balduc." Before Em could assure her she would speak with her brother, Hawisa continued, "I think he will come around, but what is most important is both he and your younger siblings have a good, safe home. Thus, you must think on your own safety so they need not worry over it."

She searched the lady's torchlit face and wondered how much she told was calculated to persuade Em to abandon her country, and if she had arrived at the solution on her own or with Dougray's prompting. Likely the latter.

*I will not be angry,* Em told herself, then said, "The same as your brother-in-law, you believe I ought to go to France."

Hawisa's smile was sorrowful. "He makes a good argument. Though I know it will pain you to leave behind all you know, I agree that until slavery is outlawed in England, it is safest for you."

"Perhaps, but I must think on it."

"Providing we are discreet to ensure Campagnon does not learn you are here, there is time since it is increasingly dangerous to cross the channel."

Then she ought to have several months in which to fully heal and be with her brother—perhaps even train with him. That last gave her pause. "Discreet?" she asked.

"Aye, away from our charges, most of whom will travel home for Christmas to be with their families. Even if we risked drawing attention to you by ordering them not to speak of our guest with the most extraordinary eyes, some would forget our warning and tell family and friends."

"And word might reach Campagnon," Em said. "How do you propose to keep me from their notice? Lock me away?"

"Of course not, but you must be separated from them so they

not happen on you. Hence, one of the tower rooms will serve. Access to the roof will allow you to be outside and passages within the walls will permit Eberhard and others entrusted with knowledge of your presence to visit. You are well with this?"

*As well as possible,* Em thought. "I am, my lady."

"Good, and fear not you will be trapped inside. There will be opportunities to go riding."

"Much appreciated." Em glanced at the lady's belly that had yet to swell noticeably but would before Em had to decide whether to make a new life in France. "I am happy for the child you and your husband have made. I shall pray for an easy birth and a healthy babe."

"I thank you, Em."

"And..."

"And?"

"'Tis too long without speaking, but not too late, I pray. Much I am aggrieved by the unkind, selfish things I said when I revealed to Ebbe you knew I was with Campagnon upon Balduc. I understand why you did not tell him, and that it was for the best." She pressed a fist to her chest. "I was so angry and vengeful, and when you would not commit to the rebels joining Harwolfson upon Darfield..." She shook her head. "I behaved as a child. Hopefully, one day you can forgive me."

Hawisa drew Em's fist from her chest and gently opened her fingers. Hooking her own over them, she said, "Understandable and forgiven—if ever forgiveness was needed." She kissed Em's cheek. "Now, I am sure Sir Dougray prepares to depart. Let us see him away, hmm?"

"I am here," his voice sounded from the right and they swung toward the one ascending the steps, mantle riding his shoulders, both arms visible.

How long had he been there? Em wondered but did not ask. What was heard was heard, and none of it would surprise.

"You save us a visit to the stables," Hawisa said and, as she stepped to where he had halted on the landing, once more rubbed her shoulder.

Would it forever trouble her? Em wondered.

"As I have duties to attend to, I shall wish you Godspeed and leave you to speak your farewell." She looked to Em. "Do you return to the donjon the way we came, you ought to cross paths with no one."

Em nearly protested and followed, not because she did not wish to be alone with Dougray but because too much she wished it and might make more a fool of herself.

When Hawisa was gone, Dougray drew near. "It sounds as if the two of you have reconciled. I am glad."

Em clasped before her hands that ached to reach to him lest this was the last time it was possible. He might return to Wulfen Castle ere she departed for France or other parts of England, but he might not—whether ill befell him in hunting the resistance or he stayed away. "I am pleased to see you one last time," she ventured.

His eyebrows rose. "You will not be here when I return?"

Her heart soared. "Then you *will* return."

"Of course. I have family here."

Family...

"I will not abandon you, Em. Though I have kept my word to Vitalis to give you into Lady Hawisa's care, if you agree to leave England, I will myself deliver you across the narrow sea."

She moistened her lips. "If I do not agree?"

"Wulfen's lady believes the same as I that you will return if forced."

"Then you have discussed this with her."

"Aye, and my brother. All are in accord. You cannot be forced."

"What if I cannot be persuaded?"

"Then it is very possible Emma Irwindotter will break the hearts of Eberhard, Tristan, and Flora when once more she falls prey to Campagnon."

*What of your heart?* she ached to ask. *Might I break a small piece of it?*

Determinedly turning her thoughts from his heart to the others', she longed to declare she would not break them, but her eyes… Ever her eyes.

She drew a deep breath only to have it turn into a sob. Dropping her chin, she shook her head, silently entreating Dougray not to offer comfort.

But he stepped nearer and set his hand on her arm. "I know I seem unfeeling, but I seek to—"

"Make right what your people made wrong, this I know. And that you are honorable and…" She swallowed hard. "Everything—everyone—will be lost to me. I will be alive and free, but utterly alone, Dougray. Is that better than being Raymond Campagnon's plaything, suffering his foul moods and cruel words? His…"

"Em!" he said with such desperation, it did not sound like him. With that other Norman so near in her thoughts, she had to look up to assure herself it *was* him.

Even in the absence of daylight and in the deep of shadow, those were his golden eyes and hair catching moonlight. It was Dougray who cared enough to deliver her to France, and that was much, but it was also all. Or so she thought until he lifted her chin, lowered his head, and closed his mouth over hers.

Moving his hand to the back of her neck, he drew her nearer and deepened a kiss that could not possibly be that of a boy. The soft of his lips, rasp of his whiskers, and heat of his breath made her quiver, go light of head, and mouth go dry.

As if he were wine to her thirst, she swept her arms around his neck, pushed onto her toes, and leaned into him.

Every place they touched, warmth. Not fire, but the promise of it.

"Em," he spoke into her.

"Dougray?"

His hand moved down her spine, gripped the small of her back, pressed her nearer.

Deeper the kiss, deeper the warmth, and now tinder and flint birthed sparks.

She did not realize her feet had left the rooftop until he turned her back against the wall alongside the embrasure.

Of a sudden, what had felt wondrously right felt wrong, as if—

Nay, this was Dougray. *Him* kissing her. She opened her eyes and strained to see his face, but his hair curtaining them cast all in shadow. *His* hair. Hence, *him* holding her against the wall. *His* hand on her waist sliding up her side. *His* body going still. *His* voice speaking her name as he lifted his head and torchlight touched his bearded face. *His* face.

And yet this was *her* shaking, not with passion but fear. *Her* breathing hard and fast, not with longing but in preparation to push him away. *Her* hands no longer clasped around his neck but splayed upon his chest.

"Forgive me," he rasped and released her and dropped back. Shoulders rising and falling with breath, he raised his arms to the sides, his one palm open as if to show it held no weapon. "I know better than to do that."

Better than to give her a man's kiss she had wanted? Better than to touch her and explore her curves as she had wanted?

She opened her mouth to call him back, but movement drew her regard to the shaking hands she held before her as if to ward him off.

She closed them, dropped them to her sides, and pushed off the wall. "Naught to forgive. 'Twas me. I thought… It was dark and the wall…"

"I know." He lowered his own arms. "I know it is not me. It is him. You cut away his mark, but he is beneath your skin and likely ever will be."

"I *will* be rid of him, Dougray. I just need—"

"—to leave England. *That* is what you need. Pray, reconcile yourself, and when I return I shall see you settled in France and a new life begun."

"Alone," she whispered.

"Not alone. I will find you a good home with good people."

"Your family?"

Dougray stared at the woman who would be breaking his heart a second time if he loved her as he had Adela. But this tearing inside was something else. Had to be. And if it was not, he must make it other than love—especially after all he felt kissing and holding and touching her.

"Is it your family you speak of?" she repeated.

That had occurred to him, and he believed his mother and Godfroi would welcome her into their household, but there were two great obstacles. First, he must reconcile with Godfroi. But even were forgiveness gained, and knowing the man who had raised him as a son it would be, the other obstacle was insurmountable. With reconciliation came a lifetime of interactions with his family, even if he settled outside of Normandy, and there would be Em.

Though tempted to lie so sooner she would agree to remove her heart from England, in the end that would be cruel. "I think not," he said, "but many are the D'Argent acquaintances and allies. All will be well."

He knew she did not believe him, but there was naught else to be said and a long, hard ride ahead. "It is past time I depart, but allow me to escort you to the donjon." He started toward the stairs.

"Nay."

He looked around.

"I wish to stay awhile longer to watch my brother and his friends return and what comes after," she said, not with self-pity but determination. "Worry not, I will be discreet as Lady Hawisa instructed."

"As you wish."

He was halfway down the steps when she called, "Dougray?"

He turned to where she stood atop the roof.

"It *was* more than desire, was it not?" she asked.

Despite this ache, he smiled. "It was, Em. And ever shall be." Then he continued his descent.

He did not look back when he rode from Wulfen Castle, but he knew she was atop the gatehouse. Would she be there when he returned?

*Lord, let her not behave rashly. Let her accept France is best. Between now and my return, continue to heal her of Campagnon's abuse. She is not for me, but perhaps one day she can find happiness with one whose longing for her does not frighten.*

*I AM NOT AS BROKEN as he fears,* Em told herself as she watched the mist part for Dougray and the lightening sky give further form to his figure as he distanced himself.

"From me," she whispered. She believed it *was* more than desire he felt, but he was right. Campagnon *was* beneath her skin. Given time, she would remove him so completely it was possible Dougray could forget the one who came before him and see and feel only her. Still, she had seen his face, the hand he raised as if to calm one slipping over the edge. And she had heard his regret for doing with her what he knew better than to do.

She was not as broken as he thought, but whatever he felt for her would be given no opportunity to grow into the love she felt for him.

Feeling the scrape of nails moving from collarbone to neck, she stilled that hand and pressed it against her skin to keep it from her shoulder.

Campagnon's mark was gone, but how was she to pry the miscreant from beneath her skin?

More prayer? she wondered as the rider went from sight. Was

that all that was left to her? Nay, she had what had passed between Dougray and her. It could find no good end, but hope could be picked from its remains. She who once could not bear to be so near a man she could see her reflection in his eyes had this eve drawn so near Dougray that even had there been abundant light, little sense could have been made of her reflection. Aye, hope that one day there would be another she loved.

"Lord, keep Dougray safe," she prayed. "Guide him, let whatever task is set him be done as You would have it. Let him number no more losses. And when he returns, let me give answer that does not burden but allows him to let me go wherever I decide."

She nodded. "And help me free my mind of Campagnon so never again I put the sins of one on another as I did Dougray."

# CHAPTER TWENTY-TWO

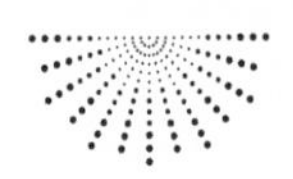

Lincolnshire, England
Early December

No Edgar, and no nests of rebels to scatter in William's direction. The latter not because they could not be found. Because they could so easily, unlike the Aetheling who appeared to have left his supporters to fend for themselves in countryside overrun by Normans who put to the sword even those merely suspected of aiding the resistance.

It was not only Vitalis's men Dougray had let be the one time he tracked them and came face to face with their leader. A half dozen others of greater numbers he had deemed of too little threat to warrant revealing them. It would be different did he not know the king's journey back to Yorkshire following Stafford had been so fraught with petty resistance, it had pushed him over a line from which it was unlikely he would be pulled back. Were Dougray one to blunder, he would not know what was not meant for him.

Overtaking William's army a sennight after departing Wulfen Castle as that great force continued its struggle to forge a path back to York, he had been summoned to the king's tent, doubtless to report on his lack of progress with Edgar. There should have been a guard posted outside to announce his arrival, but the man had slipped away—to relieve himself he said upon his return, and with the urgency of one appealing to another not to reveal him.

Dougray had held it close, just as he held close several minutes of a conversation overheard between William and one of his advisors. The king was done chasing and defeating the Northern rebels across inhospitable lands only to have them rise up again when he withdrew. Hence, he would deprive the rebels of those things necessary for their survival, which meant depriving innocents as well.

After assuring Vitalis that Em healed and, following a near tragic detour to Gloucester, was delivered to Lady Hawisa, Dougray had warned the Saxon warrior of the harrying to come.

Vitalis had searched for the lie on Dougray's face, closed his eyes so long one might think he slept, then thanked Dougray and said he and his men would do all in their power to aid their people.

"The rebel camp upon Wulfenshire," Dougray had suggested with little thought.

Dousing surprise, Vitalis had said, "If Lady Hawisa is willing, mayhap use can be made of it," then added, "Like your brothers, you are not very Norman, Dougray D'Argent." Then he was gone.

Now again, Dougray, Maël, and Guy were in the camp of the Danish allies who had proved that, beyond giving aid in laying ruin to York, they were of no use to the resistance. This time, Campagnon was absent from the Normans in the midst of Danes, having earned William's displeasure by disappearing with his men for several days during the withdrawal from Stafford. It had occurred to Dougray the knave's detour had something to do with Em and he might have been nearer than believed during her escape to Gloucester and Dougray's retrieval of her.

He could only pray Campagnon had no evidence of her

journey to Wulfenshire. But now was not for praying in Em's direction. Now was for redeeming himself in William's eyes after failing to deliver Edgar. Now was for gaining the reward promised him, though he knew not what that would be. Hopefully, a purse of coin rather than land taken from another, not only to secure his future but ensure Em a good situation in France so never again she suffer depraved men.

"The earl comes prepared to talk," Maël said drolly.

"Indeed," murmured Sir Guy.

Two score strong, the Danes approached on foot. Though armed and armored, they lacked shields. At the fore were men holding aloft the poles to which a great canopy was attached, men carrying a table, a man shouldering an elaborate chair, and another with a squat bench under his arm. And so began negotiations the Danes had surely awaited, throughout which Dougray would stand, even if the bench was not intended for their leader's feet.

He shifted his regard to the earl advancing ahead of his warriors. He was of good size, but like many an aging soldier, indulged in much food and drink. However, the young man striding just behind and to his right was fit. And recognizable, though he might not have been had not Em revealed the Dane whom Dougray put to ground at York was the earl's son.

Recalling though marriage had been proposed, the offer had become one of *bedmate* when Em revealed she did not meet the requirement of chastity, it took determination for Dougray to maintain a passive expression as father and son neared.

He was not here to seek recompense for an offense dealt her. He was here to offer recompense for those who had given the resistance false hope that led to the recent uprisings and could lead to more if the Danes continued to toy with desperate Saxons. William wanted them to withdraw, and Dougray must see it done.

As the canopy was erected twenty feet distant, he considered the earl where he halted opposite, then the restlessness of the

Dane's men—not unlike the score of Norman warriors at Dougray's back. As told by the banners flown, they were here with peaceable intentions but prepared should the wrong corner be turned.

Once the poles were secured, the table was set beneath the canopy with the chair on one side, the bench on the other. Next, two cups were placed atop the table and filled with wine.

"The name of King William's envoy?" the earl asked.

"Chevalier Dougray D'Argent."

The man's eyebrows jumped. "I have heard of your family. Your sire is Hugh D'Argent?"

Feeling Maël stiffen, Dougray said, "Chevalier Hugh was my uncle. He fell at the battle of Hastings."

"Such a pity so many died for... What is it you Normans call him now? William the Great?"

Ignoring that, Dougray nodded at the man to his right. "Here my cousin, Chevalier Maël D'Argent."

The earl smiled. "I understand your sire was a formidable warrior and trainer of men of the sword."

When Maël did not respond, the Dane shifted his regard to the man on Dougray's other side. "This is?"

"Sir Guy Torquay," Dougray said and silently added, *Also a cousin,* though he had yet to reconcile that—more, Michel Roche. But he would.

"Chevalier Guy," the earl said. When Guy responded in kind, the older man swept his hand at the Dane beside him. "My son, Bjorn, beloved albeit misbegotten."

Showing no evidence of the injury dealt six weeks past nor recognition of the one responsible, the young man said, "Much honored, Chevaliers."

Were that true, it was because he and his fellow Danes, weary of evading open battle and having accepted how slight the possibility of placing their king on England's throne, hoped to be compensated for their crossing to England and loss of warriors.

"And so?" the earl prompted.

"And so," Dougray said.

The Dane frowned. "You are here to negotiate peace in the name of your king, are you not?"

Dougray shrugged. "Where there is little strife, what need for peace?"

The earl's face darkened. "We both know Le Bâtard wants us gone from England, so all that remains is the question of what he will pay for our absence." He gestured at the table. "Let us discuss it."

"We shall leave you to it," Maël said.

The earl and Dougray stepped beneath the canopy, but unlike the Dane, Dougray remained standing.

The man settled in his carved chair. "You need not stand for me, Chevalier." He gestured at where Dougray stood behind the bench placed before the table. "Lest this take much time, make yourself comfortable and join me in raising a cup to our successful negotiation."

Dougray removed his mantle and dropped it on the bench, crossed his one arm over his chest and gripped the elbow of the other. "I shall stand."

As expected, what had escaped notice came to notice as evidenced by the earl's widening eyes. "One armed," he said and looked around at Bjorn, proof the young Dane had noted his opponent's loss that night at York.

Bjorn slid his gaze from Dougray to his sire, wrinkled his brow. He was not certain here was the warrior who bested him, the loss of an arm hardly exclusive to Dougray. Or were he certain, he was unwilling to acknowledge it in front of his fellow Danes who, unlike the earl, might be unaware their leader's son had fallen to a one-armed man.

The earl cleared his throat. "You look familiar, Sir Dougray. Perchance you were among the Normans we defeated at York, one of those who fled to fight another day?"

"I was at York, but not that day." The man had his answer, as did his son. "Now tell what you believe to be the value of withdrawing from the King of England's shores."

The earl ordered his men out of hearing distance, excepting his son. Dougray did the same, excepting his cousins. Then the Dane said, "Think on the fall of York, and there you will find the value of our absence."

And so negotiations began in earnest, Dougray standing throughout and sipping wine while time and again the earl rose from and dropped back into his chair, pounded a fist and slapped a hand on the table.

It took longer than anticipated, the Dane a stubborn man made more stubborn knowing the king's envoy was likely responsible for his son's injury. But ere the sun set, it was done. The earl believed he had doubled what William was willing to pay, oblivious to having settled for less than half of what the king had authorized. Still, they were generous terms for men who would surely be dead had they not sidled away from battling William and his forces.

A horde of silver would be paid to King Sweyn, a somewhat less substantial sum paid directly—and secretly—to his brother, the earl. It was hoped but not expected the earl would quickly take his fleet back across the sea. He would not risk it with winter chilling the timbers of his ships and causing them to groan and creak at anchorage. Thus, he accepted William's offer for his army to forage along the coast providing they departed England by winter's end.

A portion of the silver given into the earl's keeping, the rest to follow within a fortnight, Dougray said, "Godspeed," and turned away.

"Was it you, Chevalier?" Bjorn asked.

Dougray looked across his shoulder at the one who had stepped alongside his sire. "It was. You live because you have honor, Bjorn, as evidenced by not trying to take what was refused you." He paused, considered that the young man had deemed Em suitable as a bedmate. Or might it have been his sire?

Dougray glanced at the hard-faced man. Thinking it likely the earl, he continued, "It shall make you a man above other men."

The corners of Bjorn's mouth curved, then his brow lowered. "You speak of the Saxon girl—the rebel."

"I do."

"Why concern yourself over what befalls one who is your enemy?"

"Because first she is a woman vulnerable to the whims of men. Fortunately for you, you proved not such a man." Dougray inclined his head and strode from beneath the canopy.

It was time to return to York where the king had ordered the castles rebuilt to once more establish that city as a Norman stronghold. Soon, in the absence of a miracle, the harrying would begin.

And God—and Vitalis—help the innocents.

# CHAPTER TWENTY-THREE

Wulfen Castle
Wulfenshire, England

"My lady wife thought you would be up here," Guarin D'Argent said in her language.

Em had sensed the one who ascended the ladder to the roof was not Eberhard who joined her here from time to time, but thought it would be Hawisa or her housecarle, Ordric.

These weeks, often she had been in the company of the Lord of Wulfen when she accepted invitations to partake of meals with his wife and him in the solar, but never had she been alone with him—nor feared it. Just as Dougray was unlike any man she had known, so was his eldest brother. And she did not doubt he was in love with Hawisa though she heard no declaration of great feeling. It was in the eyes he traveled over his wife, the touch of their hands, the lean of his body toward hers, and deep murmurs that made his rebel bride smile and blush.

No cause to fear Guarin D'Argent, and yet this was so unexpected and awkward, Em knew she must look a frightened rabbit where she had set her back against the wall. Moments earlier, she had stood in the embrasure, mantle hugged about her to ward off December's chill as she watched the boys and young men fly out the great doors of the hall into night that would soon become day. As ever, Eberhard had been among the first to cross the inner bailey and would be among the first on the training field.

"May I approach?" the Lord of Wulfen asked.

"Of course. You but surprised me. I expected to see you on the steps below, not here."

He strode forward, and the lowering moon lit the silver of his hair that was even longer than when she had seen him on the battlefield at Darfield. Such a handsome man he was—though were there any more pleasing to the eye than Dougray? Certainly not to her.

He halted within reach, and she saw he wore only a long-sleeved tunic and chausses tucked into calf-high boots. No mantle nor undertunic visible beyond the open neck of the over tunic. He must be cold with the breeze stirring the air atop the roof, but he would be warm once he joined those gathering outside Wulfen's walls.

"Why do you seek me out, Baron?"

"My wife has proposed something, and though I do not know I agree, I see the possibility of good."

Em straightened from the wall. "In what?"

"If not a cure for your restlessness, a balm to it. Lady Hawisa tells there are few who can run as fast and as long as you. Hence, she believes you would enjoy running the wood with our charges."

Em caught her breath, exhaled on the words, "I would."

"Then you shall."

Amid the joy, a question. "But as ever I am to be garbed in men's clothes and beneath a hood when I leave the donjon, how is this to be?"

"You shall come to the gatehouse when all are gathered in the training yard preparing for the run, hair bound up beneath a cap. Ere the last half go from sight, you shall give chase. As there will only be the light of the moon and stars, and you will be overtaking those bringing up the rear and picking off those ahead, there should be no opportunity for any to look near on you."

So much excitement rippled through her, she could not think what to say.

"On the return, you will end the contest at the tree line. There, Sir Ordric or I will collect you and return you to the donjon."

"What if I overtake the leader? Will it not appear peculiar when I drop back?"

"Considering the lead which those at the fore shall have, and near always the leader is Eberhard, it is not likely. Even so, you will have to be discreet when you end your run."

"I can do that."

"Then it is decided. It is too late this day, but on the morrow."

"I thank you, my lord."

She expected him to leave and wished it so that she might loose a smile whose width she had not felt since seeing Tristan and Flora at play with their cousins, but he said, "Have you thought more on France?"

This past sennight, several times Hawisa had asked the same of her. She had shrugged it off, preferring not to speak of it lest the turmoil banging harder at her insides since Eberhard began encouraging her to do so made her speak harsh words. Did the lady now send her husband for an answer denied her? Or was he the one pressing for an answer?

Em drew her mantle closer. "Must I think on it now when 'tis even more dangerous to make a crossing than weeks past?"

"The sooner you determine your course, the sooner plans can be laid to best keep you safe. As already told, you have a greater chance of remaining free of Campagnon if you go to France. Do you not, a convent in the south of England should keep you from his notice."

"A convent?" she exclaimed.

"Aye, where your siblings could visit without fear of revealing you."

And Dougray? she wondered. Might he visit her as well? She thrust out the hope with the reminder he could never be hers, whether of her own doing or his.

"I speak not of taking vows," his brother continued, "but of living in a community of good women until Campagnon departs England or slavery is outlawed here."

"Which may never happen," she said, "and when you speak of *good* women you forget many will not be good to me for fear of these eyes."

"There will be some, as ever there have been and ever there will be, but I believe most will embrace you."

Would they? Was this the answer to a runaway slave? Would it become the permanent answer to one who had minutes earlier thrilled to a run in the wood? And what of the cost of feeding, housing, and clothing one who had not the coin required? Could she pay it by working in the kitchen or cleaning the rooms of noblewomen?

She swallowed. "Would there be work for me?"

"Only if you wish it. The Wulfriths will provide whatever you need."

*Dear Lord, this is no place for pride but gratitude,* she spoke heavenward. *Let me not offend.* "You are generous, Baron Wulfrith. Pray, bear with me. There is even more to consider now."

He inclined his head but did not withdraw.

What else had he to tell? Something he was reluctant to speak? "Have you word of Dougray?" she asked.

"I do not."

Unfortunately, there were other things to fear besides ill befalling the man she loved. "William?"

"Only that he rebuilds York so it not easily fall again."

She moistened her lips. "As you linger, you have something else to say."

He started to step nearer then settled back into his heels.

*Lest he frighten me,* she realized. Angry with herself for causing him to believe her weak, she stepped nearer. "I am not afeared of you, Baron Wulfrith."

"I am glad," he said, then, "I linger because of Dougray, a beloved brother. You care much for him, do you not?"

"I..." Nay, she would not lie. "I do, hopeless though it is."

"It does seem hopeless. Still, I must ask—among the hopelessness, do you count that he is a Norman who aided in conquering your country?"

It *was* as she had regarded Dougray, but no longer. It mattered not he was Norman. It mattered not he had fought at Hastings. He had become more to her. He had become...everything.

"I must defend him," his brother misinterpreted her silence. "Never did he wish to cross the channel and fight for our duke. *An ill and unjustified business destined to shed the blood of thousands and subjugate innocents,* he said of William's ambitions. And yet he fought for his liege, you will argue." He nodded. "He yielded to persuasion, betraying his beliefs and conscience in the hope of gaining lands to win the hand of a woman his illegitimacy denied him—a woman who proved unworthy of him."

The one of whom Michel Roche had spoken in the kitchen that morn at Stavestone, she knew.

"Great my brother's regret for what he did and terrible the price he paid. Can you not forgive him as my lady wife forgave me?"

Tears sprang to her eyes. "He is forgiven, Baron Wulfrith. Long forgiven."

Relief eased his face. "I am pleased, Em." Once more silence fell between them, then he said, "I must speak of your recovery at Stavestone."

She frowned. "What of it?"

"Last eve, I received a missive from its lord, a man whose name I know well the same as all my kin."

"Michel Roche."

"You know who he is to Dougray?"

"The one who sired your brother."

He nodded. "He sends word he comes to Wulfen Castle to deliver your friend, Margaret, into our care as directed by Dougray."

She shook her head. "I doubt your brother intended he deliver her himself."

"As thought, but since Dougray did not prepare me to meet again the man who was given the Duke of Normandy's blessing to wed one believed a widow, mayhap you could tell me what to expect from what you witnessed at Stavestone."

She tensed. "It is not for me to do."

"I would not ask were it possible to pose the same to Dougray. Will you not tell how my brother received the one who brought him into being and how they left it?"

Still she hesitated.

"Em, no matter how sore Dougray is from meeting his sire, I believe he would be well with me knowing what to expect when that man brings Margaret into my home."

*His* home. Months past, she would have resented him laying claim to Saxon holdings. No longer, at least not one of the family D'Argent. "I shall tell what I overheard and observed of Michel Roche and your brother. Since you are for the training field, when would you like to speak?"

"My lady wife and Ordric will supervise the morning run. Hence, I would speak now, and as I anticipate it will take some time, methinks the solar best providing you are comfortable there."

She was. Again, because of who he was.

An hour later, morning light pouring in through the windows, Em rose with the baron from the large table near the hearth.

"I thank you," he said. "Ever I have believed Michel Roche a good man, little different from all good men who fail at living sin free. It is a relief to know he would have been a worthy father to Dougray had he the opportunity."

"'Tis not too late," she ventured.

"That is Dougray's decision." He came around the table. "I will escort you to your chamber."

"Not necessary, my lord, I am familiar with the wall passages now." She moved toward the tapestry that hid the entrance and paused. "Is it permitted to explore the underground passage to the wood?" She had been through it only once when Hawisa was betrayed by her own and led her people to safety near the waterfall where now Wulfen's charges ran.

"It has been reinforced," he said. "There are three gates placed down its length, and its final coursing has been rerouted distant from the falls. I hope you will not be offended, but just as the passage is Wulfen's greatest defense under siege, allowing for escape or to gather a great number of soldiers at the backs of the enemy, it is also our greatest vulnerability. Hence, it is not for exploring."

She was not offended, it being imperative Hawisa and her husband protect their people. "I understand, and I thank you again for the morrow."

"I shall send my lady wife to you to discuss the details."

Though their audience was at an end, Em smoothed her tunic and, wishing it a gown better fit for her next words, said, "For you and your wife alone, I would have you know I love your brother and wish I did not for what I cannot have. But I accept it and, regardless whether I remain in England, will be a burden to him no more."

She was glad for the distance between them so she did not have to look near on his pity.

"I thank you for your honesty, Em. Truly."

*I will not cry,* she told herself as she climbed the steps to her chamber. *I have no cause. The Lord has provided far more than expected. He has righted my world. It is not perfectly straight and can never be, but providing I stay ahead of Campagnon, I will want for naught.*

"For naught," she said aloud and put Dougray from her mind.

For the moment.

# CHAPTER TWENTY-FOUR

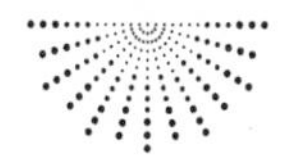

City of York
Yorkshire, England

"I am pleased, Sir Dougray, and that is good since it offsets my displeasure."

Dougray was not surprised he had not done enough to redeem himself, but he was disappointed. Negotiations had gone better than expected, neutralizing the possibility the Danes would further aid the resistance and costing William fewer coins. But still there was Edgar who had either found a deep hole to go down or returned to his exile in Scotland.

The latter, Dougray guessed. He was young and a fool, but surely not so young and foolish not to accept once more his bid for the crown was lost to the might of William. As ever it would be, Dougray believed, and all the more likely after what was to come. Still, that did not mean the Aetheling would not try again. Had he not evaded the king's men when Dougray uncovered his hiding place, the greatest threat to England's peace would be locked away with his head firmly on his shoulders since William exercised restraint where fellow nobles were concerned.

"Naught to say, Sir Dougray?" his liege prompted. "No questioning my disappointment despite your success with the earl?"

Dougray glanced at Maël and Guy who had been present when he entered the tent outside York's walls. He had believed them also summoned to give account of negotiations with the Danes, and all he had told they confirmed when questioned, but were they privy to what William alluded to?

Slight shakes of the head indicating they were ignorant, Dougray guessed the king referred to Edgar. "Your Majesty, I shall set out this day to discover the Aetheling's whereabouts. If he remains in England, I will find him."

"The little worm," William muttered and strode forward. "Had you not once delivered him and were I not fair certain he has returned to Scotland, much more he would figure into this, but it is a lie and the breaking of the law that concerns me."

Dougray went cold.

The king nodded. "The things we do for love, hmm? Of course, I assume love is what you feel for the slave-turned-rebel."

How much did he know? That she had been injured at Stafford and conveyed to Stavestone? Unlikely. And surely not that she had escaped Dougray en route to Wulfenshire. It had to be his rescue of her from the slavers, and all because he had left a man alive to tell the tale of the witchy-eyed slave and one-armed chevalier.

Keeping his gaze from Guy lest he implicate him, Dougray said, "I happened upon a young woman being abused by her captors, a slave I was acquainted with whilst Sir Raymond was keeper of Castle Balduc. As any man of honor would do, I gave aid."

William crossed his arms over his chest. "It is fortunate those you slew were Saxons and of a trade I find repulsive, but unfortunate one was left alive to see tale carried to Campagnon."

Wrong though it was to slay a defenseless man, it would be better had he done so to protect Em.

"Thus," William continued, "you obstructed the slavers in returning the woman to her master and gaining their reward in accordance with England's laws."

Dougray shifted his jaw. "The laws of King Edward and King Harold's England."

"The laws of *my* England until *I* change them," William snarled. "You are not well with that, Chevalier?"

"I also find slavery repulsive, my liege. Hence, I would be a coward to say I am well with what I am not."

"Because you feel for this young woman."

"Non, because it is wrong."

"And all the more wrong because this young woman suffers, eh?"

Dougray drew a long breath. "Oui, but as told, it is not all self-serving. Just as your lands in Normandy are free of the godless trade and all the more prosperous for it, so should be your English lands."

William uncrossed his arms. "You think to tell me what is best for my kingdom?"

"I but concur with your God-given conscience, Your Majesty. As your priests tell, slavery is an affront to God. For this, the anointed King of England finds it repulsive the same as I."

One moment William looked as if he might strike Dougray, the next he laughed. "Praise the Lord I like you, Dougray D'Argent. I shall forgive you for aiding a slave when you should have been sniffing out Edgar, the same as I forgave Campagnon for searching her out when he should have been hunting down rebels, but what cannot yet be changed must be enforced. Where is Emma Irwindotter?"

Dougray kept his expression impassive, but as he summoned an answer the king would not like, William said, "Let me save you another lie that will please Campagnon and anger me. Had I to guess, it would be that you delivered her to the Lady of Wulfen who trained her into a rebel, and there she will be found when I give Campagnon leave to collect his property."

"When you—?" Dougray snapped his teeth.

"He and his mercenaries benefit me, Chevalier. Just as I require men of honor like the D'Argents, I require ruthless men who, if ever they had honor, now but dream of it. So I shall allow Campagnon to ride on Wulfen Castle."

Dougray folded his hand into a fist, felt the absent one do the same.

"And to ensure the gates open to Sir Raymond, I will accompany him."

Dougray glanced at Maël and Guy. Both sought to cover expressions of alarm, but there was something shining from the former's eyes—distaste, doubtless that another Saxon woman had laid siege to the affections of a D'Argent.

"As work progresses well in restoring York and plans to forever end the resistance are soon to be set in motion," William continued, "I can spare a few days to see this Wulfen Castle of which men speak and observe those being trained to defend my England." He smiled. "So now the question, what are you to do?"

Already Dougray's mind worked that. Even if he reached Wulfen first, he could not ask Guarin and his wife to refuse the king and his mercenaries entrance. To do so would make traitors of them and see the demesne forfeited. He could take Em out through the underground passage to the wood, but where to deliver her that William's reach did not extend, defiance of him rendering Dougray an enemy?

The king chuckled. "Quite the quandary, so allow one bâtard to aid another."

"My liege?"

"First, let us humble you as ever my wife humbles me. Admit you love the witchy-eyed woman."

Dougray ground his teeth. For Em, such a lie he would tell—were it a lie. And it was not, he accepted. This love *was* different from what he had felt for Adela, not because it was something less, because it was something more. No longer was it a young man's heart that ached for a woman. It was that of a man finding his way back to the good of him ere the two great losses he had blamed on innocents.

Imagining the distaste sure to rise on Maël's face, Dougray said, "I love Emma Irwindotter."

William chuckled. "Nearly crippling, is it not?"

Dougray knew the tale of the Duke of Normandy and the niece of the King of France, it being said when William heard she had rejected his pursuit due to his illegitimacy, he had ridden to her sire's home and taken a whip to her. Though he was not shy about being baseborn, woe to any who sought to wield it as a blade against him. It was rumored he had left the lady in a sobbing heap and returned home to set his mind on another bride. But then came word Matilda would have him, and he had set aside her offense and wed her.

By many accounts, it was a good marriage lacking infidelity on either side, and Matilda was so esteemed her husband entrusted her with administering Normandy in his absence. William the Duke…the Conqueror…the Great…loved the same as Dougray—or as far as such a man could love. But unlike Dougray, he did not love someone who could do more than *nearly* cripple him. Dougray loved someone whose brokenness could break him more, whether because once more she fell into Campagnon's hands or he tried to make a life with one ruined for great intimacy.

Closely watched by one overly observant, Dougray said, "As you wished, I am humbled and raw for it. Thus, greater the quandary of what to do with what will be done if you allow Campagnon to take Em and further abuse her. Pray, tell how you would aid your fellow bâtard."

"Fellow," William mused, then said, "Your *king* and Campagnon, accompanied by a sizable escort, shall depart for

Wulfen Castle ere dawn on the morrow. I give you this lead to do with as you will."

Dougray frowned. "What do you suggest?"

"Naught, since I do not believe you would heed me as I would not heed those who warned me away from my lady wife. Just as it was for me to decide, it is for you to determine your chance of success and if she is worth the price of defying the law of the land should you fail."

*Are Em and I an amusement?* Dougray pondered, but it mattered not. If this was a chance to save her, he would take it. And of further advantage, it gave him leave to depart England without gaining royal wrath by refusing to participate in the plan to forever end the resistance.

"I thank you for the lead, Your Majesty."

William smiled. "Then it is unlikely I shall see you upon Wulfenshire."

Nor would Campagnon, Dougray thought, though that did not mean the mercenary and he would not meet between there and the coast. "Unlikely," he agreed. "Now with your permission, I shall depart."

"Your Majesty," Maël said, "I wish to accompany my cousin."

"You may. And you, Sir Guy? Would you accompany your…" The king looked to Dougray. "I believe you know."

"I do."

"Of recent, oui?"

Dougray considered his newly acquired cousin who appeared as tense, then the cousin he had known all his life whose furrowed brow evidenced he sought to make sense of the exchange.

Dougray nodded. "Of recent, Your Majesty."

"Hence, more to the lie, hmm?"

"Indeed, but I am to blame, not Sir Guy."

"Again, it is good you are due grace." The king returned his regard to Guy. "What say you?"

"Do you allow it, Your Majesty, I shall accompany him."

"I can spare you, and mayhap you will prove useful to his cause. And not for the first time."

There being little doubt the king had pieced together events between Stafford and delivering Em to Wulfenshire, Dougray was more eager to get astride lest William reconsider aiding one whose lie could be deemed treasonous.

"Take your leave," William said.

Dougray bowed, then followed by Maël and Guy, ducked to clear the tent flap tossed back by a guard.

"Another D'Argent ensnared by a Saxon woman," Maël muttered as he drew alongside. "For how easily they draw Normans of good sense onto crooked English paths, I begin to think it not exaggeration they are sorceresses."

If not for Em's eyes, Dougray would have thought little of his choice of words, but he halted and Maël came back around, as did Guy. But the words Dougray intended to speak were swallowed when William called to him.

Dougray turned. "My liege?"

"Think well on the reward you would ask of me for ridding England of the Danes on less generous terms than believed possible."

That struck Dougray as peculiar since he had expected to be told what his reward would be were it anything beyond redemption for being unable to discover Edgar's whereabouts and forgiveness of the lie.

William glanced between Maël and Guy, said, "I wish you and your cousins Godspeed," then motioned to his guards and strode toward his destrier flanked by two of his companions astride warhorses.

No surprise when Dougray looked to Maël and found his cousin's lids narrowed. No surprise when Maël looked from Dougray to Guy and said, "Cousins?"

Dougray had known his kinship with Guy would have to be revealed but not expected it done this day. Thus, somewhere between York and Wulfen it would be told, and told again to Guarin. As for Dougray's reward…

Considering what lay ahead, it was of no consequence.

Or was it?

~

Wulfen Castle
Wulfenshire, England

GUARIN WAS glad he was prepared to receive Michel Roche. He only wished Em had mentioned how great the resemblance between father and son. Not that he had been so young when the man entered his mother's life he did not remember the golden hair matched by golden eyes and the height and breadth, but even two hours after the baron's arrival, it unnerved him to look upon the man of fifty years that Dougray would become.

The Baron of Stavestone eased back in his chair. "Though it was the attack on the village that delayed the journey to deliver Margaret to you, again I apologize."

"Not necessary," Guarin said. "Regardless the day, we are grateful for the service you provided so Dougray could keep his word to my wife's old friend." He glanced at the only other occupant of the solar and knew despite Hawisa's solemn expression, she worried over Vitalis and those who remained his side. "But you must know I am curious about something."

"Many somethings, I wager," the man said.

"True. Though Em told some of what went between Dougray and you, I would know the reason you escorted Margaret here when you could have given the task to trusted men."

The baron reached to his goblet, drank, then returned the vessel to the table and fingered its stem. "I could have and nearly did, but I hoped if I established contact with the one first I knew as a wee lad of bared teeth and flying fists who feared I was as much the enemy as the brigands who attacked his mother, the door opened to Dougray would remain ajar." He looked up, and there was moisture in the old warrior's eyes. "You remember me, do you not, Guarin?"

"I do, Baron Roche, and I hold no grudge though much my mother and brother have suffered for your indiscretion ere the marriage that was to have made you my father. Regardless, good came of that sin—Dougray who is as much my brother as Cyr and Theriot."

The baron rocked his head. "Ever I shall regret their suffering, just as ever I thank the Lord for providing my son with a family who sees him first as one of their own—even Godfroi who forgave as I do not know I could have had Robine ever truly been mine."

Guarin liked this man, certain if not for the woman between Godfroi and Michel the two men could have been great friends, but it was not for him to hold open the door to Dougray.

"I know you are honorable," he said, "just as I knew had you not risked your life to deliver my mother out of the hands of brigands, when my sire returned he would have been dealt a blow worse than the loss of the use of his legs. Likely, he would have mourned a wife and sons. Much is owed you, but I can aid with Dougray only if he wishes it. He must decide between knowing you better and knowing you no more."

The baron smiled sorrowfully. "I have heard it said there can be no harm in asking for something beyond one's reach that is within another's reach—that there is naught to lose—but that is not so. There is the loss of hope, though I have only myself to blame for letting it in after all these years."

"I believe Dougray will come around," Hawisa spoke as rarely she had since settling at the table, and Guarin did not know whether to be glad she saved him a response that would have been long in coming or vexed she sowed hope Roche might never see flower.

*Glad,* he determined, even were she wrong. Here was the heart of his warrior bride revealed to a stranger and a Norman though —like Dougray—Roche appeared far more a Saxon.

"Even if never I see him again," the baron said, "I thank you, my lady." He pushed back his chair. "As it will be an early day for my men and me, I shall avail myself of that chamber now."

Guarin hesitated over the offer that sprang to mind, then said, "It was a long journey. Linger a few days, rest, and observe our training of England's future."

Roche looked to Hawisa.

"Pray, remain a while," she said.

"I would like that. Much gratitude, Lady Hawisa...Baron Wulfrith." He stood, as did his hosts.

When Hawisa returned after escorting him abovestairs and ensuring the squires who provided food, drink, and pallets to his men performed their duties well, she crossed to the table on which Guarin had opened the demesne's journals, came around to his back, and wrapped her arms around him.

He looked up over his shoulder. "Wife?"

"You were angry with me."

"I was." He smiled. "And then I was not."

"Why?"

He lowered the quill, turned on the bench, and drew her down onto his thighs. Settling a palm against the child growing inside her, he said, "I thought it wrong to give Roche hope that might later pain him more than accepting its loss this day, but then I realized the woman's heart known only to me and Eberhard, and on occasion Cyr and Theriot, had shown itself to a Norman stranger."

"A Norman, aye, but one who fought the side of the Saxons."

As first told by Em and this eve confirmed by the baron.

"Though methinks more dark days ahead," Guarin said, "men like Michel Roche give me hope for a united England ere our children are grown."

She touched her mouth to his. "As you and all those of your family give me hope."

"All?" He drew back. "This from my lady wife who is no nearer to embracing Dougray than Maël?"

She raised her eyebrows. "This stubborn Saxon is nearer than you think."

"Is she?"

She slid her hands over his shoulders, pushed her fingers into his hair. This time when her mouth met his, it was with the urgency of one who did not tease nor merely suggest.

Guarin returned her kiss, matched her fervor, and when she rasped, "I love you as never shall I love another," carried her to their marriage bed.

# CHAPTER TWENTY-FIVE

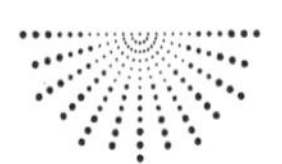

This day she bested all but three of those who began the run ahead of her, Eberhard in the lead as usual. Having gone from sight of those behind, she veered off course and slowed as the land before the castle appeared between the trees ahead.

Since it would be a quarter hour or more before Baron Wulfrith or Ordric appeared to return her to Wulfen, she halted. Hands on hips, she collected her breath and counted off the youths and boys coming after her.

There being thirty who trained at Wulfen, when a dozen had passed, Ordric appeared mid-pack, meaning Baron Wulfrith would bring up the rear, challenging boys and the occasional youth to push himself harder. And they would, none wishing to disappoint him.

When the last of the runners swept past followed by Guarin D'Argent shouting encouragement, Em lowered to her haunches against a tree and watched them grow distant as they traversed the meadow amid dawn's first light to reach the castle whose torches would soon be extinguished.

Was Michel Roche yet atop the gatehouse whose steps she had watched him climb when she slipped into the outer bailey? She had not seen him upon his arrival on the day past, only knew of it from Hawisa who had delivered Margaret to the tower room she was to share with Em.

Would he depart this day? Why this worry he would without them meeting again? Why this desire to speak with him? And of what would they speak?

She would apologize for making it difficult for his son to keep his word to Vitalis—and to him for causing him to depart Stavestone to deliver Margaret here.

Em frowned. Surely that had not been necessary. And yet, rather than entrust Margaret to others, he had journeyed with her. All these years he might have wished to distance himself from the son denied him to keep what remained of his heart intact, but now that contact was established, likely he longed for more, even were he ill received by Dougray's brother. And that she did not believe of Guarin D'Argent.

A sound, possibly of a large animal, stilled her thoughts. Closing a hand around her dagger's hilt, she listened. Not a large animal but two or more. And not animals at all, she knew when she caught the voices of men. Were they of Wulfen? Men-at-arms patrolling the area?

Hoping they altered their course, she touched the cap beneath which she had tucked her hair and drew her dagger from its sheath.

When they continued in her direction, she bent low and hastened to bushes dense enough to conceal her. Slipping into them, she caught her breath over the prick of thorns. Blessedly, as Baron Wulfrith or Ordric would soon come for her, she would not long suffer the discomfort should the approaching men linger.

Movement to the far left and the lightening sky showed there were two. When they were less than thirty feet distant, one of the men said, "Imagine being forced to wed a Saxon woman who thinks herself a man."

The other chuckled. "A woman like Hawisa Wulfrith... No

hardship once she learned to obey her master. And there would be joy in the teaching."

One moment Em felt the warmth of her exertion, the next the chill of a winter day. She knew those voices, though it was the second that yanked her back to Castle Balduc. She did not recall the Norman's name, but she remembered the decayed teeth he spoke past, foul breath, and cruel hands on her when Campagnon was nowhere near to prevent others from attempting to sample what belonged to him. These men come unto Hawisa's wood might walk on two legs, but they were animals. And they were here for her. Was Campagnon as well?

Digging nails into her palms to keep from reaching to her scarred shoulder, she drew measured breaths.

*Lord, do not let me suffer them again—more, Campagnon,* she beseeched silently. *Send them opposite.*

At twenty feet, near the tree where she had crouched, they halted and she saw the glint of weapons on their belts. Though neither had a sword or dagger to hand, they could be wielded inside a moment.

She grew colder yet at the realization whether it was the baron who came for her or Hawisa's housecarle, the man might fall victim to these two because of her.

Now she began to shake and nearly whimpered when the bushes rattled.

"Listen!" one of the men rasped.

Hoping to calm her body, Em squeezed her eyes closed.

"Just a breeze," the other man muttered.

Silence. No movement toward her, but neither away.

After a time, one of them said, "Do you think the witchy-eyed one is here as Campagnon believes?"

Unable to draw sufficient air through her nose, Em pulled shuddering breaths between clamped teeth.

"Likely," said the one whose voice was most familiar. "For that, he sent us ahead."

A grunt. "Dangerous, this. It is one thing to cross a one-armed D'Argent, but this Guarin they call the *wolf?"*

Anger clipping through Em, welcome for the distraction that further eased her shaking and pressure on her teeth, she opened her eyes. Dougray would kill them were he here. Just as he had defeated the slavers, so he would defeat these mercenaries.

"Ah, but the reward," the worst of them said.

"Reward? Do you truly believe he will share what he would not before?"

They spoke of her…

"Best we pull back ere the sun shows," one said, then they moved away.

When they went from sight, Em wrapped her arms around her head and thanked the Lord.

Minutes passed, then once more she heard movement. Had Campagnon's men returned?

"Where are you, Em?"

She lurched upright, stumbled sideways, and once more felt the prick of thorns as she set eyes on Guarin D'Argent.

Of a sudden, he was before her, lifting her from the bushes and stiffening when she threw her arms around him.

"Ca-Camp," she gasped.

He jerked. "Campagnon?"

She nodded.

"He is here?"

She shook her head.

"Then what, Em?" he growled.

*Cease,* she silently commanded. *You are not a child. You are not helpless. Be what Hawisa and Vitalis made of a beaten, runaway slave.*

It was not easy to let go of solid rock and return to what felt like sand, but she unhooked her arms and stepped back. Noting his hand on his sword, she said, "Two of his men." Her words barely a whisper, she cleared her throat. "I heard them coming and hid."

He swept up the dagger she had dropped and offered his other hand. "The sooner you are within Wulfen's walls, the sooner my men and I can indulge in the sport of unexpected prey."

She gripped his hand, and he frowned over the face she turned up.

Realizing how pricked she was, she said, "Thorn bushes, naught compared to what could have happened."

"For that, much I shall enjoy this day's hunt." He passed her dagger to her. When she sheathed it, he started to draw her from the wood.

A branch snapped, and of a sudden his sword was before him and she was behind—and praying this time the animal was four-legged, even were it a boar.

"Show yourself!" Dougray's brother demanded.

A rustle sounded from the right, then silence as if whatever was there dared not breathe.

"Draw your dagger and remain here," the Baron of Wulfen said low and lunged.

More rustling and branches snapping as a figure of exceeding height, narrow breadth, and balding head emerged from behind a tree.

Recognizing him, Em nearly choked. Though he had a sword to hand, he sprang opposite to take the same path as his fellow mercenaries.

The one who had fallen behind the others, likely due to the need to relieve himself, was fortunate to be gifted with long-reaching legs, more that he was but one of several trespassers. Hardly had Guarin gone from sight than he returned.

"Almighty! There could be others, and I dare not leave you unprotected."

Was that what Waleran had hoped—to circle back and take her once Guarin was distant?

Trembling, Em returned the dagger to her belt. "I recognized him as well. His name is Waleran. If he heard us, and I believe he did, he shall confirm to Campagnon I am here."

"Not if I bring him to ground." Guarin took her arm and hastened her across the meadow.

Shortly, he gave her into Hawisa and Margaret's care. And departed Wulfen Castle.

CAMPAGNON WOULD HAVE SENT men ahead, of that Dougray was certain. Thus, Maël, Guy and he had paused on the journey only to water and feed the horses—and themselves. But it was Dougray and Guy alone whom Hawisa greeted in the great hall, Maël having veered toward Stern Castle to do his cousin's bidding. Grudgingly.

It was one thing to learn how Dougray had gained another cousin, another to learn what now Dougray hoped to gain.

"So soon returned to us," the Lady of Wulfen said as the weary travelers halted at the center of the hall. "I am pleased." She held out a hand.

"I thank you, my lady." Dougray brushed his lips across her knuckles, then introduced her to Guy. Catching the slight widening of her eyes ahead of her welcoming the chevalier to Wulfen, he guessed she knew this was no mere chevalier but kin.

"Those at training told my brother is hunting," Dougray said.

Hawisa's smile thinned. "So he is," she said with what sounded disapproval.

Had husband and wife argued? "When do you expect him to return, my lady?"

She clasped her hands beneath her abdomen, and he noted the swelling above. Though still slight, no longer could it be thought the result of a hearty meal. The babe pressed its way into the world.

And Dougray was struck by the desire to have this for himself.

It might not be possible, but it would not be for lack of effort. For that he was here.

"I believe the Baron of Wulfen will return soon," Hawisa said. "He is keen on this particular prey."

"Then a fine meal we shall enjoy this eve."

There was something sly about her laughter, but it was lovely, another thing he wanted—for Em. "Ah nay, Dougray. Guarin hunts animals, but they are not for the table."

Understanding struck, though not as hard as it would have had he not guessed Campagnon had sent men ahead. And now he knew what had sounded like disapproval had not been directed at the lady's husband but those who trespassed on Wulfrith lands.

"Campagnon," Dougray said.

She inclined her head. "At least three of his men in the wood during the morning run." Her brow creased. "Worry not, but it was Em who sighted them."

"How?" he barked.

She turned. "You brought the chill inside. Let us speak before the fire and see you refreshed with drink and viands."

It did not take long to reel out the tale though it felt an hour, Dougray being eager to verify Em was well. Then it was his tale he unwound—the one begun with William before the long ride and the one to come that would soon see the Lady of Wulfen welcoming more Normans into her home.

"I thank you, my lady. Now—"

She held up a hand. "There is another thing you should know. Michel Roche himself delivered Margaret to Wulfen Castle." She glanced at his cousin.

Something Dougray had not expected, nor to be tugged between gratitude and disappointment that he had not been here when the Baron of Stavestone appeared. "That was good of him."

"He has not departed, Dougray."

Once more, he was tugged between gratitude and

disappointment. As the only other occupants of the hall were two servants, he asked, "Where is the Baron of Stavestone?"

"He enjoys the hunt as well."

Dougray frowned. "I would not expect my brother to welcome his company."

"As Wulfen lands are not the only ones to suffer the trespass of mercenaries, Roche is not merely company. During the retreat from Stafford, Campagnon heard there was a woman at Stavestone with mismatched eyes. By the time he arrived, Em was gone. The baron permitted him and his men to verify no such woman was inside his walls and provided a night's lodging, but upon departing Stavestone, they attacked a village."

Feeling Guy's anger rise with his own, Dougray said, "Then the hunt is Baron Roche's due," and wondered if any of Campagnon's men would survive. Best none, for much Dougray would be tempted to slay those eager for the reward Em had told Hawisa she overheard Campagnon offered the man who recaptured her. Not that it would be murder, but neither would there be mercy.

Dougray stood. "As I would like to speak with Em, I believe Sir Guy can reveal the purpose of my visit."

"I will take you to her," Hawisa said, then to Guy, "I will not be long in returning."

At the tower room to which she led Dougray, she tapped on the door.

Margaret opened it, smiled at Hawisa and a bit more at Dougray.

"She sleeps?" Hawisa asked.

The woman nodded.

Hawisa motioned her forward, and Margaret stepped from the room. "I leave her to you, Dougray."

Though he believed he had given his brother's wife cause to trust him alone with Em, it was unseemly. Still, he was grateful.

As the door closed, he strode to the bed where Em lay on her side with knees drawn up, dark hair spilling over the pillow, tresses pooled between nape and upper back.

Dougray stared at the woman whose breath gently moved the blanket drawn over her shoulder. Just as the loose fist tucked beneath her chin was thorn-pricked, so was her face. Surprisingly, her brow was smooth as of one whose sleep is untroubled. Also of note was the absence of shadows beneath her eyes, evidencing her stay at Wulfen had been peaceful before this day. Though it made him loath to awaken her, they must talk.

"Em?"

When she did not respond, he nearly lowered to the mattress, but he feared her reaction after what she had witnessed this day. He touched her shoulder. "It is Dougray."

Her eyes opened, gaze shot up him. No fear, no alarm, only disbelief, then she gave a cry and sprang onto her knees. Landing hard against his chest, she wrapped her arms around him.

He could not move. After what had happened on the gatehouse between them, and what she had faced in the wood this day, this he did not expect. He knew she was not untouchable, but perhaps here proof that, given time, she would be entirely touchable. But even if never, he was decided on her future. Rather, *their* future.

She raised her face. "You are truly here."

"I am. For you."

She smiled, showing so many pretty teeth he wanted to kiss her. "How did you know? 'Twas only this morn…" Her smile faltered. "Or was it? Have I slept—?"

"Aye, this morn, and Lady Hawisa told me all."

"Then you are not here because of Campagnon?"

"That miscreant did bring me to Wulfen since he follows the men sent ahead to ensure you do not slip away ere he arrives with the king."

Releasing him, she sat back on her heels. "Surely William does not come for me?"

"He wishes to look upon Wulfen and see the work done here, but he does intend to uphold England's law regarding slavery."

"Heavenly Father." She sent her gaze around the chamber as if to search out a hiding place. "I cannot stay. To do so would endanger all here. When shall Campagnon and the king arrive?"

"Likely the morrow, but—"

"Then I must leave."

As she dropped her legs over the mattress, Dougray jutted his chin at the chairs before the brazier. "There is something we must discuss."

Em considered the man she loved. Though she believed he would aid her in fleeing the one who would order Hawisa and her husband to yield her to Campagnon, something in Dougray's expression gave her pause.

She touched the mattress. "Sit beside me."

After a hesitation, he lowered.

"Ere you speak, I have an answer for you, Dougray. I will do as you wish and leave England—will go to France or wherever you think best."

He lifted her hand and ran his thumb over her knuckles. "I know not whether the best place for you is England or France, Em."

If the former, then he concurred with his brother a convent would serve. Though she balked at confinement and feared she would not long tolerate it were she made to feel more an object of derision than a sister in Christ, perhaps it was the place to start. On occasion her siblings could visit, and perhaps Dougray.

"Much depends on who is the best person at your side," he continued.

"You," she said and quickly added, "whether it is to France you deliver me or I remain in England."

"I speak beyond France and England. I speak beyond days and weeks."

"I do not understand."

"I speak of marriage."

Nor did she understand that since it sounded as if he meant to make her his bride. She believed he felt more for her than desire, but enough to risk the king's wrath and defy the laws of England which would require he flee her country and eschew his own? It was too great a sacrifice, and though she did not believe herself as broken as she had given him cause to think, even greater the sacrifice of taking a badly used woman to wife.

"Em."

Realizing she had lowered her eyes, she returned them to his.

"You know I speak of wedding you, do you not?"

"Me?" The word was nearly all breath.

"You. This day."

She wished his smile was not taut, that this one to whom she believed she could be a wife in the fullest sense truly wished to be her husband. It would make what he was willing to sacrifice less painful—were she to accept.

Looking to her hand in his, she struggled to suppress the longing to feel his blunt fingers and broad palm sliding over her jaw and around the back of her neck to kiss her.

"Em?"

On the verge of tears, she said, "I thank you. Simply knowing you would do that for me makes me feel more whole."

He released her, and just as she wished, moved his hand to her jaw and tilted her face up. But that was all.

*For the best,* she told herself as he searched her moist eyes.

"I shall save you as well as I can, Em."

"Why?"

"As you know, I care for you. Beneath my protection, I believe I can return you to a good life, in time perhaps better than the one Campagnon stole."

Certain he could not know the magnitude of that sacrifice, she said, "I am grateful, but I must decline. Did you wed me here in England and were we captured—"

"Lady Hawisa has revealed the consequences of wedding a slave," he spoke over her.

And still he thought to save her? Chest aching, she said, "Then you know you would jeopardize your own freedom—that if you wished to stay with me, you would answer to Campagnon, that if you could not tolerate it and must leave me to him, never could you wed another being bound to me with holy vows?"

"Em—"

"And were we to have children, they would belong to him."

Something glanced across his eyes, and she guessed he had been unaware of that last. "It would never get that far," he said gruffly.

"But the law—"

"I would break it, just as I would this day in wedding you—in speaking holy vows that give me the right in the sight of God, the Church, and all men of good repute to be the only man with whom you lie."

He made it sound simple, but it was far from that. It was not merely labor Campagnon wanted from her. If he had to make her a widow to satisfy the carnal, he would. "Nay, Dougray, it is an unnecessary risk. All I require is to enter a convent else go across the sea. You need not wed me for that."

He leaned nearer. "Were we captured ere reaching our destination, I would be held accountable and, regardless of my punishment, you would be Campagnon's again once he can prove he owns you. If you are my wife, a thief I would be but, of greater import, your husband. And I believe the king more likely to intercede on our behalf."

"*Our* behalf? I am a rebel, a slave, a commoner. Though William may esteem you and your family, you will be tainted by your association with me."

"I might agree had not the king warned me Campagnon and he were to ride on Wulfen Castle and gave me a half day's lead.

William is a dangerous man, but in some small measure, he is sympathetic to our cause."

"Again, 'tis not *our* cause, Dougray. You must cease binding yourself to me. Were you to suffer for aiding me, I would..."

He lifted her chin higher, moved his eyes over her face with all its thorn pricks. "What?"

Great was the impulse to press a hand to her heart lest it leap out and betray feelings which his sense of obligation would make him more determined to bend her to his will. Thus, rather than admit it would break her heart, she said, "You have been very good to me. Never would I forgive myself."

"Call me selfish," he said, "but *I* could not forgive myself did I not do everything in my power to ensure never again you suffer Campagnon. Hence, en route I sent my cousin, Maël, to Stern to deliver Father Fulbert to Wulfen."

*I could more than love him,* Em thought. *I could love him fiercely, and that I dare not.*

She drew his hand from her jaw. "I will not wed you, Dougray."

"Em—"

"I will not!" She thrust up off the bed.

He also stood, but before he could argue further, a sound from beyond the window turned them in that direction.

Someone cursed—loud and venomous.

He took a step toward the window, then as if realizing the chamber afforded very little view of the inner bailey, altered his course and paused at the door. "I believe my brother returns with the trespassers."

Unless Waleran was among them and he had died resisting his pursuers before alerting any that Campagnon's slave was here, there would be no leaving Wulfen. Lest those who aided her were punished, she would have to face Campagnon and his king and hope the latter was as sympathetic as Dougray believed.

"Rest, Em," he said. "When I come again, we will resolve this."

"Only the matter of my departure," she said.

A muscle at his jaw jerked, then he was gone.

She sank down on the bed. She should have been long gone from Wulfen before Dougray's return. But even were Waleran silenced, with Le Bâtard and Campagnon soon to arrive, it was too late to devise a means of escaping alone and unnoticed.

"Lord, methinks the end is near," she whispered. "Let it not prove ill for the man I love."

# CHAPTER TWENTY-SIX

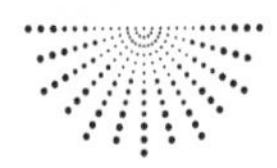

Here a face Dougray knew, and he was ten-fold more grateful Em had escaped those who stalked her.

"Robert," he named the man as the Baron of Stavestone could not do though twice the mercenary had been a guest in his hall.

"Oui, that is it," said Michel who had good cause to want Robert dead the same as the other mercenary who had fought Guarin rather than yield.

"Robert tells there are a dozen more mercenaries in my wood," Guarin said, "but thus far, no sign."

Dougray glanced at his brother, Guy, and Michel, then looked nearer on the man he hunkered alongside in the dim cell cut from rock beneath the outer wall.

Teeth partially bared, lids narrowed, Robert glared.

"A dozen, you say." Dougray chuckled. "The downfall of many a liar is the tendency to so greatly exaggerate it renders the words they vomit unbelievable. Thus, I wager no others spy on my brother's lands."

"A wager you would lose," Robert spat.

"Even did I, what sorry tale might they carry to Campagnon of your fate and that of your companion? That you parted company and have not been seen since? Not unusual in a wood teeming with wild things. That they believe you slain by men of Wulfen? Not unusual with trespassers mistaken for rebels. Hence, whatever the task Campagnon set you, you have disappointed him, and can hardly be missed."

Dougray waited for the mercenary to turn threatening, to warn the one named Waleran who evaded those of Wulfen had recognized by sight, voice, or words it was Em in the wood. But Robert made no threat as he should for leverage against death. Thus, it was unlikely he knew his fellow mercenary had witnessed what he and his companion had not.

*Unlikely,* Dougray mulled, then determined one more push might cause the man to speak and leaned nearer. "It appears you are also done for, though not honorably with a sword in hand. I am thinking such a coward deserves to swing from a rope."

Robert's teeth scraped across one another, then he jerked at the chained strung from manacled wrists to bolts in the wall on either side. "A pity," he bit. "I had hoped to be present when Sir Raymond makes good his promise to pass around his whore when his collar is once more around her pretty neck, her leash in hand. Know you what I would do with that collar and leash?"

His head struck the wall hard, as evidenced by a crack echoing around the cell. Gasping and blinking, he looked to Dougray's bunched fist, then laughed past yellowed teeth rimmed in red. "I believe Campagnon is right in believing she is here. Tell me, whoreson, how many times have you had that dirty little wench?"

This time it was a blow to the nose that knocked his head against the wall, making him shout amid a spray of blood. If not for those who dragged Dougray back, a third blow might have forever silenced the miscreant.

"Cease!" Guarin barked on one side of him.

"Enough, Son," Michel rumbled low.

*Son.* More than his brother's rebuke, that word spoken for him alone made what boiled ease. Still hot enough to burn but not splash on those it should not.

As Dougray stared into eyes whose color mirrored his own, he wondered why he did not lash out at the man who claimed him as if ever he had been present in the life of the child Robine birthed.

"Forgive me," Michel Roche murmured. "I speak with the heart rather than mind."

Looking to his brother who continued to grip his other arm, Dougray put between his teeth, "I suppose we must keep him alive?"

Guarin glanced at Robert whose nose and mouth dripped blood onto his tunic. "We are D'Argents. We take life only in defense of our own and the lives of others."

Dougray did not believe those first words were meant to hurt Michel, but knew they did. And for some reason, that further cooled Dougray's ire. "So we do," he begrudged.

Guarin released him, jutted his chin at Robert. "Too, I would not be surprised if William wishes to speak to the mercenary in his pay who ought to be hunting rebels rather than trespassing on one of his barons."

*True,* Dougray acceded as Michel loosed him. And since William had provided Dougray time to reach Wulfen ahead of him, he would not be pleased Campagnon sought to go around him.

Guarin turned aside. "Come. If Maël delivers this day, and great ill would have to befall him does he not, we must prepare for the arrival of Cyr and Father Fulbert."

Just as when Dougray had revealed his intentions earlier, he caught no censure in his brother's voice. Like Hawisa, the eldest D'Argent worried over the consequences of wedding Em, but unspoken was his understanding this was no mere rescue. What had glanced across those green eyes was acceptance Dougray was moved by love as Guarin had been in sacrificing his family name to take his wife's—a blow weathered for a woman he wanted above all else.

Though Dougray had been certain he knew what love was before his life became entangled with Em's, Guarin's sacrifice had baffled—even disgusted—the same as Cyr's with Aelfled. He had thought it unhealthy obsession, possibly even bewitchment, but now...

As he followed his brother from the cell ahead of Michel and Guy, he wondered if his feelings for Adela, stirred in the crucible of youth, had sprung from such untoward things. Certes, what he felt for Em was different—higher, wider, deeper. And worth losing all, including his dignity and freedom.

THE BRIDE SAID *NAY.* Worse, now it was known Waleran had escaped capture, neither would she depart Wulfen.

Silently, Dougray berated himself for believing fear for the tale being carried to Campagnon would cause Em to accept his offer of marriage. Long he had known she was no longer the hunched young woman whom that miscreant had named *Wench,* but he had not expected her to stand firm when faced with being reunited with him. She was resigned to whatever she might suffer lest any who aided in her escape, including Fulbert and Cyr who awaited them in the solar, were punished.

He stepped nearer. "There is no time to argue, Em. Should King William and Campagnon not arrive this eve, they shall ere noon on the morrow. If you will not wed me, we must leave now."

She raised her chin higher. "I am done running from Campagnon and endangering all between him and me. I will stand before him in sight of your king and demand he produce my papers to prove he has the right to ill use my body."

Dougray looked to Margaret who stood beside the window

and saw she pressed her lips in an expression of regret. Other than by force, she did not believe Em would depart Wulfen.

He returned his regard to Em, searched for a way around her determination, and reached to her.

She glanced at his hand. "I say one last time—no more shall I run from him."

He groaned. "Though great the longing to bind, gag, and drag you across the channel, I will not. Now take my hand. There is something I must tell you."

Hesitantly, she set cool fingers in his.

"I thought I knew my heart ere you, Em, what it wanted and needed—"

Sudden movement reminded him they were not alone, then Margaret hastened past, yanked open the door, and closed it behind her.

He smiled. "What I believed best for this heart was a woman named Adela for whom I betrayed my conscience in seeking my fortune so this misbegotten warrior would prove worthy of a noble lady otherwise out of reach. Instead, I lost a sword arm—and the love she professed when she saw I was no longer whole."

Anger flashed in Em's eyes.

"When she wed a nobleman with lands aplenty, bitterly I isolated myself, believing my heart so broken never would it mend. And so it was."

Em's eyes moistened.

Thinking it possible now he was breaking her heart, he stepped nearer. "But that was the heart of a boy. This..." He pressed her hand to his chest. "...is the heart of a man—stronger, more certain, more fierce, more desperate to spend its every beat upon you."

A small sound escaped her, and he felt her trembling move from her palm to his heart.

"A man's love is what I feel for you, Em."

A tear spilled onto her cheek.

"Is what you feel for me a woman's love?"

"I believe so. Though I began to feel for Vitalis what I thought was love, it was not like this."

Refusing to allow jealousy to take hold of him, he said, "What is this love like?"

"More," she said with wonder, "as if not even the moon will shine do you go from me."

He drew her closer. "If you will not wed me here, let us leave now for France and we will speak vows there. I do not know what life we will make, but we will be together. Each night you will fall asleep in my arms and each morn awaken there. If you can give more, gladly I will give back and, God willing, we will be blessed with children. If you cannot, I will be as content as possible holding you."

She set a hand on his jaw. "I wish to believe you speak in truth rather than to move me to your will."

"I reveal my feelings to gain your cooperation," he admitted, "but that makes them no less true. I love you and would spend the best part of my life with you."

She swallowed loudly. "I thank you, and I pray it is possible, but not because once more I flee. Because in facing Campagnon, the lord provides a way past him."

"Em—"

She set fingers against his lips. "Pray with me. Add your voice to mine in beseeching light for us amid this darkness."

He hesitated. Never had he prayed with one other than a priest, and even then few were the words he himself addressed to the Lord. It would make him uncomfortable to do so as if they were man and wife kneeling alongside their bed ere slipping beneath the covers. But until she was free of Campagnon, this was as near as they would come.

"Will you, Dougray?"

He would. And more.

He took her hand and led her to the bed where they knelt.

"Lord, in Your sight alone, I take this woman, more pure and lovely than any I have known, for my wife."

Em snapped up her chin, looked to the one whose words sought to wed him to a woman in the ways of old as King Harold had done with his first wife, Edith Swan-neck, whom he had renounced to gain the throne of England. Less than a year after taking another wife in the manner approved by the Church, he had died at Hastings, having yielding up his beloved Edith for naught. Would this handfasting prove for naught?

"Em?"

Rather than refuse him, she said, "I would have your word this is between us and God alone."

"You have the word of a D'Argent."

"Also the word of a Roche?"

His eyes flickered, but he nodded. "And a Roche."

She pulled the end of the ribbon with which she had gathered back her hair, and as tresses caped her back, began to wind the narrow strip around their joined hands as was tradition. Then she lowered her chin and closed her eyes. "Heavenly Father, in Your sight alone, I take this man, worthier and more whole than any I have known, to be my husband this day, this night, and however many more days and nights you gift us. Even if they are no more or few, I thank you for aiding him in putting me back together and for every moment between now and our last. Wife and Husband."

"Husband and wife," Dougray answered. "Ever and ever, here on earth and there above. Amen."

They remained thus several minutes, during which Em added to her prayers, then she unwound the ribbon and sat back on her heels. "I could die this day and be happy as I thought never to be again."

"As could I, but our end will not come this day nor the morrow."

She wanted to remind him of Campagnon, but he needed no

reminding. That man would remain between them unless the Lord did a mighty work.

"Will you come to the solar, Em?"

Where his family, Eberhard, and Father Fulbert expected to witness a marriage of which the Church would approve though not the laws of England.

"I think it best I remain here."

"You fear being pressed to wed me in public?"

"As I will not be moved on this, nay. What I am is tired and cautious in making those in the solar more complicit. I shall eat my supper here."

"As you will, my lady."

She startled. "Lady?"

*"My* lady, the wife of a chevalier."

"None can know," she reminded him.

"Not yet." He pulled her up and drew her against him. "A kiss to seal our vows, Lady Emma?"

She slid her arms around his neck and offered her mouth.

It was a hungry kiss, but it more thrilled than frightened, and she parted her lips and kissed him back, breathed his breath, gave him hers. And when he ended it, she said, "It is different when there is love. Given the chance, I will be a wife in full to you, Dougray. Bear with me, and in time I will see and feel no other but you."

He kissed her brow. "If the king and Campagnon do not appear this day, may I come to you this eve?"

"Th-this eve?"

"Only to hold you. For now."

"What of Margaret?"

He smiled crookedly. "I forgot about her. Regardless, I shall pause to wish you a good eve." He released her and was halfway to the door when she felt the soft between her fingers and looked to the ribbon that had handfasted them. When Eberhard had gifted it a sennight past, having purchased it from a traveling merchant, he had said it was the same shade as her one blue eye.

"Dougray!" She hastened forward and held up the ribbon. "Keep it for me—for us."

He raised his eyebrows. "I think you ought to keep it for us."

"Nay, you." She frowned. "What is it called when a lady gives something upon her person to her champion at tourney?"

"A favor."

She nodded. "I would have you wear it in remembrance of me."

"Remembrance? You are not forgettable, Em, will be with me always."

Suppressing the longing to go into his arms again, she said, "As you will be with me. Will you wear it?"

He raised his hand. "As my lady wishes."

She wrapped the ribbon thrice around his wrist and finished it with two knots. "I will see you this eve," she said, then leaned up and brushed her mouth across his.

When the last of his footsteps sounded on the stairs, she closed the door and whispered, "I love. Am loved. Pray, Lord, make a way."

# CHAPTER TWENTY-SEVEN

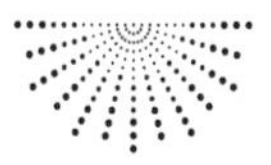

Nicola the Reckless, as dubbed by Guarin years past, once more earned the name that made her smile and laugh though their mother told it should cause her to blush, lower her eyes, and strive to be worthy of the title *Lady* and the name D'Argent.

No easy feat being the lone female child in the midst of four older brothers and a cousin. Add to that those their uncle had trained into warriors within their home and the abundance of male influence far outweighed her lady mother's, especially as Robine had few friends left following revelation of her tryst with Michel Roche.

Thus, it was hardly surprising the youngest of the D'Argents, now ten and seven, had defied Cyr when he refused to allow her to accompany Father Fulbert and him. Following their departure of Stern, she had struck out on her own, arriving at Wulfen a half hour behind them whilst Dougray was abovestairs attempting to persuade Em to wed him. Upon his return to the solar, he found her in the midst of disapproval so thick it felt a fog.

Whatever had been told her about Michel Roche, whose name she would recognize, could not have satisfied. Now, more than standing witness to her brother's wedding, she would wish to learn of the circumstances that brought their mother's indiscretion face to face with the result of that indiscretion. But that must wait.

"Truly, she refuses to wed you after we came all this way?" Nicola exclaimed, peering over her shoulder as Hawisa led her toward the tapestry to escort her to a tower room by way of the wall passages.

"Truly," Dougray said. "There will be no wedding to miss out on, little sister."

"Very well, but why must I leave?" She pulled free of Hawisa. "Why can I not dine with you and speak of the arrival of the king and that vile Campagnon?"

"Because you are more girl than woman," Guarin said harshly where he stood beside the hearth. "Because you crossed unsettled lands without an escort."

"An escort I would have had if—"

"Because to ease your aunt and sister-in-law's concern, I had to send a man across the darkening of day to assure them you are safe. Because you are impulsive and reckless. Because whatever shall be said here is not for one who will only hinder if she does not harm."

Each punctuated sentence caused her jaw to drop a degree, and now nearly all those pretty teeth were visible. As was the flood of tears.

"Come, Nicola." Hawisa cupped her elbow. "It was a long ride, and you are weary. Let us leave the men to their talk."

A tear fell from an eye that was the same green as all her silvered dark-haired brothers. "I am sorry," she said and looked from her sister-in-law to Dougray. "I wished to be here for you and Em."

It gladdened him she was eager to accept into their family the slave who belonged to Campagnon, though it did not surprise. Unlike he who had held in much the day they arrived upon

Wulfenshire and passed the night at Castle Balduc, his sister had not disguised her outrage over the treatment Em suffered that evidenced slavery enjoyed a brisk trade in England.

"I did not mean to be…" She cleared her throat. "…a burden."

Not for the first time, he saw her glance at Guy, but for the first time her cheeks spotted. It was shame enough being upbraided in the presence of strangers, but more the presence of one who moved the woman she was becoming.

Dougray strode to her, halted, and set his hand on her arm. "You should not have done as you did. None of us could bear to lose you, and that you risked, Nicola. I thank you for wishing to be with us, and were Father Fulbert to do as summoned"—he glanced at the big man near Cyr—"I would have you remain, but the best place for you is abovestairs the same as Em."

Her lips moved in a prettier direction. "I thank you, Brother," she said and turned.

It was then Dougray saw the Lady of Wulfen's eyes upon him, but not his face—rather, his wrist bound with a hair ribbon.

Her frown eased, then yet another lady found something over which to smile.

"May I visit with your Em?" his sister asked as Hawisa drew her toward the tapestry.

*My Em,* Dougray mused. *So she is.*

"You may not," Guarin said. "There are consequences for disobedience and recklessness, and this is one of them. You shall remain in your chamber, and if I suspect you stepped outside it, you will be locked within until this business with Campagnon and the king is finished."

Her eyes widened, and Dougray expected her to argue, but she closed her mouth and went behind the tapestry.

"Now we talk." Guarin motioned to the table, at one end of which were stacked journals.

Much was required to administer Wulfen's lands, Dougray acknowledged as he and the others settled at the table. Though

Hawisa resented losing Castle Balduc to the son of the Norman she had slain at Hastings for attempting to ravish her, it seemed a good thing that chevalier would soon claim his sire's reward. Unless he proved vengeful…

Though Theriot was acquainted with Estienne Lavonne and did not believe the man would retaliate—at least, not in any way ruinous—it remained to be seen.

A quarter hour later, Hawisa returned. In response to her husband's raised eyebrows, she said, "Best I take her in hand." She looked to Cyr. "'Tis in her blood. If she is not taught how to make good use of what courses her veins, it could be the end of her and possibly others." Her gaze swung back to Guarin. "Will you allow it?"

A growl sounded from him. "Nicola at Wulfen?"

"Discreetly, the same as Em, but training beyond the morning run."

At his silence, she said, "It began with you when you taught her the bow and a dagger's throw to provide a release for all inside her wanting out and to give her a means of defending and providing for herself. It was enough then. It is not enough now in this England where men like Campagnon take and abuse what they want. As lovely as your sister is, until such time as she makes a good match, she must protect herself from herself—and predators. And I speak not only of weapons but awareness, control, strategy, stealth."

Guarin nodded slowly. "The king will not like it."

More than not like it, Dougray knew. Though Hawisa had proved exceedingly worthy at wielding weapons and training women in the ways of the warrior whilst rebelling against William, upon yielding to him, the king had refused to permit her to gift her Wulfrith training to others of the fairer sex. But surely she did and would continue to do so.

Hawisa lowered into the chair to the right of her husband, raised and dropped a shoulder. "For that, William will not know."

She flicked her gaze to Michel and Guy. "I pray I am not mistaken in believing what is spoken here remains here?"

"It stays, my lady," Michel said.

"It concerns me not," Guy agreed.

"Husband?"

Guarin looked to Cyr, then Dougray and Maël. "What say you? Do we give Nicola what she wants and my wife believes she needs —and with which I agree grudgingly? Or do we wed her to a man who, if she does not break him, may break her?"

"Forcing us to break him," Cyr said, also grudgingly.

"Bad all around," Dougray concurred.

"Maël?" Guarin put to him.

Their cousin, sitting well back in his chair, stretched his legs longer. "She is a D'Argent, but more she is your sister. It is not for me to set her on any path."

"She has been as much a sister to you as to us," Guarin reminded.

"So she has, and I care much for her, but I will have no say in this. However, as best I can, I shall support whatever you decide."

"Father Fulbert?" Guarin asked.

The priest, recently wed to their widowed aunt ahead of Church reform that would bar men of God from taking wives, leaned forward. "Though Nicola is of good heart, much she challenges my lady wife. Thus, I do not know warrior training will be of greater benefit than detriment. It could make her more reckless."

Guarin sighed. "A decision that ought not be made quickly, so let us return to the more pressing matter." He jutted his chin at Dougray. "If Em is determined to stand before Campagnon and the king, I agree we step back. So tell, when, where, and how do we step forward if she is unable to extricate herself?"

Something else that must be thought through, but could not be set aside. Whether William was now a single stride from Wulfen's walls or thousands, he was coming.

"England's roads and woods have never been so dangerous. Much unseen and unheard can happen on and in them." Dougray sent his gaze around the table, and not one of those present asked his meaning. And that meaning?

Were he to lose Em to Campagnon, he would take her back. Then to France husband and wife would go, never to return.

~

No William this eve. The morrow, then.

Middle night two hours distant, Dougray eased open the door.

The light of a puddling candle lit Em where she sat on the bed, knees clasped to her chest, raised lids revealing glittering eyes. "I began to think you would not come," she said low lest she awaken Margaret who slept in the chair before the brazier.

Dougray entered, closed the door, and crossed to the foot of the bed. "There was much to discuss. Though they are not outside the walls, soon they shall be."

She reached to him. "I know we are not alone, but lest this is all we have left to us, will you not sit with me awhile?"

He came around and, when she scooted to the center of the bed, lowered to the warm place she had been. It seemed wrong to do so with his feet and legs encased in boots but more wrong to remove them though her hair ribbon evidenced he could be with her this night.

"Draw nearer," she said.

"Only possible if I remove my boots."

"Why would you not?"

"As you say, we are not alone."

"Margaret's sleep is of the deep as I pray one day mine shall be," Em said.

He would make it so, Dougray determined, then dragged off his boots, swung his legs onto the mattress, and leaned back against the headboard. He wanted to pull her against his side and settle her head on his chest so she might sleep the night through, but just as he felt Campagnon's presence, surely she did.

And yet she ducked beneath his arm, turned into his side, and settled his hand on her waist. "I will not be afeared of you, Dougray," she whispered, "not this night, not any night. I will not count the seconds and minutes ere you sleep so I can slip away and find my rest in the farthest corner lest too soon I come to notice."

He was mildly surprised by words that better explained her awakening at Stavestone, but not by greater desire to ensure Campagnon never again harmed her or any woman. And come the morrow, no matter William's part in the attempt to reclaim Em, by day's end she would be free of the Norman who was among the worst of those who trespassed on England.

All was in place. God willing, those who aided Em and him would pass unscathed through the needle's eye of the king's patience.

Em drew her hand over his wrist, slid her fingers beneath the ribbon, and settled their tips below his knuckles. "I love you, Dougray."

"I love you. Now sleep."

"I am afraid to, not because I shall find myself here with you when I awaken, because I might not."

He kissed the top of her head. "I must rise early, but I will not leave without awakening you."

*Not for a parting kiss,* he told himself. *For the first of many kisses we shall share on the morrow.* "Sleep now, my lady."

It was an hour before her breathing turned slow and even, then Dougray also slept and was awakened only once when she stiffened. But he had only to tell her he loved her and she drifted off again.

Love would heal her, he assured himself, just as it had healed him.

# CHAPTER TWENTY-EIGHT

The nooning hour came. The nooning hour went. Then the patrol, among them Eberhard, pounded over the drawbridge bearing tidings William and his entourage of six score were sighted between Balduc and Stern. If they maintained their current pace, they would be outside Wulfen's walls two hours hence. If they put spurs to their mounts, within an hour.

When the great doors had been flung open to admit the patrol, Em had risen from before the hearth with the talkative Nicola. Now that the warriors gathered around the high table had their report, Eberhard descended the dais.

Dragging her gaze from Dougray who had kept his word to awaken her before his departure this morn, Em opened her arms to her brother.

He embraced her fiercely, in a strained voice said, "'Tis not too late to allow Sir Dougray to take you from here."

"Nay, I would finish it this day," she said, then recalling his attempt upon Darfield to slay the one who abused her, drew back. "You must promise to go nowhere near Campagnon. No matter the outcome, you will be strong and not deny me the happiness of knowing yours is a good life here upon Wulfen."

His mouth twitched. "You would not wish me to lie, so do not ask that of me. I know I am yet as nothing against seasoned warriors, but I am no coward."

Then as feared, what was healed between Hawisa and him might turn diseased again, the lady having assured Em she would set Ordric near Eberhard to prevent him from succumbing to foolishness.

Em inclined her head and stepped back. "You are your own man," she flattered though it was mostly his due. "I but hope whatever comes to pass, you will not forget there is still Tristan and Flora."

His jaw shifted. "I will see them again, as shall you."

"Of course we shall."

"Squire Eberhard," the Baron of Wulfen called. "Choose four to serve at high table, six to serve below the salt."

"Aye, my lord."

"And from the moment our king enters, speak Norman-French only, even those not yet proficient."

"Oui, my lord."

Guarin D'Argent raised an eyebrow. "Lesson eight, Squire Eberhard."

To Em's surprise, her brother's mouth lightened. "When finding one's self at great disadvantage, woo the devil so he not look to your backside."

The baron nodded. "Of great import this day."

"Indeed, my lord."

"What does it mean?" Em whispered as Eberhard strode opposite. Though she had been given lessons to sharpen her mind during rebel training, this one seemed part riddle. However, she made sense of it a moment later.

When a hand touched her arm, she remembered she kept company with Dougray's sister. "My eldest brother is adept at wooing," Nicola said. "Had I to guess, he tells your brother there is strength and gain in letting a powerful enemy believe he is worthy of high regard."

As thought…

"Oh, to be gifted such learning and make use of it beyond the duties of a lady," Nicola bemoaned, then wrinkled her nose. "I know I sound spoiled, and having been born to privilege ought to sit at my embroidery frame without complaint, but…" A half-hearted shrug. "All my life I have stood on the woman's side of this fence, so near the other side I hardly notice the planks barring my way, so near it is no strain to see much of what is denied me for being born fifth rather than fourth, so near I can scale it…with my fingertips touch the forbidden." She shook her head. "I do not wish to be a man, but like you, I would know better how to protect myself in the absence of a champion."

Em wondered how it was possible to like the young woman so much and so soon. Nicola did not yet know a handfasting made them sisters, and yet every word, smile, and gesture since Em was invited belowstairs to partake of the nooning meal was delivered as if this noble lady and this slave were equals.

Eyes stinging, Em realized she was near to tears.

"Selfish, petty Nicola!" the young woman berated and set a hand on Em's shoulder. "Forgive me for filling your ears with whining. But fear not, you could not hope for better champions than my brothers and cousin. All will come right, and that dirty Campagnon will scoot off with his tail between his legs." She turned thoughtful, added, "That is, does he live."

A bubble of laughter escaped Em. "I thank you, Lady Nicola. Your kindness gives my heart ease." Still, it beat hard and she was too warm for the end of autumn that had caused her to seek the fire.

She plucked at the gown that had belonged to Michel Roche's wife and which Hawisa had instructed her to wear now her presence at Wulfen was to be known to all. So much curiosity had thrummed from the boys and youths during the meal, especially those near enough to confirm her mismatched eyes, she had sought to distract herself by conversing with another curiosity—Nicola, who appeared merely amused by the attention.

Em tugged at the bodice again, ran her finger from one side of the neck to the other.

"You are well?" the younger woman asked.

"Only frightened."

"Only?" Nicola took a step back and ran her gaze down Em. "That is a fine gown but aged and not well enough fitted to show your figure at its best." She placed splayed hands on either side of her waist as if to measure it, reached them forward and touched Em's sides, nodded. "And your hair..." She considered the braids tautly worked back off Em's face. "Methinks Eberhard's lesson eight applies here. We have an hour, mayhap more."

"For?"

Her smile was so bright, one might think to shade their eyes. "You do not look a slave, but just barely a lady."

"I am not a lady," Em said, then recalled she was that to Dougray. When it was revealed to others, it was as she would be titled.

"Nicola!" called Hawisa, who had moved from her husband's side.

The young woman spun around. "Sister?"

"I am pleased Em and you become friends."

"So we do," Nicola said when Hawisa halted before them, "and great friends we shall be."

The lady inclined her head. "There is much to do in preparation to receive..." Anger pulsed amid her hesitation. "... our *guests* whose numbers we underestimated. Hence, may I entrust Em to you?"

"Of course! I was about to suggest she accompany me to my chamber."

"For?"

"As you know, I packed well for my journey to Wulfen."

Understanding brightened Hawisa's face. "You are clever, Nicola. Methinks something must be done about that."

"Done?"

The lady waved a hand. "Something we shall discuss later. Now take Em and Margaret abovestairs, and let us see how adept you are at wooing..." Another hesitation. "...Le Bâtard."

~

"DO NOT LOOK, EM."

She had to. Lifting the skirt of the gown fashioned from fabric heretofore unimaginable, Em stepped around Nicola who had hastened to the window at the sound of approaching riders.

"Non!" The other woman tried to catch her back.

She slipped free, and two more strides delivered her to the unshuttered window through which a cool breeze entered Nicola's tower room. High and situated at the front of the donjon, it allowed one to see much of the land between the castle's outer wall and the wood.

Scores of mounted warriors rode on Wulfen amid streaming pennants that proclaimed the usurper had arrived. Doubtless, he was the figure at the fore, and somewhere amid horse flesh, emblazoned tunics, flashing armor and weapons was the one who had bought her at auction.

"Raymond Campagnon," she forced his name across her tongue.

"Come away, Em."

This time she did not pull free.

Nicola returned her to the center of the room and considered her handiwork. "As I was saying before I interrupted myself, a fine job we have done." She nodded at Margaret who stood to the side, then moved her eyes over Em's face. "Most unfortunate those scratches, but they have lightened and a bit of powder will mostly cover them." She clicked her tongue. "Oh, to have a mirror. Much confidence it would give you. Though you were lovely before, now no one would believe you other than a lady."

When Em's attempt to smile failed, Nicola hugged her. "You belong to us now—even if *I* must kill that vile creature."

Her first words swelled Em's heart. Her last words made her smile. "I think you would try."

The young woman stepped back. "The same I would have done your rebel Vitalis had he been responsible for Guarin's near mortal injuries."

Imagining this young woman of dark, silvered hair and lithe figure drawing a sword on the immense fiery-haired Saxon warrior, Em nearly laughed. Never could Em defeat him, and more impossible it would be for a lady, even one born a D'Argent.

"If you saw Vitalis, Nicola—"

"I have seen him, but just because a man is as big as a bear does not mean he cannot be felled by a fawn. And as you must know, the bigger the beast, the harder he falls."

Em knew, but still it was laughable—until she heard the great quiet where moments earlier the din of boys and youths sounded as they clashed over weapons or wrestled one another.

Now the shouts of their trainers, doubtless commanding them to present well in welcoming their king. Next, the clang of portcullis chains. Then the clamor of drawbridge chains.

Someone patted Em's arm, and she opened her eyes to find Margaret alongside. Eyes wide, she raised her eyebrows.

"Pray for me," Em rasped.

"I sh-shall."

"She speaks!" Nicola exclaimed. "You speak!"

Margaret pressed her lips.

"You are not mute. You simply choose not to talk. Why? Are you a nun, this a vow of silence? Or do you penance for sinning?"

The woman crossed her arms over her chest.

"Very well," Nicola said on a sigh, "keep your secret, though I shall pry it out of Em."

"I know no more than you," Em said, then asked, "Will I see Dougray ere I go to the hall?"

Nicola's brow rumpled. "Unlikely now the king is here."

As thought, Dougray having all but said it this morn when he told her he wished to kiss her not as if it were the last time but as if the first of thousands of kisses across their lives.

"But Margaret and I shall accompany you," Nicola assured her.

Em lowered her eyes and tried to marvel over the soft, luminous gown that was the color of new pine needles, the hem of its long sleeves and skirts embroidered with flowers of orange and yellow. "It is kind of you to allow me to wear this, but I am curious why you brought so fine a garment to Wulfen."

"As told, I do not care to be a man. I like pretty things, so when I travel I bring at least one fine gown should there be an occasion to wear one." She touched the sleeve. "Aunt Chanson and I worked this several months past. She hopes to display me in it should my brothers find worthy suitors. Me…" She smiled wide. "I like wearing it."

Of a sudden, the noise in the outer bailey moving toward the inner increased, and Em shuddered, certain the king and the most esteemed of his entourage passed beneath the portcullis toward the donjon.

"Your hair," Nicola exclaimed and drew Em to the table. Urging her onto the stool, she said, "Make haste, Margaret. I am thinking three braids each side met at the nape and bound with a ribbon, the tail uncrossed." She bent near Em. "You will look the lady, speak the lady, and behave the lady no matter what Raymond Campagnon says or does. Do you hear me?"

Her words were so forceful, Em momentarily forgot Dougray's sister was younger than she. And she realized that, for as playful and light as Nicola presented, she had great depth.

"I hear you. I will be the lady for your King William."

"*Not* for King William, though his audience you must play to. Do it for you and Dougray."

"Why are you so kind to me?" Em asked.

"Because already I love you—though not yet as much as my sisters, Aelfled and Hawisa—as one day I shall love Theriot's wife. And if ever Maël recovers the heart lost at Hastings, I shall love his wife as well."

Em stared. Did Nicola know of the handfasting?

"I think this will be a lovely gown in which to speak vows with Dougray," Nicola said. "You may have to keep it." Then she swept up the comb and, drawing it through loosed tresses, began to hum loudly as if to muffle the voices outside.

## CHAPTER TWENTY-NINE

Did it bode worse that Campagnon rode directly behind William as if one of his companions?

No sooner did that concern settle amid rising bloodlust than another raised its head. Behind the mercenary came one whose mount quivered more than the others.

It had been night when first Dougray looked upon the man, but it was the aged merchant of much weight who had imprisoned Em in Gloucester and tasked slavers with delivering her to Campagnon.

"Who is the slovenly one amongst warriors?" Cyr spoke low where he stood alongside Dougray at the bottom of the steps.

"He to whom Em and Eberhard sold themselves into slavery."

"Almighty. Though Campagnon is absent papers, here proof she is a slave."

Dougray nodded. "Though she would not have denied it, his witness provides less room for William to give aid should he be so moved."

"He is moved," Cyr said, "else he would not have sent you ahead."

"Unless he knew Campagnon had also sent men ahead to

ensure none stole Em away," Dougray said and half hoped his brother would protest, but neither did Guarin believe their sovereign above such games. Returning his regard to the score of mounted men who advanced on those descended from the donjon, Dougray said, "I am glad you are here, Cyr."

"As am I, Brother."

Dougray was grateful for their time alone whilst breaking fast this morn. Long an apology was due the second-born whom Dougray had blamed for the loss of his arm. Though he had told himself Cyr persuaded his landless sibling to join the conquest of England, and it was true he had moved him in that direction, it was hope of winning Adela for a wife that landed Dougray on England's shore. Thus, the one responsible for his loss was the one who compromised his beliefs for gain and, in the midst of battle, let down his guard.

"Eyes forward, Dougray," Guarin spoke from his other side, alerting him once more he erred in letting down his guard.

Returning his attention to the king, he found William watched him, a frown gathering his eyebrows. Likely, he questioned Dougray's presence at Wulfen.

When the king raised a hand, causing the score of men who had accompanied him inside the walls to halt their mounts, Guarin called, "Squires, attend your king and his escort," and the eleven youths forming a line to the right hastened forward—ten to tend to two horses each, the most senior to tend William's destrier. The latter was Eberhard who had given Guarin his word he could be entrusted with so great a duty in the presence of the king he hated and Campagnon whom he hated more.

Dougray watched Em's brother and saw him firmly set his eyes on the man who could save or destroy his sister.

Halting beside William, Eberhard said in finely-accented Norman French, "Your Majesty, permit me to tend your destrier."

William eyed him. "You are?"

"Squire Eberhard."

"Saxon name. Of whose house are you?"

"The venerable, mighty house of Wulfrith."

William glanced at Hawisa who stood on Guarin's other side. "So here the false son of Roger Fortier who named himself Wulf."

The youth inclined his head. "Once more Eberhard, Your Majesty. And of recent, Eberhard Wulfrith."

William's eyebrows jumped. "Are you?"

"Oui, my liege. I am as a son to Baron Wulfrith and his lady wife."

"Born common?"

"Born common."

"Orphaned?"

Eberhard hesitated. "Orphaned, Your Majesty."

"Your sire fell at Hastings?"

"He did."

"You blame me for his death?"

A longer hesitation, then more honesty than many would venture. "He would yet live had you not crossed the channel, but with prayer and godly guidance, I draw nearer to reconciling myself to the present as my noble sire and lady mother impress upon me. As what is done cannot be undone, Normans and Saxons must look to the future—an England at peace."

"Beneath my rule," William tested him.

Did the youth's eyes waver? "Beneath the rule of my king, William the Great."

The conqueror chuckled. "I almost believe you, lad. When next we meet, I expect the Wulfriths to have delivered you firmly to my side along with the other Saxons with whom you train."

"I do not doubt it will be done, Your Majesty."

When the conqueror looked to his men and the other squires who awaited the passing of reins, Dougray shifted his regard to the man whose gaze he so intensely felt his muscles ached.

Campagnon smiled larger. Whether or not he believed Em was

here, he exulted in the honor of the king's accompaniment, believing if he did not win this day, he would win the morrow.

William slapped the reins in Eberhard's hand. "Dismount!" he commanded the others, then landed his feet near the squire's. "There is no finer steed in all of Christendom, lad. Do not disappoint me." He strode toward Guarin and Hawisa.

His welcome to Wulfen was brief because he made it so. As the squires led the horses back toward the stables, William stepped past the Lord and Lady of Wulfen. "Sir Cyr, Sir Dougray."

"Your Majesty."

He looked between the two who stood behind and to the sides. "Sir Maël, Sir Guy."

"Your Majesty."

Returning to Dougray, William said low, "As I find you at Wulfen, I assume you sent Campagnon's slave distant."

"It pains me to disappoint," Dougray said. "Emma Irwindotter is yet here, Your Majesty."

Never had he seen surprise so greatly open the king's face it made him seem more flesh and blood than stone. Then William narrowed his eyes and said, "I understand the men Campagnon sent ahead failed him, Waleran having overtaken us and reported his sighting of her in the wood."

"They did fail him, Your Majesty, and one yet lives though great the temptation he not."

"Imprisoned?"

"Oui."

The king turned thoughtful. "Is he of Normandy?"

"Flanders, my liege."

"Ah." William nodded. "Keep him locked up a sennight, then see him transported to the coast and put on a ship."

Dougray inclined his head. Since the mercenary was not of Normandy, of little esteem for failing Campagnon, and likely owed coin for uprooting rebels, this suited the king well.

"Now tell," William said. "Why is the slave here when you were provided adequate time to take her distant?"

Here confirmation he had sought to aid in accord with a conscience that warred with the need for slave trade revenues?

Dougray cleared his throat. "She wearies of running and fears endangering any accused of aiding her. Thus, she trusts you to be fair in determining her fate."

The king snorted. "That might appeal were I unaware she is a rebel who recently betrayed me at Stafford where she was injured."

Of course he knew of that.

"Hence, I am only as merciful as you have been useful to me and for the bond of Les Bâtards. Unfortunate for her, she tossed out that mercy in thinking to stand as a man who faces his enemies rather than flee as a woman ought. There is only one Hawisa Wulfrith, and I tolerate her because she is the last of a great line and I have hope she shall begin breeding Wulfriths for me."

Then he did not know Dougray's sister-in-law was with child. However, were the observant William not told, soon he would note the slight change in her face if not her figure. What, then? Would he order her to depart Wulfen and live at Stern separate from her husband? Even so, that did not mean she would.

The king looked to her. "Had I to guess, already your brother has got her with child—God be kind, the first of many boys to protect England for the generations born of my blood." He took a step back. "As I am here to see all that is Wulfen, let us be done with this matter of Campagnon's slave."

"Oui, Your Majesty."

William gestured Guarin and his wife ahead, and all entered the great hall which received them with an abundance of lit candles, rushes strewn with herbs, tables and benches positioned below the dais, platters of bread, meats, and cheeses, pitchers of wine and ale to fill Wulfen's best goblets and cups, and squires and pages standing at attention.

At the center of the hall, the king halted when the aged warrior who had declined to greet his sovereign outside rose from a chair before the hearth.

The others ceased their advance and silence fell.

"King William." Michel inclined his head.

"Methinks I see my old friend and advisor," William boomed, then veered toward the man Dougray would not have expected to be recognized after so many years, especially at a distance and looking more a Saxon than a Norman.

Did the king recognize him because he knew the one who sired Dougray would be here? Or had the youth William was when his vassal gained his permission to wed a woman believed widowed been so esteemed he remained memorable despite the passage of twenty and five years?

The two embraced and the sound of the king clapping Michel on the back resounded around the hall. "Too many years, my friend!" he boomed and drew back to look upon a face aged ten or more years beyond his own. "As you had yet to present yourself to one once your duke and now your king, I began to wonder if you had gone too Saxon to be my man again."

So he had, but Dougray prayed Michel would not confirm it and this reunion would work for the good of Em.

"Forgive me, Your Majesty, but care of my wife's people and floundering health has kept me from pledging my fealty in person. You did receive Stavestone's tribute, did you not?"

"I did, and it was generous."

"As is your due."

If one did not know Michel—not that Dougray truly knew him—one would not think him opposed to the conquering of England, so genuine did he sound. Likely, even had they seen him fighting the side of the English, they would think he but resembled another.

"My due, indeed." William turned. "See here Michel Roche, Baron of Stavestone," he announced. "Once amongst my most loyal subjects of Normandy, and now again."

Dougray was tempted to look upon Campagnon's reaction to learning the man he and his mercenaries had wronged was so esteemed, but he need not. He could feel the miscreant's churning.

Urging Michel forward, William said, "For what do I find you at Wulfen?"

"Justice…restitution. I but pause here in the course of pursuing men who attacked a village upon Stavestone after availing themselves of my food, drink, and lodging." His gaze touched Dougray, moved to Campagnon.

Was the knave's hand on a hilt? If not, certainly his mind. Smug and triumphant he had ridden into the castle where he had never been welcome, but now his belief he could better Dougray had to be shaken. And far more it would be were he to learn that to which he must be unaware—great the ties of the king's old friend to Dougray.

"Tenacious as ever, Roche," William said as they neared the dais. "However, as far east as you have come, surely you have lost the scent of those villains."

"So I feared." Michel ascended the dais behind William. "But your arrival changes all."

"Does it?"

"It does."

William settled in the high seat a squire pulled out for him and gestured at the chair to his left. As Michel lowered, the king called, "Join us for a brief repast, then we shall tend to the day's business."

Those of Wulfen and of William became as waves, the weaker ones breaking upon the lower tables, the stronger ones breaking upon the high table, the latter comprised of Guarin, Hawisa, Cyr, Dougray, Maël, Guy, and Father Fulbert.

Though Campagnon, Waleran, and the merchant seated

themselves at the nearest table below the dais, whatever hope they had of listening in on the king's exchange with Michel was disappointed by voices too low to be heard above the din of thirsting, hungering, and boasting. Neither could Dougray hear what went between the two, and likely much of it escaped Guarin though he sat to the king's right.

*Lord,* Dougray silently appealed throughout a meal less brief than the king commanded, *let more good come of Michel fathering me than saving my life upon that bloody meadow. Let whatever goes between those two save my wife.*

~

As if of one body, Nicola, Em, and Margaret were on their feet the moment the first footfall sounded outside the chamber. And there all three stood, shoulder-to-shoulder when the door opened.

Hawisa's stern face eased as she took in the one standing between the other two women. "God's sweet earth, Nicola, what have you done to our Em?"

*Our Em.* Momentarily, the fear lancing its recipient's breast subsided. So sincerely the lady had spoken, Em wondered if this was how Eberhard felt to belong to Hawisa and she to him—to be part of this family.

Nicola stepped forward. "Margaret and I sought to make it more difficult for our half-noble misbegotten king to see this common legitimate woman as the property of an ungodly mercenary. We succeeded, did we not?"

"Beyond all expectations." The lady stepped near Em. "I knew you to be lovely, but many a man's jaw will go loose when you enter the hall."

Em moistened her lips. "'Tis time?"

"It is. I shall deliver you belowstairs where you will stand before the king, Campagnon, his fellow mercenary who saw you in the wood, and the Gloucester merchant by way of whom you and Eberhard sold yourselves into slavery."

That last nearly made Em choke. It was terrible enough she must face the first two, but also that man?

"Be strong," Hawisa said. "Be respectful and precise, speaking only when required to answer, and do so in Norman-French. Do not let your gaze stray to Campagnon except when he is permitted to speak directly to you. Then you will keep your chin up, eyes on him as if you look upon a lesser."

"Will that not offend the king that I, a commoner—?"

"Only if you look upon Le Bâtard as if *he* is common. Campagnon…" She shrugged. "Methinks it will amuse William, and that is a good thing with a man who believes all inferior to him."

"Will Dougray be present?"

"Your greatest champion is there now, exercising much control in being so near Campagnon." Her lips curved. "I believe the ribbon you gave him—that around his wrist which he is wont to look upon—is of good benefit."

Did the lady think it a favor? Or something more?

It mattered not as long as neither Le Bâtard nor Campagnon knew its real significance.

"England is very broken," Hawisa said, "and we fool ourselves in denying she was broken ere *he* came. That there is a man belowstairs who owns you as he would a horse is proof enough, though there is more. For it, we must accept neither Edgar the Aetheling nor a grandson of Gytha is any more worthy of ruling our people than that grasping Norman who took the throne from Harold. Accept it, and when you stand before him, as best you can think only of fixing this one thing this one day. You know what that is, aye?"

"My freedom."

"Which is your future." Hawisa opened her mouth as if to say more, glanced at Nicola and Margaret and added, "With Dougray."

Em could not suppress a sob.

"Let it out," Hawisa said, and when another sob escaped, asked, "More?"

Em shook her head. "I am ready for William."

The lady snorted. "I said the same to Sir Maël upon Darfield when he came to deliver me to his king who was to decide my fate. The chevalier told me no one is ready for Le Bâtard, and he was right. But that does not mean, dear one, he cannot be bested in things of no great consequence to him that are everything to us. Do as I have told and greater your chance of never again running from Campagnon."

"I shall."

"And be assured that should ill befall Dougray, allowing Campagnon to take you from here, the D'Argents and Wulfriths will take you back."

At Em's widening eyes, Hawisa added, "England remains greatly unsettled. Sneeze too loudly, and one might find one's self ambushed."

"Dougray," Em said.

"Be assured, his family will not hesitate to do as he asks."

As Em struggled to control her emotions, Hawisa kissed her cheek. Then the lady motioned the other two near.

They closed their eyes, bowed their heads, and Hawisa said, "Lord, attend to Your daughters' groanings and pleadings. If 'tis not in Your will to free our people of Norman yokes, may it be in Your will to free this woman from this one yoke that offends thee for stealing her purity. We ask for Your justice, Lord." She squeezed Em's hand. "Amen."

The others echoed her, then Hawisa said, "Em, behind me. Nicola and Margaret, behind Em. She stays between us until Le Bâtard orders otherwise." Upon the threshold, she turned. "I do you ill insulting him behind his back, Em. You must empty your head of that name now. No matter how much he insults and demeans, speak naught of him being baseborn nor even allude to it."

"I will hold in all and prove myself worthy, my lady."

"As many times already you have done, Em. This, however, is of greatest import."

"I understand."

"Follow, ladies," Hawisa said. "We go in together. Lord willing, we come out together."

## CHAPTER THIRTY

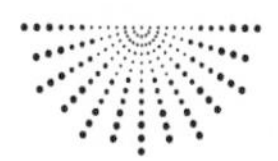

He knew it was her, though the woman he loved was more felt than seen. And she stole his breath—ashamedly, in that moment more for how beautifully she was transformed into a lady than that she looked a meal entering a den of ravenous beasts.

Three paces behind Hawisa, Em was followed by Nicola and Margaret who moved left and right as they came off the stairs. Unhurriedly, the four advanced on the dais whose table had been set back to accommodate the high seat moved to the front and into which William had dropped minutes earlier, warning if Wulfen's lady did not soon appear with the slave, he would send men abovestairs.

Whereas Dougray stood to the right of the king between his brothers, cousin, Michel, and a king's guard, to the left stood Campagnon, the merchant, Waleran, and another of the king's guard. And lining the wall beyond them were Wulfen's housecarles, squires, and pages.

Ordric and Eberhard were at the center of those who stood at attention, the jut of the young man's jaw evidencing the effort required to maintain control. Should he seek to slay Campagnon as denied him at Darfield, Hawisa's housecarle would swiftly escort him from the hall. William would wonder at that, and wonder could lead to revelation he was Em's brother should the merchant look near on one more changed by the years than the sister. As there seemed no gain in revealing their kinship, great the trust Guarin placed in the youth.

Hawisa halted a dozen feet from the dais. As the other women stilled, Dougray looked to Campagnon. His eyes were all for the woman who made the slave she had been at Castle Balduc seem a shadow of this one. Doubtless, his mind was alight with plans for returning her to her former state.

*No more will he touch you,* Dougray silently vowed, *even do I lay down my life to sooner see him face God's judgment.*

"Nearer, Emma Irwindotter," the king commanded.

She stepped alongside Hawisa who looked behind and nodded at the other two. Immediately, Nicola moved to Em's side and Margaret to Nicola's side. Then the Lady of Wulfen closed her left hand around Em's right.

William chortled. "Are battle lines being drawn, Lady Hawisa?"

"We but seek to protect our own, Your Majesty."

"*Your own?* I believe Chevalier Raymond disagrees."

"Then he is not of the faith, and methinks the sooner you send the heretic from your side, the sooner God will bless your kingship."

The silence that followed surely alarmed Guarin, but then William slapped a thigh. "The lady plays with us, Campagnon. Fear not, it is as a fellow sister in Christ she claims Emma Irwindotter. Eh, Lady Hawisa?"

"That is so, Your Majesty, but it ought not be of relief to your hired killer. Fornicator and ravisher that he is, more frightened he should be."

"Your Majesty!" Campagnon cried. "For what do you allow this traitor to speak ill of a Norman long loyal to you?"

The mail worn beneath William's tunic ringing, the king rose to his good height. Turning to Campagnon, he stepped near enough bodily odors would assail the nostrils. "A *mercenary* long loyal to my *coin.* To say otherwise suggests you think me a fool."

"I do not think you a fool, my liege. Never would I, but…"

"But?"

"My men and I have served you well, and better we shall in the days ahead when the last of the rebels water the soil with their blood. Pray, forgive me for spilling anger due those who reject you though they claim to be your liegemen."

William further scrutinized him, then descended the dais.

Silently, Dougray beseeched Em to be strong, and as if heard, she raised her chin and pressed her shoulders back.

The king halted before her, swept his arms behind, and gripped a wrist in the long fingers of the opposite hand. "You have stunning eyes, Emma Irwindotter. Though surprisingly beautiful, they must seem more a curse than a blessing."

With scant volume, she said, "At times, Your Majesty, but I remind myself it was with great thought and purpose God set them in my face."

"What purpose that?"

Her left hand scratched up a fistful of skirt. "Mayhap so one day—"

"Speak louder. I am not the only one who wishes your answer."

Her chest expanded with breath. "Mayhap these eyes were given me so one day I—"

"Your Norman French is passable, but the common in your voice vexes like a fly one cannot slap away."

She cleared her throat, more succinctly said, "Mayhap these eyes were given me so one day this Saxon commoner—"

"Commoner become slave, turned runaway and rebel."

Her throat bobbed. "That I am."

"But not a lady."

"Not a lady," she agreed as if the ribbon around Dougray's wrist were merely a favor.

"Still, your effort to appear of gentle birth in the hope of moving me to your side is admirable. I am guessing aid was given by your *sisters in Christ.*"

"They have been very kind to me."

As if moved by the strain in her voice, Nicola closed a hand over the one gripping Em's skirt.

Immediately, William stepped to the side, caught up the younger woman's other hand, and brushed his lips across her knuckles. "I understand you remain unwed, Lady Nicola."

Her smile was so tight it had no bow. "I do, Your Majesty."

He drew back and considered her figure. "Strange a husband cannot be found for such a beauty. Do your brothers continue to neglect their duty, be assured your king shall remedy the matter."

Her lashes fluttered, and Dougray knew she sought to veil her emotions. "You are kind, Your Majesty, but surely you do not suggest being unwed is a disease."

"Not a disease, but where Nicola D'Argent is concerned, an affliction in need of ministration."

Her smile thinned further. "Then I must seriously appraise the suitors recently presented by my brother."

A lie, Dougray would wager.

"Many contend for my sister's hand," Guarin said when William looked around. "A decision will be made soon." Likely another lie.

"I am gladdened, Baron. Just as I would have more Wulfriths and Wulfrith-trained warriors to protect my realm, I would have more D'Argents."

"You shall, Your Majesty."

William turned to Margaret. "Who are you?"

"She is—" Nicola began.

"She can answer for herself," William snapped.

"Non, she cannot. Margaret is mute."

The king blinked, shrugged. "What is this mute to you?"

"M-my maid."

Another lie, but better Margaret be associated with Nicola than the rebel Em.

Abruptly, William returned to Em. "For what do you keep your king waiting on an answer?"

Dougray growled low and felt Cyr shift as if preparing to drag him back.

But Em had not lost her place in the conversation, which might have made her seem unworthy of William's time. "Mayhap God's purpose in gifting me with such eyes was so this day I would stand before the conqueror and beseech him to bless our country as Normandy is blessed—that no man, woman, or child be sold to another formed in God's image lest they be treated the same as animals. Worse, less than animals."

"I am not unaware some slaves are subjected to treatment no better than that dealt animals, but less than animals?"

She inclined her head. "I would like to believe there are more good masters than bad, but I have no experience with the first. What I have suffered, a good master would not do to an animal that bears his weight league after league, pulls his plow acre after acre, not even one who comes to his table to sustain the lives of those who bled and carved it." She stood taller. "I speak of violation, the use of a slave's body, whether the yoked is an adult or child, to satisfy the carnal, the lustful, the unholy."

"These charges you level against Sir Raymond Campagnon?"

"I do."

"Then you do not deny he bought you at auction and you belong to him?"

*Steel yourself,* Em counseled as she moved her gaze past this beast's face to that one's. And quivered as she was abandoned by the curious peace she had been gifted when Hawisa and Nicola took up her hands.

Campagnon made no attempt to lighten an expression that told when he had her alone, he would do worse than when he boasted an audience of mercenaries goading him to subject her to harsher lessons.

Bile stirring, fearful she would mess the king's boots, she averted her gaze and landed on Dougray. From the set of his face and body, he struggled for control. For that, had Michel Roche moved behind him—to aid D'Argent kin should his son not behave?

Em looked back at Le Bâtard and saw impatience rumpled his brow.

Before she could form words to ease it, Campagnon called, "Look upon her shoulder, my liege. There you will see a mark that verifies that to which this upstanding merchant of Gloucester attests."

Hoping the anger flashing across William's face was sown by Campagnon, Em said, "I do not deny your countryman bought me at auction, nor that if I lower the shoulder of my gown you will see his mark adorned by the cross of crucifixion—rather, would see it had I not cut it away."

William's startle was so slight, she doubted others saw it. "You flayed it from your flesh?"

"I did, in the hope it would aid in forgetting the same day he bought and inked me, upon the road to Wulfenshire and beneath the eyes of God he introduced a maiden not yet ten and six to the appetites of a godless man."

A choked sound flew her gaze to Eberhard, and a thousand times more she hated he was here. Fortunately, not only did he bear no arms the same as all those not of William's guard, but Ordric had set a hand on his shoulder.

"You seem to have shocked Squire..." The king frowned. "... Eberhard?" No sooner said than William's eyebrows soared as if he understood something he had not before. But when he spoke again, he did so only for her ears. "The merchant presented me your original bill of sale with your mark upon it and that of your brother—a boy named Eberhard."

Though a fairly common Saxon name, he knew. And from the whistle of breath drawn between Hawisa's teeth, the Lady of Wulfen's hearing was acute.

Em inclined her head.

"Hmm," he grunted, then said loud, "Let us return to the matter of your freedom. You do not deny you belong to Raymond Campagnon?"

"I do not deny he purchased me. I deny I belong to him. Every coin he gave has been repaid ten-fold in labor, one-hundred-fold in the abuse of my body."

"Your Majesty!" Campagnon exclaimed. "No matter how long or hard a slave labors, she does not purchase her freedom unless her master agrees."

"Silence!" William commanded and motioned to the merchant. "Bring here the document granting the right to sell this free woman at auction."

The man of sizable girth hastened from the dais and set a rolled parchment in his palm.

As Em watched the king read it, she refused to look to the merchant though she felt his gaze.

William looked up. "Your name and mark are alongside your brother's. Proof you were not forced into slavery."

"Not so, Your Majesty. We *were* forced into it."

"By whom?"

She stood taller. "The Duke of Normandy."

"What say you?" he demanded.

"I speak of the one who came across the sea to take a kingdom and whose victory decimated the lives of thousands, causing a great loss of menfolk that led to the loss of homes and the ability to stave off starvation. Oui, my brother and I sold ourselves, but only to ensure the survival of our siblings. And many others have sacrificed the same. Labor for coin to feed, clothe, and house loved ones. Labor so we might ourselves be fed, clothed, and housed. Labor, your Majesty, not..." She swallowed.

Something flickered in the conqueror's eyes—something human, she prayed. "Even so, no provision in this document grants you the right to earn your freedom, Emma Irwindotter." He returned it to the merchant and waved him away. "So what would you have me do?"

"Find in favor of a Christian whose beliefs and rights have been violated repeatedly by one who but professes to be of our faith."

"You make it sound simple, but were I to free you, numerous others would demand the same."

"Years past it was done in Normandy, and there you were but a duke. Now all of England is yours, and you are a king."

"A fair argument, albeit inaccurate. I am king and England is mine, but not all of it. And by *all* I mean its people." He stepped nearer, and his ale-scented breath fanned her face. "Rebels are the reason I am unable to follow my God-given conscience and end slavery here, the cost of defending England in pursuit of peace and prosperity unconscionable. To pay my army, revenue is had where it can be found, and a good source is slavers who pay for the privilege of conducting their heathen trade."

Hope that had fluttered in Em's breast ceased fluttering. Ever his answer had been *nay*. Hence, the only good of this day was none knew of the handfasting—providing Dougray would let her go without challenging Campagnon.

Unable to resist looking to see how he received William's refusal, she noted his jaw was clenched. And his brothers, cousin, and Michel Roche were prepared to prevent him from aggressing against Campagnon or his king.

"Hold!" William said, and she saw he had followed her gaze. "I forget Sir Dougray is owed a reward." His eyes returned to hers. "Do you feel the same for him as he feels for you?"

Amid gasps, mutterings, and the shuffling of bodies long at rest, her mouth went drier.

"Do you?"

He knew she did, just as he knew the one who had played Hawisa's son was her brother.

"Speak!"

"How could I not feel for so honorable a man? Though I am Saxon to his Norman, he sees me as worthy of gentle affection regardless of the color of my eyes and no matter my body was fouled by Campagnon."

His smile told he was pleased. "You heard that, Campagnon?" he called. "Your fellow Norman values your slave more than his destrier."

The face of the one she loathed darkened further. If not for the powerful company he kept, already that violence would have emerged. He would have her to ground and—

*Do not think there,* she told herself.

"And yet," the king mused, "I question if he values her enough to take her not to mistress but to wife."

Hawisa's hand grip Em's more firmly, then Nicola's tightened.

"You dare suggest D'Argent wed her?" the mercenary erupted. *"My* slave?"

"Careful," William rumbled. "You forget whom you serve at his pleasure."

Campagnon muttered something, but whether the king did not hear or merely let it pass was unknown. "Tell, Sir Dougray," he said, "would you make this woman your wife were I to grant permission?"

"Non!" Campagnon took a step toward William.

"One more word," his liege snarled, "and I *shall* allow it."

The mercenary clamped his teeth the same as others in the hall who roused.

"Oui, given permission, I would wed Emma Irwindotter," Dougray said.

As Nicola gave a squeak of joy, William said, "Truly, this woman in lieu of the reward promised you, which could be land and a lordship?"

Em knew her heart yet pounded, but no longer did she feel it, so great her dread that should Dougray choose her over what first brought him to England, ever he would see her as a sacrifice.

"Truly, Your Majesty."

She did not know if he had hesitated, only that once more she felt the working of her heart though no less the dread.

"As Father Fulbert is here," he added, "I would wed her this day."

Em nearly looked to the priest she had noted before the hearth when she entered the hall, familiar not only for having accompanied Dougray and Cyr to Castle Balduc but his height and breadth that made him appear as much a Goliath as Vitalis.

"You are clear what would be required of you, Chevalier?" William said with warning.

Em saw Dougray tense. "Your Majesty?"

"As she is Campagnon's property, until I outlaw slavery in England, where he goes, she goes. Hence, where she goes, you go."

Em's knees weakened. Seeing Dougray's face had darkened, she imagined the color fleeing hers had found its way to his.

"That is my understanding," he said, "though I submit—"

Campagnon laughed, reminding Em of the chase he liked which she, unable to submit to him, had indulged for as long as her strength did not fail. "You want her, have her, you misbegotten son of a whore, and ever you shall answer to me."

"Lord," she breathed, even more grateful for the hands holding hers.

Though Campagnon had spoken without permission, it was not with words William rebuked him. One moment laughter bubbled from the mercenary, the next he gulped it down as two of the guard answered the sweep of the king's hand.

Campagnon backed into the table, but before he could slip past the merchant and Waleran, he was gripped both sides.

"Must I see you gagged as well?" William demanded.

"Pray, Your Majesty, forgive me for blood that runs as hot as yours when men take what belongs to you."

"So my blood does," the king said, "but unlike you, I answer to no one."

*Not even God,* Em thought.

He jutted his chin at Dougray. "Continue."

Muscles aching from the effort to keep himself from Campagnon, grudgingly grateful for the presence of kin, and less resentful than expected for that of Michel, Dougray said, "I do not believe Sir Raymond has any right to Emma Irwindotter. Therefore, where he goes, the woman I would wed does not go, nor I."

"Whence comes this belief?" William asked, almost kindly. Certes, Campagnon erred in naming the one who sought to free Em a whoreson. William had spoken of the bond of *Les Bâtards,* but one did not speak such in the presence of a powerful man offended by those who believed a noble born out of wedlock was a lesser being.

"Though the merchant has verified children desperate to save their siblings sold themselves," Dougray said, "as yet no papers have been produced to prove Raymond Campagnon owns this woman."

"She admits he purchased her at auction."

"I do not dispute that. I question the absence of papers proving he yet owns her. Does he not submit them because it was agreed she could work off the coin paid? Or because now the papers are valid only to the one to whom he sold her?"

Though Campagnon held his tongue, so greatly he seethed his breathing was heard.

"An interesting observation, Sir Dougray. Sir Raymond, where are the papers documenting ownership?"

The man hiked his upper lip. "Stolen upon the isle of Axholme to which you sent me to spy on the Danes."

"You accuse Sir Dougray of taking them from his fellow warrior?"

"I do. Aided by Sir Maël and Sir Guy, he rendered me unconscious. When I regained my senses, I discovered the papers stolen from my purse."

"And yet only now you speak of it. Sir Dougray, what say you?" Almost immediately, William tossed up a hand. "Non, I shall have my answer from Sir Maël, though mayhap he has not earned my trust as well as believed."

Dougray's cousin stepped forward. "Upon Axholme, circumstances necessitated we subdue Sir Raymond lest we be discovered and slaughtered, Your Majesty."

"What circumstances did you withhold from me?"

"Emma Irwindotter was among the Saxon rebels who met with the earl. When Sir Raymond recognized her, he would not be dissuaded from recovering her. Lest our mission was utterly compromised, we were forced to quiet him."

"And took the papers," the mercenary said as if his behavior were justified. "Admit it!"

Dougray felt cornered. The absence of documents supported the argument Campagnon had no right to Em, but if the king believed the mercenary had them upon Axholme, Maël and Guy could be held accountable for their loss alongside the one who had seen them burned by Em.

Before Dougray could determine the direction to turn, William said, "I am aware the leader of the Rebels of the Pale was upon the isle, daughter of Irwin. Why were you there?"

"Admit it, D'Argent!" Campagnon demanded. "Admit you took the papers."

"Silence!" William shouted. "As the papers are gone, we have only your testimony this woman still belongs to you, and much I question the word of one so obsessed with a Saxon he nearly sabotaged the task set him by his king."

As Dougray thanked the Lord for this mercy, William repeated, "Why were you there, Emma?"

"I was but one of many who accompanied my leader. It was for a good showing, Your Majesty, that is all."

"Are you Vitalis's lover?"

Her lids sprang wide. "Non!"

"But you wish to be Sir Dougray's lover? His wife?"

"With your permission, I would match my life to his."

"And there the question—will I permit it, making you Sir Dougray's reward, or will I return you to Sir Raymond as punishment for betraying your king?" He shrugged his mouth. "To ensure never again you cause me trouble, I lean toward the latter."

"I am in need of a lady's maid." The words bounded from Hawisa. "Do you allow Em to serve me at Wulfen, I shall keep her close."

He snorted. "And reform her rebel ways as you have reformed yours, my lady?"

She did not flinch. "As I have, and as I shall do with this young woman."

He looked between Dougray and Campagnon. "As told, a reward is due D'Argent, but methinks the crown best served were the reward a lordship—lands, title, a Saxon lady in need of a firm hand to ensure her and her people do not stray from Norman rule."

"I prefer Emma Irwindotter's freedom, and that I be permitted to wed her, Your Majesty."

The king sighed. "Two warriors, both useful when they are not shirking their duties in pursuit of a woman who is not at all useful. How am I to decide?"

"With your conscience you say is God-given," Em answered as she was not meant to.

Dougray ground his teeth. It was bold, and even were it not, William's conscience would play little to no role in the decision. Thus, since the king wanted this matter resolved quickly,

Dougray beckoned forth what paced the back of his mind as it had since that night at Balduc when Campagnon humiliated him in front of his slave.

He considered all sides of it and decided. Since William enjoyed setting warriors against each other as done at Darfield when he forced Hawisa to meet at swords with her traitorous housecarle, here a means of resolving the matter in a way that would appeal—and more importantly, might ensure never again the mercenary presented a threat to the woman Dougray loved.

## CHAPTER THIRTY-ONE

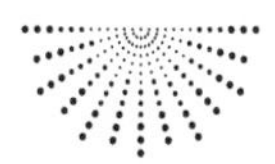

"At such a time as this, is it not often best to let the sword decide, my king?"

William narrowed his eyes at Dougray. "You would set your sword against Sir Raymond's?"

Hearing Em's breath catch, Dougray hoped she would not speak words that would reflect a lack of confidence in his ability to triumph over one who had the advantage of all four limbs. "I would, my liege, my reward the opportunity to win—not be given—Emma Irwindotter as my bride."

A smile plucked at William's mouth. "What think you, Campagnon? If Sir Dougray is victorious, the woman is freed and may wed him. If you are victorious, new papers of ownership shall be issued you."

"No drop of sweat will I spill to gain what already belongs to me!" the mercenary snapped.

"Sweat?" Dougray pounced. "We are not youths at training, Campagnon. Sweat is where it begins. Blood is where it ends."

"Were I of a mind to fight you, it would be *your* blood."

"So you say, but I think you fear me—do not believe your skill equal to mine."

"I but protect my reputation, whoreson! It is one thing to cross swords with an inferior two-armed warrior, another to engage an inferior, one-armed man whose service to his king is the picked-clean bone of tracking rebels for better men to slay."

Though not long ago, Dougray could have been roused, he kept control. "Your excuse for leaving your blade sheathed entertains, but I believe our king tires of this. Let us be done with it."

"I agree," William said. "Sir Maël, see them armed."

"Your Majesty!" the mercenary protested as Dougray's cousin strode toward the table beside the great doors where weapons relinquished to the king's men were laid out. "As long as England's laws are in place, I cannot be deprived of my property without just cause. The law is very clear—"

"Since when does William the Great, King of England, Conqueror of Saxons, and Duke of Normandy, live by the laws of others?" William demanded. "I may require it of my subjects, but such does not apply to God's anointed one. Now if you wish to face Sir Dougray empty-handed, superior warrior you believe yourself to be, I am well with that. The sooner this is done, the better."

As a seething Campagnon was released to follow his opponent from the donjon, Dougray looked to Em whose eyes were large and arms stiff at her sides where she continued to hold to Hawisa and Nicola.

*Lord, strengthen my sword arm,* he silently beseeched, *steady my hand. Firm my feet. Let this be the first day of her return to freedom.*

"Non!" William called. "I will see it fought here."

As surprise sounded all around, Dougray turned and saw Campagnon also pivot.

"Your Majesty, ours is a civilized hall," Hawisa said. "We do not—"

"It shall be done, Lady. Order your servants to move the tables and benches."

Anger flushing her face, she released Em and called, "Attend!" When men emerged from the corridor leading to the kitchen, she directed them to move the tables and benches against the far wall and sweep away the rushes.

"The rushes stay," William countered.

"But they are a hazard to swift movement, Your Majesty."

"As such, will make the contest more interesting." He looked to Em. "You shall stand at my side, the sooner I may award you to the victor." He turned toward the dais. "Follow."

She glanced at Dougray, and he saw her uncertainty. But then she smiled as if confident he would triumph. He was capable, he did not doubt, but more capable he would be had he continued training with his brothers rather than aid in ending the rebellion.

He inclined his head, and Em, Nicola, and Margaret followed the king.

"Only the rebel Emma Irwindotter," William commanded without looking around. "Lady Nicola and Margaret who speaks not, join Father Fulbert at the hearth."

Em drew her hand from Nicola's and said something low, then continued forward with a glide in steps taken beneath the luminous skirt.

Having collected Dougray's and Campagnon's swords and daggers, Maël halted alongside his cousin. "I think you must kill him," he murmured as he passed the sword.

"As he must kill me if he thinks to take back Em." Dougray thrust his sword in its scabbard.

Maël pulled one of two daggers from beneath his belt and extended it. "A pity William does not order armor donned and you were required to relinquish the dagger strapped to your arm."

"Is that a lack of faith in my skill, Cousin?"

"It is not. I but wish to avert trickery to which dishonorable, desperate men turn when failure is imminent."

Dougray returned the D'Argent dagger to its sheath. "Even does he resort to trickery, I shall best him."

"Then God be with you." Maël's eyes flicked downward. "And your Saxon lady."

Whether he thought the ribbon a favor that would become more once this day was done or believed already it was more, Dougray could not know. What he knew was his kin remained nearly as elusive as he had become following the loss of his sire at Hastings. Nearly.

Maël had been angered when Cyr wed a Saxon, disgusted when Guarin did the same, and now seemed resigned Dougray had also found a woman to love in this conquered country.

What next? Acceptance should Theriot take a Saxon bride? Might Maël finally emerge from the depths to which he consigned himself and sink his own roots in English soil? Or would he forever remain in William's service, whether in this country or Normandy, a man alone with none to aid in battling his demons?

"I thank you," Dougray said, and as he followed his cousin toward the dais, saw Waleran had descended and leaned near Campagnon. Ill afoot there? Likely preparations in the event Campagnon failed, meaning Em would not be entirely safe until those who sought to allow her tormentor to reach beyond the grave were also taken to ground.

Dougray placed himself in front of the king who stood before the high seat with Em behind and to his side. Though he held his gaze to William, peripherally he saw Waleran retreat and Maël pass sword and dagger to Campagnon. Moments later, the mercenary also stood before the king.

When the last tables and benches were against the wall, the Lady of Wulfen passed so near Dougray her sleeve brushed his. "Return him to the devil," she rasped, then ascended the dais to Guarin's side.

"I do not require death decide this match," William said loud, "only victory beyond question. Regardless whether it is the grave that ends this dispute or bitter defeat, it is done this day. Come the morrow, we return to ending the rebellion by whatever means I deem necessary."

Those last words chilled but did not surprise. This was only a distraction—even entertainment—for him. When he returned to York, he would finalize his plans for the harrying.

"Agreed, Sir Raymond?"

"Agreed," the mercenary lied.

"Agreed, Sir Dougray?"

"Agreed," he said and assured himself it would be a lie only if he failed. But even were he unable to free Em, his kin would—for her, for him, for Eberhard.

William swept a hand forward. "Chevaliers, show these boys and youths what is expected of Norman warriors and is now expected of those born Saxon."

As Dougray turned, Campagnon said, "What of shields, Your Majesty?"

Of which he knew a one-armed man could not avail himself unless he chose one over a sword, Dougray brooded, and not for the first time wondered what made a man like Raymond Campagnon. Were such beings born into the world evil? Or if one went far enough back, might they discover depravity was learned at the knee of another depraved soul or depraved circumstances?

Certes, Dougray knew where his own depravity had begun and how hard it was to climb back into the man he had thought no longer existed following the great battle.

"Surely those who train at Wulfen ought to see the true reach of an accomplished warrior?" Campagnon pressed when no answer was forthcoming. It was to Dougray's advantage the knave further alienated the king in trying to shame his opponent. William might toy with others in this way, but it was his prerogative.

His face revealed that, as did his words. "The true reach of an accomplished warrior is what I shall show these boys and young men—how a Norman-trained chevalier who lost an arm serving his liege yet excels, even against a two-armed opponent who sells his sword arm to make his way through life." He smiled. "Positions!"

Feeling Campagnon's seething as they moved to the center of the hall, Dougray considered the floor covering. Recently strewn with herbs to mask the scent of whatever had been deposited there by animals or men deficient in manners, the rushes were fresh enough to mostly stick beneath the feet rather than slide. Those at the center would provide the surest footing since a great number of boots had passed over them. Too, during the meal, tables and benches had been set left and right to avoid blocking the passage from doors to dais, keeping it mostly clear of dropped and slopped food and drink.

"This eve, she is mine again," Campagnon said low, his smile revealing a rotting tooth. "Be assured, great pleasure I will take scouring her mind and body of you."

Were the taunt not expected, Dougray might have struck before William ordered the contest commence.

"And when she thinks the worst is done and tries to crawl into a corner—"

"Make ready!" the king called.

Dougray was grateful the command granted permission to set a hand on his sword a moment after he did so—and that the promise he would soon be swinging it kept it sheathed.

As the offender stepped opposite, he chuckled as if he knew how far he had pushed his opponent. Blessedly, not as far as at Castle Balduc when, distant from the warrior he had been, Dougray had reacted to Em's abuse with little thought and no strategy.

Since he dare not make that mistake again, nor that of pride that cost him an arm, he drew his sword and silently began citing lessons taught him as he had moved from squire to chevalier beneath the tutelage of both uncle and sire.

*Feet shoulder width apart,* he heard Hugh instruct as he kicked

Dougray's feet wider. *Lead foot pointing toward your opponent, rear foot angled outward. Back straight and slightly forward. Shoulders and hips level but loose. Never rigid. Loose. Fluid.*

Dougray raised his sword to the middle position and angled it upward, then weighted his back leg that would launch him at the mercenary whose own stance Hugh would rebuke for being too narrow for a fight not yet begun.

*Attend to your opponent,* he reminded himself as Campagnon also raised his blade to middle position.

*Think victory, feel victory, seize victory,* Hugh spoke from the grave, whereas Godfroi sent from across the sea, *Engage the mind ere the muscles, my son.*

*My son.* As if Michel Roche had not seduced Robine D'Argent. As if her misbegotten son were his own.

*I will live to make it right,* Dougray silently vowed. *I will, Father.*

"Gird your fear!" the king commanded as if he had received training from Hugh who believed fear a weapon all its own, the need to survive making one capable of the unimaginable.

*Courage is spawned by fear,* his uncle had said. *When the latter raps at your door, embrace it as the most loyal of friends, letting fear—the desperate desire not to die—form you into something to be feared.*

"Gird your strength!" William demanded. "Gird your resolve! And..."

As Dougray awaited the final command, he studied Campagnon to discover vulnerability beyond a stance that remained narrow.

The mercenary should be doing the same, but his gaze was on the dais. As told by his smile, he looked to the woman he believed would depart Wulfen with him.

"Begin!" William bellowed.

Dougray lunged, swept his blade behind, up, down, and landed it on Campagnon's before the mercenary could reach full extension. The impact snapped his opponent to the side, exposing his left arm and leg.

The former tempted. Were it disabled, the mercenary could not simultaneously wield sword and dagger the same as Dougray, but the leg more greatly benefitted Campagnon. Thus, Dougray reversed his swing and arced it downward.

Campagnon reacted in time to avoid a slash to the thigh that could have opened a major vein, but still the blade found flesh. Blood darkening the cut edges of his lower tunic, he shouted and jumped backward.

As the slice opened up other targets on Dougray's body—legs, chest, and neck—it was fortunate his calculation proved accurate that if he did not land a mortal blow, he would have time to recover.

Following through with his swing, he stepped into it and turned, closing his body and briefly exposing his back. When once more he faced Campagnon, the mercenary sprang and swung wide.

The tip of his blade opened Dougray's tunic and scored his lower ribs, but he felt only the sensation of cool air and moisture. As often happened when men battled, discomfort would come when the cool sweat of victory or the bone-shaking chill of pending death doused the fire coursing their veins.

*Victory,* Dougray told himself and slammed the flat of his sword against the flat of his opponent's.

Campagnon answered with a sweep that freed his blade, next a thrust targeting the heart.

Dougray countered, nearly sending the other sword flying, then they circled each other. As they exchanged tight, swift strokes, the ring of steel on steel was like a wildly tolling bell, the hall and its occupants a blur, the trampled rushes scenting the air in preparation to mask the smell of poured blood.

Amid shouts, the spray of saliva, and the mist of sweat, the warriors moved right, Dougray forcing Campagnon back, then left, Campagnon forcing Dougray back. They parted and circled again. Backward swing met backward, forward swing met forward, side swing met side.

Despite the loss of Dougray's lower arm, the two were well matched, meaning the victor could prove the one who possessed the greatest endurance.

*Hastings,* Dougray told himself. From morning through afternoon, he had battled. In between putting Saxons to ground, he had snatched a full breath here, a moment's rest there. This was nothing compared to that. And yet where Em was concerned, it was everything.

*Em.* Forcefully, he told himself he needed to be here with her, not upon that bloody meadow. And it was not a Saxon he must put to ground but a Norman who was more an enemy than the man who had taken an invader's sword arm.

A shout tightening Dougray's chest and abdomen, he put the full strength of his body into his next swing and more forcefully deflected Campagnon's blow.

The mercenary staggered and regained his balance, but continued backward toward the dais as if seeking time in which to recover.

Dougray followed. Narrowly, Campagnon turned aside a blow aimed at the great vein in his neck, then thrust his second arm forward, gripped Dougray's hand beneath the sword's crossguard, and attempted to wrench it to the side.

He had the advantage. Had he possessed it a moment longer, he might have untangled his sword and landed *his* blade to the great vein. But just as he was versed in making use of all his limbs, so was Dougray. Leaning hard into their crossed blades, he landed a kick to Campagnon's abdomen.

The mercenary lurched sideways, and though he tried to take Dougray with him, his hold loosened and their swords parted.

The rushes near the dais, dark with what appeared to be blood but had to be spilt wine, dropped Campagnon to a knee, eliciting gasps from boys and youths mostly forgotten until now. However, as Dougray raised his sword to execute a backward swing, his adversary threw himself to the side, rolled, and stumbled upright.

"Oui, run!" Dougray called. "That is the only way ever again you shall sell your sword arm to support your miserable existence."

The taunt proved effective, causing the mercenary to charge.

Dougray returned to the middle stance. Lest he was watched for signs of his next move, neither by expression nor tension did he reveal himself. Only when Campagnon was nearly upon him did he move.

He did not attempt to match the sword swing powered by the force of the other man's advance lest the impact send him reeling backward. Instead, he ducked low, launched to the side, and cleared the descending blade.

As he straightened and came around, the imbalance of his one-armed body denied him the opportunity to deliver the edge of his blade to his opponent's back. Still, he executed the move well enough to cause the mercenary's feet to skitter.

Campagnon arrested his flight just short of Waleran, cursed, and came around. "Trickster!" he cried.

"Skill!" Dougray corrected. "But were it trickery, it would not justify your failings nor make you look more than you are before your equals and betters."

Campagnon stared out of a face so bright it appeared he spent too many hours beneath the summer sun.

"Cease your cowering!" Dougray beckoned with his sword. "I have a reward to claim."

The mercenary lunged, pumping his sword arm and reaching for his dagger.

Dougray ran to meet him, swung up and back, and feinted to the right before their swords met. Spinning around, he folded the flat of his blade across his body and thrust his elbow up into the mercenary's temple.

Campagnon cried out and jammed the tip of his sword to the

floor to remain upright. As he shook his head to set aright whatever was knocked askew, Dougray glimpsed the crimson of the mercenary's split open temple. The brow would have been better, causing blood to run into the eyes, but there was further gain to be had.

Dougray sprang. As his prey tried to get his sword aloft and raised the dagger-wielding arm to protect his head and neck, the tip of Dougray's sword hooked the short blade from the mercenary's fingers and sent it across the rushes. Dougray continued past, arced down and up and drove the pommel of his sword into Campagnon's back.

He heard breath rush from the mercenary, and when he came around saw Campagnon gripped his back, next heard the whistle of air resistant to being drawn into lungs. Then once more the knave dropped to a knee.

The fiery taste of victory tempted Dougray as it had at Hastings. But just as then when relief, transformed into pride, caused him to rejoice before its due, here and now his battle was not done.

He started forward. And at his back heard the creak of the dais, the crack of bone on bone, a grunt.

"Waleran!"

There were other warnings alongside Em's and the thump of boots, but he needed no others to reveal what came for him. Here, before the king and men relieved of weapons, it should not be necessary to guard his back, but with Campagnon's champion present—a man not right in the head—Dougray was in grave danger the same as the one who had taken a strike to the kidney and was not yet fully upright.

As Em was nearer Waleran who could more easily attack her than the man who wished her for his wife, Dougray pivoted.

Sword before him, Campagnon's man came at Dougray, leaving behind one of the king's men who sought to regain his feet.

But the contest was now between Dougray and Waleran.

*Slow of wit but swift of foot,* Em had cited this man's weakness and strength. As shouts and the pound of boots sounded behind, it was the weakness Dougray focused on. Reserving strength for finishing off Campagnon, he met the man's crazed eyes, then feinted as if to strike from the left, swept his sword right, and brought it down on Waleran's.

Edge met edge, jolting them to a standstill, then Dougray slid his sword down the other, put weight behind a thrust, and scraped the tip of his blade off and inward. It opened Waleran's belly, but before Dougray could fully twist aside to avoid the recoil of his opponent's weapon, that blade sliced the inside of his upper arm.

Like the first slice he received, he hardly felt the physical pain of this one, but the emotional…

Horror that his sword-wielding days might truly be at an end gave him pause he could ill afford though Waleran dropped and began fouling the rushes.

The hilt remaining firmly in his grip, Dougray silently demanded, *Now Campagnon.*

He brought his sword around and thanked the Lord it swung true. Waleran's blade had not cut to the bone, and likely not deep into muscle. God willing, the injury was all surface.

An instant later, there was Em's tormentor charging ahead of D'Argent kin, contorted face revealing pain—bared teeth evidencing determination to reach Dougray before he fully recovered.

*Fly, else you are dead!* his uncle's voice resounded across the years.

*Godspeed, my son,* Godfroi encouraged.

Dougray lunged to fend off an attack too soon come. But it did not arrive.

Campagnon's feet went out from under him, not from fouled rushes but a force that slammed him to the ground two strides from his opponent and sent him face down and his sword plowing the rushes. That force was the man who had fathered a misbegotten son given the name D'Argent.

"Cease!" the king commanded.

Dougray skid to a halt the same as Guarin, Cyr, and Maël opposite, but just as at Hastings, Michel did not falter. Rising from Campagnon's back, he dropped his knees to the floor on either side, drew back the arm hooked around the mercenary's neck, gripped the jaw, and shouted, "For sins against me and mine!" And wrenched Campagnon's head opposite.

## CHAPTER THIRTY-TWO

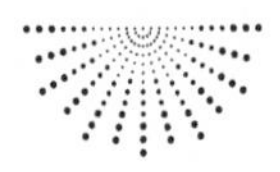

A moment earlier, Em had longed to bring a blade to hand and avenge the injury done Dougray's remaining sword arm. Now she wondered if the snap of bones amid the rising din was mere imagining. It had to be, and yet as that sound moved from her head to the soles of her feet, it whispered, *You are free.*

But was she?

Dougray was the superior warrior, but it was his father who denied Campagnon victory which might have been his had his opponent erred in the slightest.

"Roche!" William descended the dais—tall, broad, muscular, and fearfully god-like in the power he exuded that could prove a giver of bondage as easily as freedom. Or a giver of death as easily as life.

When Dougray's sire pushed upright, Em looked to Eberhard.

The strain on his face had eased, and he smiled—not so broadly he appeared to delight in the death of another, but there was triumph along the edges. He had not been the one to wreak vengeance, but it was enough another ensured never again Campagnon harmed anyone.

"Never again," she breathed. But what of Dougray? If he lost his sword arm…

Her knees gave.

If not for an arm around her waist, she would have dropped. "'Tis over," Hawisa rasped and drew the younger woman against her side.

"Dougray," Em gasped "His arm—"

"He has movement. Methinks it did not go deep."

"But—"

"For what did you interfere, Roche?" the king demanded.

Standing in front of the motionless body of Raymond Campagnon, it was some moments before the baron answered. "Your Majesty, when you were a youth and I a young man, you asked when it was acceptable to ignore the bounds set by those to whom you must give a good account. My answer now is the same as then—providing you have the courage to accept the consequences, overstep to avert ponderous treachery and see justice denied given its due."

He inclined his head as if to indicate he possessed such courage. "Campagnon conspired with his man to deny Sir Dougray the hand of Emma Irwindotter. Now ponderous treachery is averted. Campagnon and his men attacked a village upon Stavestone after availing themselves of my hospitality. Now justice is served." He glanced at his son. "No matter my punishment, my only regret is denying Sir Dougray the satisfaction of landing the final blow."

Em looked to her husband. Despite blood on his upper sleeve, he continued to grip his sword. She raised her gaze higher and knew much went behind his stony face. Anger toward his sire? Anger toward himself for not being the one to slay Campagnon? Anger for taking a blow that threatened his ability to defend himself and others? Might he steel himself for a terrible pronouncement? Did he begin to feel his injuries?

"I pray he can forgive me," Michel said, then added, "for all."

Not only for this day, Em realized.

"And I covet your forgiveness as well, Your Majesty...for all."

Again, not only for this day.

"All, Baron Roche? Might you look more Saxon than Norman not only for having lived long amongst the people of this land?" William narrowed his lids. "Would it benefit your king to know what *all* is?"

Michel raised his eyebrows. "Only if you wish to live in the past as long ago I advised against when you had to choose between the dark behind and the light ahead. As then, the present is where the future begins. And hope."

William's chest expanded, then he strode to the left of Dougray where the convulsing Waleran had gone still. He prodded the man with a boot. Receiving no response, he moved to Campagnon and prodded him harder. Also dead.

He stepped before Michel. "A troublesome *present,* this. Two mercenaries worth scores of slain rebels lost to me."

"After what transpired this day and in the days before, methinks you must agree there are better, more worthy men to serve you, my liege. Oui, these two were dangerous to your enemies, but they were just as dangerous to those loyal to you."

William put his head to the side. "Are you loyal to me?"

"I am, Your Majesty."

He turned to Dougray. "Are you my man? In this present, through the morrow, into the future?"

"I am, Your Majesty," Dougray said gruffly, and Em guessed pain was upon him.

William sighed. "Though this contest did not find its proper end, I grant your reward. Now a question—is it to be the same as whilst Sir Raymond lived? Do you still wish this rebel for a wife rather than land and title?"

"Emma Irwindotter is my greatest wish, Your Majesty."

As her heart leapt, something drew her gaze to Dougray's cousin. The ruined side of his face in shadow, she would have thought him most handsome if not for the disapproval darkening the visible side.

"Then as payment for my forgiveness," William said, "she shall renounce her rebel ways, and you shall have her."

Em drew a sharp breath and turned into Hawisa to muffle a sob.

"All is well," the lady said at her ear.

"Sir Dougray, attend your betrothed," William ordered, then gave a snort of disgust. "As told Baron Wulfrith, Wulfen is no place for women. Just as he must address your sister's lack of matrimony, he must remedy this."

Em drew back from Hawisa and turned to Dougray as he stepped onto the dais.

He halted before her, said softly, deeply, "It is done."

She knew if she succumbed to the longing to be nearer he would hold her, but from the grip of his teeth, he was in pain. Blinking away tears, she looked to his bloodied sleeve. "Your arm?"

"Not deep." He raised it, opened and closed his hand, causing the ribbon trailing his wrist to swing.

"Still, it must be tended lest—"

"Now this business is done," William said, "I would see all of Wulfen, Baron Wulfrith."

"Oui, Your Majesty." Ordering the housecarles to assemble the boys and youths in the training yards, Dougray's brother strode toward the doors.

"A word, Baron Roche," the king ordered.

"I am well," Dougray rasped and folded Em's hand in his and turned.

Whatever was put to the Lord of Stavestone, he responded with nods and words too low to carry. Then William commanded his men to accompany him from the hall, and called, "I shall send my physician to tend your injuries, Sir Dougray. As for land and title, I do not believe you will lack for either. Indeed, you may even gain a new surname the same as your brother."

Dougray felt Em's startle. Or was it his own, replete with understanding?

"And Father Fulbert," William said, "see Sir Dougray and Emma Irwindotter wed forthwith."

When the doors closed behind him and the last of his men, including Maël and Guy, once more Hawisa called for servants, this time to remove the fallen warriors and clean away evidence of what had transpired in her formerly civil hall.

As Nicola and Margaret hastened forward to aid her, Michel approached the dais. "Forgive me, Dougray. As upon Hastings, I could not risk doing naught. Though I believed you would prevail, I dared not believe wrong."

Though it had offended when Michel toppled Campagnon, resentment eased as Dougray looked upon the man who had likely saved his life during the great battle and, possibly, this day. Twice in dire circumstances, Michel had acted the father long denied him—just as Dougray knew he himself would do for sons and daughters who came of him and Em to ensure loved ones outlived them.

Loved ones... Was love what the man who sired him felt?

"Dougray," Em entreated as if fearing he would reject Michel.

"I know," he said and stepped with her from the dais to stand before the Baron of Stavestone. "I thank you for that day and this."

As the older man searched Dougray's eyes, gratitude pooled in his. "I could not be prouder of you, nor more thankful the loss of the woman I loved and the son we made benefitted you beyond what I could have offered. Truly, you are worthy of the name D'Argent."

Dougray hesitated, said, "As I wish to be worthy of the name Roche."

Michel exhaled sharply. "If worthy of the D'Argent name, beyond worthy of Roche."

Dougray inclined his head. "I thank you."

"You need not take my name," the baron said, "but I wish to make you heir to Stavestone."

That to which William had alluded, perhaps even required of his liegeman. But then, Roche had no other children to—

Not true. What had Guy said? Introducing Dougray to the Baron of Stavestone could hand him more loss than already he knew.

"I am honored, but you have Guy," Dougray said.

"So I have, but even when I knew you not, you were first in my affections and ever shall be. And I wish it thus, as does our king. However, Guy will not be empty-handed. Boltstone lies north of Stavestone, upon which William wishes a castle raised. When the one who keeps it for me passes, your cousin can hold it for you. I believe he will be well with this."

"Will he?"

"Were he not, he would not have forced us on each other. He is a fine man."

"Indeed, but consider this—you are not so old you could not father a legitimate heir." And quite possibly with the woman he had delivered to Wulfen, Dougray mused, having several times seen them looking upon each other and quickly away.

"I am not, but should I, still I would have Stavestone go to my firstborn. And William wishes it as well."

"As he wishes me to take your name."

"Methinks that negotiable."

Dougray breathed deep. "I shall think on it."

Michel looked to his son's arm. "Ere you wed, that must be tended."

No sooner spoken than the great doors opened and the king's physician entered with a leather bag slung over one shoulder.

Jasper D'Arci was a peculiar man. Though of noble blood and possessing the build of a warrior, it was medicine he wielded—or mostly. The sword and dagger on his belt were not pridefully worn. They ensured any who came between him and his healing came no more. For it, there was none the king trusted more to heal bodily miseries and bind up wounds.

"Sir Dougray," he called, "I understand there is a sword arm that needs saving."

Dougray's heart felt as if it knocked on a stout door. Most of his memories of Hastings following the battle consisted of blurred images, whether they weaved drunkenly or flashed frenziedly before him, but what he remembered clearly was Jasper D'Arci pronouncing Dougray's left arm beyond saving and instructing that it be removed at the elbow.

But this one he would not lose. "Not saving, D'Arci," Dougray said. "Only tending the same as my ribs."

"I shall be the judge of that." The man nodded at the fireplace. "Upon the bench where the light is good and fire abundant."

The latter lest cauterizing was required.

A short while later, D'Arci rose from where he had lowered to inspect the injuries revealed by the removal of Dougray's tunic. "Had the blade gone much deeper, this arm would require saving. But only tending is needed."

Standing over her husband's shoulder, Em loosed a breath, and she was not alone. Hawisa, Nicola, and Margaret also breathed out fear and breathed in relief.

"A score of stitches, a half dozen to your ribs, and a fortnight of rest should see you fit again." D'Arci smiled faintly. "Wulfenshire is a good place to recover." He nodded, and Dougray guessed what he did not say—better here than where next William rode to further impress on the rebels the conqueror was in England to stay.

When the physician put needle to flesh after ordering his patient to drink a goblet of mead to dull the pain, Dougray closed his eyes. Feeling Em's hand on him, he questioned if he had done all he could to end the rebellion. As there seemed few things in life could not be done better given insight and another chance, he knew the same as D'Arci that it had not been enough for William nor the rebels. If the Lord did not pull the king back from the brink, terrible days lay ahead. And what beyond those? Light or greater darkness?

*Light, Lord,* he prayed. *Peace...prosperity...our peoples made one.*

FOLLOWING a meal that began at dusk and ended two hours later, William had surprised all by declining to pass the night at Wulfenshire. The signs were there—that he ordered no tents erected outside the walls to accommodate the bulk of his men, he commanded them not to let pass their lips more than two tankards of ale, and provisions for the return journey were secured before he presided over supper.

Signs, and yet it was expected he would take the solar that night and be in the saddle before dawn. Instead, he had shoved back the high seat, thanked the Lord and Lady of Wulfen for their hospitality, congratulated Dougray on his marriage, and announced England needed him in the North.

He and his men, including Maël and Guy, rode out beneath a sparsely clouded, moonlit sky. A half hour later, Dougray answered Em's summons delivered by Margaret who approached those gathered before the hearth—D'Argents, Wulfriths, and a Roche, the latter's face brightening at her appearance. Though her eyes had not strayed to Michel, a flush had crept her neck and spotted her cheeks as she gave the ribbon around Dougray's wrist a tug and jutted her chin heavenward.

*Heavenward, indeed,* he thought as he paused on the chamber's threshold to take in the candlelit woman who awaited him at the center of the room. Her hair was loose, a robe belted about her waist, and the ring provided by Hawisa winked on her hand.

No longer Emma Irwindotter but Emma D'Argent. More, *Dougray's* Em, as it seemed she had been since first he set eyes on her and it was not a Saxon he saw but a woman in need of saving. It had been momentary only, his loss of an arm yet too raw to blind him to the enemy. Was he blind now? He did not believe it. In fact, he did not think ever he had seen more clearly.

"Do you intend to stand there all night?" she said almost breathlessly. But not with passion. With uncertainty that could easily become fear.

She girded herself to be his wife in full, and for that he was grateful for every ache behind every stitch and bruise that allowed him to think as clearly as he saw.

When he stepped inside and closed the door, her smile was brave rather than beckoning, and as he neared he saw her throat convulse.

Halting, he set his hand on her jaw. "What I intend is to fall asleep with you at my side and awaken to find you there, just as I did last eve and this morn."

"Aye, but this eve…" With trembling hands, she parted the robe and let it slide back off her shoulders.

"Em," he groaned and pulled up one side pooled in the crook of an arm to cover breasts he dare not look near upon. "We ought not."

She caught her breath. "You do not want me because of—"

"Non, not him. Never him. But we should not hurry this, and need not now we have years ahead of us."

Tears glittered in her eyes. "I am not as broken as you fear."

He tilted her face higher. "Dearest Em, you are so well-mended, I do not doubt it was done by the Creator's hand, but that does not mean this is the time for two who have become one in heart to become one in body."

She blinked. "Truly, you do not think me terribly broken?"

"I speak as I find, love."

"Then…I can do my duty."

"Duty?" He shook his head. "It ought not be that, but answered longing—*mutually* answered longing."

With a determined glint in her eyes, she settled her body against his. "I wish your arms around me."

*Arms.* Spoken as if he were whole, but then he had never felt as perfectly pieced together as he did in this moment. With her.

"I long for you, Dougray."

Fatigue and pain were naught compared to desire that made him consider his longing for her *was* mutual—that she was ready to seal their marriage with consummation. Feeling the beat of his heart, he looked to her throat and would have kissed it had not his eyes strayed to her bared shoulder. There the scar.

Seeing her gaze had followed his, he lowered his head and set his lips to the ridged, pitted skin.

When her sharp exhale shifted the hair at his temple, he straightened. "My arms shall be around you, Em. This night and every night I will hold you. Certes, it will be among the most difficult things ever required of me not to make love to you, but—"

"Though now we are wed by a priest, you will not be one with me?" she said.

He touched his thumb to the corner of her mouth. "I do not know it is possible to entirely snuff out that knave, but I will not replace him, Em. And do we move too quickly..." He shook his head. "We will not go there until you are more ready. *Mutually* answered longing."

Her lashes fluttered. "What if I am never more ready?"

"I will hold you still, love you still, protect you still. I give you the word of a D'Argent. And a Roche."

She shuddered. "You know not how much I love you."

"As you know not how much I love you. But we will learn each other." He slid her robe up over her shoulder and began tugging at his tunic ties. "I am in need of rest."

She pushed his hand aside. "This is my duty as well. A good place to begin, do you not think?"

Not for him, but though the ache of her touch in relieving him of tunic, boots, and chausses made him numb to his injuries, she was right. It was a good beginning. God willing, one day even more effortlessly she would touch him.

With Dougray clad in undertunic, Em in her robe, they gained the bed. As she settled her back against his chest, she drew his arm around her and pushed her fingers through his.

Just the two of them. And he wished it ever this way, that what went across this land being pounded beneath William's army would never again touch them. But it would.

"No matter what comes, you are mine, Em."

"I am." Her voice drifted across his senses like the smoke of the extinguished candles. "As you are mine, but..."

"But?"

"Am I worth it, Dougray?"

He drew her nearer, smiled into her hair. "You are worth all, dearest rebel—all I am and all I will become with you at my side."

# EPILOGUE

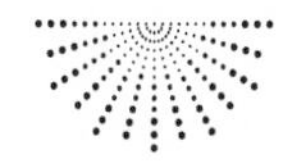

Normandy, France
Early Spring, 1070

Home.

Dougray urged his destrier into the outer bailey behind Cyr and Aelfled. As when first he set eyes on the place from which he was three years absent, his soul lightened further. Yet still it felt weighted by the anvil that forged King William's newest war machine.

No matter the good of Dougray's return to the D'Argent family home, it was impossible to leave the past months on the other side of these walls to be collected when what must be done here was done. The scale of what he did not wish to accompany him inside was too great—and greater for the woman seated before him.

Though ever innocents suffered in times of war, the number afflicted during William's harrying of the North was unconscionable—even were a man's conscience no bigger than a grain of sand. But rather than break Em, she had put her mind and hands to saving what could otherwise prove beyond saving, and was stronger for it.

Execution of the conqueror's plan to end the rebellion might number weeks, but it was naught compared to its effects that would be felt for years to come. While much of northern England had smoldered and thousands of Saxons suffered the first throes of famine, the king had returned to York to celebrate the Savior's birth and the third anniversary of his coronation—pleased, it was said, as if what he wrought was good in the sight of the Lord.

Then in the new year, he had divided his army into contingents of modest size to furtively search the forests and mountains for remaining pockets of resistance. While those forces covered hundreds of miles, uprooting and slaying Saxons, other forces destroyed all means of sustenance to prevent rebels from supporting themselves against their Norman king and to strike such fear in the English all yielded.

Just as William would not outlive tales of his atrocities, neither would his ancestors, and of his own people who yet named him *William the Great,* now many did so grudgingly and out of fear. Though there was consolation in knowing when he passed from this world, he would stand before one more powerful than he and answer for all whom his ambition had condemned to suffering and early deaths, there was more consolation in the here and now.

Not all who fled their decimated homes could be saved, but the people of Wulfenshire, including the new Baron of Balduc, aided refugees by the scores. Abbess Mary Sarah and the D'Argent and Wulfrith women led the way, and their men followed. It was not enough, thousands upon thousands yet destined for death, extreme poverty, and slavery, but they were not alone. As best they could, others across England aided their fellow man.

A squeal of delight sounded ahead, and Cyr and Aelfled's eleven-month-old son pushed to his feet atop the saddle and appeared above his father's shoulder.

Arm firmly around him, Cyr chuckled as the babbling boy

jabbed a finger in the direction of the donjon visible above the inner wall.

Home. Though Soren could not yet comprehend it, this Normandy stronghold and its lands was his future the same as Cyr and Aelfled's—as well as the latter's grandmother who shared the saddle with the younger woman. At last, Godfroi's heir had brought his family home to fill it with long-awaited joy. And come summer, were England settled enough, Guarin would journey here to reunite with his parents and introduce his wife and the child with which Hawisa yet burgeoned.

Would Theriot and Maël accompany them? Only God knew since Saxons were not the only casualties of the harrying. Normans suffered as well, whether at the hands of rebels resolved to fight to the death, mercenaries who used the license to devastate to enrich themselves with plunder, or the king who tolerated no objection to the means by which he crushed the resistance—as Dougray himself might have suffered if not for the injury Waleran dealt him. By the time his sword arm was fully healed, the harrying was done. Even so, he had remained at Wulfen and resumed his training to better compensate for the loss of an arm and aid with the refugees.

As the small entourage passed beneath the inner bailey's portcullis, Soren squealed again.

Grateful for the distraction, Dougray looked to that for which it appeared his nephew reached.

Flanked by chevaliers and servants, Godfroi's wife stood on the donjon's lowermost step, the yellow veil covering her hair dancing in the breeze, eyes bright as they moved over old loves and new loves, mouth bowing as she lingered on the son she had surely prayed would break his vow to never again darken her home.

"My mother, Robine," Dougray said as that lady shifted her regard to her second-born who held the first of her grandchildren.

Em looked around. "She is beautiful."

"As are you." He kissed her cheek and marveled though he had known he would love her more with the passing of years, he had not expected to love her this much more so soon. What he felt for her was far greater than that felt for Adela. This was knowing and being known as he had never known nor been known.

When they reined in, Robine sprang off the step. Pebbles skittering beneath her slippers, she halted alongside Cyr's mount. "Well come!" she exclaimed and reached to her grandson. "Pray, come unto your grandmere, little Soren."

Another child might have ducked beneath his father's chin, but not Soren the bold, and certainly not with Cyr between him and that flirtatious yellow veil.

"Yewo bud!" he exclaimed as Cyr lowered him. "Yewo bud fwy!"

He thought his grandmother a bird, and as soon as her hands were beneath his arms, he snatched hold of those yellow wings, sending her restraining circlet to the ground. As he shook out the veil and laughed, Robine drew her to him. "Long we have awaited you, precious one," she crooned.

Cyr dismounted and kissed her cheek. "It is good to be home, Mother."

"Such a blessing you are returned to us," she said, then her smile faltered. "Have you word of Theriot or Maël?"

"No new tidings. We can only wait."

She drew a shuddering breath. "Guarin and Hawisa?"

"They are well. A few more months, and you shall have another grandchild."

Her smile returned. "What of my Nicola?"

"Happily unwed though the king strongly suggests the new Baron of Balduc for a husband."

She gasped. "William thinks him a good match for the sister-in-law of the woman who slew his sire at Hastings?" She shook her head. "If that does not put him off, then perhaps the reason she departed Normandy."

Cyr grinned. "Does he not know already, Nicola shall inform him of that scandal—and make more of it than it was." Speaking naught of the training his sister received from Hawisa, he took his mother's arm. As he turned her and Soren toward his wife, Dougray dismounted and lifted Em down beside him.

"Mother, here my lady wife," Cyr said as he also set his wife to her feet.

Robine's veil in one of Soren's fists, her braid in the other, Dougray's mother stepped near Aelfled. "How I have longed to meet the heart of my Cyr and mother of my grandchild. I love you already, Daughter."

Soren babbling between them, they embraced.

"And this is Aelfled's grandmother, Bernia," Cyr said.

The old woman was greeted warmly, and when Dougray led Em forward, he saw what seemed a smile in Bernia's unseeing eyes.

Robine kissed Soren on the cheek, passed him to Aelfled who gently pried his fingers from his grandmother's braid, then took a halting step toward Dougray.

"First, mother and son," Em said and drew her arm from his hold.

Pushing his short mantle back off his shoulders, he strode forward.

Robine fell into his arms and clung to him as if he were the only driftwood in all the ocean. "Returned to me at last, beloved!"

He hugged her tighter. "Pray, forgive me for the pain I caused you."

His mother dropped her head back. "I am the one in need of forgiveness. I promised myself I would not do this—need not, having been prepared for your return, yet I crumble."

She knew nearly all, Dougray having sent across the winter ocean word of all that had transpired which would one day see him succeed as Baron of Stavestone and promising he and his wife would accompany Cyr and Aelfled.

"Everything has come right," he said, "or shall if father can forgive me."

She smiled. "He has missed you. If not for poor sleep last eve, he would have come outside to greet you."

Dougray tensed. "He is unwell?"

"His back troubles him, but otherwise he is hale. He awaits you and your brother in the hall."

"Then allow me to introduce my wife so we may join him."

Dougray started to draw back, but she said low, "What your missive revealed of what Michel did for you made my heart hurt more for all the years you were parted and happy you found each other. I feared he would turn bitter and hard. Is he truly as you told?"

"We cannot know all his years before, but if he is bitter, it is in such small measure it casts no darkness across him. He is a good man, and I am honored to acknowledge him as my sire."

"Then you will take his name as the king wishes?"

"Providing I have the blessing of the father who raised me." Dougray glanced at Em who was the only one near enough to hear them. Encouraged by her smile, he said, "How did Godfroi receive the tidings?"

"Much time he has spent at prayer accepting it is God's will you and Michel meet, and as ever he has done since the Lord returned him to me, he has risen above the hurt. Thus, no matter another has a claim on you, he does not begrudge it. Indeed, he praises the Lord, knowing had not Michel sought you at Hastings, you could have been lost to all. And had not his nephew brought you together following the battle of Stafford, you could have fallen to that mercenary at Wulfen. What matters most is you remain as much Godfroi's son now as before and just as loved."

"You are also well with this, Mother?"

"I am. There is just one thing I would have you know do you not already."

"Tell."

"Never did I regret the babe born of my sin. What I regretted was that he, an innocent, suffered the cruelties of others, many of whom have sinned more greatly than Michel and I."

"Be assured, I know this. Ever I have felt loved."

She kissed his cheek. "Pray, make me known to your Em."

Dougray introduced the woman his mother had years earlier assured him would come into his life and prove more true than Adela.

Robine exclaimed over Em's wondrous eyes, then welcomed her into their family the same as she had done Aelfled, naming her a daughter. Shortly, trailed by chevaliers and household servants, they ascended the steps to the hall.

Godfroi D'Argent was not seated on the dais but before the hearth in an armchair less imposing than the high seat, and the blanket ever draped over his lap was absent, the chausses covering his legs beneath the tunic evidencing how lax and still his lower limbs.

Dougray understood what it meant, just as Cyr must. This was no mere homecoming. This day, ahead of his death, Duke William's baron ceded his title to his heir.

Fear bounded though Dougray. Did Godfroi suffer more than back discomfort?

"Sons, daughters, grandchild," he called, "well come."

Despite the emotion straining his voice, he sounded hearty, and his upper body appeared as broad and muscled as ever. God willing, he but wished to pass the reins to Cyr to show confidence in him.

As all advanced, Soren continuing to chatter over the veil, Godfroi's gaze touched all. But it was Dougray he lingered over longest, eyes moving from his third son's face to the empty lower sleeve to the D'Argent dagger.

They halted before him, and Robine stepped to her husband's side.

Reaching up, he covered the hand she set on his shoulder. "See how our family has grown, my love. Praise the Lord for His abundant blessings." He reached to Cyr.

His second-born strode forward, lowered to a knee, and pressed his mouth to his hand. "Beloved sire, I am gladdened to return to your hearth and bring my family to dwell alongside Mother and you."

Godfroi smiled. "I see before me my once merciless son now a man ready to shepherd our family and people."

Cyr inclined his head. "I pray I give you no cause to regret it is not Guarin who succeeds you."

"Never could I regret so worthy an heir." The baron gestured to his right. "Stand at my side."

Cyr did so, then Godfroi reached to his third son.

Dougray squeezed Em's fingers, released them, dropped to a knee, and kissed the hand extended to him. But unlike Cyr, he kept his head bowed. "I am returned as once I vowed never to return, Father."

Godfroi set his other hand on Dougray's head. "I could not be more grateful the Lord has answered my prayers."

Dougray's chest tightened. "I beg your forgiveness for the wrongs I have done you."

"Forgiven, my son. Now rise and stand by my side. Though much needs discussing, all can wait until I have looked close upon and praised the Lord for every blessing rendered unto me this day."

As Dougray stepped alongside Cyr, he considered Em who stood on one side of Aelfled. Now it was her braid Soren gripped, his other hand waving the veil before the face of his great grandmother on the other side as if to tempt her blind eyes to sight.

*I love you,* Em mouthed, and Dougray wondered if this would be the night they had long moved toward. They were so near it was possible here the wait would end. It seemed right to him, but it had to be right for her.

"Come forth, Lady Aelfled," Godfroi beckoned.

She said something to her grandmother, then stepped before her father-in-law. Hardly had they begun to speak than Soren began wiggling down his mother.

Godfroi was entranced by the child who sought his lap, and for some minutes forgot all others as he spoke slowly and intently to the boy who would carry his name into the ages.

Appearing equally delighted, Soren chattered as he explored the old man's face and tugged and poked at him, then the little boy presented Godfroi with the yellow veil.

In that moment, Dougray cast off the weight of England's suffering, firmly placing himself here and now—and in the future with the hope once more Em and he would cross the channel to themselves present a child to its grandparents.

Soren settled on Godfroi's lap, and as he pointed at and named things in the hall, Aelfled, Bernia, and Em became acquainted with their host who received them warmly.

The feast that followed lasted for hours. Afterward, while the women settled in chambers abovestairs, Dougray and Cyr joined their sire in the solar. Much was discussed, including Dougray's future as the Baron of Stavestone. Clearly, it was difficult for Godfroi to speak of Michel, but he asked questions and responded thoughtfully to answers.

Night had long fallen when Dougray ascended the stairs to the chamber where he had passed endless months during his recovery that, unbeknownst to him, saw a horrified Adela bedside. Though his mother had denounced her love as being unworthy of her son, he had not believed it. But that was long before he met the woman with whom he would grow old…the woman whose arms awaited him…the woman worthier of his love than he was of hers.

He paused outside the chamber. "Lord," he rasped, "You knew I would rue the path upon which I set myself. You knew I would rage at being thrust off it. You knew my resentment would fall upon You and those I love. You knew there was something—someone—better for me. And so I thank You for this path I no longer walk alone. Even if You do not further bless Em and me with children, it is enough."

He breathed deep, raised his head, and opened the door.

SHE HAD KNOWN he was there, his shadow in the torchlit corridor sweeping beneath the door and across the floor to her toes.

*This eve,* she told herself again as he halted just over the threshold to look upon her where she had lowered to the foot of the bed after pacing away chill bumps that could not be blamed entirely on the brazier's inability to vanquish the cool of the night.

*Aye, this eve.* So close they had come to consummation these past weeks that there could be no question both were ready for their courtship to end and marriage to truly begin.

As Dougray closed the door, he lowered his gaze from her bared neck to the cleft of her breasts between the robe's lapels. She was bare beneath and yet he did not draw near.

"You are beautiful, Em."

She smiled. "Will you not come to me, Husband?"

"I would, but are you certain?"

"I believe I have been ready for some time. Let us prove me right, hmm?"

He hesitated, then strode forward.

Em tensed when he halted before her, and his frown revealed he noticed. Wishing she had gained her feet so she did not feel small and vulnerable, she started to rise, but he dropped to a knee just as he had done his father.

Gripping her cool hands, he said, "Perhaps we ought to wait awhile longer."

"Nay, I am done waiting. I wish to be your wife in full."

"Em—"

"Is a maiden, even one pleased with the match made for her, truly prepared for the nuptial bed? I think not, and yet your mother, who clearly loves your father, has given him five children."

Seeing Dougray's struggle and knowing he ached to embrace her as much as he feared doing so because of the man who had failed to retake his property, she said, "There is something you ought to know, then I shall speak of it no more." She swallowed. "Fighting him was impossible though ever I tried. But despite my every loss, after that first time I was barely present."

His frown deepened.

"I went to God, and He covered my eyes and ears and shrouded my body until it was done. But with you..." She shook her head. "I need not hide in Him. It will be us alone, and I shall be fully present with the man I love."

Though his expression lightened, uncertainty continued to lurk there.

"Be present with me, Dougray. Show me what is on that other side of us." She touched her lips to his. "Make love to me."

"Em, you know not how I want—"

"I do know. I want it too."

He searched her eyes—brown to blue, blue to brown—then pulled her up and closed his mouth over hers. His kisses had become more passionate of late, but there was more than the promise of something beyond this one, as further evidenced by his fingers grazing her shoulder and the robe falling around her feet.

Dougray was not as easily unclothed, even with both tugging at ties and raising and lowering garments between kisses and caresses, but at last they gained the candlelit bed, and the urgency of getting there had them drawing quick, sharp breaths.

Quaking with the effort to move slowly, he said, "I would

savor this," and trailed his lips from her mouth to her ear, neck, and the base of her throat.

Lingeringly, they touched and explored as they had not done before. Then when Em asked it of her husband, they went where they had not gone before. And became one in body.

Afterward, they held each other, neither speaking, only feeling what was savored and would be savored throughout their lives.

It was Em who finally pulled free. Urging Dougray onto his back, she rose up over him. "Very much I like this other side of us. And you, Husband?"

He laughed. "Surely that question is well answered," he said, then more seriously, "Tell me I did not hurt you."

Now she laughed. "Surely *that* question is well answered."

"As thought. I but wish to be certain."

"Then be certain. This night was so far from fear and pain I feel almost a stranger to who I was before you. With you, I was present, and we were utterly—wonderfully—alone."

He pushed his fingers into her hair. "I love you, Em."

"I love you." She lowered her head and kissed him as he kissed her, lingeringly reveled in the sensuous rasp of his beard, then tucked herself against his side and set her cheek on his shoulder and a hand over his heart.

There the ring he had placed on her finger months past and later had set with a D'Argent blue sapphire.

"How was the meeting with your sire?" she asked.

"Better than hoped. Godfroi accepts Michel will be a part of our lives henceforth and is glad for it."

"What of taking the Roche name?"

"It saddened him, but he said if it is as William wishes, it is for the best."

Loving the thud of his heart beneath her palm, she said, "We shall be Dougray and Em Roche. That will please Michel."

"It will."

Then soon they would depart Wulfen and, as planned, first

journey to Gloucestershire to reunite with her siblings and aunt. Hopefully, Eberhard would be able to accompany them.

"Are you also glad Stavestone is to become our home, Husband?"

Slow to answer, finally he said, "I am pleased it will become our second home."

By the light of the one candle that remained lit, she met his gaze. "Second?"

"You are my first home, Em, as I would be yours."

She smiled. "You are my first home and shall ever be, my love." Then she sighed, closed her eyes, and fell deeply…restfully… asleep in her husband's arms.

*Dear Reader,*

*Thank you for reading Sir Dougray and Em's love story. If you enjoyed the third Wulfrith origins tale, I would appreciate a review of NAMELESS at your online retailer—a sentence or two would be lovely, more if you have time.*

*As for Sir Guy... Those who have blessed me with their readership throughout my romancing of the Middle Ages will recognize him from LADY OF CONQUEST. Since that book's release, often readers have requested his happily ever after. Thus, in preparation for love long awaited, I wrote him into NAMELESS. Being mostly a Seat-of-the-Pants writer, never did I expect him to play a significant role, but it wasn't enough for him to be Dougray's friend. He had to be more. And so he is. Patience, Sir Guy, methinks your tale draws nigh.*

*For a peek at the fourth book in the AGE OF CONQUEST series featuring Sir Maël D'Argent and Mary Sarah, an excerpt of HEARTLESS is included here and soon will be available on my website:*

*www.TamaraLeigh.com. Off to finish that story for its Spring 2020 release...*

*Pen. Paper. Inspiration. Imagination. ~ Tamara*

For new releases and special promotions, subscribe to Tamara Leigh's mailing list: www.TamaraLeigh.com

# HEARTLESS EXCERPT

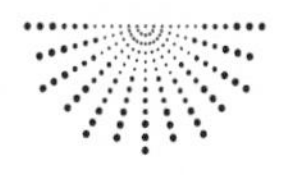

THE WULFRITHS. IT ALL BEGAN WITH A WOMAN

From USA Today Bestselling author Tamara Leigh, the fourth book in a new series set in the 11th century during the Norman Conquest of England, revealing the origins of the Wulfrith family of the AGE OF FAITH series. Releasing Spring 2020.

## PROLOGUE

Westminster Abbey, England
December 25, 1066

William seethed. And well he should. Even a bad king, which he could prove, ought not suffer so inauspicious a coronation.

As if turned to stone where he faced an anxious audience of Normans and Saxons about whose feet a haze of smoke had begun to drift, only his eyes stirred when he caught sight of one of two D'Argents who had accompanied a dozen of his personal guard outside.

Chevalier Maël, returning to the chapel by way of a side door, inclined his head, assuring his liege and what remained of his guard there was no need to halt the ceremony that would see the Duke of Normandy crowned King of England. Rather, no need yet.

The service, conducted by an English archbishop, had proceeded smoothly and according to long-established tradition —William prostrated before the high altar, anthems sung in praise of the one who would be king, and his oaths sworn to govern his subjects justly and defend the Church—but the next part had shattered the solemnity, causing the congregation to tense in anticipation of fleeing hallowed ground.

The archbishop had asked if the people would accept William as their king, and the Norman bishop of Coutances translated his words into French as done throughout the ceremony.

As if of one accord, hundreds of nobles had shouted their approval, but the man who would rule would be a fool to believe the enthusiasm of his fellow Normans was matched by Saxons who had lost their country when King Harold fell at the Battle of Hastings two months past.

Doubtless, some of the latter were well with being a beaten people since there was gain to be had in turning against one's own, but most were not. Hence, the need to protect themselves from further loss made those who believed England's throne stolen feign acceptance of the thief.

Unfortunately, the shouts of Saxons elevated by Normans had caused the soldiers stationed outside to suspect an assassination attempt against their liege. For that, they set fire to nearby buildings. Or so said those intercepted by the duke's personal guard.

Maël did not believe it, nor had his cousin, Theriot.

Had the soldiers truly feared William's life was in danger, sense and loyalty would have demanded they hasten inside to defend him. Hence, much coin Maël would wager the mercenary soldiers seen emerging from homes and shops with bulging sacks had used the din inside the abbey as an excuse to return to burning and pillaging. And too great the temptation for many of those pledged to the duke not to enrich themselves as well.

When the man soon crowned king learned his forces, rather than rebellious Saxons, were responsible for the disturbance, he would have much to say about the near ruination of his coronation. But it would be naught compared to his wrath if it did prove necessary to halt the ceremony.

Having alerted William it was safe to proceed as the captain of the duke's guard asked of him, Maël was eager to return to Theriot to aid in ensuring those out of control were brought under control before Saxons fleeing ruined homes and businesses were moved from fear to anger. If that happened, rioting would ensue. And slaughter.

Maël had no love for the people of this land, having lost to them what had once been nearly unimaginable, but further bloodshed—especially that of folk not given to warring—benefitted none.

He turned, but as he started back toward the side door with the archbishop's words trailing off and the bishop beginning his translation, movement where there should be none made him pause.

Narrowing his eyes on the dim balcony to the left that provided an unobstructed view of William before the altar—and a path for arrows and blades—he searched for the source.

Utter still, but something had been there. Had a bird found its way in and could not find its way out? Had a rodent scurried across the rail?

The rising shouts and cries of those in the streets beyond the chapel and sharpening scent of smoke causing the congregation to grow more restless, Maël hesitated. He was needed outside, but more so here lest the coronation was interrupted not by the actions of greedy men but an assassin.

Bypassing the side door, he nodded at one of the king's guard whose presence there ensured the congregation remained seated. Hoping the man had not allowed someone to gain the balcony unseen, he stepped onto the tightly-turning stairway and drew the dagger he continued to don only so none question its absence from a warrior no longer worthy of so fine a weapon.

As the stairway had been constructed without regard to defense, there was no room to wield a sword effectively. Thus, the D'Argent dagger it must be.

It was wrong it should fit his hand so well, and the price paid for the momentary comfort was vivid recall of his sire awarding it to his only son. Rather, *legitimate* son.

Shoving aside memories of that prideful day his accomplishment was honored by the man who had demanded that if Maël could not prove the worthiest of the family D'Argent he would be *among* the worthiest, he ascended the stairs cautiously to hear and not be heard above the holy words intoned.

But he was expected by the two who stood center of the balcony in the light of a single torch at their backs. Ladies, as told by veiled hair, embroidered skirts beneath mantles fastened with silver brooches, and noble bearing. *Saxon* ladies as told by their presence in a city recently surrendered to Normans. But they were far from harmless, the same as their children, a handful of who had…

Maël tossed out another memory best not dwelt upon and, seeing no others here and the women's weaponless hands clasped at their waists, strode forward.

Their faces were mostly in shadow. However, as he neared he discerned the one on the right was elderly, a hunch to her shoulders and pale braids beneath her veil grey rather than blond. The taller one was young, and if the loose, darkly gleaming hair caping her shoulders was to be believed, yet a maiden.

From her sharply drawn breath, he knew the moment her eyes made sense of the side of his face denied the benefit of shadow. It was the same reaction of nearly all the fairer sex—*and* the not so fair—who looked upon a visage so ruined it mattered not the other side remained mostly unspoiled.

The king's physician had assured Maël that, given time, the livid and swollen flesh would heal sufficiently so the monster made of him would once more look the man, but it was assurance he had not sought nor wanted. Worse should have been done him, and not merely the loss of a limb as suffered by his cousin. Rather, the same loss as his sire who spilled his life at Hastings and, possibly, another cousin whose body had not been recovered from that godforsaken meadow.

Thrusting aside more memories, he halted a stride from the women. "What do you here?" he demanded with only enough volume to be heard above the voices of the men of God and the congregation's increasing restlessness which boded that, regardless of the remaining guard, they would make for the doors if what transpired outside was not soon resolved.

"What do we here, Chevalier?" the old woman scorned in a voice still melodious despite its creak and well enough accented it was obvious she was familiar with his language. "We mark this momentous day in the history of *our* country by bearing witness to what goes inside this *English* abbey."

Unlike the Saxons below who feigned acceptance of William, she was openly disaffected, embracing the prerogative of the elderly who oft believed they had little to lose—unlike her companion who set a hand on the other woman's arm as if to calm her. For it, she was jabbed with an elbow, causing her to snatch her hand back.

Maël shifted his regard to the younger one's face, and immediately the glitter in her eyes extinguished.

As her proud bearing did not falter, he was certain she had not lowered her lids out of fear or deference. More likely she sought to hide something. Unfortunately, it was impossible to look nearer on one whose features were mostly obscured the same as the older woman's. However, of note was hair peaked on her brow, dark eyebrows, a generous mouth, and was that a cleft chin?

She might be pretty, she might not, but unlike life before the great battle, it was of no consequence to one whose once handsome face had given him the pick of women worth courting.

Returning his attention to the old woman, he said, "Who are you?"

She snorted. "I would think it obvious we are Saxons."

"Your names," he growled.

She put her head to the side. "For what would you know? So you might further persecute us the same as your countrymen outside these walls who set fires and pillage though the people of this city surrendered to Le Bâtard?"

The young woman sucked breath between her teeth, stepped in front of the other one, and raised her gaze to Maël's. The glitter there of such height and breadth it bespoke large eyes, she said, "Forgive my grandmother. So dear and great the number of those lost to her at Hastings, it is difficult to see any good come of the rule of your people."

Though her Norman-French accent was somewhat aslant, her voice was beautifully precise as of one given to much thought ere letting that thought off her tongue.

When he did not respond, she set her chin higher. "Have mercy, Chevalier. Of an honorable age, my grandmother is of no harm to you nor your duke."

"Her *king,*" he corrected.

"Her king—*our* king," she said, then stumbled forward a step.

Certain a blow had landed to her back, Maël bit, "Cease, old woman, else your granddaughter's pleading is for naught."

So quickly that one came out from behind the young woman, had Maël lacked training in swiftly assessing a threat, impulse might have caused him to make use of his dagger. The old woman was empty-handed, but were it not impossible for her to escape following a struggle sure to draw the guard's notice, whatever blade she wore on her girdle would be out.

Without regard to his own dagger, she stepped so near its point grazed her mantle. "Nithing! Thief! Murderer!"

Maël wavered between delivering her to the king's guard and yielding to the younger one's request by escorting them from the chapel.

An instant later, the decision was snatched from him by a rise in the commotion outside the abbey that was answered by a congregation which, as if having held its breath, expelled exclamations and cries. Then came the sound of boots and slippers across the floor.

Maël strode to the railing. Though William remained flanked by the archbishop and bishop, monks, and personal guard seeded amongst the latter, all was chaos below. Even before the doors were flung open to permit the panicked to flee, it was obvious the smoke's penetration of the chapel had intensified. But the duke did not stir, determined to allow naught but the certainty of death to prevent him from departing Westminster without the crown, ring, sword, scepter, and rod of the King of England.

More smoke entering by way of the congregation's exit, Maël swung around. Having sensed no movement about the women, he should not have been surprised they were where he had left them, but he was—until he realized they had no cause to join the frantic exodus. They had not slipped past William's guard to ascend the same stairs that delivered Maël to the balcony. There was a concealed door here that, had the trespassers been of murderous intent, could have seen an arrow sighted on William below.

Thrusting his dagger in its scabbard, he strode back. "Show me, and you may depart the way you came without consequence once I seal the passage behind you. Refuse me, and the guard will detain you and themselves discover its location."

As expected, the old one said naught. As hoped, the young one said, "We are without choice," and turned and strode past the torch.

Maël gripped the older woman's arm through her mantle to hasten her.

"You dare!" she snarled as if not only were he the enemy but beneath her. Though commanding and well-spoken, she was mistaken to assume he was less noble than she, but he let it pass and allowed her to wrench free.

She huffed and, less hunched than before, hurried after her companion.

The passage in the far corner was accessed by an empty sconce. When turned to the right, the wooden panel whispered inward to reveal descending stairs.

Entering, the young woman reached behind, but once more her aid was spurned, the old woman slapping aside her hand.

"We must make haste," the dark-haired one entreated.

But the old woman turned back. Torchlight now on her face, Maël's in shadow, she said, "I pray it was one of mine who spoiled your comeliness." She coughed, surely from the smoke. "Most unfortunate he did not also gut you."

Though she meant to offend, he was in accord.

"Go," he said, and when she gave her back to him, closed the Saxons into the darkness. If the stubborn old one continued to refuse aid offered her and was injured, it was on her.

Maël straightened the sconce and engaged the lever that locked it in place to prevent it from being opened from the inside again.

When he descended the narrow stairs, the last of the congregation were coughing and loudly clearing their throats as they shoved past William's guard amid smoke that was as eager to enter as they were to exit.

As he moved past doors soon to be shut to allow the officiating clergy to complete the coronation, he looked behind.

No longer did William appear turned to stone, his color high and shoulders and chest rising and falling rapidly. Doubtless, of the reward soon to be distributed to those of greatest worth in seeing him take England's throne, many would be denied for making a mockery of his ascendancy that could prove impossible to remove from memory.

Though Maël believed his own reward secure, he would decline and return to Normandy. Or so he planned, unaware his efforts in the riotous hours ahead would see many of those responsible for the abomination dropped to their knees before a wrathful William—and Maël elevated not to the lordship he politely refused after Theriot accepted lands for his brother, but to something of greater import to the King of England.

A position fit for one who had betrayed his family in proving incapable of keeping his word and remembering where his loyalties lay.

A position requiring him to ensure no murderous Saxon, Norman, or otherwise thwarted his liege's plan to bring England fully under control.

A position that could render him bereft of family and friends.

That last was due him, but God help him did he become as heartless as the king he served.

HIS FACE. Beneath silvered dark hair that did not belong on a young man, she had thought it so handsome as to be nearly beautiful—until long strides carried him fully into torchlight to which she and her grandmother had turned their backs at the realization there was no time to retreat.

For a moment, Mercia had thought herself afforded a glimpse of evil disguised as a thing of beauty to seduce women otherwise destined for heaven, but his mask had not slipped—indeed, was no mask at all, merely a ruined face. Considering how fresh the scar lightly scoring the left side and grossly ridging the right, she guessed it dealt two months past during the great clash now known as the Battle of Hastings.

Might one of her grandmother's sons fallen there been the one to disfigure a Norman unworthy of such a face? Might it have been Mercia's own sire? Unlikely and never to be known, not even when the old woman made good her promise to answer a question that was not to be asked of her again.

"There!" that one said, voice roughened less by age than the smoke of precious things devoured by fire. She pointed at the two-storied inn on the opposite side of the street where the rendezvous had been set in the event her men drew the attention of Normans. And so her escort had, no trace of them at the back of the stables where they had aided the two women in dismounting.

"Praise the Lord," Mercia breathed.

The escape from Westminster had been perilous. Amid smoke and great heat, screaming, shouting, cursing, even laughter, they had run street to street, turning back here, turning aside there. And once it had been necessary to crawl to escape the notice of Normans whose stuffed sacks were beginning to move their victims from fear to anger as evidenced by Saxons arresting their flight, making weapons of whatever was brought to hand, and setting themselves at thieves and murderers.

"Halt!" her grandmother commanded.

"For what?" Mercia exclaimed as she slowed. "The inn is just ahead." And as far as she could see, the only people about were few and Saxon. As told by the many they had passed and those who fled ahead of them, the foolishly curious were drawn to the commotion around the abbey, the wisely fearful determined to put distance between themselves and danger.

"Here!" the old woman repeated and turned into an alley between buildings.

Mercia followed and was unprepared when her grandmother spun around and backhanded her.

She cried out, stumbled sideways into the building, and slid down the wooden slats onto her knees.

"You dare!"

Quelling the impulse to raise an arm to shield her head lest the attack had only begun, berating herself for not expecting it ahead of forgiveness for what instinct demanded she do to keep them safe, Mercia pressed a palm against lips whose blood she tasted on her tongue.

She had known her grandmother's ire was not all for the chevalier, having been subjected to it when jabbed with an elbow, struck in the back, and hand slapped away, but as there had been no further show of aggression during their flight, she had thought that the worst of it. So now the question—was this the true end or only the beginning? If the latter, she would suffer it without protest.

The hem of the old woman's soiled, embroidered skirt sweeping the dirt, she stepped near. "Never are you to name me *grandmother,* neither in private nor public, and yet you did so before our enemy."

"In the hope of calming his impatience and rousing sympathy so he would let us go," Mercia apologetically defended.

"And had he not—had he dragged us before others and I was recognized—what then? All I have done to keep you safe would be for naught were it known you are of the blood of my son."

*Which son?* Mercia longed to ask.

"And then for you to speak to that knave of my great loss and beseech his mercy!" She spat on the ground, snatched up her granddaughter's chin, and hissed, "Show me."

Lowering her bloodied hand and curling fingers into the slick warmth, Mercia watched the aged eyes move over her mouth.

"Regrettable." It was said with what sounded sincerity. "But deserved for speaking of me as if I am a helpless, senseless old woman—worse, acknowledging Le Bâtard as our king."

"Gran—" Mercia nearly named her that again as if the title of kinship were more familiar than that by which ever she addressed her. Seeing the old woman's teeth begin to bare, she hastened, "Forgive me, Countess. I did not know what else to do to free us of him. But see, we are here now, and soon we shall be safe in Exeter."

The old woman's gaze wavered and lips quivered, then she released Mercia's chin. "Safe for how long?" she rasped. "Le Bâtard will set his army at that city's walls as well...will not be content until all of England bends the knee."

"We shall beat him and his kind back across the sea," Mercia said. "That is as you told, and that Harold's son will take back the throne. He will, will he not?"

As if the old woman needed to hear those words, her shoulders and back straightened. "Aye, Harold's son will sit the throne, and all the higher it will be upon the bones of the usurper." She nodded. "I will see it done ere I breathe my last, as you shall see it done. This I vow."

Would they? Mercia wondered and startled when her grandmother reached a hand to her. Though no frail thing, it was not for a lady of years to bear the weight of one of far fewer years. However, lest Mercia offend, she placed a hand in the extended one, pressed her bloodied hand to the ground, and pushed upright.

"Mercia," the older woman bemoaned as she looked near on the damage done. "Your lip is cut and begins to swell. I..." She swallowed loudly.

"'Twas deserved," Mercia sought to console her though little of her heart was in it. She had been disrespectful as never before, but the humbling of one of two vengeful Saxons had surely moved the chevalier to allow them to depart the way they had come.

Raised and educated in letters and numbers at a convent that had aspired to shape her into a woman afeared of displeasing the Lord, next tutored in the ways of the nobility while tending the lady of a great house that would have become greater had

King Harold been the victor at Hastings, Mercia had learned to read women and men and to flatter and be flattered as necessary.

Having sensed the chevalier on the balcony was not given to the behavior of fellow Normans who threatened to ruin Le Bâtard's coronation—hopefully, *had* ruined it—she had trampled pride nearly to the point of scraping and bowing. And for it, this.

But she would not have her grandmother know how great her resentment. Blessedly, it would ease as it must, the countess's loss of loved ones so great she could not be blamed for grief-induced rage. It was her due as it was not Mercia's whose own loss remained uncertain and could never be that of a loved one.

Blinking away moisture brightening her eyes, her grandmother said, "Aye, deserved, but I am glad for the disrespect shown me."

Mercia startled. "I do not understand."

"Though I know you to be of fine demeanor and sharp intelligence, I was unaware you could be so wily."

"Wily?"

"A kind word for deceitful," she misinterpreted the question, and as Mercia struggled against revealing how much it offended, continued, "Of good benefit to our cause."

"What benefit?"

The woman's pale eyebrows arched. "You shall not accompany me to Exeter."

Mercia nearly choked on saliva. "Then my punishment is to be parted from you?"

"Not punishment. Reward. A pity I took you from the convent rather than see your profession made, but you were raised well enough to play the part so none need discover your true purpose."

Mercia knew that were she to look wide and deep, she would find the answer to her questions in words already spoken, but she needed to hear them. "What part and what purpose, Countess?"

"I shall send you to Wulfenshire."

Still no direct answer, but she would not have to look as wide and deep as before. "Why must I go so far and for what?"

"'Tis where you are needed, and as God has made a place for you there, it is surely His will."

Head buzzing, heart pounding, flesh prickling, Mercia clamped her teeth lest she spill words and was dealt another blow.

"Mercia," her grandmother murmured as if to herself. "Though few know what you are to me, that name could prove your undoing in the midst of our enemies. You must take another, and methinks a Biblical one best serves where you go."

Somewhere upon Wulfenshire, which was far northeast of the city of Exeter where her grandmother intended to journey without her.

"Have you a name to mind, Mercia?"

"I...must think on it."

"Best one similar to your own so you not neglect to answer to it."

"Wise," Mercia croaked, and fearful of the pressure in her chest where screams circled, lowered tear-stung eyes.

An aged hand settled on her arm. "Look at me, Granddaughter."

Never named that, neither in private nor public, Mercia flew her gaze to rheumy eyes darkened by sorrow amid vengeful resolve.

"Other than the danger which names present in the face of our enemies, they are no longer of great consequence. Who you are inside is who you must be." She stepped nearer. Skirts brushing Mercia's, she cupped her granddaughter's jaw. "Never forget—ever embrace—you are Saxon. Strong of mind, body, and spirit. True to the blood, the bone, the marrow."

Mercia shivered. These the words with which her grandmother had rallied thousands of noble and common Saxons since the flower of England were slain upon the meadow of Senlac.

Thus, it mattered not she remained unaware of the part she would play. It was enough to know she was to aid in overthrowing the usurper.

No mere companion, Mercia of Mercia.

A rebel.

*Dear Reader,*
*I hope you enjoyed this excerpt of* HEARTLESS: Book Four in the Age of Conquest series. *Watch for its release in Spring 2020.*

***For new releases and special promotions, subscribe to Tamara Leigh's mailing list: www.TamaraLeigh.com***

# AGE OF CONQUEST PRONUNCIATION GUIDE

Aelfled/Aelf: AYL-flehd
Aethelflaed: EH-thul-flehd
Aetheling: AA-thuh-leeng
Alfrith: AAL-frihth
Balliol: BAY-lee-uhl
Bernia: BUHR-nee-uh
Bjorn: BEE-yohrn
Boudica: BOO-dih-kuh
Campagnon: CAHM-paan-yah
Chanson: SHAHN-sahn
Cyr: SEE-uhr
D'Argent: DAR-zhahnt
Dougray: DOO-gray
Ebbe: EH-buh
Eberhard: EH-buh-hahrt
Em: EHM
Emma: EHM-uh-leen
Estienne: EHs-tee-ihn
Fortier: FOHR-tee-ay
Fulbert: FOO-behr
Gerald: JEHR-uhld
Gloucester: GLAH-stuhr
Gloucestershire: GLAH-stuhr-shuhr
Godfroi: GAWD-frwah
Gospatric: GAHS-paa-trihk
Guarin: GAA-rahn
Guy: Gee
Gytha: JIY-thuh
Hawisa/Isa: HAH-wee-suh/EE-suh
Hugh: HYOO

Jaxon: JAAK-suhn
Lavonne: LUH-vahn
Maël: MAY-luh
Maerleswein: MAYRL-swiyn
Mary Sarah: MAA-ree-SAA-ruh
Merle: MUHRL-uh
Michel: MEE-shehl
Nicola: NEE-koh-luh
Ordric: OHR-drihk
Pierre: PEE-ehr
Ravven: RAY-vihn
Raymond: RAY-mohnd
Rixende: RIHKS-ahnd
Robine: rah-BEEN
Roche: ROHSH
Roger: ROH-zheh
Sigward: SEEG-wuhrd
Sweyn: SVIHN
Theriot: TEH-ree-oh
Torquay: tohr-KEE
Waleran: VAHL-ehr-ahn
Wulf: WUULF
Wulfrith: WUUL-frihth
Vitalis: VEE-tah-lihs
Zedekiah: ZEH-duh-KIY-uh

## PRONUNCIATION KEY

VOWELS
aa: arrow, castle
ay: chain, lady
ah: fought, sod
aw: flaw, paw

eh: bet, leg
ee: king, league
ih: hilt, missive
iy: knight, write
oh: coat, noble
oi: boy, coin
oo: fool, rule
ow: cow, brown
uh: sun, up
uu: book, hood
y: yearn, yield

CONSONANTS
b: bailey, club
ch: charge, trencher
d: dagger, hard
f: first, staff
g: gauntlet, stag
h: heart, hilt
j: jest, siege
k: coffer, pike
l: lance, vassal
m: moat, pommel
n: noble, postern
ng: ring, song
p: pike, lip
r: rain, far
s: spur, pass
sh: chivalry, shield
t: tame, moat
th: thistle, death
t~h: that, feather
v: vassal, missive

w: water, wife
wh: where, whisper
z: zip, haze
zh: treasure, vision

## AGE OF CONQUEST GLOSSARY

ANDREDESWALD: forest that covered areas of Sussex and Surrey in England
ANGLO-SAXON: people of the Angles (Denmark) and Saxons (northern Germany) of which the population of 11th century England was mostly comprised
BLIAUT: medieval gown
BRAIES: men's underwear
CASTELLAN: commander of a castle
CHAUSSES: men's close-fitting leg coverings
CHEMISE: loose-fitting undergarment or nightdress
CHEVALIER: a knight of France
COIF: hood-shaped cap made of cloth or chain mail
DEMESNE: home and adjoining lands held by a lord
DONJON: tower at center of a castle serving as a lord's living area
DOTTER: meaning "daughter"; attached to a woman's name to identify her by whose daughter she is
EMBRASURE: opening in a wall often used by archers
FEALTY: tenant or vassal's sworn loyalty to a lord
FORTNIGHT: two weeks
FREE MAN: person not a slave or serf
GARDEROBE: enclosed toilet
GIRDLE: belt worn upon which purses or weaponry might be attached
HILT: grip or handle of a sword or dagger
HOUSECARLE: elite warrior who was a lord's personal bodyguard
KNAVE: dishonest or unprincipled man
LEAGUE: equivalent to approximately three miles
LIEGE: superior or lord
MAIL: garments of armor made of linked metal rings
MISCREANT: badly behaving person

MISSIVE: letter
MOAT: defensive ditch, dry or filled with water
MORROW: tomorrow; the next day
MOTTE: mound of earth
NITHING: derogatory term for someone without honor
NOBLE: one of high birth
NORMAN: people whose origins lay in Normandy on the continent
NORMANDY: principality of northern France founded in the early tenth century by the viking Rollo
PARCHMENT: treated animal skin used for writing
PELL: used for combat training, a vertical post set in the ground against which a sword was beat
PIKE: long wooden shaft with a sharp steel or iron head
POLTROON: utter coward
POMMEL: counterbalance weight at the end of a sword hilt or a knob located at the fore of a saddle
PORTCULLIS: metal or wood gate lowered to block a passage
POSTERN GATE: rear door in a wall, often concealed to allow occupants to arrive and depart inconspicuously
QUINTAIN: post used for lance training to which a dummy and sandbag are attached; the latter swings around and hits the unsuccessful tilter
SALLY PORT: small hidden entrance and exit in a fortification
SAXON: Germanic people, many of whom conquered and settled in England in the 5th and 6th centuries
SENNIGHT: one week
SHIRE: division of land; England was divided into earldoms, next shires, then hundreds
THANE: in Anglo-Saxon England, a member of the nobility or landed aristocracy who owed military and administrative duty to an overlord, above all the king; owned at least five hides of land
TRENCHER: large piece of stale bread used as a bowl for food
VASSAL: one who holds land from a lord and owes fealty

## ALSO BY TAMARA LEIGH

## AVAILABLE IN: EBOOK, PAPERBACK, AND AUDIOBOOK

~

**CLEAN READ HISTORICAL ROMANCE**

THE FEUD: A Medieval Romance Series

***Baron Of Godsmere: Book One***

***Baron Of Emberly: Book Two***

***Baron of Blackwood: Book Three***

LADY: A Medieval Romance Series

***Lady At Arms: Book One***

***Lady Of Eve: Book Two***

BEYOND TIME: A Medieval Time Travel Romance Series

***Dreamspell: Book One***

***Lady Ever After: Book Two***

STAND-ALONE Medieval Romance Novels

***Lady Of Fire***

***Lady Of Conquest***

***Lady Undaunted***

***Lady Betrayed***

~

**INSPIRATIONAL HISTORICAL ROMANCE**

AGE OF FAITH: A Medieval Romance Series

***The Unveiling: Book One***

***The Yielding: Book Two***

***The Redeeming: Book Three***

***The Kindling: Book Four***

***The Longing: Book Five***

***The Vexing: Book Six***

***The Awakening: Book Seven***

***The Raveling: Book Eight***

AGE OF CONQUEST: A Medieval Romance Series

***Merciless: Book One***

***Fearless: Book Two***

***Nameless: Book Three***

***Heartless: Book Four*** (Spring 2020)

**INSPIRATIONAL CONTEMPORARY ROMANCE**

HEAD OVER HEELS: Stand-Alone Romance Collection

***Stealing Adda***

***Perfecting Kate***

***Splitting Harriet***

***Faking Grace***

SOUTHERN DISCOMFORT: A Contemporary Romance Series

***Leaving Carolina: Book One***

***Nowhere, Carolina: Book Two***

***Restless in Carolina: Book Three***

~

## OUT-OF-PRINT GENERAL MARKET REWRITES

***Warrior Bride*** 1994: Bantam Books (Lady At Arms)

*****Virgin Bride*** 1994: Bantam Books (Lady Of Eve)

***Pagan Bride*** 1995: Bantam Books (Lady Of Fire)

***Saxon Bride*** 1995: Bantam Books (Lady Of Conquest)

***Misbegotten*** 1996: HarperCollins (Lady Undaunted)

***Unforgotten*** 1997: HarperCollins (Lady Ever After)

***Blackheart*** 2001: Dorchester Leisure (Lady Betrayed)

***For new releases and special promotions, subscribe to Tamara Leigh's mailing list: www.TamaraLeigh.com***

# ABOUT THE AUTHOR

Tamara Leigh signed a 4-book contract with Bantam Books in 1993, her debut medieval romance was nominated for a RITA award, and successive books with Bantam, HarperCollins, and Dorchester earned awards and appeared on national bestseller lists.

In 2006, the first of Tamara's inspirational contemporary romances was published, followed by six more with Multnomah and RandomHouse. Perfecting Kate was optioned for a movie, Splitting Harriet won an ACFW Book of the Year award, and Faking Grace was nominated for a RITA award.

In 2012, Tamara returned to writing historical romance with the release of Dreamspell and the bestselling Age of Faith and The Feud series. Among her #1 bestsellers are her general market romances rewritten as clean and inspirational reads, including Lady at Arms and Lady of Conquest. In late 2018, she released Merciless, the first book in the new AGE OF CONQUEST series, followed by Fearless and Nameless, unveiling the origins of the Wulfrith family. Psst!—It all began with a woman. Watch for Heartless in Spring 2020.

Tamara lives near Nashville with her husband, a German Shepherd who has never met a squeaky toy she can't destroy, and a feisty Morkie who keeps her company during long writing stints.

Connect with Tamara at her website www.tamaraleigh.com, Facebook, Twitter and tamaraleightenn@gmail.com.

For new releases and special promotions, subscribe to Tamara Leigh's mailing list: www.tamaraleigh.com

Made in the USA
Middletown, DE
09 January 2020